Praise for Peter Murphy's *Lagan Love*

"The best books are not forgotten because you can never stop thinking beyond the story. This is true of *Lagan Love*. Murphy is a natural storyteller. I look forward to reading more."
– *Examiner.com*

"*Lagan Love* is more than your ordinary novel and Mr. Murphy is a skilled writer with the ability to tell a story that teaches a life lesson everyone can benefit from."
– *Simply Stacie*

"Old Ireland myths, a beautifully woven background, a cast of unique and adept characters set the tone for this phenomenal story of love, loss, and hunger.... With twists and turns, erotic scenes and magic, *Lagan Love* is a fascinating read."
– *Minding Spot*

"*Lagan Love* is as complex as love itself, particularly when artists and simply men and women are competing for the affections of the same person — even if only to be in control. Murphy's style is as complex as his characters, but readers will be absorbed in the forlorn myths and legends created and expounded upon."
– *Savvy Verse and Wit*

"Peter Murphy spins an exciting story of romance and the problems with it, making *Lagan Love* a unique novel with plenty of twists and turns underneath it all."
– *Midwest Book Review*

BORN & BRED

Also by Peter Murphy

Lagan Love

BORN
&
BRED

A novel by
Peter
Murphy

The Story Plant
Studio Digital CT, LLC
P.O. Box 4331
Stamford, CT 06907

Jacket design by Barbara Aronica Buck

Print ISBN-13: 978-1-61188-116-5
E-book ISBN: 978-1-61188-117-2

Visit our website at www.TheStoryPlant.com

First Story Plant Printing: March 2014

Printed in the United States of America

0 9 8 7 6 5 4 3 2 1

For the wayward children of strife, everywhere.

Happy will they be who lend ear to the words of the Dead.
—*Leonardo da Vinci*

CHAPTER 1

On the night of August 10, 1977, Daniel Bartholomew Boyle made the biggest mistake of his young life, one that was to have far-reaching consequences for him and those around him. He might have argued that the course of his life had already been determined by happenings that occurred before he was born, but, poor Catholic that he was, riddled with guilt and shame, he believed that he, and he alone, was responsible. He had been dodging the inevitable since Scully got lifted but he knew it was only a matter of time before it caught up with him. Perhaps that was why he paused in front of the old cinema in Terenure after weeks of skulking in the shadows. Perhaps that was why he waited in the drizzle as the passing car turned back and pulled up beside him.

"Get in the car, Boyle."

Danny wanted to make an excuse—to say that he was waiting for someone—but he knew better.

It wouldn't do to keep them waiting. They weren't the patient sort, twitchy and nervous, and single-minded without a shred of compassion. He looked around but the streets were empty. There was no one to help him now, standing like a target in front of the art deco facade of the Classic.

The cinema had been closed for over a year, its lights and projectors darkened, and now lingered in hope of new purpose. He had spent hours in there with Deirdre, exploring each other in the dark while watching the midnight film, stoned out of their minds, back when they first started doing the stuff. He used to do a lot of his dealing there, too, around the back where no one ever looked.

"Come on, Boyle. We haven't got all fuckin' night."

Danny's bowels fluttered as he stooped to look inside the wet black car. Anthony Flanagan was sitting in the passenger's seat, alongside a driver Danny had seen around. He was called "the Driller" and they said he was from Derry and was lying low in Dublin. They said he was an expert at kneecapping and had learned his trade from the best. Danny had no choice; things would only get worse if he didn't go along with them.

"How are ya?" He tested the mood as he settled into the back seat beside a cowering and battered Scully. He had known Scully since he used to hang around the Dandelion Market. He was still at school then and spent his Saturday afternoons there, down the narrow covered lane that ran from Stephen's Green into the Wonderland where the hip of Dublin could come together to imitate what was going on in the rest of the world—but in a particularly Dublin way.

Dave, the busker, always took the time to nod to him as he passed. Dave was black and played Dylan in a Hendrix way. He always wore an afghan coat and his guitar was covered with peace symbols. Danny would drop a few coins as he passed and moved on between the stalls as Dylan gave way to Horslips, Rory Gallagher, and Thin Lizzy.

The stalls were stacked with albums and tapes, josh sticks and tie-dyed t-shirts with messages like "Peace" and "Love," pictures of green plants and yellow happy faces along with posters of Che, whose father's people had come from Galway.

The stalls were run by hippies from such far-out places as Blackrock and Sandyford, students from Belfield and Trinity, and a select few from Churchtown. They were all so aloof as they tried to mask their involvement in commercialism under a veneer of cool. Danny knew most of them by sight, and some by name. On occasion he'd watch over their stalls when they had to get lunch or relieve themselves. He was becoming a part of the scene.

**

"Hey Boyle!"

Danny had seen Scully around before but they had never spoken. Scully, everyone said, was the guy to see about hash and acid, and, on occasion, some opium.

"You go to school in Churchtown?"

Danny had just nodded, not wanting to seem overawed.

"Wanna make some bread?"

"Sure. What do I have to do?"

"Just deliver some stuff to a friend. He'll meet up with you around the school and no one will know—if you're cool?"

Danny had thought about it for a moment but he couldn't say no. He had been at the edge of everything that happened for so long. Now he was getting a chance to be connected—to be one of those guys that everybody spoke about in whispers. Sure it was a bit risky but he could use the money and, besides, no one would ever suspect him. Most people felt sorry for him and the rest thought he was a bit of a spaz.

"Could be a regular gig—if you don't fuck it up." Scully had smiled a shifty smile and melted back into the crowd, checking over each shoulder as he went.

***

As they drove off, Scully didn't answer and just looked down at his hands. His fingers were bloody and distorted like they had been torn away from whatever he had been clinging onto.

Anto turned around and smiled as the street lights caught in the diamond beads on the windshield behind him. "We're just fuckin' fine, Boyle. We're taking Scully out for a little spin in the mountains."

His cigarette dangled from his thin lips and the smoke wisped away ambiguously. He reached back and grabbed a handful of Scully's hair, lifting his bruised and bloodied face. "Scully hasn't been feeling too good lately and we thought that a bit of fresh air might sort him out, ya know?"

"Cool," Danny agreed, trying to stay calm, trying not to let his fear show—Anto fed off it. He briefly considered asking them to drop him off when they got to Rathfarnham but there was no point. He knew what was about to go down. Scully had been busted a few weeks before, and, after a few days in custody, had been released.

It was how the cops set them up. They lifted them and held them until they broke and spilled all that they knew. Then they let them back out while they waited for their court date. If they survived until then—well and good. And if they didn't, it saved everybody a lot of time and bother.

Danny sat back and watched Rathfarnham Road glide by in the night. They crossed the Dodder and headed up the hill toward the quiet, tree-lined streets that he had grown up in. As they passed near his house he thought about it: if the car slowed enough he could risk it—just like they did in the pictures. He could jump out and roll away. He could be up and running before they got the car turned around and by then he would be cutting through the back gardens and could easily lose them.

"You live around here, don't ya, Boyle?" Anto spoke to the windshield but Danny got the message. "And your girlfriend—she lives down that way?"

Danny thought about correcting him. He hadn't seen Deirdre since the incident in the church but there was no point. They'd use anybody and anything to get to him. He was better off just going along with them for now.

He briefly thought about asking God to save him but there was no point in that, either. They had given up on each other a long time ago. He turned his head away as they approached the church where he had been confirmed into the Faith, so long ago and far away now.

**

He had dipped his little fingers into the old stone font and made a wet cross on his forehead, his chest and each of his shoulders. His granny had often told him that the font was used in the Penal times when the faithful were banished to the mountains and the English spread their "Enlightenment" with muskets and swords. He had blessed himself like the generations had done before him, entitled by patriotism and Catholicism, rising up from the bogs of hopelessness to shake off the Imperial yoke. And back then he believed every word of it.

"The long arm of the Devil is always reaching out to knock unwary souls from the narrow path that leads to Heaven," she always warned him. "And the fires of Hell burn brighter every time a soul falls."

He had been fascinated by that and once held his finger in the flame of a candle to see what it was like. And though he quickly pulled it away, he had a blister. "Let that be a lesson to you," his granny chided as she smeared butter on it. "Now you can imagine what it's like to have your whole body burning—for eternity."

***

Anto lit another cigarette; the bursting match filled the car with sulphur, the red and yellow glare briefly brightening the side of the driver's impassive face. "You don't mind if I smoke, do you, Scully?"

Scully didn't say anything and just shook his downturned head.

"C'mon, Scully. Don't be like that. We're all still friends." Anto handed his cigarette packet back over his shoulder. "Here, give Scully a smoke—and have one yourself. We're all good mates here. Right? Just a bunch of mates taking a drive in the mountains."

Danny took the packet and fished two out. He held one toward Scully and when he didn't raise his head, searched for his mouth. He struck another match and held it out as Scully turned his head. His face was bloody and swollen. His nose, snotty and flattened to one side. He was missing more teeth than usual and he had been crying, probably for his life. He sucked the flame toward the tip of the cigarette and nodded at Danny but his eyes were resigned.

"There's the old church where we all went to Mass. Isn't that right, Boyle?" Anto reached over his shoulder and took the pack from Danny. "That was where we made our Confirmation and all that shite?"

Danny just nodded as old memories flooded back.

**

He had blessed himself with deliberate care under the supervision of Mr. Patrick Joseph Muldoon, his National School teacher, who had spent most of 1966 teaching Danny and his classmates how to be really Irish as the country got ready to celebrate the once derided martyrs of the Easter Rising—those who had died so Christ-like. By 1967, Muldoon's vocation was to ready them for Confirmation, that they might be a credit to their Church, their parents, and, of course, to Patrick Joseph Muldoon, once from a small biteen of a place in the bogs beyond in Mayo.

But when the Confirmation class went to Confession, he caught Danny blessing himself with his left hand and wacked it with a leather strap. "For the love of God, Boyle, what kind of way is that to be blessing yourself and you about to make your Confirmation? What kind of a Catholic are you?" Danny didn't dare answer, burning as he was with shame, the lingering effects of Original Sin. Muldoon had taught them about that, too. That's why they had to have the love of God beaten into them.

He was smiling as Danny stepped inside and took his place with his classmates. All the boys were dressed in dark suits with ribboned medals on their lapels, looking for all the world like little gentlemen.

And the girls looked like flowers in A-line coats over lace-trimmed satins and white stockinged feet in black patent-leather shoes. They weren't women yet, but some of them were beginning to attract attention in the way they stood and eyed the boys who smiled back nervously. Some of the boys even blushed and fidgeted until someone broke the tension by whispering: "I hope the bishop asks you!"

They had all been drilled in the Catechism but when the moment came—when the bishop walked among them and stopped, searching for doubts and unworthiness—none of them wanted to be tested. There was so much riding on the day. It was the day when they took their place in the One, Holy, Catholic and Apostolic Church.

It was also the day when friends and families bestowed their blessings in a much more tangible way. The previous year, some of the boys made over five pounds. Danny knew that he would do better. His father had already promised him a fiver—the next time he came home—to make up for not being able to make it over for the big day. "Things are a bit slow right now," he had told him when he made his weekly phone call. "But I'm just going down to see a man who knows a man who heard of a fella that might be hiring. Things are going to pick up, you'll see."

His father often made promises like that and usually forgot about them, but this time Danny was sure he'd come through. It was his Confirmation, after all, and the Holy Ghost was involved. He'd move his father to do the right thing. Besides, his granny said they would go and visit his mother in the hospital and Danny could show off to all the nurses and the patients. "They all have lots of money," his granny assured him, "and they'll be delighted for you, on your big day. Now stop fidgeting and pull up your socks. And make sure you take the pledge."

***

"I didn't grass," Scully suddenly announced to no one in particular, as if the enormity of his plight had finally seeped through all of his pain and nausea. "I swear to ya, I didn't tell them anything. They tried to make me but I just told them a load of shite, ya know. I just gave them names of people I made up. Ya know I'd never grass. Ya know that, don't ya?"

The Driller and Anto exchanged glances but said nothing so Danny stayed silent, too. The Devil was coming to collect his due and there was nothing any of them could do about that. Scully was done-for but there might still be some hope for Danny. There had to be. Sure he had strayed from the path, but it wasn't all his fault.

**

When the Confirmation ceremony reached its apex, Dr. John Charles McQuaid, the archbishop of Dublin, ascended into the elevated pulpit. He rose like an apparition without seeming to move his limbs under his dark robes. He looked to the ceiling and then down on them all for a moment like he was thinking about withholding Confirmation.

Danny had overheard his granny say that he was like that: "Cold and remote but, God love him, he grew up without his mother's love to soften his world. But it's a pity that he doesn't pay more attention to what the Sacred Heart of Jesus used to say about Love and being nice to everyone—especially poor sinners."

Danny never knew what to say when Granny spoke like that. He just listened and stored it all away to consider when he was alone and his face couldn't be read. But none of that would get in his way today, not when being a Catholic finally paid off.

The archbishop was talking in a low stern voice: "I promise," he intoned and paused until they repeated it. Danny joined in and raised his voice above them all, vowing with all of his heart: "to abstain from all intoxicating drinks, except used medically and by order of a medical man, and to discountenance the cause and practice of intemperance."

When he'd finished, Danny's heart soared up around the columns, searching for an open window, to fly out, all the way to the Heavens. The small fiery tongue of the Holy Ghost had descended upon him and kindled his soul and he wanted to feel that way forever.

But, by the time they got out of the warm stuffy church, the boys were tugging at their fresh white collars, loosening their stifling ties, while the girls hopped from foot to foot, trying to skip the pinch of new shoes. Muldoon was organizing them for photographs. First the whole class and then a series of each newly-confirmed with attending parents and himself—prominent for all posterity.

"If you don't mind," Granny Boyle had asked with polite insistence, "Danny and I would rather it was just the two of us."

Muldoon smiled like he'd been slapped but stood back without comment. The old principal was retiring that summer and he was next in line for the job. He didn't want to risk any more complaints reaching the parish priest's ears. "Not at all Mrs. Boyle, and may I tell you that I've never seen Master Daniel looking so well turned out. He's a real credit to you."

"He's a credit to the Sacred Heart of Jesus, that one. A pure angel if ever there was one, no matter what slandering sinners would say about him." She stared Muldoon down as she arranged herself for the camera. She had never gotten over it—the day Danny came home in tears.

**

"What's the matter pet?"

Danny was still shaking as he told her about what had happened at school that day.

They had been having a serious discussion about what went on in the local dances. None of them had been to any, of course, but most of them had older brothers and sisters.

Geraldine Wray was talking about "the Lurch"—the latest dance craze. Muldoon listened with growing indignation and puffed himself up a little more. He blamed television, the world's latest intrusion on Ireland. He had one but he only watched RTE. His students, though, watched the BBC and ITV, watching shows like *Top of the Pops* and no good could come of that. He had warned them it was a bad influence. "God bless us and save us," he declared when he had heard enough.

"Everybody's doing it," Geraldine assured him.

Muldoon puffed himself up a little more. "I don't care if the bishop and the reverend mother are doing it."

"I can just see those two at it," Danny piped up in a flash. He had a bit of a crush on Geraldine and never missed a chance to be in the same conversation, but it went wrong. Muldoon turned on him with a face like thunder. "May God forgive you for saying such a thing. That's a mortal sin—that's what that is—and you just weeks before your Confirmation. I've a good mind to call the archbishop myself and . . ."

Granny gritted her teeth as Danny relayed it all.

"Oh, did he now?" she stroked Danny's face. "You go on up and have a little lie down in your bed while I go and have a word with the parish priest. I'll not have that *bog-amadán* talk to my grandson like that. Go on now, and here," she handed him a small plate of chocolate biscuits. "Just mind you don't get any on the sheets."

**

"Big smiles for the camera, now."

Granny composed herself. This was one of those great moments that would live on long after she had gone to meet her maker. She would have a few bones to pick with Him when she got there but for now she smiled and held Danny close to her. *Please God,* she whispered through her smile. *Look after my Danny when I'm gone.*

She had great faith in God but she also had a healthy fear of the Devil and there were, God forgive her, times when she wasn't certain which one would win out in the end. But she kept her doubts to herself and went along with the current of the times.

Besides, she reminded herself as she shook hands with neighbors and friends, *God tests the faithful but doesn't stint on their rewards.* He had given her Danny, the apple of her eye and the only thing the world hadn't torn from her. She was there for His angel when those who should weren't. She accepted the job with joy, and dread. She knew far too well that the wickedness in the world would be out to destroy Danny, just like it had done to Jesus—and Padraig Pearse.

***

When they got to Killakee car park, the Driller pulled over and turned the car toward the twinkling lights of the city below and waited for Anto to break the silence.

"It's nice up here, isn't it lads? I like to come up here to think, ya know?"

"I think we'd have a nicer view over by the wee wood," the Driller disagreed and nodded in the direction of Cruagh Wood, off in the darkness.

"What do you think lads? Do you think we should go for a walk in the woods?"

Scully said nothing but pleaded with Danny with his swollen, puffy eyes.

"I'm fine here," Danny answered, hoping that if they waited in the car park, someone might drive by, maybe even the Garda.

Anto was probably just trying to frighten the shite out of them—and he was doing a great job. Every time Danny let his mind wander into what might happen, he had to clench his arse.

But it was all just for fuckin' show—it had to be. They weren't going to whack the two of them. They might just be making a show for Scully's sake, but Danny had done nothing wrong. Sure he owed them some money, but he was going to pay them, one of these days.

In the back of his mind, Danny had always known that life was out to get him. Despite all the talk about God loving them, and all, he knew better. His God stalked the streets looking to mete out punishment when he could and there was nothing anyone could do about that.

"Always thinking of yourself, Boyle. Didn't anybody ever teach you to be considerate of other people's feelings? Like Scully, here. Don't you think that he might like a walk in the woods?"

"But it's still fuckin' pissin' down with rain. Maybe we should just go back down and come out another time?" It was a long shot but Danny had to try. If he could just get back to the city, he'd change everything. He'd even start going to Mass again. And he'd go to Confession and clear his slate. He prayed silently into the dark desperation that swirled around him. Maybe, if he prayed hard enough?

Anto nodded to the Driller who started the car and took the road that led toward the wood. "Ya, maybe you're right, Boyle. What do you think, Scully? Do you think we should come back on a nicer day?"

"I didn't grass anybody. They tried to make me but I just told them a load of shite, ya know? I wouldn't grass you'se guys. Ya know that, don't ya? You'se are my mates. I'd never fuck you'se over. You know that, don't ya?"

Anto seemed to be thinking about it and nodded when he was done. "Of course we do but we just had to hear it from your own lips. You know that we're just trying to remind you of what would happen if you did."

"I know that Anto, that's why I'd never fuckin' grass you, ya know. I'm not mad, ya know?"

"Ya," Danny joined in, careful not to implicate himself with his enthusiasm as a rush of forgiveness flowed through the car. He whispered his thanks to the side window and resisted the urge to bless himself.

"Okay," Anto turned around and smiled at them both. "But let this be a lesson for you—the both of you'se. We have to stick together. Right?"

Danny and Scully nodded as they drove off, but the Driller pulled over when they got to the woods. "Well now that we've all kissed and made up, I need to take a leak. Anybody else?"

"Ya," Anto agreed. "We're all cool now. Right Scully? Boyle? No hard feelings? Let's all get out. We can have a few hits, too, and put the whole fuckin' thing behind us. I don't want to smoke-up in the car, in case we get pulled over on the way back."

They all got out and stretched in the damp mountain air. Perhaps, Danny wanted to believe, it was all going to be okay; Anto was just sending them a message. He could be like that—very dramatic.

They stood in a row, pissing up against the boles of trees, careful to stand with the wind behind them. Danny stood next to Scully and had almost relaxed when the Driller stepped up behind them and popped two shots into the back of Scully's head.

Scully fell forward, his own piss still dribbling between his fingers. He twitched a few times and then grew still. Anto approached and nudged him with his foot before looking into Danny's face. "It wasn't personal, Boyle, ya know that? It's just business. We have to maintain loyalty. Scully knew that, ya know?"

Danny didn't speak and just nodded as he kept one eye on the Driller who still held his gun ready.

"And now we should commit our dear departed friend to the ground," Anto continued like he was saddened by what had just happened. "And, when all the fuss has died down, we'll come back and put up a nice little cross, or something. Scully used to be a good mate; it's the least he deserves. Did you bring the shovel?" he asked the Driller who was still standing over Scully, ready to shoot again if he moved.

"No! Fuck-me. I left it in the car. Here," the Driller held out the gun, cold and hard in the softness of his damp leather gloves. "Hold this while I get it."

Danny fingered the cold metal, still reeking of death, and thought about it. He could pop them and get the fuck away without anybody knowing. He'd always wanted to be a hero—just like his grandfather who had fought off the Black and Tans.

**

"He would have been so proud of you, Danny boy," his granny had reminded him the day he was Confirmed. "I'm sure he's boasting about you right now with all of his old friends and comrades."

She had brought him to the Garden of Remembrance because that's where his spirit lingered. It was where she came to talk with him when the spinning of the world got too fast. He never spoke to her, she wasn't crazy—like some people—but she always said that she found peace and calm in his silence.

She wanted to share that with Danny but he was too young still.

And too full of wonder, as he stared into the pool, at the mosaic on the bottom, ancient Celtic weapons, forever beyond use.

He watched his granny's reflection walk to the other side of the cruciform, and, with the sunlight reflecting on the water and the brilliant white fluffy clouds just beyond her shoulders, she looked like a guardian angel. But he could tell that she was tiring. The long bus ride from Rathfarnham and the short one across the river and up to the "Square" had taken their toll.

When he looked up she rearranged herself and beckoned: "Come on now and sit down with your granny and enjoy a little bit of the peace and quiet they all died for."

The sun was flittering through the fresh green trees and Dublin rumbled by outside without deference as Danny nestled in beside her and stretched his legs in front of him. He admired the sharp crease on his long pants. His shoes were a bit dusty and his socks had rolled down to his ankles. His ribbons fluttered under his nose, tickling as they passed. He was almost a young man now, almost ready to make his own way in the world, still clutching the envelope that Granny had given him on the bus.

"Go on," she smiled. "You may as well open it now. Only give it back to me afterwards so I can keep it safe until we get home. It's not much now, but it's the least you deserve."

Danny nearly piddled when he saw the two five-pound notes tucked in the folds of a handwritten letter that said how proud she was of him; how he was the reason that she was happy to get up every morning even though everything else she had loved had been taken from her. Her handwriting never varied and flowed until it carried him along to where she reminded him to stay close to God—that the Devil was never far away.

Danny read it slowly and deliberately before putting it back in the envelope which Granny tucked into the folds of her bag and looked at all the memories that swirled around them.

"When I was a girl the English opened their jails and sent their murderers over here to plunder and pillage, and, some say, defile any young girls who might be out at night."

She fanned herself with her glove before continuing. "They were the Devil's spawn, all right, but some of the boys weren't going to let them get away with any more of that. Your grandfather was one of those that stood up to them. Even killed a few of them, too, but he got absolution for that. The priest told him to pray for their souls, every day; for the rest of his life, as his penance.

"Not that he ever talked about it, mind you, but then those that did the most say the least and that's the way the holy mother of God wants it. Maybe it was Her plan all along—that Bart would kill them and then pray for their souls. That way they could still get to Heaven. Don't you see?"

Danny nodded in total agreement. His grandfather was his idol. He was going to grow up just like him, too, and become the man that won the North back. Granny often told him that he had it in him—not like the Gombeens down in Leinster House. "Free-Staters," she called them and almost spat the words. "They were the ones who locked your grandfather up for being too much of an Irish hero—the bunch of scuts, every one of them, God forgive me.

"But your grandfather never held a grudge. 'We all die for Ireland, someday,' he always used to say when people got to arguing about it. He wasn't one for making a hash of the past, especially with those who hadn't even been a part of it."

She then fell silent among her memories as the breeze rippled the water and the flags, and the fresh green leaves, as Danny wandered among his own daydreams. After he had done all the patriotic stuff, he'd play football for Ireland and help them win the World Cup. And they would win it fairly, too, not like the English. The parish curate was starting a new team and had asked Granny if Danny could play for them. They must know how good he was, although he had never really played much.

He'd have to get a pair of boots, though. He'd get his father to buy them the next time he was over. Granny wouldn't know the right ones. He would ask his mother to ask him; she always knew how to get him to do things.

"Can we go see my ma now?"

"Sure of course we can, pet. We can get the bus just down the street and we'll be there in no time."

She rose slowly and headed toward the gate, trailing her fingers in the water for a moment before raising them to her lips, her heart, and across her shoulders.

***

"You like that, don't ya Boyle? A gun gives a man real power." Anto lit another cigarette and watched Danny's face. "Why don't ya keep it? It could come in handy, ya know?"

Danny hesitated. He could get one of them—but which one? Anto was always packing. He had lit his cigarette with his left hand. His right was still in his pocket, facing Danny. And the Driller was coming back.

Danny decided against it. He would have to raise the gun on both of them and he couldn't be sure that he would actually fire it. He might pause and that would give one of them a chance to pop him. He held the gun in his hands, turning it around before handing it back to Anto.

"Thanks, but I don't want it."

"Are you sure, Boyle? It could come in handy." Anto reached his gloved hand forward and took the gun away. "C'mon then, let's get the fuck outta here."

"But what about Scully?"

"Ah, fuck him. We'll make a call when we get back. The cops can come and pick him up."

"But won't they figure out what happened?"

"Don't worry, Boyle. They'll never be able to trace it back to us. That's why we wear gloves. C'mon, let's get to fuck outta here."

Danny sat in the back seat and looked at his bare fingers, now imprinted on the gun. Anto had him over a barrel and there was fuck-all he could do about it.

"By the way, Boyle," Anto turned when they pulled up outside the Yellow House, close to where Danny lived. "Now that Scully is no longer with us, we'll have a few things for you to do."

"I don't know if I can."

"C'mon, Boyle. You're perfect for the job. And," he paused to pull his gloves off, "we know we can trust you. Think about it and we'll be in touch."

CHAPTER 2

Danny's mother listened to the radio as she waited for the kettle to boil. The news was full of the Queen's visit to the North and Jacinta's heart grew warm with hope. They were all tired of the fighting, but her heart froze a little when the newscaster went on to report on the finding of a young man's body up near the Hell Fire Club. He had been shot in the head and left like rubbish among the trees.

Danny had been out late and she couldn't help but worry. He had become so shifty again, avoiding her eyes and any questions about how he was spending his nights.

"It's just one less feckin' drug dealer," Jerry snorted as he sat down at the kitchen table and waited for his tea.

She had seen that look on his face before. He had worn it for years when she was in the hospital, when he tried to show that he wasn't afraid. "The sooner they all kill each other the better, as far as I'm concerned. Besides, it's got feck-all to do with us."

"Maybe you're right, but did you ever wonder where Danny is getting all his money from? Every time he goes out, he buys things for himself."

"He's probably making it busking."

"Are you sure? He's got nearly two hundred under his mattress."

"Good for him. He's getting great on the guitar and he has a good voice. If only he'd sing something good, like Buddy Holly. I'm sick of all the punk shite he does."

"But he can't be making it all from that."

"He's probably got a few fiddles going—down at the Dandelion—you know? Buying and selling shit. Fair play, I say. Anybody who can make any money in this country is a feckin' genius."

"You don't think we should be worried?"

"Not at all. Danny is a good lad at heart. He'd never do anything stupid."

But Jerry wasn't so sure. If Danny was anything like him, he'd get himself into more trouble than he could handle. He was probably involved, somehow. It was the only way he could be making money like that. The Ireland that Jerry's father had fought for had become a hard place and he and Jacinta hadn't made it any easier for Danny. He knew what was going on. There were drug dealers everywhere like they didn't fear anybody.

But there were those that the drug dealers feared and Jerry knew someone who knew someone who knew them all. They might be interested in helping—for Bart and Nora's sake if not for Jerry's. He'd have to convince them, though. He had blotted his copybook with them before.

*

Danny lay in his bed, listening to them. He had hardly slept. He didn't dare. He was haunted by Scully's bruised and swollen face, and that look in his eyes—like he was just resigned. And afterwards, he almost seemed relieved that all the running and hiding was over, lying by the bole of a tree as his blood trickled from his head and mingled with own piss still dribbling off down the hill.

Danny retched again but his stomach was empty but for the bile that churned like a knife. It had all seemed like a game up until now, playing the hard chaw. He wasn't going to be like his father, catholically bowing and scraping to bishops, priests and all those that carried out their will. Beaten down from the beginning, but, in the back of the car, he had prayed like a sinner and made promises into the dark.

He was ashamed of that. Despite all of his posturing and protestations he was just like the rest of them, a craven Catholic to the core, trapped in the limbo of Purgatory, lost and alone now, betrayed by hubris and delivered to the Devil.

No one was ever going help him—no one ever had. His granny said she was but she was just doing it so everybody could say what a great woman she was, raising a child at her age. His prayers had never been answered and it was stupid of him to think they might. He was cut off from all that.

He wished he could go down and tell his parents what happened but they had never been the type of parents that could make things better. Usually they just made things worse. They had never really been parents to him when he was growing up. His father had been in England and his mother was in St. Patricks' Mental Hospital, even when he was Confirmed. But his granny had taken him to see her, just like she said she would.

**

"He gave the little wealth he had," they used to chant in unison as they approached the front door, almost skipping along the path.

> To build a house for fools and mad
> And showed by one satiric touch

No Nation wanted it so much
That Kingdom he hath left his debtor
I wish it soon may have a better.

Granny had taught him that verse when they first started to visit, when Danny was very young. It made it all a bit more normal and she always said that she loved to hear him laugh and sing. "The great Dean Swift left the money to build it when he died," she had explained. She had given Danny a copy of *Gulliver's Travels*, too. Sometimes he brought it with him and pretended to read while his mother and his granny stared at each in stony silence only broken now and then by banalities.

"Oh, Danny, pet! I thought you'd get here much earlier." His mother was agitated and lit another cigarette from the lipstick stained butt of the last. "I was even starting to think that you might have fallen under a bus or something." She wore a skirt and blouse and had her hair brushed out. And she wore makeup. Usually she just wore her worn out robe with curlers in her hair. "But I'm so glad that you're finally here. Come here to me," she beckoned, "so that I can hug the life out of you."

Danny waited for his granny's nod of approval before nestling into his mother's arms, feeling her cold cheek against his, and the soft warmth of her tears. He wanted to say something that would make her happy but he was unsure. His granny told him he had to be polite to his mother but she didn't want him to get too close—for his own sake. She told him that his poor mother was not well, God love her, and that she couldn't be a real mother to him right now.

"So did you have a nice day?"

"I did, Ma, it was very nice."

"He took the pledge too," Granny interjected as she reached out to extract Danny.

"Look what I have for you. Come here and see." His mother pulled him closer again and reached under her cushion for her beaded purse, one of the items she had made during arts and crafts.

She had made one for Granny too, though she never used it. She also made covers for bottles—to turn them into lamps. Danny had one in his room, a wicker of colored plastics with a soft heart-shaped cushion edged with white lace.

She drew a clean, fresh pound note from her purse and held it up. "This is for you, pet, to celebrate the day. And," she was enjoying herself and her smile almost chased the furrows from her brow. "Your Uncle Martin sent you this." She reached back into her purse again and pulled out a bright ten-shilling note. "He wanted to see you today but he couldn't wait. He was here for over an hour," she paused for emphasis. "But he said to tell you that you're to phone him and he'll take you to the Grafton. You'd like that, wouldn't you?"

His granny reached from behind him and took the money just as Danny's fingers reached it. "I'll put it with the other money I'm keeping safe for you. Don't forget to thank your mother."

His mother watched and a twinge of annoyance flashed across her face before she swallowed and pushed it back down inside of her. "I wanted to go and see you at the church but they wouldn't let me. They said I wasn't up for it."

Her eyes filled with tears as the flickers of old regrets rose and she struggled like she was trying to avoid sliding back into the darkness inside of herself.

"There's no need to be upsetting yourself," Granny soothed. "I was there with him and we're both here now."

For a moment, his granny softened and reached out to touch his mother's hand. "So! Are you feeling any better? I think you're looking better but you're very thin. Are they not feeding you at least?"

"Better?" Danny's mother answered without taking her eyes from his face. "All they do is give me pills and tell me to pray to God."

"Prayer is the best medicine," his granny soothed, even as she stiffened.

"Could you not have a word with them?" his mother pleaded. "At least to get them to let me out once in a while? For Danny's sake."

"And why would they listen to me; I'm just an old woman. And besides, Danny's well looked after, now."

Danny rose and walked to the window like he wasn't listening and watched their reflections and the breeze running free on the grass outside. It was a nice view when the sun was shining but it could get very damp and grey when it rained and sadness hung in the air.

"Would you mind if we came in?" asked the nurses who had gathered in the doorway. "We just want to say congratulations to Danny on his big day."

They squeezed into the room crinkling their starched white linens, followed by two nuns draped in flowing black whispers. The nurses took turns squeezing him and slipping coins into his hand but the nuns just patted his cheek and handed him little medals—St. Christopher and the Sacred Heart of Jesus.

"God bless you, Danny!" they all agreed and told him he looked like a saint–or an angel.

"I'm afraid it's getting late and we should be leaving," Granny announced when the fuss died down, and while the presence of the nuns would discourage Jacinta from protesting. "I have to get Danny home in time for his tea."

"But we only just got here," Danny said, forgetting his manners and his vague understanding of the situation.

"Now Danny," the nuns admonished.

"But I've hardly had a chance to see him." Jacinta rose to take him in her arms.

"You mustn't get excited," the nuns reminded her. "What would the doctor say if he knew?"

The nuns pried them apart, faces stoic beneath their veils, and ushered the nurses out.

Danny's mother smiled wearily as if there was nothing she could do. Even Danny could see that. He wanted her to say something so he could spend a few minutes with her alone but she had begun to shrivel again.

"Can I just say goodbye to Ma before we go?" He knew if he pleaded just right that he would get his way and Granny and the nuns would withdraw to the hallway outside.

But they left the door open.

"It's so good to see you, Danny boy. I can't believe how big you're getting. Did your daddy call you?"

"He did, last weekend, and he says he'll be home soon and that he is going to give me a fiver."

"Ah, that'll be grand."

"But I really want him to buy me a pair of football boots, you know, like the ones Johnny Giles wears."

"We'll ask him, then. I'm sure he'll know the right ones." But she didn't sound convincing. Her face was sad, almost without hope.

Danny searched for something to change that: "And when he comes I'm going to ask Granny if he and I can come and see you on our own." It was all he had to offer.

"Ah, that would be lovely. That gives me something to look forward to." She reached out to take him back into her arms.

"Danny," his granny called from the doorway. "We have to leave now."

Danny hesitated but his mother just nodded. "Go on now, Danny boy, and don't be keeping your granny waiting. There's a good boy."

He turned again from the doorway but his mother had her head down, like she might be falling asleep, except her shoulders were shuddering a little. "Bye Ma," he called as the nuns closed like a curtain between them, muffling any answer she might have made.

**

"When I grow up," Danny announced when they were back home, as he dipped his chips into the broken yolks of his fried eggs, "after I'm finished being the president and playing football, I'm going to become a doctor. But not the type that just give people pills and lock them up. I'm going to be the type of doctor that actually makes people better."

"I think you should be a priest, instead," Granny answered without turning around from her sink of soapy dishes. She said she wanted to tidy up before they had the cake she bought—just for the day that it was. It was yellow and spongy with a soft cream layer in the middle. It had hard, sweet icing with lemon jelly wedges coated in sugar. Granny would even let Danny pick them off her slice. "A priest can do far more good than a doctor."

"Father Reilly said that only the doctors can help Ma. I asked him at Confession."

"I'm sure he meant something else. Only God can help your mother and not before she lets Him."

"Why doesn't God just mend her now?"

"Ah, Danny, you don't understand. God works in mysterious ways."

"Does He not love Ma?"

"Of course He does. Why would you even think such a thing? He loves us all."

"I pray all the time, for Ma to get better, but sometimes I don't think He is listening."

Granny stopped what she was doing and swatted the stray strands that had wisped around her face.

"God is always listening, Danny, and He is always watching us. That's why we have to be good all the time. But sometimes," she paused and waited for his frown to lift, "he lets us try to find our own way back to Him. He wants us to have free will so that we come to Him of our own accord."

"But what about Ma? She doesn't have free will anymore. She isn't even allowed to leave the hospital anymore."

"Ah, Danny, sure you don't understand yet. When you're bigger you will but for now you'll just have to believe me that God knows what is best for all of us, even your mother—God love her."

The kettle began to whistle and Granny fussed with the teapot. "Come on now and let's have some cake."

Danny was easily deflected and devoured his cake with enthusiasm. When he had finished his second slice she ushered him off to brush his teeth and say his prayers. "I'll be up to tuck you in, in a minute."

**

But when she got to his room he was fast asleep. He looked like an angel with his fists rolled up beneath his chin, the little medals the nuns had given him peeping out from between his fingers. She gently stroked his hair and fought to keep her heart from bursting.

You will look out for him after I am gone? she whispered into the unanswering dark.

God, who knew what was best for them all, and kept His thoughts to Himself, had given her a great many challenges in life. But He had given her Danny, too, to lighten the burden no matter how dark the days became. He was that small candle that burned when her heart and mind grew dark with sorrow.

And fear and doubt. She'd had conversations with Davies, the solicitor and long-time friend of her dear, departed, Bart. There was nothing else to be done. She'd have to let Danny's father back into his life. She could make conditions, but she would have to allow it.

And you'll make sure that no harm will ever come to him?

She didn't hesitate to make bargains with God, assured as she was in her faith. When she needed something she asked because when He needed her to step in and take care of His little angel, she didn't hesitate.

Naturally she had confidence in Him, but sometimes she wondered if He wasn't distracted by the multitude of conflicting prayers and personal requests. Things were allowed to happen that were obviously going to come to a bad end—like Jeremiah and Jacinta, who should never have been brought together. Her son had a weakness for drink and Jacinta had a feeble mind.

But they did, and they gave into temptation and had to be married before she began to show. That, Granny decided, was her role in life—to help to iron out the wrinkles in the Great Plan.

She sat for a while gently stroking Danny's hair. He had come into the world just after Christmas, a few weeks before he was expected. Jeremiah and Jacinta had been arguing all night. Jacinta had a visit from her sisters. They were on their way home from the dance and brought her fish and chips.

**

"We saw Jerry down in the pub." They masked their delight in sharing bad news with a veneer of seeming concern. Jacinta had married above her station, showing them all up, even if she had hitched herself to Jerry's falling star. "He spent the whole evening going around flirting with all of the women there."

"And him with an expecting wife at home."

"Not a shred of shame in him either."

"What was he up to?"

"Maybe we shouldn't be telling you all of this but it's better that you know now."

By the time Jerry got home she had worked herself into a right state.

***

Danny also knew that he had literally fallen into the world, expelled by his mother in a fit of rage.

He had heard the story often, whispered by grown-ups who overlooked his small presence, like he was too young to understand.

The story went that his mother had lifted a heavy skillet to rap his father across the head and the strain of it was too much and she expelled Danny, just seven and a half months after the wedding.

They said he didn't seem to mind and for the first few months he slept for most of the day.

His granny said it was because he never enjoyed a moment of peace inside of his mother as she was the type of woman that could never be at ease. Even when she was sleeping she fretted and twitched over every little slight, real or imagined. Even carrying Danny, while other women had a glow about them, Jacinta had a scowl.

Danny had also overheard that it wasn't a planned pregnancy, that it was more of an unfortunate accident in a lane behind the dance hall. He had heard whisperings that his mother had been drunk and eager and his father had been drunk and thoughtless. He had no idea what any of it meant but apparently, "they had been eyeing each other for a few weeks." He heard that his father thought she was a fine-looking thing and his mother knew that he came from a few "bob"—Danny's grandfather was a minister in the government at the time, and a veteran of the War of Independence.

His granny said it was what was to be expected. She often said that she knew that Jeremiah was lost the day he came home drunk, at eighteen, with his Confirmation Pledge in tatters around him.

That he should fall prey to Lust was inevitable, and when the news reached her, she chided him for a while and then arranged for a nice, respectable wedding while her future daughter-in-law could still be squeezed into a white dress.

**

"I have had a quiet word with Father Brennan," she had announced as cordially as she could manage.

She had brought Jerry and Jacinta together over tea at Bewley's, in a booth where they could keep their business to themselves. "He can fit you in on the third Saturday in May."

Jerry stirred his tea without looking up while Jacinta devoured sticky buns. Neither of them even offered a word of thanks but Granny Boyle didn't care. The holy mother of God would grant her all the thanks she needed. "And then you can have a nice weekend on the Isle of Man."

Jerry lit another Woodbine as Jacinta stared at the empty plate. "Are there any more of those sticky buns?"

Granny Boyle forced a smile as she beckoned a waitress. This was going to take all of her patience so she turned her gaze on her son. "Your father is going to have a word with someone in the Public Works Department, too."

Jerry looked at her for a moment and shrugged. "I was going to reapply," he protested softly.

"There's no time for that anymore," Granny cut him off. It was still an open sore between them. He had failed in his first year at UCD much to the consternation of his father, causing the poor man to turn purple. "He's a thundering disgrace to us all," he had bellowed when he heard about Jerry and Jacinta. "First he drinks himself out of college and now he takes up with the daughter of some common laborer from God-knows-where. We should send the pair of them off to England and be rid of them."

"Now Bart," Granny had soothed. "He's made his bed and we're not going to turn him out over that." She folded her arms to let him know the matter was decided and he better just get used to it.

"Very well but don't expect me to pay for the wedding."

"You won't have to," she reminded him. She had her own means. Her father had left her money when he sold up the old place. She had always kept it separate and apart.

The wedding went well and the weather was fine. Bart behaved himself and even danced with his daughter-in-law and her mother. Granny let him have a few whiskeys in the bar before the reception so that he could put on his public persona. He made a very good speech, too, and only mentioned re-election twice.

And when it was all done, Granny sat back as the young people danced the rest of the evening away. She had done all she could and now it was up to Jeremiah and Jacinta, though she would be there to help them every step of the way—for her unborn grandson's sake if not for theirs.

But as Granny spent the summer making plans, arranging a nice flat for the newlyweds on the Terenure side of Rathgar and prodding Jacinta in the direction of motherhood, Fate played its own hand and took Bart. He died of a heart attack at the Galway races after a day of longshot winners.

"Fate is fickle," she reminded her son as they walked along behind his hearse.

***

"They found a young fella named Declan Scully shot dead in the mountains," his mother told Danny as she poured a cup of tea and placed it in front of him. "Didn't you know somebody by that name?"

Danny didn't look up as his parents sat and waited. "I haven't seen him in a few years. The last I heard he was into drugs."

His parents said nothing but he could sense them exchanging glances. He knew they wouldn't force the issue. They couldn't; he could turn it back on them so easily. "Did they say who did it?"

"No, but the Garda said that it might be linked to the killing down in Rathgar, a few months ago."

His mother hovered but Danny didn't answer. Instead, he reached across and took a cigarette from her pack and lit it with one of her matches, filling the kitchen with the acridity of sulphur.

"Whoever it was should be given a feckin' medal," his father added as he gulped some tea and raised his newspaper. "We should get rid of all these little feckers, once and for all."

"Don't be talkin' like that. What if it was our Danny?"

"And why would he get caught up in that shite? He's not that stupid. Isn't that right, Danny?"

Danny agreed but didn't raise his head. He couldn't be sure what his eyes might tell them.

He had to get away from them. He wasn't a part of their world anymore. He had to get back to where he could hide away until he sorted it all out. He'd go down to the Dandelion while it was still there. His whole world was changing and he needed something to hold onto.

"I'm going out."

"Where are you off to now?"

"I'm going to busk for a while and then I got to look after a few stalls."

"Will you be home for your dinner?"

"I don't know."

"You won't be late, will ya?"

"I told ya, I don't know."

"Well, I'll leave something in the oven and you can heat it up when you get home."

*

His parents watched in silence as he finished his tea and swung his guitar over his shoulder. His jeans were soiled and his denim jacket was tattered and frayed around the collar. His hair was long and greasy and he hadn't had a bath in over a week.

"I'm worried about him," Jacinta said after she heard the front door close.

"He's not going to listen to either of us."

"What are you saying—that we should just give up on him?"

Jerry lit another cigarette and shrugged. "Why are you asking me? How would I know what to do?"

"'Cos you're supposed to be his father."

"Right, like the little bollocks would listen to me, anyway."

"But we have to try. We can't just turn our backs on him. He needs us."

"What he needs," Jerry paused to stub out his cigarette. Her face was lined with worry so he had to sound reassuring.

He knew what he had to do but he couldn't tell her. Not until he had it all sorted, anyway. He had let her down so often, but not this time. This time he'd come through for them all. "Is a good, swift kick up the arse."

*

Jacinta couldn't let it go at that. She had to do something. She went down to the church to have a chat with Nora. She would know what to do. She always did before.

Jacinta blessed herself at the old stone font and stepped inside. The church was almost empty, just a few old people seeking solace in the shadows, every little noise they made echoing to the wooden beams above.

She made her way through the flickering shadows to the little side altar and lit a tea candle from the sputtering flame of another. She knelt in the first pew and lowered her head and prayed to the statue of Mary, standing forever between them and God, almost shapeless in her long white shift, under the pale blue mantle, her sandaled foot crushing the serpent that slithered around the world.

Jacinta always prayed there; it was where Nora would find her when she came.

Nora would listen to her and the news she brought. She would never speak but Jacinta could always feel her censure. She and Jerry had always been a disappointment to the old woman but she never spoke about that anymore. Instead she would just listen as Jacinta poured out all that troubled her.

And even when Jacinta was finished unloading her burdens, the old woman would not speak. She didn't have to. Jacinta knew she would intercede on her behalf, interceding with God's own mother, interceding on behalf of her daughter-in-law who could never be strong enough to bear her own burdens.

Jacinta knew her mother-in-law had never approved of her but she'd still help—for her grandson's sake if nothing else. That was Jacinta's one solace: Nora Boyle would never turn her back on them. She would move the powers of Heaven and Earth for her grandson.

"It's Danny," Jacinta spoke softly, keeping their business private. "I'm worried sick about him. I think he's into drugs again and I worry that he'll end up like the poor Scully boy they found dead this morning."

Nora didn't answer so Jacinta continued.

"I know that Jerry and I are to blame. We should have been better parents for him but we're trying now. Please, Mrs. Boyle. Is there anything you can do to help us?"

Nora didn't answer and Jacinta waited. Her mother-in-law liked to make her wait. She probably wanted her to know that things took time, that she couldn't just ask and have everything put to right. She and Jerry would never learn anything if all of their problems were solved whenever they asked.

No. Nora Boyle would make her wait for a little while so Jacinta prayed and dedicated her rosary to the Blessed Virgin, saying each prayer slowly so the words would not get all jumbled together.

"Hail Mary, full of grace. Our Lord is with thee. Blessed art thou among women and blessed is the fruit of thy womb, Jesus. Holy Mary, mother of God, pray for us sinners, now and at the hour of our death. Amen."

CHAPTER 3

Fr. Reilly waited for her by the door. He had seen Jacinta deep in prayer and didn't want to intrude. Instead he pottered around, rearranging pamphlets and tidying up the noticeboard until she rose and came toward him.

"Mrs. Boyle. Are you well?" he whispered as he held the door open for her, letting the sunlight into the shadows.

"As good as can be expected, given what's happening."

"Yes, Mrs. Boyle," Fr. Reilly agreed as they walked from the church. "I did hear the news. It's shocking to think that we have gotten to the point where human life means so little."

It was all the comfort a childless man could offer. He glanced across at her, wondering how she was dealing with it, her being a bit delicate, and all. He saw the same fear he had seen in the faces of parishioners before. Fear and doubt about how to steer their children through a world that had changed so much. Evil was washing over Ireland again and there was nothing he and all the priests and bishops could offer but to cling to the Faith–a Faith that had never delivered them from the pain and anguishes of the past, but it was all they had.

"It is, Father, and the ones who killed him were probably not much older, themselves."

He had no answers, nor did he have anything new to assure her. "I suppose that all we can do is to stay strong in our Faith–to show the young people that it still matters–that God is still there–and that they can reach out for His divine mercy and forgiveness."

He once knew Danny well. He used to come to him for Confession. But that was before that ill-conceived call to the house. He hadn't thought about how it might look; he was too concerned with what Danny had said.

Every Saturday night, his grandmother used to queue to put him in Fr. Reilly's box before joining the line for Fr. Brennan's. "Sit there and be quiet," she'd announce in a penetrating whisper, to let Fr. Reilly know he was there waiting alone in the muffled darkness as Fr. Reilly heard the confession from the other side; a doleful litany of human frailties. He hoped that Danny wasn't listening; that he would be distracting himself with a thorough examination of his own conscience, just like he had been taught.

Until it was his turn, and Fr. Reilly would lean against his side of the grill, with his hand to his face, so he wouldn't recognize the boy he knew so well. It was the same thing most weeks but one night stood out.

**

"Bless me Father, for I have sinned," Danny had whispered. "It has been a week since my last confession."

"Go on," Fr. Reilly always had to coax it out of him.

"Father I've been having impure thoughts and I've been dishonest in my dealings with others."

Since his Confirmation, Danny was no longer content with little venial sins and offered up things that were far more mortal. He was going through that age when boys often confused the murmurings of their bodies with the whisperings of the Devil. Fr. Reilly had heard it all before.

"I see. Go on."

"I told my granny that I'd no homework so that I could watch TV."

"Well that's not right. You must strive to be honest—and to be responsible—in all of your dealings."

"I will, Father."

"And what about the other part?"

"Father?"

"The part about the impure thoughts."

"Oh those, Father. They just pop into my mind. I can't help it."

"I see."

They both hesitated on their sides of the grill.

"And I stole a few apples from the shop," Danny blurted out as if to move things along.

"Well that's not a good thing, either. Remember what happened to Adam and Eve?"

"Yes, Father. Afterwards, I wanted to give them back but I was afraid of getting caught."

"Well, are you sorry for your sins, at least?"

"I am indeed, Father. Every one of them."

"Well then, say three Our Fathers and ten Hail Marys and try to remember the story of Adam and Eve because Sin is how we got thrown out from the Garden of Eden."

"I will, Father."

Fr. Reilly lowered his head and mumbled in Latin, cleansing Danny's soul of impurities.

"Is there anything else?" He asked after a few moments, as Danny lingered. "Is there something else you need to get off your mind?"

"Father, I've been praying to God to help my ma but He still hasn't done anything yet. Is there something else I should be doing? I mean, I've tried to be good but it doesn't seem to be working."

Fr. Reilly raised his head and leaned closer to the grill. Even in the gloom, Danny's boyish face was clear, his deep brown eyes sparkled as his full lips whispered.

"God works in mysterious ways," Fr. Reilly decided from all the thoughts he considered. "And it's hard to know what He has in store for us all. Sometimes, He tests us to see if we're worthy. That's why we must go on developing our faith in Him and trust that everything is going according to His plan."

"But my ma is so unhappy. Sometimes I worry that she might go and kill herself."

"Don't be thinking like that. Have you prayed for her?"

"I have, Father, every night and every morning but I don't think it's doing any good. I think maybe God has forgotten about her."

"You can't be thinking like that. Maybe He is just testing you, like he did with Job."

"But my ma is suffering so much, Father. Couldn't you have a word with Him and see if He can do anything about it."

Fr. Reilly was silenced for a while until the penitent on the other side coughed a few times to remind them that she was waiting.

"Listen, my son," Fr. Reilly whispered urgently. "We'll talk about this another time instead of staying in here all night. People might start thinking you have lots of sins. Go on now and don't forget to say your penance. And say a few more for your family."

***

After he called the house that night, Nora Boyle started bringing Danny to Fr. Brennan and avoided him altogether, barely nodding to him as they passed on the street. She never forgave him and he could feel her scorn when she passed nearby.

"Poor Declan's funeral will be on Tuesday. They'll bring the remains in on Monday evening. Perhaps you would mention it to Danny in case he wants to attend?"

Jacinta just nodded, deep in her own thoughts. "I will, indeed, Father. I'll mention it to him when he gets home." She wasn't sure if Nora would be happy that Fr. Reilly was getting involved but Nora, like God, worked in mysterious ways.

*

Nora Boyle wasn't happy as she lingered in the flickering shadows by the small altar, kneeling, with her forehead resting against her wrists, rosary beads trickling through her fingers as she whispered.

Her mind was a bit of a muddle. She had always thought that things would have been very different by now. She had always tried to do her best but she had a few regrets, too. She had made her fair share of mistakes and there were times, God forgive her, when she had been less than she might have been, especially with Jeremiah.

She had done well by Danny, though. No one could argue with that. She had given him a solid basis of what was right and wrong and now it was up to him; she couldn't lead him anymore. The world had changed far too much for that. She couldn't even make her way to the Garden of Remembrance anymore.

That might have bothered her but she knew Bart would come for her though it was taking him a lot longer than she'd expected. He must have met up with some of his old friends.

She wanted to talk with him about what they should do with Danny. She didn't want to make the same mistakes she had made with Jeremiah. After she'd banished him to England he seemed more and more shrivelled each time he came back for weekends, in his long tweedy coat, reeking of resignation and cigarettes, his teeth and nails turning browner and browner.

But what else could she have done? He had picked his own path and all she could hope for was that one day, like the Bible's prodigal, he would return. So when he was home, she insisted that he spend time with his son. She had him take the boy to Milltown, to watch the Rovers. Or, if it was raining, she'd send them off to the Grafton Cinema. Danny loved his cartoons and always came home with wonderful stories about Bugs Bunny, Tweetie Pie and Sylvester, and Danny's favorite, Daffy Duck.

Or if the weather was finer, she'd send them to the zoo though, as she found out later, they only ever walked around the outer fence.

**

"It is better this way," Jerry always insisted. "It's like we're on a real safari. Inside it's just like all the animals are in prison but from here, with the bushes and all, you can hardly see the cages. It's like the animals are pacing back and forth like they know we're hunting them."

"Can't we just go in the next time?"

"Don't be asking me for stuff like that Danny. I don't have money for that kind of thing. People like us just get to stand outside and look in. That's the bit they don't tell you about in school. But don't worry, the priests say that the poor get to Heaven easier, especially if they become poor giving all their money to the Church." He stopped as Danny's eyes welled up. "I'm sorry but I'm just trying to warn you, Danny boy, so you'll know what to expect."

They always stopped in Ryan's on the way home, a warren of old wooden snugs for every type of drinking. Danny always wanted to go into the little rooms with the window that opened over the bar. They reminded him of confessionals.

"That was great all the same, wasn't it Danny?"

Danny looked over the four empty lemonade bottles, knee-deep in the torn wrappers of four potato chip bags. His father was glassy and ruddy and pleading desperately with his eyes.

"It was brilliant, Da, but couldn't we just go inside one of these days?"

"I told you. I'm not made of money, son."

"Uncle Martin took me inside last summer."

"Well you've seen it then so we can stop coming."

While Danny struggled to control his tears his father peered through the cloud of smoke between them. "Ah, not you too, Danny? You're looking at me the same way your mother did." He shriveled a little more into the wood panel behind him, another sad and beaten man.

**

Nora had had to find someone else for him to look up to, so, when Martin had asked if he could take Danny to the pictures—for his Confirmation, she didn't hesitate, even when he asked if she'd mind if they went for something to eat afterwards.

She approved of Martin; there was something different about him—not like the rest of his family. She'd never heard a bad word spoken about him though he did like to keep to himself, but that, she assumed, was a personal choice and one that she admired. Danny liked him a lot and that was good enough for Nora, though she did ask him to tell her all about it.

Danny said it was much better with Martin—that he'd brought him for burgers and chips. His father just used to take him to the pub and buy him lemonade and crisps. Wimpy's was much better.

**

Danny's smile had broken into a huge grin when his stacked plate was placed on the table in front of him.

"It's all right," Martin had agreed. "But in America they have these huge burgers. I'm going to go there, to New York, as soon as I finish school and all. And you can come and visit," he added when Danny's face clouded.

"I don't know if I will have the time. I'm going to be busy when I grow up."

"Oh really?"

"Ya. I'm going to become the president first, and make the British give back the North. Then I'm going to play football for Ireland."

Martin smiled and watched Danny chew on another big mouthful that pressed against the inside of his soft downy cheek.

"How're things going at school? Have you had any more trouble with the Nutgrove crowd?"

They had been picking on Danny for months, waylaying him on his way home from school, or from the shops. When his granny heard about it she confronted them on the street, warning them that she would have the Guards on them if they didn't stop. "I'll have the lot of you in the Borstal. Let that be fair warning. Go on now and never bother my grandson again. If one of you as much as touches a hair on his head . . ."

They scattered and left him alone for a while but Martin knew that someday Danny would have to fight his own battles. Perhaps, Martin considered, he would get Danny some boxing gloves and teach him how to use them. That's how he survived. He never went looking for trouble but when it found him he could send it home with a black eye and a bloody nose. He had gained a bit of a reputation as a hard man. Maybe it was enough to protect Danny, too, at least until he got a bit older. Maybe he should drop by and pick him up after school a few times so that everybody could see them together.

"Uncle Martin?" Danny asked after a few moments of silence. "Do you think that God doesn't like my ma?"

Martin never really thought about stuff like that anymore and paused before he answered, to find the right words. "Danny, I don't know, but everybody says that God's supposed to love us all."

"Why do you think that my ma is always sick?"

She had always been sickly, as long as Martin could remember. His mother always referred to her as "that poor little creature" and Jacinta was never expected to help out around the house. His other sisters always complained about that. "How come she never gets asked?"

"Because she gets nervous and drops things," their mother would answer impatiently.

"She only does that to get out of doing anything," Brenda would reply.

"And to get attention," Linda would chime in.

Martin was the youngest so his opinions hadn't really mattered. He had always known that Jacinta was nervous but he'd never believed there was something really wrong with her until she got put in the hospital. Then he wondered if he shouldn't have been a little nicer to her, all along. He felt bad about that but he was young and couldn't do much about anything. He'd make it up to her when he was older.

"I don't know, Danny, I think she is getting better."

"My granny says she's a lost cause."

"C'mon now and finish your chips. It's getting late and your granny will be getting worried."

He waited until Danny turned back to his plate; he didn't want to show his concern. He knew how hard it was to grow up with parents but it must be awful to grow up without them. He wanted to tell Danny the truth—about everything, but what could he say? Instead, as they rode on the upper deck of the bus, all the way out to Rathfarnham, they talked about the cartoons and all the crazy things they had seen.

"Do you remember when Daffy Duck tried to shoot Bugs with the gun and Bugs stuck his carrot in the barrel? That was so funny."

**

As Martin walked back toward Terenure, he kicked his trepidations along in front of him but he couldn't do it: he couldn't shatter Danny's innocence. Life would do that, and probably brutally, but he couldn't.

His own was shredded but he was okay with that. He was different. He had always known it but only in the last few years had he gained the ability to articulate it, even if only to himself.

He had gone to a priest, too, when his questions were bigger than his answers. And he was given the same old advice: Faith, Hope, Love and lots and lots of Prayer but it all lost its lustre as he grew into the world. It was a hard place where those who were different were singled out for special torment.

That's why he took up boxing. He hated fighting, but growing up in Dublin demanded it. Boxing made him feel confident but most of all, it made sure they left him alone.

Danny was easy prey, wide eyed and trusting and coddled by his grandmother, and the street scuts were like piranha. He'd need to defend himself, and, in time, he'd need to grow a hard shell against the world and that was the greatest sadness of all—that it was the actions of other children that often shattered the innocence of childhood.

"It's about time you got here," his sisters greeted him when he got home. "The Lamb of God keeps phoning for you."

"Don't call him that. He's your nephew, for Christ's sake."

"He would be, if that old bitch would let us near him."

Martin answered when the phone burred again. Danny was calling to thank him for the evening out.

"Thanks Uncle Martin, I had a great time and the cartoons were so funny. I was telling Granny about them and she says that I'm the luckiest boy in the world to have an uncle like you."

His manners were polished, probably at Granny's insistence, and Martin admired that.

"You're more than welcome, Danny, and do you know what I was just thinking? We should do this every week, you know? We can go to the pictures and then go for burgers. You'd like that, wouldn't you? And then we can talk about things like mates."

"I'd like that." Danny's voice was echoic, like he was holding his hand around the phone so no one else could hear their conversation. "But we can't go on Fridays anymore."

"And why's that?"

"Because we had meat on a Friday and Granny would kill me if she found out."

"Well, we'll just have to keep that our secret." Martin hadn't even thought about it. He'd have to be more careful. "Maybe we'll do it on Saturdays instead, in the afternoons. They have lots of Westerns on in the afternoon."

"In the Grafton?"

"No, but it's good to see different kinds of films."

"Well okay, but I'd prefer the cartoons. Do you think that my granny will say yes?"

"Don't worry about Granny. I'll have a word with her and I'm sure she'll agree. Anyway, go on to bed now and I'll talk with you next week."

Martin was sure that Granny wouldn't be a problem. He'd heard that she was unwell. His sisters went as far as saying that she was dying—and not before time—but Jacinta didn't want Danny to know, not until he had to. Until then, Granny would need his help with Danny. Granny had always liked him, saying he was "a cut above the rest" and Martin liked her for that.

"Good night, Uncle Martin."

"Good night, Danny. And don't forget to brush your teeth."

He couldn't let his sisters know that he was helping her. "She was the one that broke them apart with all of her meddling," they always said when the old woman was mentioned. "And she drove poor Jacinta into the asylum, even if it is only for treatment. It's not like she's really mad or anything."

"Ah, but maybe she is better off in there—her being so delicate and all."

"Of course she's better off in there. Not like the rest of us trying to find husbands and the pickings of men getting slimmer each year."

The years were taking their toll on his sisters, but Martin had little pity for them. They had all been in a hurry to leave school assured that their youth was all they needed—and that it would last. They were, as they often boasted, not the learning type. Martin was ashamed of them and the reputations they cultivated. "I hear your sisters are all rides," cruel voices would jibe as he passed on the street but they never dared to say it to his face. He'd burst them if they did.

He couldn't wait to get away from them all and their narrow little minds. He'd show them all though—after he had made it big in New York. He'd come back and rub their smug little faces in their own shitty little lives.

But he'd look after Danny until then—at least until he was able to look out for himself.

**

Nora still remembered how happy she was the day that he dropped by.

It was a Sunday and she had been listening to the radio and the news just made her angry. The government was caving in to the British again and rounding up the men who had tried to get guns into the hands of those who'd defend the poor people of the North.

It had split "the Cause" and the country. The Republic that Bart had fought for was being taken over by Gombeens and Quislings, again. He said that it might. "We can only lead the people to the water," he used to say, "but we can't make them drink." It was his favorite saying when he was out canvassing in the pubs, buying drinks for feckless voters.

"Now Nora," he would remind her when she chided him. "The people want politicians now and have no time for statesmen. But we can rest knowing that we did our part, however it might turn out."

She missed him more and more as his like became fewer and fewer.

"Are you sure that I'm not putting you to any bother?" Martin had hesitated when she insisted that he come in for a cup of tea and have a little chat while Danny was out playing football. "I could help you make it, if you like."

She always thought he was such a fine young man. It was hard to believe that he was from the same parish as the rest of them—let alone the same family. "We can have chocolate biscuits, too, as long as we leave a few for Danny. He does love his chocolate biscuits."

"Okay, so?" Martin agreed, and followed her into the kitchen and helped as much as she let him. He handled the Belleek with care and that brought a smile to her face. "They've been in the family for years. I don't get much cause for using them anymore. Danny's not ready and would probably chip them."

"They are very fine," Martin agreed as he placed the delicate cups on the thin saucers on either side of a platter of biscuits and carried the whole tray into the parlor. "Can I pour for you?"

"Well now," she beamed as she settled into her musty old Queen Anne. "This is a treat—a fine young gentleman over for tea. I haven't had the likes since . . ."

"Ah now, Mrs. Boyle, it's me that should be thanking you for all you have done for Danny. He always has a good word for you."

"And well he should, but he is a little angel, my Danny. And he speaks very highly of you, too. It's all 'Uncle Martin said this' and 'Uncle Martin did that.' It's very good of you to take such an interest in the boy."

"It's my pleasure, I can assure you."

"Well it's still very good of you. There's not many your age that would do that. Most of them are off chasing girls and learning to drink pints. Do you have a girlfriend?"

"I don't," Martin hesitated for a moment. "I think it's best to leave all of that until after I do my exams, you know?"

"And you're right too," Granny gushed to put the young man at ease. "There's plenty of time for that later. Here," she held the plate between them. "Have another biscuit and don't worry; I have put a few aside for Danny so you can eat as many as you like."

"Ah thanks, Mrs. Boyle. That's very kind of you."

Granny nibbled her biscuit and watched Martin over the rim of her teacup but he didn't look up.

"I'm a bit worried about Danny," she finally announced to break the settling silence of the afternoon. "Something happened recently that has me a bit uneasy."

"About Danny?" Martin sat forward on the edge of his chair to be closer.

"Yes. It was very strange. I was just sitting here when someone called on the telephone. I don't get many calls that late; it was almost half-past-nine."

Martin nodded in commiseration but not so much to cause distraction.

"'Hello' says I, dreading that it might be bad news—that late in the evening, you know?"

Martin remained still until she continued.

"'Hello,' says he. 'It's Father Reilly here. Is it too late to talk with Danny?'"

"What was he calling about at that hour?"

"True for you, Martin, calling like that and putting the fear across me and me having a few troubles right now. Anyways, I told him that Danny was in bed and he shouldn't be calling this late. But he says that he and Danny had a little chat and that he was thinking about it and wanted to make sure that everything was okay. 'Why wouldn't it be?' I asked him and then I asked him why he left it so late to call."

She watched Martin closely and nodded at his reaction. He was nobody's fool and she liked that.

"Anyway, he told me that he had been trying to come up with the right things to say."

She waited again as she studied Martin's reaction. She didn't want to think badly of the poor young priest. She wanted to believe him. She could just picture him, sitting by the phone, twisting himself into knots. "He's very young, you know? And he gets terrible shy around people. I usually avoid him in case he starts piddling himself." She never told him her confession—he'd be too shocked by what she had to say.

Instead she went to Fr. Brennan, the parish priest, who was old enough to understand her motives, and wise enough to see her wisdom. She had done what she had to do and, if penance was required, she'd leave her house and her bonds to the Church—after Danny was finished with them.

Fr. Brennan always gave her absolution with a smile, and well he should. It was the least he could do for all that she and Bart had done in the service of the Lord.

They had him installed as parish priest and it wasn't a bad parish. He made a good living out of it and he could look after his curate who, God love him, needed looking after—fresh faced from the seminary, full of Jesus and looking after the sick and the poor.

That was all very well, but, as Fr. Brennan often confided to Granny, someone had to pay the bills: mortgage and heating, the cost of wine and hosts, candles burning like they grew on trees, and all the other costs of the ritual to remember a poor man's supper.

Bart had known Fr. Brennan since his days on the run when the priest's family often sheltered him. Fr. Brennan often reminisced about that when he came by on Thursdays for afternoon tea.

Granny looked forward to his visits. It was good to be able to talk with someone who knew and understood. He often said that Bart and Granny had been his closest friends for years, and that they were very generous, too. Always ready to help out when a young girl had to be sent away before her shame was there for all to see. They used to send them off to England—to convents where they could leave their babies in the good care of the nuns—but they needed the fare.

She had faith in the parish priest but she wasn't sure about the curate.

**

"Of course," Granny continued when she returned from her thoughts. "I wouldn't let him talk with Danny at that hour. Says I, 'I'm the boy's guardian and you can tell me whatever it is that you wanted to say to him.' At first he was reluctant and said that it was a confessional matter and that he couldn't discuss it with me. Can you believe it? And me the child's only love in the world. Present company excepted, or course. Then I said to him: 'You can tell me or you can tell Father Brennan.' That put the skids under him, I can tell you," she nodded in satisfied agreement with her own sentiment. "Then he tells me that Danny was asking him about God and why He doesn't help his mother."

She paused again to pour more tea but it wouldn't warm her. Despite her best efforts the past was reaching out again like a restless ghost. She had been putting off thinking about it but now she had to face it: she was going to die and Danny was going to be left alone in the world.

"Has Danny ever mentioned any of this to you?"

Martin had been watching her, like he could sense some of the things that passed behind her impassive face. "He did, yes, but I told him not to think about stuff like that. I told him he was too young to understand, but that, in time, when he was bigger, it would all make sense to him."

"You're a very wise and decent young man, Martin, and I thank you for saying that to Danny."

"You're welcome, Mrs. Boyle, and it was no bother at all. Danny's like a little brother to me."

"Well I'm so glad that he has you in his corner."

"Mrs. Boyle. Would you mind if Danny and I went out every week to see a picture? I can take him out for burgers and chips after, too, if that's all right with you?"

"I don't mind a bit as long as you let me pay for both of you."

"I wasn't asking you to do that, Mrs. Boyle."

"I know you weren't and that's why I'm happy to offer."

"Well," Martin rose to take his leave. "In that case I'll be very happy to accept, and this way Danny will have someone to talk with. Someone else," he added so as not to give offence.

"Grand so," Granny agreed as she showed him to the door. "And God bless you, Martin, for doing this."

"It's no bother, Mrs. Boyle. Danny and I are becoming mates, you know?"

"I do indeed," she reached out and placed a ten-pound note in the young man's hand. "That's for the next time; only don't be going for burgers on a Friday. People might start thinking we're Protestants."

CHAPTER 4

Fr. Reilly's late night call had not sat well and Nora Boyle had called the Bishop about her concerns. And while they both agreed that there was nothing to worry about, he did. "I'm so glad that you told me, Mrs. Boyle," he had said as he held the bridge of his nose between his fingers to deflect a nagging headache. "No. Not at all, Mrs. Boyle. You did the right thing and I'll make sure that there's nothing in it. And thanks very much again. I couldn't function without the help of concerned people like yourself. I'll have him in for a little chat and we'll get to the bottom of this in no time."

As he waited for Fr. Reilly, the Bishop sat at his desk and reviewed his appointments for the rest of the morning. He had his nephew, followed by the meeting he was dreading, but he still had time for a midmorning coffee and another quick scan of the newspapers before he had to face it all. His housekeeper brought his caffè latte, an affectation that had survived from his days in Rome when he was young and full of vigor. When he sent her over there on her pilgrimages, she took time from visiting churches to learn how to make coffee properly and now took great pride in it, buying beans from Bewley's and grinding them herself, filling the palace with the aroma of the piazzas and the memories of warm sunny days. She was everything a man like him could want in a widow.

It was, he often reminded himself, when his mind would wander down paths he hadn't chosen, a perfect situation.

They were very fond of each and they were far too wise to do anything to complicate that. She kept his loneliness away with her endless bustling and fussing and he provided her with security and status—he baptized every one of her nieces and nephews and was godfather to more than he could remember. Mrs. Power kept all their names and birthdates and gave them to his secretary when it was time for him to send his heartfelt blessings.

His secretary was a good convent girl who had found love in the arms of a man she met when she was away at university in Belfast—her people were from up around that way. He served in the RAF and didn't survive the War. Mrs. Mawhinney took the job with the Bishop when she was done mourning him. She liked to paint in her spare time so he sent her to Rome, too, but on a different pilgrimage. She always came home with armfuls of pictures and postcards to study and copy in her spare time.

He was, in the oddest of ways, a very contented man in a world full of misery and strife.

He scanned the headlines in *The Irish Times*, a paper he distrusted but read to keep informed. It had a long history of reporting things that, to his mind, would have been better left in the hands of those who actually steered the ship of state.

Not that he was against open dialogue and people having a say, but he had seen what could happen when moral authority ceded to populism. Europe had torn its self apart following Pied Pipers and Generalissimos. Even Ireland wasn't immune with "the Troubles" in the North boiling up again, the old simmering sore that incited acts and reactions that were a shame to God and man.

His old friend, Seán Lemass, was remembered in the editorial and not too kindly either, but that wasn't the worst of it. The "Contraceptive Train" had pulled into Connolly station the day before. The Irish Women's Liberation Movement had gone to Belfast to bring back the dreaded contraband and flaunt it before the *Humanae Vitae* of all that was holy.

"What kind of women are these?" he asked Mrs. Mawhinney when she stuck her head around the door.

"They are the product of the changing times, Your Grace."

"You're not condoning them, are you?"

"Of course not, Your Grace, I was merely answering your question."

"What's the world coming to when our own women are out acting like hussies? I blame television, you know. Is there to be no end to the corruption it spreads?"

"Apparently not, Your Grace."

The Bishop stopped fuming for a moment and tried to read her face. She was an educated woman who still took courses down at the university. And she painted. She would know something of the minds behind it all.

"How is it that we're supposed to lead such people?"

"It was Gandhi, Your Grace, that once said: 'There go my people. I must follow them, for I am their leader.'"

"You're not suggesting . . . " He couldn't even finish the thought.

"Of course not, Your Grace. I just came in to tell you that Father Reilly is here."

"Grand. Show him in on the hour."

The Bishop was never sure of her but knew her to be an informed and considered woman. He'd wait until his mind was calmer and broach the subject with her later. It was good to have an ear in all camps.

He had a few moments to compose himself and rearrange his thoughts. His nephew was a good lad but he had to check, just to be sure. Bart Boyle was an old friend and a good man—the likes of which would not be seen again. They had often played a bit of golf when time permitted. It gave them a chance to consult and compare their agendas over a couple of balls of the best malt whiskey in a private room in the clubhouse.

Bart was a bit of a rogue whose private commitments to the teachings of the Church were a bit slack but publically he never put a foot wrong. And he was generous whenever the Bishop asked—with his own funds as well as the public purse.

His widow kept his generous spirit alive, often delving into her own savings and still capable of reaching the ears of cabinet ministers and the like. She wasn't complaining about his nephew—she just thought that the Bishop should know.

He put the *Times* aside. He would scour it later for more whispers of dissent. It was essential that he be informed. That way he could help to formulate a better way of dealing with all the change the times brought. They couldn't rely on the old ways of censure and excommunication anymore. They had enough problems getting people to come to Mass without banning them.

Not to mention they weren't getting as many vocations as they once were. Since Vatican II priests and nuns were starting to leave the Holy Orders. It was still just a trickle but it was unheard of in his time. Yes, the Church was facing difficult times.

It was different when he was a young man in Rome and they were guided only by the word of God. Not directly, of course. God spoke clearly through his servant, Pius XI. The Bishop had once brandished the *Divini Redemptoris* as proof and still had an original copy somewhere among his papers.

He also had a copy of *Mit Brennender Sorge*, too, but he avoided rereading it. It made him feel that they had been caught between two stools and that was heresy against their "infallibility."

His nephew entered on the hour and took his seat on the other side of the desk. He waited like a schoolboy while Mrs. Power fussed around with her tray. He declined coffee but accepted a cup of tea. He had never been to Rome, despite the Bishop's urgings. "All roads . . . you know? Especially for a man of the cloth," he often coaxed, but his nephew was one of the "New Breed" that wore their hair far too long, wisping out from behind their ears and falling across their forehead.

But God had called him and the Bishop wasn't going to question His wisdom.

"Are you well, Patrick?"

"I am indeed, Your Grace. Thanks for asking. And I hope that all is well with yourself?"

"As well as can be expected," the Bishop laughed to ease the mood. "And don't be calling me 'Your Grace.' We're family."

His nephew nodded and sipped his tea while the Bishop appraised him. He was nervous and fingered his unruly fringe as he waited for his uncle to continue.

"I thought it was time that we had a little chat." The Bishop was casual, hoping to put the young man at ease. "I like to hear from the men who do the real work, you know? I've been spending too much time up at the Diocese."

"It must be very taxing on you."

The Bishop couldn't help but think the comment was loaded but continued regardless. "I envy men like you. Young and fresh from the seminary, and out among the flock."

"It is a blessing."

Again the Bishop wasn't sure. He never really understood his nephew. He was a decent enough curate, but he played guitar and often wore a turtleneck instead of the crisp white collar. Father Brennan had complained when he started pushing for "Folk Masses" and the like.

**

"What's wrong with the ordinary Mass that you and I were born and bred on?" he complained when he phoned. "Is it not enough that it's in English now? What will they want from us next—get rid of the choir and replace them with a ceilidh band, or worse, a mop of rock and rollers?"

It took all of the Bishop's persistence to calm him down. "You and I are from the old days but we have to change with the times, too."

"So are you saying that we should allow it?"

"I'm not going to start telling you how to run your own parish, Dan. You've been doing well without my interference but I would ask you to remember what it was like when we were young and the Church was run by men we thought were so old. We couldn't wait to be rid of the lot of them. Don't you remember, Dan?"

"I suppose, but these young bucks are going to be the ruin of us."

"My nephew will do fine. Let him do these things now and he'll grow tired of them. He'll get older and wiser, just like the rest of us."

"I hope you're right on this."

"Time will tell, my old friend, time will tell. Do you know what I was going to ask you?" he wanted to shake hands on their agreement. "Would you have time to get in a bit of fishing next week? We haven't had the rods out in years. There's a house I can get the use of, up near Lough Sheelin . . ."

Father Brennan ceded, and for a while his church was full of bearded young men, and women in short skirts, singing about Jesus like he was a pop star. But he didn't mind anymore. They filled his plates like good Catholics had done for years, even during the bad times.

**

"And how is Father Brennan?" the Bishop asked.

"He's grand, Uncle. Can I tell him you were asking after him?"

The Bishop nodded as he relit his pipe. He didn't smoke very often—only when he wanted to be very careful. Young priests were like foals and were easy to scare. "And yourself? How are things with you?"

"I am well, Uncle." His nephew sipped his tea again, looking like he might make a dart for the door.

"You're probably wondering why I asked to see you."

"I hope it's not because of something I've done wrong?"

"Wrong? Not at all. What would go and put that in your head? I'm just doing my job, you know? As your uncle, as well as your bishop."

He leaned forward to span the formality between them.

"These are difficult times to be a priest, what with Vatican II and all that's going on in the world. What with students protesting and women burning their underthings in public—not to mention the pill? Mark my words. We'll look back at it as the Silent Holocaust, you know?

"And then there are the Troubles. At times like this it's very hard to hear the voice of God and some are getting lost." His face clouded over as he thought of his next appointment—the priest that had to be moved on. The Bishop couldn't allow it to spread. That poor man was lost to them but there was still time for those like his nephew. He had to reach out now, while he still could. He had to be there to offer a helping hand when they wavered on the path, where any misstep could lead them right into the middle of a bog.

But he had to be careful too, and not push them over the edge.

"Priests of today are under a lot more pressure. In my day we never had to encounter the type of defiance we see all around us, at least not from the man in the street. Lawyers and the likes have always been a bit uppity. And don't get me started on the poets and writers! A thundering disgrace, every one of them. Like that whore, God forgive me, that wrote *The Country Girls.*"

"That would be Edna O'Brien," the young priest interrupted.

The Bishop sat back and looked at him. His nephew wasn't being defiant; it wasn't in his nature. But he was being elusive. It was hard enough to have these types of talks and the Bishop was running out of patience. "And how's that young grandson of Bart Boyle's. Do you ever see him at all?" He was tired of pussy-footing around and drove to the heart of the matter.

"Danny?" His nephew shifted a little in his chair. "He's in confession every week and takes communion every Sunday without fail. He made his confirmation a while back."

"That's the one. Keep an eye on him for me, will you? His Grandmother is a great friend to us and to me personally."

"I'll keep a special eye out for him."

Again the Bishop tried to read beyond the words, but his secretary knocked on the door to let him know his next appointment had arrived.

"Let him cool his heels in the study for a while." He spoke in a voice that carried before she gently closed the door again.

It would allow his next appointment more time to reflect. Not that he had any choice—it was what the Bishop had to offer or deal with the Garda. The Bishop was dreading it and wanted to have a quick drink to steady his nerves—so he could mask his revulsion with compassion. It was not for him to judge—but there was the good name of the Church to think about. Something had to be done.

"Would you care for a quick nip?" He winked at his nephew. He knew he wasn't really the type that would go wrong but he'd keep a closer eye on him for a little while, just to be sure.

"It's a bit early for me."

"Go on with you. It's not often that I offer."

"Okay then."

The Bishop came around from behind his desk and sat on the straight back chair beside the young priest. Times were changing. His day was in the past, and, if he was the man he had always believed he was, he wouldn't become like Dan Brennan: grumbling and complaining when the world spun too fast. They needed the new breed to have meaning in the world, even if they ruffled a few feathers. He downed his whiskey in one and watched his nephew grimace as he tried to swallow his sippings.

God, how was one so young and innocent ever going to survive?

"I don't want to rush you, Father," the Bishop smiled as he took away the glasses and secreted them back into the drawer of his desk, "but I have someone waiting."

He strode forward again and took the young priest's hand and pumped him up again. "Look after them for me, will you? They're your flock now and I know, just by looking at you, that God chose well when he picked you for His work. And if ever you have something on your mind, you just come over and we can have a chat about it. I'm your bishop but I'm your uncle, too. Come over any time you like."

He hugged the young man briefly and patted his back as he walked him to the door, shifting the weight of their common cross more toward the younger man's shoulders.

***

Father Reilly had nursed his embarrassment on the bus ride home. He had been "called into the office"—an ignominy the Bishop liked to mete out when he wanted to chuck on the reins of his power.

His uncle was a decent enough man but one from the old school in which priests, like all men, just kept things to themselves and got on with the job. There were no grey areas in the Bishop's thinking. Just the complete contrast of black against white.

Nor was there room for doubt. He didn't tolerate those who strayed from the path: "You don't choose the priesthood as you might choose to be a doctor, or a lawyer. We are selected by God himself, and, as He doesn't make mistakes, any failing is ours and ours alone."

Patrick Reilly had grown up with comments like that, chiding him and prodding him. But he would have to stand his ground against his uncle, politely standing up for all that would have to change if they were to have any meaning in the lives of those they served.

He was a bit ashamed of himself, too, for thinking like that. That kind of thinking might just be Pride, or the chaffing of his collar.

It had been so easy in the seminary, spending hours reading and studying. That's all he ever wanted to do—to have his nose in a book. But his mother was insistent; they had been blessed with good fortune and it was the least that he could do.

His father felt differently. He took Patrick aside one night before he left, to have a few pints before he made his way in the world. His father drank Guinness while Patrick stuck to shandies—but even then he got a bit tipsy.

**

"I just wanted to know, from your own lips," his father asked after all the other rituals had been observed: the weather had been discussed as well as the politics of the day, and the price of tea in China, "that this is something you're doing for yourself. I know that sometimes your mammy, and your uncle, too, can be a bit pushy. I just want you to know that if it doesn't work out, I'll have money to send you off to university. You could become a teacher or something and have a normal life."

"Are you against me going, Father?"

"Not at all. I just want you to know that you have a choice."

"Thanks but I have made my mind up."

"Right so," his father agreed, happy to let the delicate matter close. "But if you ever change your mind—the offer will still be open."

The changing times had taught him to keep his thoughts to himself, but sometimes he couldn't help but see himself in his son's eyes; the young man he once was, growing up on the farm when life was simpler. "I suppose," he laughed and ordered another round of drinks, "that some of us are born to be farmers and some of us are born to be shepherds." He raised his glass between them. "May I wish you the very best of luck."

***

Nothing in the seminary had prepared Patrick Reilly for parish life where the children of Ireland murdered each other like common criminals. He had been led to believe that he would be guiding trusting young boys and girls from the protection of innocence to their places as good Catholics.

He didn't dare speak of it from the pulpit. He had learned that lesson after Bloody Sunday. The people didn't want to hear messages of Love and Tolerance—they wanted God's vengeance on the heads of those who trespassed against them.

They didn't see them as children but rather the spawn of the unworthy—those that lived off the dole and raised their broods out of wedlock. He would never be able to get them to see it any other way. They couldn't. If they did they would have to admit that they had failed as a society.

But he would do what he could. He would reach out and make himself accessible to those that others shunned; it's what Christ had asked them to do. *Judge not*, he reminded himself, but when it came to Danny Boyle he couldn't help but wonder if things couldn't have been done better.

Not that he was criticizing his grandmother—she had done what she thought was right.

**

"He gave the little wealth he had . . ." Danny had chanted in a singsong but his granny didn't join in. She had been distant for days. Danny had used up his little bag of tricks but nothing worked. Sometimes she even seemed impatient with him.

But his mother was getting better. Over the last few visits, he had noticed the change. She was always dressed in something nice with her hair brushed and shining. Maybe his deal with God was working.

"I promise," he had added to his recent prayers, "that if you let my ma come back to live with me that I will become a priest."

"Good afternoon, Mrs. Boyle, Danny." Martin stepped across the path that led to the front door.

"Martin!" Granny seemed happier. "It was good of you to come."

"Is everything all right? My sisters said you phoned."

"We'll talk about it later." She nudged Danny toward the door but he saw her try to catch Martin's eye unnoticed.

"Fair enough then. How are you, Danny, and would you ever hold the door for your granny?"

"He's losing his manners," Granny rolled her eyes a little. "Maybe you could have a word with him."

Danny hung his head and held the door as they passed by, entwined in their conspiracy. The whole world was changing, and sometimes it felt like it was turning against him.

But his mother was delighted to see him and rose from her chair in the crafts room where she had been weaving plastic strands to pass the time.

"Danny! Come here and give your mother a big hug and a kiss."

She squeezed him tightly and wrestled him onto her lap, his weight almost crushing her and his long legs dangling out before him. "You're getting so big," she laughed as she struggled for breath. "Maybe from now on I should be sitting on your lap. Are you well?"

"Well enough," Danny pouted a little. "But I really wanted to go to the pictures and instead Granny said we had to come here, and Uncle Martin and I always go to the pictures on Saturdays."

"Now Danny." Granny admonished as she lowered herself gingerly into a chair.

"Okay, but I really miss the pictures."

"Sure we'll see them another time." Martin stood behind Granny's chair and his face was almost stern.

"Martin?" Jacinta moved and dislodged Danny from his perch. "I've no cigarettes left. Would you be a love and run to the shop down the street? Maybe you could bring Danny, too, and get him a chocolate bar." She nudged Danny toward his uncle. "You'd like that, wouldn't you, pet?"

"Why doesn't Martin go and I'll stay here?"

"Because," Martin coaxed. "I wouldn't know what to get you. C'mon now."

Martin waited for a moment but his sister just stared back blankly.

"Here. Take this," Granny held up a pound note and snapped her purse shut. "Go on now and get them."

**

Granny must be getting bad, Jacinta thought to herself with her head averted, avoiding confrontation. She was on her best behavior. She had to be. She was on trial and her release depended on it. She was nervous but determined to look and act like the worst was behind her. She even crossed her ankles and sat straight with her hands nestling in her lap.

**

Granny didn't notice; she was deep in her own thoughts, a dark and dreary place of late. Her last visit with the doctor confirmed her condition was no better, and was probably getting worse. She might not even see out the year. There wasn't much time to put everything in place. She had spoken with the solicitor and was making provisions for them all. She would let Jeremiah come home as soon as she could have someone find him a job. And then Jacinta might be able to come out on weekends—with her doctor's agreement—something Granny had already sought. It would be better for Danny if they all seemed more like a family.

**

"And how are you, Mrs. Boyle?" Jacinta interrupted her thoughts.

"I'm well enough, all things considered. Have you had any news of my Jerry?"

Jacinta almost smiled; he would always be her Jerry. "I did. He phoned last week and said he had a bit of a surprise but he couldn't tell me about it."

"He's a great one for surprises."

"He said he might be able to come over in a few weeks."

"It'll be nice for Danny to see him. He hasn't been over in months."

"It'll be grand for all of us and it'll be nice for him to spend some time with you, too." Jacinta was determined to build on any reconciliation. Jerry had told her that Granny was going to find him a job, at home. He also told her that Granny didn't have long to go and they should all be nice to her.

"It will if he has developed a bit of sense." Granny settled herself but her breathing was labored.

"It will be good for Danny, too, to have a man around now that he is starting to get all grown up."

"There is that. He's a bit more than I can manage these days."

"You've been very good all these years and I'll always be grateful to you but maybe it is time to start taking it a bit easy."

Granny's face flickered for a moment before she smiled. "Jacinta?"

"Yes Granny?"

"Would you like me to have a word with the doctors about you? Maybe, if they don't mind, we could see about having you come home at weekends for a while."

"Oh Granny," Jacinta slid from her chair and kneeled before the old woman. "I'd give everything for a chance to do that." She took the old woman's hand in hers and raised it to her lips. "I promise that I will do my very best, so help me God."

Granny raised her hand and placed it on her daughter-in-law's head. "We'll need all the help He can give. But I don't want you to say anything to Danny just yet—not until we get everything arranged."

"Oh, Granny," Jacinta purred as she took Granny's hand and stroked her own cheek with it, the dry wrinkles rough against her moist cheek. "May God bless you for doing this."

"I'm just doing what's right for my Danny."

"I know and I won't let you down."

"It'll just be for the weekends at first, mind you. Until we see."

"Oh thanks, Granny. I won't let you down ever again."

"Get up now before someone sees. Get up quick before they get back."

**

"We should be getting ready to leave," Granny decided after Danny came back. He was in a much better mood and ruffled their entante, fussing for attention and pestering the two women with his string of questions.

"But I only just got here," Danny complained and slumped into a chair where he sat with his arms folded before him. "Can't we just stay a little longer?"

"Could we please?" Jacinta joined in. "Just for a few minutes."

"Oh very well," Granny ceded and struggled to get out of her chair. "Martin, would you be a good man and help me up?"

Martin obliged and offered his arm. "Why don't you and I start walking and Jacinta can bring Danny and catch up with us."

"You're very kind," the old woman agreed and shuffled away under her burdens.

**

"Danny, you have to be nicer to Granny Boyle because she is getting very old."

"But I am nice to her, all the time."

"Of course you are, pet, but Granny's not able to keep up with you anymore—now that you're getting so big." She hugged him again and couldn't contain herself. "And if you're good I might have a big surprise for you."

"Are you going to take me to the pictures someday, when you're all better?"

Jacinta laughed and tousled his hair. "Of course I will but, what I wanted to tell you is that Granny is going to ask the doctors if they'll let me out—at least for the weekends for now."

"That's what I've asked God for, after I say my other prayers."

"Well you must have God's ear, then." Jacinta laughed again as all of her clouds began to blow away. "Come now. Let's go so we don't keep Granny waiting."

**

Granny was standing outside with Martin by her elbow.

"I think this is very good of you, Mrs. Boyle. I think it's the best thing for Danny, too."

"I hope you're right." She paused to examine his face. "But there's something I need you to do for me."

"Anything, Mrs. Boyle."

"I want you to keep an eye on them all. I can trust you."

"Thank you very much Mrs. Boyle, but I'm not sure what it is you're asking me to do."

"I want you to go and see my solicitor and he can explain it all to you."

"Is there anything wrong? You're not ill, are you?"

"You're not getting rid of me just yet. I just want things to be in order for when Danny is older; you know what I mean."

"I do, Mrs. Boyle, and I'll be more than happy to oblige."

"You're a fine young man, Martin, God bless you. And not a word to anyone now—I'm counting on you."

"You can rely on me."

"Here," Granny handed him a five-pound note. "Take Danny to the pictures so that I can have a bit of peace and quiet when I get home. Only mind you have him back before ten. He has to have his bath tonight."

CHAPTER 5

Danny liked busking under the awning, outside Arnott's on Henry Street. Saturdays were the best. That's when the older women would be out shopping. He did his best to look sad-sack as they passed and sang songs to remind them of the times when they had their own children to look after. They were stoic about it, hiding behind their bustle, but Danny knew: old women could never ignore him for long.

He was stoned again. It was the only way he could deal with all that had happened. It made it feel more dreamlike, like at any moment Scully would walk by, the hole in his head miraculously healed and his face no longer bruised and swollen. The horror had not subsided, nor the waves of panic and fear.

He strummed a few chords, G, D, and an A minor 7th, then G, D, and C, searching for a song that would make it all go away, even if only for a while. Something penitent that even God might hear. It was starting to sound reverent so he followed along until it became *Knocking on Heaven's Door.* He sang it slowly for Scully, and for himself; behind his dark glasses, his eyes began to well-up. God would never forgive him and Danny could never go back to what he had once believed in; he had spent too much time poking holes in all of that. He was alone to face the burning fire that was waiting for him, and, because he couldn't talk to anybody about it, he sang about it instead.

Sometimes he got through to them. Some of the old women took pity on him and foraged in their purses for a 10p, or a 20, and on occasion a 50p-piece. It was the only communion he had with the world—through the hearts of the mothers of Henry Street. It allowed him a chance to relive his innocence until some young culchie in a Garda uniform would move him along, officiously, to the point of ridicule.

I am outcast from the garden, he smiled as stern faces passed by and almost laughed aloud. Now, when he remembered being happy, it was in the garden of the hospital, but not as it really was. It was warm in his memories, and sunlight fell like a cheesecloth curtain.

His mother sat in a deck chair, in a fresh, spotted blue dress and gently fanned herself with one of her beaded purses. His father was there, too, wearing a clean white shirt, looking relaxed as he sipped tea from Granny's finest china. She was there, too, sitting in the shade of the wall looking tired, clutching her grey cobweb shawl around her shoulders and when he tried to walk toward them, she refused to look at him.

He shook his head to clear the tears rising up from his soul. One of these days he'd get his shit together and drop out of the scene. It was getting far too heavy. He'd quit the business and get on with his life. He'd quit smoking, too, and get fit again. He might even start playing football again, like he did when he was a kid.

*

Anto knew the voice rising above all the singsong and murmurings of the crowd and stopped at the corner of Moore Street and waited for Danny to finish. He stood back into a doorway and lit a cigarette. He wanted to let Danny know that he wasn't happy about the way things had gone down with Scully but he had no choice. It was the way things had to be in their business—he couldn't afford to allow anyone to step out of line and Scully knew the score.

When Scully first got lifted, Anto wasn't too concerned. He was a mate and had been for years; he'd never grass. But whispers started to reach him that cops knew all about him and were looking to link him to the incident in Rathgar. Anto had nothing to do with that—that was the Driller. It was some issue that had spilled over from Derry. The Driller explained that the orders came from "the Boys" and had nothing to do with business, but the cops thought otherwise. The dead man was one of Anto's dealers and he had burnt the wrong people.

Anto hated "the Boys." They claimed that they were clamping down on drug dealers but in reality they were just shaking them down. That's why he took up with the Driller. It was better to be in bed with the devil. And besides, the stories of what he'd done in Derry discouraged anyone from having a go at Anto. It was all becoming too complicated; a tangled web of intrigue and shifting loyalties that left him longing for the days when things were simpler.

He had known Danny since they were kids, since his father got steady work at Hughes' Dairy and the family moved from the Northside into a house on Dodderdale. Anto hated it. All of his old friends wanted nothing more to do with him and he found the Southsiders too full of themselves. They looked down on him, and, for the first few months, he had to fight just to be left alone. His father wanted them all to have a new beginning and when he found out, he put Anto on the parish football team. That was where he first met Danny.

He almost smiled as he remembered the day when they huddled beneath a tree as it pissed down with rain, coming down in sheets across the open spaces of the Phoenix Park. Father Reilly had an umbrella but the boys just stood under the tree with their hair slicked to their heads and their faded green shirts darkening with damp. The rest of them complained, but not Anto; he was far too tough for that.

**

"When do you think the others are going to show up, Father?"

They had left far too early and two boys had missed the bus but Fr. Reilly had wanted to be safe rather than sorry. They had to take two buses, the first into the Quays and the other out to the "Park." He had to come up with a better way. He even asked Fr. Brennan if the parish would consider getting a minibus, so that he could drive them around instead. "A minibus? Are you mad? Where do you think the parish can find that kind of money? We barely have enough to get by and the little that's left over goes to the diocese. Minibus! Are you having me on, or what?" Fr. Reilly had tried to argue that it would be so handy and that they could also use it to drive the old people around, too. They could even take them on excursions. "Father," the older man reminded his young curate, "the only transportation we offer is from this world to the next." He walked away laughing to himself and shaking his head.

"I'm sure they'll be along soon, Anthony," Fr. Reilly responded absentmindedly as he peered through the rain.

"I hope so—we only have ten." Anto looked to the priest like he could make them appear.

"No, we have eleven. You forgot to count Danny."

"Oh yeah," Anto grinned at the others around him. "Still, I hope the others get here soon. These wankers are good—they're unbeaten."

"Language!" Fr. Reilly admonished. "And remember, we're all the same in the eyes of God."

"See," someone whispered when he rejoined the boys under the other tree. "I told you everybody does it."

"I don't."

They all joined in, leaning closer to talk in whispers so the priest wouldn't hear. "Why not?"

"I get your sister to do it for me."

"Feck off ya bastard. If you say that again I'll burst your face."

"Now lads," Fr. Reilly called over as the rain slackened enough to coax the referee out from under his tree. "We'll start with the usual lineup but instead of Dominic, we'll have Danny play as center forward."

"But he's never played there before, Father."

"I've a feeling that he's going to do great today, Anthony."

Anto looked over at the shiny new boots Danny's father had got him for Christmas. "He looks more like a feckin' ballerina."

"Now, now. Let's remember who we are and let's have a good clean game."

"C'mon Saint Endas," his teammates cheered as they rushed out to take their places.

"Where are you from?" their opponents asked in a disinterested way.

"Rathfarnham."

"Fucking mountain men."

"No bad language, please," the referee scolded them as he checked his watch one more time and got ready to blow his whistle.

From the kick-off they all knew what to do, except Danny who wandered back and forth along the halfway line. If he went further into his own half, Anto would berate him. "Stay up there for when we get the break. Get ready for the long ball."

"C'mon Danny," Fr. Reilly called from the sideline. "Keep at it. You're doing great."

Danny seemed happy with that and ran back and forth with enthusiasm while the other team stopped even pretending to cover him.

"That's great," Fr. Reilly reassured him. "You're doing a great job getting open. C'mon lads, Danny is open, let's start getting the ball to him."

His teammates carried on regardless.

"Move away Boyle," Anto shouted as he advanced with the ball. "Move away and take the cover with ya."

Danny didn't seem to understand and stood where he was, forcing Anto to weave around him. But the opponent didn't, clattering right through Danny as he tried to get to the ball. Danny fell to the muddy, wet ground and looked like he might cry but the ref helped him up as he awarded a free-kick to the outrage of the other team. "C'mon, ref, that's obstruction."

"Obstruction? Are you having me on? He was doing nothing of the sort. He was just minding his own business. Free kick, and that's enough lip out of you or I'll book ya." He admonished with his finger as his other hand tapped his shirt pocket where his black notebook could be seen, along with the stubby yellow pencil.

"Good man, Boyle. You're playing a blinder," Anto muttered as he set the ball and drove it into the other team's end of the field, far away from Danny. Normally they only played him on defense, against the weaker teams, and the ball never came near him. "It's because they know they're never going to beat you," Anto had once told him and Danny was convinced.

The ball sloshed back and forth in the mud and Anto and his teammates forgot about Danny for a while, but, at Fr. Reilly's insistence, they did include him in the back-slapping when they finally scored.

"Who're the mountain men now, ye bollockses?" they jeered the other team and even Danny joined in.

"What are you looking at, ya fucking queer?" one of them challenged him when he strayed too far from the huddle.

"Language!" the referee reminded them as he took out his notebook to record the scorer. "I couldn't see who got it so I'm going to put down your number," he winked at Danny and blew his whistle to restart play. He never strayed from the center circle so Anto told Danny to stay near him so that he wouldn't get run over again.

"Is he marking the fucking ref now?" someone muttered when the game was paused while Fr. Reilly tried to dislodge the ball from an overhanging tree.

"Leave him alone, for fuck's sake," Anto warned. He didn't like the way they all picked on Danny.

"Why? Is he your boyfriend now?"

"Fuck you. Say that again and I'll bleedin' burst ya," Anto challenged. They were all very brave when it came to picking on Boyle but none of them would dare stand up to him.

"Language!" the ref reminded them absentmindedly as he watched Fr. Reilly throw sticks at the lodged ball.

**

The rain stopped as the second half started and the sun struggled with the low clouds but the field was slick and the tackles were flying. The opponents weren't used to losing and were taking it badly. One of them even elbowed Danny as he ran past—a stinging blow to the back of his head when the ref wasn't looking. He was far too busy blowing on his whistle with increasing fury. The game was getting rowdy.

"It's just a game, gentlemen," he reminded them all, but they just ignored him. They were at war and it was only a matter of time until someone got hurt.

The referee nearly blew the pea out of his whistle as one of the Saints rolled around in the mud clutching his shin where the angry red rake of studs was emerging. Fr. Reilly was called to examine the wound while the referee wrote the offender's name in his notebook. "I'll have my eye on you now," he advised the lurking offender and snapped his notebook shut.

"We're going to have to play short," Fr. Reilly coached after he got his maimed player under the tree. "Anthony! Get them organized."

On cue, Anto called them into a huddle. "These fuckers are going to try to rattle us now, so don't take any of their shite. There's not long left."

"And what should I do?" Danny asked.

"Just keep doing what you're doing. Stay high and wait for the long ball."

He did for a while but in the last few minutes he came wandering back. His team was getting ready to defend a corner.

"What the fuck are you doing?" Anto asked.

"I'm better as a defender."

"Okay, go cover number seven and don't fuckin' lose him. Don't let him get a free header." They were under mounting pressure—playing a man short, and all.

When the corner was taken, it floated over them all, toward the far post where number seven waited with the goal at his mercy.

"Get to it, Boyle," Anto yelled but Danny just closed his eyes and jumped.

It was like he was hit by a wet sack of sand and he collapsed to the ground in total silence.

"Ah, Jesus! The fuckin' spastic put it in his own net," the other team jeered as they brushed past but one stopped to pat Danny on the back, even as he lay face down in the mud.

"Is he hurt?" the referee asked from the center circle.

"He'd better be," the keeper muttered as he nudged Danny with his toe. "Get up ya little bollocks, will ya?"

But the ref decided to blow his whistle and end the game.

***

"How are ya, Boyle?" Anto emerged from the crowd and dropped a few coins into the open case as he leaned closer so that no one else might hear. "I just wanted you to know that I feel bad about involving you with what went down with Scully. It wasn't what I wanted, but we all take orders from above, ya know? They were concerned that the cops might want to have a chat with you, too, and they wanted you to know what happens to those that talk back. No hard feelings?"

"No," Danny agreed as he raised his eyes and looked at his own reflection in Anto's sunglasses, nodding like a fool. What else could he say?

"Well Boyle, we appreciate you keeping your mouth shut and afterwards, when things have calmed down, we're going to want you to look after things now that Scully is gone. And Boyle," Anto paused and quickly glanced around, "don't fuck it up. And another thing, it you're still using the stuff, it would be better if you were seen buying from someone else, now and then. That way no one will suspect. Just make sure it stays now and then—otherwise you could end up busking in a fuckin' bowl. Got it? Now start acting natural before anybody looks over."

When he stepped back, Danny leaned down and picked the coins from his case. His hands were trembling. He thought about running but where could he go? He was walking down the dark paths that led to the time and place when he would lie, like Scully, dead in a ditch.

"Anto, what happened to the gun? I think I might have left my prints on it."

"Don't worry about that Boyle. I buried it in a bog. Nobody is ever going to find it."

"Thanks Anto."

"No problem, Boyle. Like I always say, we're mates and mates look out for each other, like when we used to play football together, remember?"

*

Jerry stood on the other side of the street and pretended to be absorbed in the contents of a shop window. He could see Danny and Anto's reflection in the glass while the passing crowd hid him from view. He could tell just from the way they stood, that things were tense between them.

He had heard about Anto, mostly mutterings and whispers about drugs and guns. People feared him and wondered why nobody did anything about him, but, when it came down to it, they were afraid for themselves and their families. Anto had a way of getting to anybody who crossed him and no one wanted to risk that. In the local pub, the men always said that one of these days they would get together and deal with him but Jerry also remembered when he was younger and played on the football team with Danny. He was a good player, tough and fast, and he didn't pick on Danny the way the other little scuts did. He even helped him off the field, that day in the "Park."

Jerry remembered it well. Everyone did—it was the day of Bloody Sunday.

**

"You played a blinder." Jerry had coaxed Danny off the field and used his wet hanky to wipe away his tears and snot. He was embarrassed but he couldn't let his son see that. Things were bad enough.

"But I didn't even get to kick the ball!"

"But you're making space for the others," he continued as he tried to get him to stand on his own. "That's what all the professionals do. Just like Johnny Giles. Isn't that right?" he pleaded with Anto who was standing on the other side of

Danny. He nodded a few times before he stepped back and went off to join the others. Danny waited until he was gone before he brought up the own-goal.

"I wouldn't worry about it," Jerry continued. "It could have happened to the Bishop. Besides, there's one good thing: your mother wanted to come with me but I told her to wait for a better day." He wiped the rain from his face and raised the collar of his old tweedy coat.

***

Still, he never felt that he had done right by his son. He had no idea what a father should be. His own father had been cold and remote, offering only judgements like a magistrate. Everyone else thought so highly of him but Jerry knew what he was really like.

And his mother didn't help, casting him as a prodigal in Danny's eyes. Like she had never put a foot wrong in her own life. He didn't want to think badly about her but he couldn't help it as old memories rose.

**

When they got back from the game, the kitchen was warm and steamy, smelling deliciously of bacon and cabbage; Granny's panacea for all that January could throw at them. The winter was taking its toll on her but she still had to have the dinner ready.

"You're both soaked to the skin," she chided as she handed them towels to dry their heads and ushered them to the table. "Sit down now and get that into you before you both come down with coughing and sneezing and Danny will have to be off school for a while."

"Are you not eating?" Jerry had asked when he noticed the settings for two.

"I'm not very hungry right now. I have a bit of an upset tummy. That medicine I'm on takes all the joy out of food."

"Have you talked with the doctor about it?"

"Don't worry your head about that. Go on now and sit down before your dinner gets cold. I'm going to go and watch the news. The Civil Rights people were marching up in Derry today and you never know what those B-Specials might get up to. Not to mention the Paisley mobs. He's nothing but a rabble-rouser, that one, make no mistake. He isn't even a real minister, you know? He was ordained in one of those Bible colleges they have over in America. I wonder what type of Christianity they teach over there, because there is nothing but hatred and bitterness in the man—and all those thugs that follow him." She sniffed self-righteously and left for the living room.

"You were doing great until that header," Jerry said to deflect Danny.

"Do you really think so?"

"I do and do you know what? Maybe I could start teaching you a few things—show you a few tricks and stuff. I could even show you how to head a ball."

Since he'd come home everything was getting better. Granny wasn't well but Jacinta came over every Saturday and spent the whole day with them.

"Thanks, Da. But I'm not sure if I want to stay with this team. I'm not really enjoying it anymore."

"Sweet mother of Jesus," Granny called out to them before he could answer. "Come in quick—they're after killing a priest."

They rushed in as the solemn voice of the RTE recounted the day's events: *British Forces have opened fire on a peaceful march in Derry this afternoon. Reports are coming in that they have killed a number of people, including a Catholic Priest, and injured many more.*

"Holy Mary, mother of God, have mercy on us," Granny sobbed, over and over as the evening grew darker, flickering with grainy images of bodies lying in the streets, of stone faced soldiers, with rifles ready, and the terrified survivors waving dirty white hankies as they carried the dead and dying away.

"It will mean war," Granny pronounced, her knuckles whitening as she gripped the arms of her chair.

"Maybe," Jerry prodded Danny until he turned from the screams of outrage on the streets of Derry. "You should go on up and have a bath. You got soaked today and you don't want to be getting a cold. And I'm sure you still have some homework you could be finishing."

"I didn't want him to be getting all upset," he explained after Danny had gone, but his mother didn't answer. She was rocking back and forth, kneading her bony hands and muttering about vengeance, "because that's all those godless heathens understand."

"Maybe we should turn it off now?" He was worried that she would work herself into a state.

"It won't change anything if we do. They're killing our people right there in front of everybody, as bold as brass. Poor innocent people who were just out asking that they be given the same rights as anybody else. I don't believe them when they say that they were shooting people carrying petrol bombs—they're all murderers at heart, that lot, just like the Black and Tans."

"C'mon now, Mam. Let's turn it off and have a cup of tea?"

His mother turned slowly from the screen and eyed him coldly. "Tea? Is that the best that you can do? You should be up there, right now, defending the people like your father did."

"I don't believe in violence. I don't think it will solve our problems."

"And what do you suggest we do? Sit on our arses and sing rebel songs?"

"And what'll be gained by fighting back? Sure, we can kill a few of them but then they'll come back and kill some of us and then the killing will go on and on for years."

"It's the only language they understand for all their talk about fair play and all."

"But Mam, the problem is that the working people have to see that they're all the same no matter which side they're from. And they have to realize that it's their masters who're the real enemy, not each other."

"That's fine talk coming from you. Is that what you learnt in your one and only year in university? Well let me tell you something. You can't talk to the British. They'll never listen to us. Violence is the only thing they ever understand, mark my words. That was how we got the twenty-six counties back. We fought them until they were brought to their knees. Only then would they agree to sit down and talk."

Jerry didn't want to argue. He didn't want to upset her any more than she was. Jacinta had been out for the weekend, and, for the first time, his mother let them spend the night together. She told them that she felt they were almost ready to become a married couple again.

Jerry resented that but couldn't complain—even when Granny used Jacinta as a skivvy, having her fetch and carry from the shops as well as doing the weekly wash. On the way back to the hospital Jacinta had encouraged him to be patient.

**

"She won't live forever but in the mean time we just have to be nice and go along with her. She's just old and wants everything to be her way. And don't you be fretting about me. I'm just happy that I can get out every weekend."

The doctor had told her that Granny had spoken to him about how well she was doing; how she seemed so much better and how Granny was beginning to depend on her—now that she was a bit poorly. The doctor also told Jacinta that, if she kept it up, they would see about letting her out for good.

"We can't mess that up now—after all we've been through."

Jerry wrapped his arm around her shoulders as the rain began, pulling her closer to him and steadying her umbrella between them. He didn't look at her face—at the desperation in her eyes. She would do anything to get out and his mother would see that she did.

But it was probably for the best. He couldn't look after his mother and Danny. He could barely look after himself. When Jacinta moved back they could be a family again, and, maybe by then, his mother would finally give them some credit for that.

When they got to the gate Jacinta squeezed his arm and turned away before her eyes welled up.

"Wait," he called after her. "Gimme a kiss before you go."

Jacinta came back and pecked his cheek. "Now go on and catch Danny's match; it'll mean the world to him if you're there. It'll be the proudest day of his life."

Yes. It was better to go along with things for now and not rock the boat. Maybe his mother might even leave them some money, so that they could go on being a family after she'd gone.

***

Bloody Sunday was the day that changed everything, Jerry decided as Danny strummed a few new chords. That's when the entire population of Ireland got off the fence. An angry mob razed the British Embassy and the IRA blew up an army barracks in Aldershot, killing a bunch of ordinary people, mostly women—and a Catholic British Army chaplain.

And his own mother spent her time in front of the TV, cheering them on all the way.

Jerry tried to explain that his mother was sick and that she didn't mean to say all the terrible things she was saying, but Danny told him it was okay. He said he wanted to hear what Fr. Reilly would have to say about it, first. They could talk about it afterwards.

And when they all went to Mass the following Sunday, to ask God for forgiveness, and to take care of the matter for them—unworthy as they were and prone to lusting for vengeance and all other kinds of sins, Fr. Reilly had denounced it all.

"Love your enemies," he pleaded with them. "Our Savior asked this of us and what do we do? We go out in mobs and behave like the savages they accuse us of being. We had a chance to prove we were worthy of God's love by turning the other cheek but we failed. We failed because we put our pride in country between us and God's power to forgive. I'm ashamed to call myself Irish. We're no better than the English and they barely have any religion at all."

Half the congregation had walked out muttering that they wouldn't return "until the damn young fool apologized." They even threatened to march on the Bishop's Palace and demand that the young curate learn to keep a civil tongue in his head and not be berating those who had always stood by, and supported, the Church. It wasn't for the likes of him to be telling them how they should react. The Bishop, maybe, but he'd have more sense than to be going on like that.

Danny stopped playing football after that and spent every evening with his granny, even when his mother was home. Jerry should have spoken up but didn't know what to say so he decided to wait until Jacinta was settled—she'd know how to deal with it all. In the meantime, he just made tea for the late night visitors who came to talk privately with Granny and always thanked her when they left.

He tried to put his foot down the day Danny came home and told him that a blue Cortina had followed them to Mass, and waited until they came out. But his mother just stared him down and never went to Mass again.

**

"They're spies for the British," Granny reassured Danny who was concerned for the state of her soul. "But don't worry; we'll just do what Michael Collins did to them."

"Michael Collins," Danny whispered to himself, like the very name sent a shiver down his spine.

"You're the spitting image of your grandfather, when he was little."

"Tell me about the time they thought he was dead."

His granny laughed, something she didn't do so much anymore. "Well! It was when he was on the run. He had been to a friendly house for his supper and then went up the road to a barn full of fine, warm hay. In he goes and settles down for the night—after saying his prayers, of course. But it was a cold, frosty night and all he had to warm himself was a bottle of wine.

"Now your grandfather wasn't a great man for the drinking—not like some that we know—and after a few swigs didn't he fall asleep and slept the sleep of an honest man. When he woke up the farmer was poking him with a stick to see if he was alive or dead. You see, the wine had spilt all over your grandfather's shirt making it look for all the world like he had been shot through the chest.

"'I'm not dead at all,' he tells the poor farmer. 'Not dead at all but powerful hungry.'"

"Did they take him in and give him his breakfast?" Danny asked as he did every time before.

"Sure, of course they did. Back then the people used to support the ones that did the fighting. Not like today when we all think we are so civilized. Take my word for it, Danny boy. We drove them out too late. We might be rid of the English but we will never be rid of the way they made us.

"It's at times like these," she told him, "that everybody has to look into their own heart and see what is right and wrong. I know that I've always taught you to be good and to not go around fighting and sinning but this is different. You see, if we didn't fight once in a while we never would have been allowed to have our own place to ourselves. And every once in a while, the Church closed its doors to those that did the fighting. But it was quick, too, to take charge after the hard work was done. But a lot of them know better, only they can't say. Some of them even led us into battle."

"Like Father Murphy of old Kilcormack?"

"Just like Father Murphy from old Kilcormack," she smiled and tousled his hair.

CHAPTER 6

Fr. Reilly was writing to his friend, Joe, when the two detectives called.

Writing about the death of Declan Scully let him organize his thoughts a bit and almost helped him to make some sense out of the senselessness of it all. The detectives were very sorry for disturbing him but they needed his help with their inquiries. He led them into the front room and went off to make some tea—and to compose himself.

He had done his priestly duties for poor Scully. It was easy—sadness, loss, bereavement, consolation—these things were his stock in trade and his primary purpose in the world. He shared the words that Christ had left them; the message of Faith, Hope and the greatest of these–Love. "The Virtues," he had promised the broken-hearted family of the deceased, "can be a source of strength at a time like this."

It was the same message he gave every funeral family, but this time it seemed so inadequate. "We must believe that Our Heavenly Father took Declan for a reason—that his life had a purpose and a meaning. Let us not give in to despair but take strength in the knowledge that God loves us. And when doubts arise remember that God, too, let His own son die to save us all."

Some of the parishioners stiffened a bit. He hadn't meant it to sound like he was comparing Declan Scully to Jesus Christ but he didn't know what else to say. His job was to get them through it all as best he could. The two detectives had a far worse job. They were looking into the details of Scully's death. They had just been over to talk with Danny's parents who both assured him that Danny was home with them all night—and that he hadn't snuck out between midnight and four a.m.

**

"Of course we're sure," Jerry had explained. "Weren't we up playing cards and listening to a few records until after four? We're only trying to get our Danny interested in some good music, ya know? They need all the direction they can get these days—what with the whole world going mad around us."

"Like what happened to that poor Scully boy, God save his soul," Jacinta joined in and started to cry.

"It's very upsetting," Jerry continued as he put his arm around her. "That's why we make a point of spending as much time as we can with our Danny. We even share a few bottles of beer with him, ya know? There's no harm in having a few drinks every now and then, right? What with all the other stuff they could be getting up to."

***

"Why are you telling me all of this?" Fr. Reilly asked cautiously. He could imagine what it must have been like for Jerry and Jacinta. They had enough to deal with without having to believe that Danny was involved in any way. But life as a priest had taught him that nothing was to be unexpected. "You can't really believe that Danny Boyle was involved. I've known the boy for most of his life and I can assure you that it is highly unlikely that he would ever get involved in anything like this."

"Well," the younger detective checked his notebook as his older colleague sat impassively watching Fr. Reilly. "One of the names that Mr. Scully gave us, before he met his unfortunate demise, was one Danny Boyle, whom he described as a small-time pusher."

Fr. Reilly tried not to react and betray anything until he had time to sort it out.

"What we were hoping," the young detective continued after a nod from his colleague, "was that maybe you could have a word with the parents—or better still, with Danny, himself. We don't think that he was involved directly but we do have reason to believe that he might know something about it. In previous investigations, we have found that they all knew what was going on but they were reluctant to let us get involved—even if it was to protect them."

"Like the way you were protecting Declan Scully?"

He shouldn't have said that. They were only doing their best, as they saw it. Policemen were a peculiar breed who tended to see the worst in everybody. He could understand that but he could never accept it. "I'm very sorry," he corrected himself. He had no business judging them. "I didn't mean that. I just get so frustrated with it all."

"We all do, Father, but we still have to investigate these matters—and we have to do it against a wall of silence. We get no cooperation, Father. We do try to work with some of these unfortunates, you know, and get them into treatment, and the likes. We offer protection—when they ask for it. And that's the problem, Father. Some of them are so addicted that as soon as we let them out, they go running back into the arms of the gangs. We can't just hold them indefinitely, Father."

The younger detective seemed to be in earnest but the taciturn one just sat impassively watching Fr. Reilly's face with just a hint of condescension around his mouth. "The problem lies in the courts, Father. We can't do anything that might infringe on their rights, even if it is to save their lives. It's a bad business, Father, and one that we have to deal with every day."

"I'm sorry gentlemen." Fr. Reilly thought about blessing them but decided against it. He had to be a little more careful or they wouldn't help. Policemen could be very sensitive and defensive. Not that he blamed them. He didn't envy their job: damned if you do and damned if you don't. He understood that, but he also understood that they were no Pat McCarthys either. "Please continue."

"That's okay, Father," the taciturn detective soothed. "We understand. But you must understand something, too. In our line of work we can't afford to have bleeding hearts. You have to learn how to stop bleeding on this job—otherwise you'd bleed to death, Father. Now will you have a chat with Mr. Boyle, or will we?"

If he was Chuck O'Malley, or even Fr. Fitzgibbon, Fr. Reilly might have pulled rank. But he wasn't. He was heading into unfamiliar ground. He was going onto their turf and all he had left was to appeal to their Catholicism. "But even if I talk with him I cannot repeat anything he might tell me."

"Not if it's outside the confessional, Father."

"It wouldn't matter. I'd have to maintain Danny's trust to have any hope of reaching out to him."

"I do see your point, Father. And, if you prefer, we can discuss this matter with the Bishop, directly, and let him decide what it is we all should do."

Fr. Reilly lowered his head like Judas and told them he would do what he could and let them know. He'd let the Bishop know, too. He'd get to him before the detectives and lay the case before him. His uncle was a decent man, but could be a touch unpredictable at times. Especially when he sensed defiance. It brought out the St. Michael in him. He'd have to be careful, though; the Bishop had never really got over that time he made his famous sermon—the one that troubled so many. He had even been called to the Palace for a little chat about things.

**

The Bishop's secretary had smiled her knowing smile. "Good morning Father Reilly. Are you well? Have a seat and himself will be with you in no time. Can I get you a cup of tea in the meantime?"

He was getting the wait, the Bishop's way of signalling his displeasure, but he wasn't surprised. Fr. Brennan had been fielding calls for a few weeks. The parishioners were outraged and it was only a matter of time before the higher powers became involved. "Not at all Mrs. Mawhinney, I'm grand. Is he very busy?"

"He's been on the phone to the Diocese all morning and," she paused to smile at the errant young curate, "he's in a right old mood."

"You know, Patrick," the Bishop began when he finally saw him. "The Irish are a very particular race of people. They have stood by the Church through the years of persecution, risking their very lives to hear Mass and take the Sacraments.

"And they have given their children to the missions to spread the word of God into every dark corner of the world.

They've a particular passion for the downtrodden and the exploited and the Church needs as much of that as it can get." He sipped his coffee and searched his nephew's face for some indication that he was getting the message. "But they're also a fiery people—the savagery of their Celtic ancestry is never far below the surface. And sometimes, when they're outraged, they need to blow off a little steam. It's at times like these that a good priest knows when to listen and when to talk. They're very angry right now and we both know that they've every right to be. Am I right?"

"You are indeed, Your Grace."

The Bishop noted his stilted formality. *Damn the boy for his hard head.* "Then why, in the name of God, did you have to take it upon yourself to berate them, now of all times?"

"I was just hoping to remind them of the true message of Christ."

The Bishop's eye bulged a little and his cheeks reddened but his voice remained calm and low, like he was coaxing a skittish foal. "The true message of Christ, you say? For the love of God man, don't you remember what they did to Him?"

He regretted it the moment he said it. His nephew was starry-eyed enough without putting thoughts of martyrdom into his head. And it'd look so bad in the newspapers if his parishioners crucified him. It'd be better for all concerned if any killing of his holy spirit was done quietly, behind closed doors.

"So?" he asked in the most superior tone he could manage. "How's it that you're so certain what the true message was when the Pope and all of the cardinals sit up late at night trying to understand it?"

"I'm sorry, Your Grace. I meant no disrespect with my comments. I was just hoping to remind them of the comfort the Sacred Heart of Christ offers to those in trial."

It sounded like sass but the Bishop couldn't be sure. His nephew's face was in earnest.

"Patrick, matters of Church and State have a way of making simple things complex. The people of Ireland are at a crossroads and may choose to go on without us. Times are changing and with all this talk about civil rights, the old ways are in danger of being washed away—the good and the bad. The Diocese is most anxious that we do nothing that might tip the scales even if it means relaxing the reins a bit and letting them blow off their steam. Most of them will spend their rage getting a few pints into them and singing rebel songs. And so what if they burn down the British Embassy? It can be rebuilt, but our relationship with the people might not. Let them have their rage and we'll rein them back when the time is right."

"But what about the people that were killed in Aldershot?"

"Ah! We can only assume that God took them for his own purpose. Why else would he allow a priest to die?"

"But, Your Grace, the Provos are talking about bombing the Brits out."

The Bishop paused to think. The Provisional IRA were young and hard and full of bile. And they had split from the "Officials" who had put aside the gun to unite the working men. He had seen their likes before—earnest, and driven by their cause; the most dangerous types of individuals. The types that could actually cause things to change. Church and State had worked hard to discredit them and turn the flock away from them. It would be a problem for a while, but in time, when their thirst for vengeance was slaked, they could be brought back in line. And a few dead Protestants was regrettable but better than dead Catholics.

Not that the other side wouldn't strike back, too. The Church would just have to sit back and offer comfort where it could. There was no point in trying to talk peace to any of them right now—they were deafened by their rage.

"My advice to you, Father, is to pray to God for the wisdom and guidance so that you can be a comfort to the people instead."

"Very well, Your Grace, I will."

"And you'll apologize, too, next Sunday. Or you'll be off to Timbuktu in the morning. Now get off with you so I can get a bit of lunch into me."

***

In time the parishioners accepted his apology, but Fr. Reilly never felt he re-won their trust. They tolerated him because of his collar but they put little stock in what he had to say. It was, he consoled himself, the cost of telling the absolute truth, something that he had become somewhat selective about since. He hadn't started to lie, he just became more selective in how much of the truth he revealed. It was too bright a light to be flashing in the eyes of those who were living in darkness.

It had taken some cajoling but Danny finally agreed to meet him. They walked through the grounds of Rathfarnham Castle, away from prying eyes, and where the casuistry of the Jesuits might help in getting through to Danny. He could talk to the Garda voluntarily, or they would come and get him.

"But I keep telling you, Father, I don't know anything about it."

Danny seemed to be getting nervous and Fr. Reilly didn't want to lose him. His good nature told him to believe the boy but he couldn't trust that judgement. He wasn't seasoned enough yet for these situations. But he had to be. He just had to apply his craft the way they had taught him after he left the seminary. Fr. Brennan always said that it was like trout fishing: getting someone to open up enough to share the burdens that God had put there for His own reasons.

That was another thing he didn't understand. Why was this to be Danny's lot? There was no logic behind it. Danny, God love him, had suffered enough. What more could God want from the boy?

"Well, that may be as well be, but the fact is the Garda still want to talk with you. They seem to think you have some information that might be helpful in finding who murdered Declan Scully."

He thought Danny might have winced for a second but he had his head down as they walked the stone drive; the crunching of the stones in rhythm with the song of birds, the only noises of the world outside.

This was his Chuck O'Malley moment. This was when his worth as a priest was to be really measured. This was what Christ had called him to do—to save the soul of Danny Boyle. *Who had a grandmother in Heaven and,* he almost smiled as he thought it, *she probably had a hold of God's ear by now—or at least someone that had. It was probably St.*

Jude, Patrick Reilly decided. Jude was always his favorite; lost cause that he was.

"I'm not going to grass on anyone, Father."

"Of course not, Danny. Nobody's asking you to do that. All I'm telling you is that either you go to see them or they will come and see you."

"Then I'm fucked—just like Scully."

Patrick Reilly ignored the profanity in deference to the importance of the moment—when the sinner comes to the realization that a life without God would end down in Hell. He had to choose his next words carefully. He had to let Danny know that he understood the enormity of it all and that he wasn't shocked or disapproving. He wasn't there as a judge but as an advocate: Danny's advocate before the courts of God, and man.

"Yes, Danny. It's very serious. There is no point in trying to soften the truth. Declan Scully gave them your name and you have now become what they call a person of interest. You're in very serious trouble, but you still have God to turn to."

"Him? The same God that let my granny lock my mother up in the loony bin? I'd rather stick with my mates. At least I can trust them."

"Danny, they didn't do so well by Declan Scully. You know you can't trust them."

"Then what? Go to cops and grass? And spend the rest of my days looking over my shoulder?"

"Danny. We could do a deal with them. If you're willing to cooperate with them . . . then I'm sure we can ask them to protect you properly. I have even taken the matter up with the Bishop. He's always been a great friend to your family."

The Bishop would help—after he had berated Patrick for a while, but he would help. He had promised Nora Boyle that he would. Fr. Brennan would grumble, too, but he was getting old and would forget about it when the next outrage reached his ears.

Danny seemed to be considering it, even if he still professed denial. "I used to take the stuff; I won't deny that. And I got a bit hooked—and the last time I got some from Scully, I never got around to paying for it. That's why he grassed on me. I don't know any more than that."

He claimed that he had heard that that's how things went; when a dealer got lifted he'd just give out all the names of the guys he dealt with. They never named anybody above—just the little guys below.

Fr. Reilly let it go in one ear and out the other. He wasn't dismissing it, he just didn't want to get distracted. Danny would say anything; addicts were like that. He had read up on them and the ways that were used to help them. And he read up on the impact all the years of violence must be having on their minds, too. He was going to be ready on all counts. But he'd need the Bishop and all the influence he had. It was waning but it was still potent enough to shade the thinking of policemen and judges alike. His uncle had friends who would listen to the truth about Danny Boyle. He wouldn't be left to the mercy of the way things were done—like Declan Scully. No. Patrick Reilly would not fail Danny Boyle in this, his hour of need.

"I'll go if you'll come with me," Danny finally agreed as the sun broke through again and showered them with light.

"Are you sure?"

"What fuckin' choice do I have?"

*

"I have every reason to believe that he's making a serious effort to turn his life around," Patrick assured the detective, the taciturn one who had answered the phone. "He is willing to come in, voluntarily, and answer any questions you might have."

"I'm very happy to hear that, Father. I think we all know that it's what's best."

"There is just one condition. He will only come in if I'm allowed to stay with him."

"Fair enough, Father, but I should warn you that if we find that Mr. Boyle has information he could be implicated in a murder case. Usually, people like him prefer to have solicitors."

Fr. Reilly could imagine him smirking—in his reticent way. Probably no more than a snide wrinkling of his lips but at least he had agreed. "Well, I'm sure that after you've had a chance to speak with Danny, you'll realize that he is telling the truth."

"Father, in my line of work, truth is a rare commodity but I'll be delighted if you're right."

Patrick would mention all of this to his uncle. He'd know how to deal with likes of them. He'd put them in their places quick enough. "Very good, then. I will bring him by the station tomorrow afternoon."

"Good man, Father."

*

"Who's that you were talking to?" Fr. Brennan stood in the doorway, looking more and more dishevelled. He hadn't had a bath in a few days and reeked of body odor. He hadn't been changing his underwear, either. Something would have to be done.

"I was talking with the Garda relating to the Scully boy's death."

"Are you playing the detective now?"

"Not at all, Father. I was just passing on some information to them, that's all."

"Not something you heard in the confessional?"

"Of course not, Father."

"Well, mind you don't."

"I will be very careful, Father." He had played the deferent long enough and decided to turn the table, again. "Is there something the matter, Father? You seem agitated. Is there anything I can do to help you relax? Perhaps I could pour a bath and then you could sit out in Gethsemane for a while. You'd like that, wouldn't you, Father?"

"I can pour my own bath, you know."

"Of course you can. I was just offering to be of some help."

"That's very Christian of you. Very Christian," Fr. Brennan muttered as he went to take his bath.

Fr. Reilly listened to him cross, and recross floors. He heard him open the taps in the bathroom and go to the cupboard for a fresh towel. And in time he heard the taps close and the swish as the old man lowered himself into the water. He rose and closed the door to the study and reached for his writing paper.

He finished writing to Joe and put it with the others he hadn't got around to sending. He had been avoiding Miriam and didn't know how to explain that.

He missed being in contact with Joe who always knew what

to say to cheer him up. For a long time, Joe's letters were all that kept him from going completely and utterly mad.

*

Jerry sipped his tea and eyed Jacinta over the rim. He hadn't told her about seeing Danny on the street. Even she would have heard the whispers about Anto.

No one could ever prove anything but everyone was sure that, if bad things happened in the neighborhood, Anto had something to do with it. They called him the "local general." No one was really sure about anything but they avoided crossing his path.

A year ago, some of the lads in the pub finally decided to stand up and do something about it after a night of heavy drinking. And as each drink went down, their righteous anger grew.

Even Jerry got caught up in it all; it was the first time they had included him. They had always viewed him with a touch of wariness before—him having been to university, and all. And then there was the whole thing around Jacinta in the mental hospital, his banishment to England, his drinking, and the whole stink about Danny in the church with that young Deirdre one—not that Jerry blamed him. Deirdre was a bit-of-all-right and Danny would've been mad not to take his chance with her.

But that night, even Deirdre's father started to speak to him again. He was still angry about what had happened but he had stopped blaming Jerry for that. And, as the pints were lowered, he said it wasn't even Danny's fault anymore—he'd been high on drugs. The drug dealers were the real problem and it was time the ordinary man stood up and took back the neighborhood. They were all united in that.

But nothing good came of it. A few of them were attacked a few nights later, on their way home, and left beaten and bloodied on the street; not having even seen their assailants. No one had seen or heard anything. And if they ever changed their minds, Anto would send messages home with their kids.

That was when Deirdre's father organized the Neighborhood Residents Watch Committee—or "Watchers," as they preferred to be called. It was supposed to be shadowy but everyone knew about it. They had a few late-night run-ins with local lads acting-the-tool and one of those got a bit violent. The Guards were involved but no one had seen or heard anything.

After that, Deirdre's father insisted that they get properly organized. He thought that they should wear berets, and maybe sunglasses, too, and of course, they would have to be sober when on duty.

When the rest of them made it obvious that they might not be able to get into the fighting spirit unless they had a few beforehand—Dutch Courage, and all—he laid out the trump card that established him as their leader.

The Guards had already warned him that they couldn't have drunken mobs keeping the peace, but they could see their way to supplying walkie-talkies to a few organized, responsible citizens who would report problems and not get directly involved. It was better for everyone so they all agreed.

They all felt better about it, too; even Anto, who was always privy to the Watchers schedules and simply organized his business around them.

Jerry had served his time with the Watchers until the third time he turned up drunk.

Now he was going to have to cross paths with Anto for real and calmed himself with the reassurance the forces he could call on would create more than enough problems for Anto. Enough that he would leave Danny alone for the sake of peace. They could all be reasonable about it and sort it out without any more shootings, beatings, or anything like that.

He hadn't spoken to Jacinta about any of that yet. He had let Danny, and Jacinta, down so many times before. This time he'd get everything sorted before he told her. It wasn't like he was going to confront Anto personally—he was no knight-in-shining-armor. Instead he would plead and cajole with everyone he needed.

He even thought about going to the church a few times—to have a private word with God.

He didn't have to; Fr. Reilly phoned him and explained that the Bishop had agreed to get involved. He assured Jerry that he had every reason to believe that everything would be done to portray Danny in the best light.

Jerry thanked him for that. There was no harm in having the clergy in their corner—they needed all the help the Boyle name could still afford them, and then some.

He'd still have to go and have a talk with the people his mother had given so much of her money to—the shadowy men who were still romantically referred to as the Boys, fallen as they were from the mantels of Ireland's firesides.

Rumor had it that some of them, seeking a more lucrative and reliable source of income, were dabbling in the business. The older ones refuted that and still claimed they were trying to stamp it out—that the drugs business was abhorrent to all that held the Republic dearly. Drug-dealing was another foreign influence and would be dealt with when the opportunity arose.

Now Jerry was going to give them their chance.

*

"Are you going to sit on your arse all day or are you going to do something about Danny?" Jacinta looked at him the way she always did when their problems were becoming too much for her.

Jerry drained his tea cup and stood up as straight as he could. "I'm going down to have a chat with a few people who might be able to help, if you must know. In the meantime, why don't you go out with your sisters and not spend the whole day cooped up in here? Danny will be fine. You'll see."

After he had gone, Jacinta phoned her sisters. They knew all about it and immediately agreed to meet for a bite to eat, and maybe a few drinks, too, just to help Jacinta get over it. She loved her sisters. She could count on their love and support as long as she was buying the drinks.

After that they could say what they liked about her, and Jerry, and Danny. It never lasted long before they moved on to something stupid that one of them did. But they were family and she took what little strength she could from that. Jerry was an only child.

After she made up her face, and brushed out her hair, Jacinta stopped in to the church. It was on the way to the bus stop.

"Nora," she whispered through her fingers. "Promise me that you won't let anything happen to Danny?"

A breeze fluttered through the door as someone entered, genuflected, and shuffled off to the first station-of-the-cross. Jacinta watched through her fingers and found some comfort in that. Her own Jesus had been condemned and had gone down to have his cross laid on him. But at least he had Fr. Reilly there, like Simon.

She stayed a little while longer but Nora Boyle had nothing to say.

"Very well, Nora. Work in your mysterious ways." She blessed herself again and stole a quick glance at Mary before rising and stepping outside where it was warm and full of the sounds of the world.

She would call Martin, later, when it was cheaper. By then, Danny would be back from the station. There was no point in worrying her brother before then. He'd always been there for Danny, even after she got out of the hospital. She used to be a bit jealous of him for that; Danny was closer to him than anybody else in the world.

*

When she got home, Jacinta settled by the phone. Her sisters had all agreed; Martin would know what to do. He'd always been close to Danny and if anyone could help him, it was Martin. She politely asked if he was well and how things were in his new life. She envied him, now free from shadows and rebuke. Her sister said that he had run-away-for-the-dollars, but Jacinta knew it was far more than that. Martin had a sensitivity about him and that made him different.

"And where are things at now?" he asked and she could feel his concern from three thousand miles away.

"Well I met Fr. Reilly coming up the road and he had just got back from the Garda station. He thinks they might believe Danny but that they might have a few more questions in the future."

"I'm sure they will. They will want to squeeze whatever they can out of him."

"Fr. Reilly said that the Guards told him that they had been talking to somebody called Flanagan and he said that he had heard that Danny owed Scully money and that Scully had said that he was going to kill Danny if he didn't pay up."

"Flanagan? Anto Flanagan?"

"I think so? Do you know of him?"

"I do. He's a right piece of work, that one. What was Danny doing getting mixed up with guttersnipes like him?"

"I wish I had the answer, Martin. All I know is that the Guards also told Fr. Reilly that they believed that Flanagan would say or do anything to get himself in the clear."

"Well that's good."

"It is, but they also said that Danny has to start thinking about how he is going to look out for himself."

"He's going to have to grass."

"I know, but it's what's going to happen after that that has me worried."

"Do you want me to come home, Jass?"

"I couldn't ask you . . ." She paused long enough for him to realize what she was really hoping for.

"Do you think that Danny would fancy coming over here for a while—until everything cools down?"

"I'd hate for him to be so far away but it might be what's best—after he clears things up with the Guards."

"Ok," Martin decided. "I'll get started on his application and get them to send everything to you. You just have to make sure that Danny fills it out properly."

"It's not going to cost money, is it?"

"Don't worry, Jass. I'll look after things."

"You were always like a guardian angel to Danny. God bless you for that."

CHAPTER 7

Granny had always told Danny that guardian angels would be there for him when he needed them most, even when he couldn't see them. "Sometimes," she'd say with a touch of mystery in her voice, "they will act through others."

That was what had disappointed Danny the most. He would have loved to have a glowing angel, with resplendent wings and a fiery sword, appear by his side when the other kids turned on him.

Instead, he just learned to blend in and avoid the worst of them, and, as time passed, and it became obvious, he began to wonder if there was any truth to anything he'd been told. Nobody really tried to be good anymore, and, by the time he got to secondary school, he was beginning to wonder if any of the stuff about God was true.

**

Brother Arnold was reading aloud from *Les Scrupules de Maigret* in his very best French—the way he imagined St. Jean-Baptiste might have done. Now that Ireland was in the Common Market they would all be talking French in no time—unless the "Coalition" messed it up again.

But the boys weren't listening. It was a warm spring afternoon and most of them had their faces down pretending to follow. They were really looking forward to a day off. Schools all over the city would be closed tomorrow, to mark the death of the archbishop. It was the end of an era—and the beginning of a new one, too. Brother Arnold had joined the Order to dispense pearls of wisdom to shining-faced young pupils who could never get enough. But since "Free Education" so many of his pupils were just not suited and would have been better off out working and learning trades.

"When they get it for free—they see no value in it," was the consensus in the staff room. The De La Salle Brothers had a fine tradition, but the times were changing. "They've no time for it anymore, with their rock-and-roll, and their protesting, and their 'Rights!'"

"They want to change the world so they don't have to get off their arses and do a bit of work."

"And we can't do a damn thing—if you lay a hand on them . . ."

"They should be off in the technical schools, the lot of them, so we can get back to teaching the boys that are here to learn."

"I blame the parents. None of them want to take a shred of responsibility. You hear it at the parent-teacher meetings: 'My Johnny is not getting the type of education that he deserves . . .' God preserve us from Bedlam."

Br. Arnold paused his reading to take a quick look around. Maguire and Collins were passing something back and forth, snickering softly to themselves. Br. Arnold rose from behind his desk with his book in his hand and continued his reading as he walked to the window. The mountains were closer today and he wished he was walking among them. That's where he had found contentment as a young man, walking through God's creation—just a tiny piece looking for his place in it all.

He turned casually so he could walk along the side of the desks and across the back of the room. Maguire and Collins noticed and raised their books to their faces but their snickering continued. They were poking at the boy in front of them: Danny Boyle.

Boyle had first come to the school as a polite young man, so well turned out in his new blazer and crisp white shirt, his grey pants neatly pressed and his shoes shining. He was a shy, hesitant lad who struggled in his dealings with the other boys but worked hard to improve his marks. Br. Arnold took a special interest in him, knowing his circumstances and his family's connections with the Bishop. His grandmother was a benefactor, donating generously to any appeal the school made.

But over the last two years, things had changed. With his grandmother ailing—some said she was dying—Danny's appearance deteriorated. His shirts wrinkled and yellowed, and he had outgrown his pants that now fluttered a few inches above his scuffed and tattered shoes. And where he had once excelled in his studies, he now struggled to keep up.

The staff room had been advised that there were problems at home and to give the boy some latitude. There were rumors, too, that his grandmother had given all of her savings to the Provos and times were getting tough. "The mother is not long out of St. Pat's and the father, who has a bit of a fondness for drink, lost his job when the government changed," those in the know confided.

Others said he had been caught drinking on the job. Either way it didn't matter—things weren't good at home. There'd been talk of holding Danny back for a year to let him catch up. But the fear of stigmatizing the boy lead them all to agree: "Let him sit his exams and if he doesn't do well he can repeat them next year."

Br. Arnold spent as much time with him as he could, helping Danny without drawing the other boys' attention. Children could be such a vicious lot and he didn't want the burden of teacher's pet to be piled on the boy's flagging shoulders.

When he got behind Maguire and Collins, he could see what all the snickering was about. They had been sneaking glances at a folded-out picture of a young woman, naked, with her breasts on show for the whole world to see, and her other parts, concealed only by the fold of her thighs.

Br. Arnold pounced and extracted the smut from under Maguire's book and crumpled it up like a wick.

"Get up, the two of you, and stand at the front of the class until I decide what to do with the pair of you—bringing the likes of that into school with you. You should both be ashamed of yourselves."

"It's not ours, Brother. We were only just looking at it. Boyle gave it to us," Maguire pleaded, his eyes wide and his face red.

"That's right, Brother," Collins chimed in. He was a sneaky little runt of a thing that was never far from trouble. "We didn't know what it was."

"Is any of this true, Boyle?"

"No!" Danny protested with indignation. "I never saw that before in my life."

"Are you telling me the truth, Boyle?"

"I am, Brother, on my granny's life."

"Go on then," Br. Arnold commanded gruffly as he snapped his book shut and held the wicked girl in the other hand. "Go on, the lot of you, the class is over. Except you two," he pointed to Maguire and Collins. "You two are off to the headmaster's office to explain yourselves."

**

They were waiting for Danny on the way home, leaning by the corner near the Bottle Tower, sharing a cigarette and blowing on the angry welts on their fingers. The headmaster had the same solution for every problem that landed in his office—six-of-the-best from a vicious, swishing, bamboo cane. Maguire knew that it was better to stand and face it and not flinch. Those that did had their legs whipped, too, until they stood still and took their punishment like a man. Maguire had been there often enough but Collins had tried to dodge and had two burning welts on his thighs, chaffing against his pants. They were both in a foul mood but brightened when they saw Danny approach.

"Come here, ya bollocks. Come here and get what's comin' to you." Maguire stepped away from the wall and flicked the cigarette butt into the gutter.

"Yeah Boyle," Collins joined in. "Your granny isn't here to save you this time."

**

Danny struggled to control the fear that churned in his stomach and threatened to come scuttering down his leg. He wanted to run but there was no point. They would be waiting there tomorrow, and the day after, and each day their fury would grow. No, he had to face them now and get it over with. Martin had shown him a few boxing moves—how to keep his guard up and how to throw a jab, but he hadn't really taught him how to fight.

"Leave me alone will ya? It wasn't my fault. I'd nothin' to do with it. What are you blamin' me for?"

"Because," Maguire explained like he was talking to a retard. "You could have fuckin' told him it was yours."

"Then I would have been caned."

"You're the brother's pet; he wouldn't have done anythin' to you." Maguire slapped him up the side of his head. "You could have got us off, Boyle, and now you're goin' to get what's comin' to you."

He stood closer and sneered into Danny's face. He made a sudden movement with his arm and when Danny ducked, flicked his shoulder catching Danny on the nose, causing his eyes to water.

"Magser!" Collins laughed as he swung his foot toward Danny's backside. "You're after makin' him cry. Look at him." He grabbed Danny by the hair and pulled his head up level with his own and spat in his face.

Danny's blood began to boil, melting his fear. He wriggled free and pushed Collins to the ground kicking wildly at his ribs.

"Get him Magser," the terrified Collins pleaded as he tried to roll away. Maguire stepped between them and pushed Danny back, like he expected him to run. But a red mist had descended on Danny. He jabbed as Martin had taught him and connected with something soft, even as Maguire's fist caught him on the nose. He was fighting for his life and punched away with both fists, ignoring the pain in his nose and blinded by his own tears. He backed Maguire against the wall and punched frantically for as long as he could until someone grabbed him by the collar and hauled him back.

"Hold on there, Tiger," an adult voice commanded and Danny went limp, sobbing and slobbering as he tried to control his breathing. "Calm down now before you kill the pair of them."

Mr. Quirke offered him his handkerchief and motioned for him to wipe his face. "Calm down now, Boyle, and take a few deep breaths." Mr. Quirke taught history and encouraged Danny when other's didn't. "If I were you," he advised the bloodied Maguire, "I'd get out of here while I try to calm Boyle down."

Collins didn't need any more encouragement but had to help Maguire get away, his bravado now in tatters around his ankles.

**

Mr. Quirke watched them leave with a flicker of a smile on his face. He couldn't take sides but he could enjoy the outcome, privately. He waited until Danny stopped shaking and snivelling, getting colder as his rage evaporated, and put his arm around his shoulder. "Go on home now, Boyle, and get someone to put something cold on your nose."

He saw him safely onto the bus before he allowed himself to smile fully and whistled aloud as he headed for home.

**

Jacinta didn't smile. She ran her hand through her hair and raised her eyes to the ceiling. "What on earth got into you? Brawling on the streets with a pair of guttersnipes."

"Leave the boy alone, for Christ's sake," Jerry snorted from behind his *Evening Press*. "He was just standin' up for himself—and it's about time, too."

"And what are we going to tell his granny when she sees his nose all bloody and swollen?"

"We'll tell her that he was playin' football and the ball hit him. Besides, she'll hardly notice—the state she's in."

"Jerry! Don't be talking like that in front of the child; can't you see that he's upset enough?"

"He'll be fine." Jerry lowered the paper and studied his son's face. "It's about time that you learned to stand up for yourself. The world is full of bastards who will only leave you alone if they can find someone easier. You gotta be tough to survive, son. That's somethin' else they don't teach you in school." He went back behind his paper to hide his smile.

"This is nothing to be smiling about."

"You're probably right, Missus. Is the dinner almost ready?"

**

Jacinta turned away and went back to stirring pots on the stove. She sniffed each one and added a pinch of salt here and there. Her cooking was getting better—not that they seemed to notice, shovelling it down without comment. And Granny was worse, hardly touching what was placed before her but quick to complain if it wasn't. Jacinta didn't mind, too much. Granny was clearly in pain, though she did her best to hide it.

Jacinta would never let her find out that Danny was getting into fights—it would kill her altogether and that day was coming soon enough. Jacinta knew better than anybody; she changed the old woman's sheets and washed her things.

She worried about what would happen to them all. Jerry hadn't found work yet, and, sometimes, she wondered if he was even trying. Not that she could say anything about that; Granny and Jerry were united in agreement that he was a victim of politics, just like his father before him, and Jacinta knew better than to step between them.

She still had to go and see the doctor once a week; a bitter visitation to the dull hopelessness that once was her life. He told her how happy he was with her progress, of which he always seemed to have prior notification. He even worried about regression on the occasions when she displeased Mrs. Boyle, something Jacinta was learning to avoid.

But it was worth the price she had to pay. She had Danny back—and Jerry. They were becoming a normal family again and normal families had to put up with tough times. That was one of the things they had taught her in the hospital: that life wasn't going to be rosy all the time. "That's why God made drink," her sisters agreed when they got together and tried to laugh all of their problems away, even while creating new ones. She felt better when she was with them, married with a child—even if it was to Jerry Boyle. But at least she had a man. At least there was that.

She smiled as she put their plates on the table "C'mon lads and get this into you. Go on now and start and I'll be down after I feed Granny."

"Can I bring it up to her?"

"Not tonight Danny. If she sees the state of your face she will only get upset and we don't want that, do we?"

"I guess not."

"You can say goodnight to her later on when her lights are off, okay?" Jacinta caressed his bruised face and his swollen nose. "Go on now and eat so you have plenty of time to do your homework."

"So?" she heard Jerry ask as she left the kitchen. "Tell me all about the fight."

**

"What are we going to do?" Jacinta asked when Jerry came back from the bar with their drinks.

They liked to get out every night after Granny was asleep, to relax a bit. Danny was there doing his homework and would come and get them if there was a problem. "There's no money for anything. I don't suppose you have had any luck finding a job?"

"There's no work anywhere—what with the Arabs shuttin' off the oil, and all. There isn't even any work in London and there's always work there."

"You're not thinking of going back there?"

"I might have to if things don't pick up here."

"And what about me and Danny? I don't think we should be dragging him off to London; it's no place for a family."

"You and Danny can stay here and I'll send money over."

"But what about when your mother is dead?"

"Don't be talking like that. The poor woman is bad enough without wishin' her dead."

"I'm not Jerry, but we have to face facts."

Jacinta leaned forward and raised her gin and tonic to her lips. "It's going to happen, one of these days, and we'd be better off knowing what we're going to do."

Jerry sipped his pint and fumbled in his pocket for his cigarettes. "Let's just have these few drinks in peace. I'm worn out."

"Worn out? What has you worn out now. Didn't you stay in bed until after ten while I was up tending to Granny and seeing Danny off to school. I hardly have a minute to myself, anymore. I haven't even seen my sisters in weeks."

"Jazus, Jass. You're not the only one who is suffering. It's my mother that's dying."

"I'm sorry, Jerry. I didn't mean to upset you. I know how hard things are for you right now, having your job stolen right out from under you and having your mother dying. Is there anything I can do to make things better?"

"You can give me a cigarette. I must have left mine at home."

"Don't you remember? You smoked them all."

"Shite! I only have enough for two more drinks. Unless you can make that one last the night?"

"I can do better than that." She reached into her purse and pulled out an old five-pound note.

"Where did you get that?"

"I've been saving it," Jacinta nudged him. "Go on and get your fags and get us another round, too."

She had found the money in an envelope in one of Granny's drawers. There were two more fives and an old ten-shilling note. There was a letter, too, but it wasn't her place to read it. She wasn't really taking the money—she was only borrowing it.

**

"You're a life saver," Jerry sighed as he blew a long stream of smoke above their fresh drinks, lined up, waiting.

"And we've enough for another, too." She swallowed the tang of guilt. It was another thing she had learned about in hospital: rationalization–only they were trying to discourage it. But if Jacinta was going to survive, she had to make her own rules. "Jerry? Would you mind terribly if I went out with my sisters, one of these days?"

"What do you want to be goin' out with them for?"

"They're my sisters, Jerry. I just want to see them, once in a while. Besides, I can ask Martin to take Danny to the pictures so you can stay at home and watch the racing on the telly."

"But what if my mam needs something? I don't know where anything is."

"We can give her medicine early and she'll sleep like a baby."

**

They met in town, in the usual place, and fussed over Jacinta, making it clear they still thought of her as delicate. "You're looking awful tired. You must be worn out with all that you have to do."

"And I don't suppose that himself has a job yet?"

"A job? He's just waiting for his mammy to croak so he can get at her money."

"Is that old bitch not dead yet?"

"She's too miserable to die."

"She's probably died already—only the Devil sent her back so as he could get some peace."

"Ah don't be talking about her like that. She's dying, God love her."

"Not soon enough."

"Now girls, don't be speaking too badly of her—after all, she's buying the drinks." Jacinta flourished a five-pound note, the penultimate from the forgotten envelope in the drawer.

"Fair enough then, we'll be nice—'til it's gone."

"Does she still have any money? I heard that she gave it all to the IRA"

"I heard that they pay her—for protection."

"That old bitch has bags of it hidden away somewhere."

"How do you put up with it all?"

"She's not that bad, and besides, when she dies the house will be Jerry's and mine and then we'll see who's laughing."

Jacinta was not as confident as she wished to sound. She did not believe in guardian angels; she was far more focused on the devils that preyed on her mind, just waiting for an opportunity to reach out and create havoc in her day. She did not love God, she feared Him and all He stood for—judgement and retribution. Stern and strict and remote like an overlord, He had little time for the likes of her so she had to find her own way, always careful not to get caught doing wrong. Not because it was wrong but because the punishment of God was vicious and complete.

**

Martin was far more optimistic and believed everything had a reason and a purpose in a greater plan that simply was and did not conform to right or wrong. Nor was it haphazard, simply far too complex for human understanding. He took hope from that, even if he was nervous as he waited.

He had never been to a solicitor's office before. Mr. Davies had the second floor of an old building on Dawson Street, a musty old office full of dusty old tomes and the memorabilia of a life spent in the public cause; yellowing pictures of posed smiles and formal handshakes between friends, and colleagues, and notaries. Martin recognized some of them from pictures he had seen in the newspapers, and a few from his history books.

Davies's secretary said he wouldn't be long and offered coffee but Martin declined, not wanting to have to balance the cup on his knee while he waited. He was wearing his best suit, a dark blue polyester with wide lapels and flared pants.

"He won't be long now," the secretary smiled and went back to her typewriter, tapping along with the ticking of the great clock in the corner. Martin sat and rummaged through the newspapers and magazines on the low table in front of him. He found an old and yellowed issue of *Dublin Opinion* and passed the time down memory lane.

**

"And you must be Martin," an old whiskey-red face beamed at him from the door of the inner office; a mustier place with a large wooden desk and fine old leather chairs, dense with years of pipe smoke. "Come in, come in." He ushered Martin inside and softly closed the door, muting the world outside. He sat behind his desk and deliberately composed himself. "Well now. Has Mrs. Boyle given you any indication as to why she wanted me to see you?"

"Not really," Martin was unsure and didn't want to say the wrong thing.

"I see. Well! Let me get straight to the point, then. As you know, my client does not have long and she has asked me to apprise you of her wishes for her estate, after she has passed."

Martin sat as straight as he could and held his hands in his lap.

"The house and its contents will pass to her grandson, Daniel, with a monthly provision for her son, Jeremiah, and his wife, Jacinta, to maintain things until Daniel comes of age."

"I see." Martin wanted to sound like he knew why any of this concerned him.

"However, Mrs. Boyle has some reservations about their financial acumen and has appointed you as . . . a form of guardian."

"I see, but I'm not sure I understand."

"Yes. It is a bit unorthodox but what Mrs. Boyle has requested is that you oversee the family and keep me informed of any problems that might arise. I realize," he paused as if he was studying Martin's perplexed face, "that this might put you in an awkward position but Mrs. Boyle expressed a particular confidence in you and felt that you would be the best possible influence on Danny's life."

"But what am I supposed to do?"

"Well, the house is paid for, so we have monthly allowances for utilities and other household expenses. Mrs. Boyle, however, has concerns that these monies might be misappropriated and feels that having a reliable pair of eyes on the situation would benefit everyone, particularly your nephew, Daniel."

"But what am I supposed to do? Am I supposed to tell his parents how to live their lives?"

"Not at all," Davies laughed as if to put him at ease. It was all very unorthodox but Davies understood: Jeremiah Boyle was a disgrace to his name and that wife of his . . .

The law wasn't flexible enough but he had ways of getting around it. Jeremiah didn't have the wit to object. And besides, the Bishop was onside with it all. Mrs. Boyle had made provisions for the Church too, as well as certain political interests.

Despite rumors to the contrary Mrs. Boyle still had money. She had given far too much to the "Cause" but Bart had invested wisely and there was enough for them all, as long as it wasn't squandered. "What Mrs. Boyle was hoping is that you could keep an eye on the situation, and, if any problems arise, report back to me."

**

"So you want me to spy on them for you?"

"It is not about what I want, young man. Mrs. Boyle wants to appoint you as Daniel's legal guardian until he comes of age. It is just a matter of ensuring that his best interests are being maintained."

"But I don't know anything about this stuff."

Davies smiled like he was trying to explain something to a child. "I can assure you, young man, that you appear to be more than capable. Mrs. Boyle spoke at some length about your qualities. And besides, if problems were to arise, I am here to deal with them."

"Well, I would do anything for Danny—and Granny Boyle—but I don't want to be spying on my sister, or anything."

"It is not a matter of spying on anybody. You would just be making sure that everybody is doing what they should be doing for the sake of your nephew, until he is old enough to take care of his own affairs. It is what is best—for all concerned."

Martin signed some papers and left, feeling like a Judas as he walked through the rain. He didn't need this right now.

He had just started studying at Bolton Street and the pressures of life were beginning to pile up in front of him, obscuring his view.

But he had to be there for Danny: the poor little bollocks was going to need all the help he could get.

Besides, it was only for a few years and then he would be gone. After he graduated he would be off in America and be rid of them all. Dublin was far too Dublin for the likes of him.

**

Fr. Brennan had suggested that Fr. Reilly take on the task of visiting the old and infirm of the parish. "It is the closest we can get to stepping into the footsteps of the Fisherman."

He made it sound like he was doing the young curate a favor. That it would free him up to go fly-fishing with the Bishop again was but a happy coincidence.

Not that Fr. Reilly agreed, but he accepted it—as penance for his ill-advised sermon. He was, however, trepidatious when he realized that Nora Boyle was on his list.

He hadn't seen her in months and was shocked. She had shrivelled up like a spider, pale and wan with grey stands dangling around her frightened face. The end was fast approaching and Fr. Reilly felt too young and inadequate to meet the old lady's gaze and had no idea where to begin.

"Are you well, Mrs. Boyle?"

"Of course I'm not well. What kind of a question is that and where's Father Brennan?"

"Father Brennan is away this week, on parish business, but he made a point of asking me to drop in to see you."

"Parish business? And what business does the parish have with the trout in Lough Sheelin?"

There was little wrong with the old lady's mind, nor her ears. But then again she was good friends with the Bishop.

"Well now," Fr. Reilly smiled boyishly, "It's not for a curate to pry in such matters. But tell me now, are they doing all they can for you?"

"Who?"

"The doctors."

"Oh them. They know nothing but giving people pills and bills. I was in perfect health until they got involved."

"Well I'm sorry to hear that, Mrs. Boyle. And how is your family? Are they all keeping well?"

"Them? They're worse than the doctors. Waiting and watching for the day I die. Except Danny, of course. Danny will miss me the most but I don't want you to say a word to him. I don't want to be upsetting him before his exams. Please God I will last 'til then."

"Is he taking his Inter this year?"

"Of course he is and he is going to get it with flying colors, too. He's a very smart boy, my Danny. And an angel, too."

They sat in silence for a while, Fr. Reilly groping in the darkening room for something to say while Granny Boyle made strange little sounds, like she was trying to swallow her bile. She probably thought he was an *amadán.* A total *amadán.*

"Father," she asked with a sudden urgency that startled the young priest. "You'll keep an eye on him—after I'm gone?"

"I will of course Mrs. Boyle. You've nothing to worry about."

"And what would you know about what I have to worry about? That's between me and your Boss."

For a moment he thought she was referring to the Bishop.

"I'll be seeing Him soon enough and I'll have a chance to give Him a piece of my mind." She seemed content with that.

"Well I hope that I haven't given you reason to complain."

"You? What have you got to do with what I have to tell the Lord?"

"Oh! Well, is there anything else I can do for you before you go? Have you had the sacraments?"

"Trust me Father, other than Danny, I'm at peace with life but if you have to have something to do, you can say the rosary with me. That would be a comfort. Hail Mary full of grace . . ."

CHAPTER 8

"So." Anto opened the door wider and smirked like he was dispelling any doubts he may have had, "You had the good fuckin' sense to come and see me right away. That's smart, Boyle. C'mon in and tell me how it went down with the cops."

He led Danny into his darkened room and sat back into his cold, black leather armchair. It had fallen off the back of a truck somewhere and came to Anto in lieu of an overdue payment.

He turned the stereo down a little—the new album by the Boomtown Rats—and leaned forward to pet the head of his massive black and brown dog. It lay at his feet, softly growling at Danny, but relaxed when Anto spoke again. "That was Scully's mistake, ya know? He went into hiding and we got a bit nervous. Then we started to hear rumors and we knew we had to do something. It was just business, ya know?"

Danny nodded keeping one eye on the dog. Anto hadn't told him he could sit so he stood in the middle of the room, like he was in court or something. "I told them nothing," he blurted out. "I only told them that Scully gave them my name because I owed him some money."

"And do you think they believed you?"

"I just made out like I was addicted, and all, and that I was confused. Besides, the priest came with me and he told them I was telling the truth."

"A priest, Boyle?"

"Ya, and a bishop put in a good word, too. The Bishop was a friend of my granny's."

"It must be nice to have such connections." Anto's eyes glistened in the low light and Danny knew what he was thinking and piled it on. "Ya, they can't touch me. They'll have to believe what everybody is saying about me, ya know?"

"That could come in very handy, Boyle."

"Ya." But Danny wasn't so sure. He had to be careful that he didn't jump from the frying pan into the fires below. "Only I think it would be better if I laid low for a while and didn't handle stuff. Just in case they are keeping an eye on me."

"You're right, Boyle. They'll be watching you so we'd better let them see you're clean. At least for a while."

That was the glimmer Danny had hoped for. He had pleaded his case on the way over from the Garda station, pleading into the empty darkness and despair. He hadn't pleaded with God. He told himself that he didn't need His help but, deep down inside, he just didn't feel worthy.

His father always told him that was why they taught them about Original Sin. "They get ya right from the start, like you have something wrong that only they can fix. Then they have you hooked. You've got to spend the rest of your life bowing and scraping to them and all their cronies. They're as bad as the feckin' drug dealers."

But everything his father told him was just a load of shite. His father was as lost as he was. Everybody was. That's why they made all that stuff up. There was no God and there was no Devil. There was just the luck of the draw.

If there was a God, he wouldn't have taken his mother away. He was only a feckin' child, for Christ's sake. What could he have done to ever deserve something like that? If

God was the decent, loving . . . whatever, he would have stepped in but he didn't, leaving Danny to fend for himself.

Anto nodded like he understood and took off his sunglasses. Danny could almost feel his eyes searching deep inside him. Anto always wore his dark glasses when he was out, even at night. He always wore a suit, too, and fine leather shoes. He didn't look like a drug dealer at all. He looked more like a businessman—or a pop star.

"Trust, Boyle. That's what's most important. We just need to know that we can trust you."

Danny lowered his eyes again and decided. It was all very well for the priests and the Guards to talk about right and wrong, and law, but their hands were covered in blood, too. They had all done what they had to do, and, when it was done—when the bodies were burned or buried—sanctified the cause with God and country. Just like what his grandfather had done—putting bullets in men's heads for the cause.

He would have to shake hands with the Devil and take whatever salvation Anto was offering. He would be smart about it, though. He'd play along with the Bishop and the priest for as long as he needed their help. He would be the "prodigal returned" and when things cooled down he would find a way to get out from under it all.

He'd even tell everybody that he was going to go back to school and redo his Leaving exam. He'd tell them that he was going to get a few "honors" and go on to university, just like Deirdre. That way he could get a degree and a good job, and like his grandfather, he would never speak about the days when darkness was the only light. "So? Do you trust me?"

"Well," Anto paused like he was considering it. "Like I said, you did the right thing in coming to see me before any nasty shit got spread around. I like honesty, and I like to be able to trust."

He patted the dog's head again. It rose on its haunches with its red tongue hanging to one side, its big brown eyes turned in devotion to its master.

"Are we cool then?" Danny asked in hope.

"Okay, Boyle. We're cool. But remember we might have to call on you for a favor, now and then. Nothing too heavy. We might just need you to do a few pickups for us. After things have cooled down, of course."

He rose and led Danny to the door with the dog following behind. "Go home, Boyle, and stay out of trouble until you hear from us. And Boyle, you did the right thing."

*

Nora Boyle whispered into the darkness around the small altar to the side.

She pleaded with the mother of God to intercede on behalf of her Danny who had fallen from the Grace of God and would now have to walk the world until the darkness took him.

Her very own grandson had outgrown those sunny days when God smiled down through the clouds; days when sins were so small and could easily be cleansed, days when Danny trusted in those who were there for him. But he had turned away from all of that. He had turned his back on God, despite all that she had tried to teach him.

But, she reminded himself, *it wasn't all her fault.* Things had started to fall apart when she died.

Though her funeral was a grand sight to see and she loved every minute of it.

The church was packed and everyone wore their finest. Even Fr. Brennan was moved to generosity with incense and brand new candles. It was the least that he could do for her—she had been generous enough in her will.

Her heart ached a little for Danny, sitting in the front row, alongside his parents, surrounded by priests and nuns naturally attired for the presence of death. The nuns clucked over him and patted his cheeks while the priests shook hands with his father before they all sat down, only to rise again to make way for the Bishop and his entourage who arrived just before it all began.

Her coffin was the centerpiece of it all and that made her proud. That and the fact that a disposition had been secured to have the Mass in Latin—the way God intended.

It was a High Mass, too, and Fr. Reilly led the choir; bearded or miniskirted and pitchy. She would have preferred a good choir but it was the best they could do.

Fr. Brennan was in his element and put on a grand show, talking about her like she was the mother of God himself, but deferred to the Bishop on the sermon.

When he spoke, his voice boomed causing everyone to sit up straight. Even the nuns stopped fidgeting with their beads and the men at the back stopped looking at the arses of the young women around them. When the Bishop spoke everyone listened.

Except Danny.

**

His mind was wandering and he couldn't stop it. His new suit was stiff and a bit big for him. Granny had bought it so he would look fine on the day. His shoes were tight and stiff and pinched above his heels. He would have blisters but he didn't mind; he needed to feel something. He had known Granny was dying but had gone along with everybody's wishes and pretended he didn't.

And now that she had, he didn't know how to feel.

Of course he felt sad, but he felt relieved, too. Even he noticed how much Granny suffered in the end.

That was the thing that bothered him the most: if this God they all talked about was so good and kind, why did he have to treat Granny the way he did?

But what was the point? If he said it to anybody they would only slather him with words. They had lots and lots of words that meant nothing. He had heard them so often that he had learned to pretend to find comfort in them to end the repetition. Inside, he was angry at them all, but he knew better than to let it show. They would only try to hound it out of him. That, he decided, was all that he had learned at school.

So he went through the motions, rising and kneeling when they did and sitting back when the time came. He liked the Latin Mass—it gave him time to wander through his own thoughts.

**

When they drove to the graveyard in a cavalcade of shiny cars, Danny and his parents rode in a big black Daimler, directly after the hearse, and pulled up right by the gates as everyone else parked where they could and milled around. There were men from the government: a cabinet minister, a few backbenchers, and a man representing the *Taoiseach's* office, all being cordial enough with the men from Bart's party, now banished into opposition.

A cluster of older men, who knew Bart and Granny well, came to offer their sympathies and condolences. The Bishop was there, too, amidst a flock of nuns, a couple of monsignors, and a few canons.

When the coffin was hoisted by the selected bearers—that didn't include Jerry—the crowd organized themselves by rank and privilege and followed it inside.

The delegation from the Boys waited near the gate. They would visit the grave when the others had gone and passed their time smoking cigarettes and whispering among themselves to the great consternation of the Special Branch who stood as close as they dared without seeming too obvious.

The Special Branch followed the Boys everywhere, maintaining constant surveillance—even if it meant spending hours in pubs drinking pints, but always at separate tables so as not to arouse suspicion.

The Boys didn't mind. They could keep the eyes of the law busy while others, those who were less well known, could carry on with the cause. It was the way things had been done since the movement had split and new allegiances were strained by old friendships.

Jerry and Jacinta stood over the grave, with Danny in between them, as Fr. Brennan reminded God of the faith they all placed in Him. And in the surety of that righteousness, he asked Him to grant Nora Boyle her well-deserved eternal rest.

Danny squirmed a bit as she was lowered into the ground so his father held his shoulder while his mother squeezed his hand, but Danny was just trying to find some relief from the chaffing on his heels. It was all taking so long.

When it was done, Fr. Brennan liberally sprinkled holy water around the grave and the diggers went to work, the first few shovelfuls rattling on the coffin, growing muffled as they filled the hole.

As it filled, the crowd formed a line to shake the hands of the family and to offer kind words:

"My deepest sympathies for your loss. May she rest in peace."

"She was a great character, God have mercy on us all."

"We'll never see the likes of her again."

"I'm sorry for your loss."

"God bless you all in this time of sorrow."

His mother just nodded as she stood back with her arm around Danny but his father shook each hand and muttered his thanks as the line filed past. "It was good of you to come." And to those that Granny had selected in her written arrangements he added, "You'll come back to the house?"

They were the faces Jerry had known since childhood, aged now since his father's death but enlivened by the invitation—the promise of whiskey and a chance to reminisce. "That's very kind of you. Maybe I will drop in then—just to honour their memories."

Jerry invited the Boys, too, knowing that the Special Branch would have to follow, to make things more interesting.

"Are you sure?" Jacinta asked as they climbed into the back of the long black car.

"Ah sure why not? Mam and Dad would enjoy this. And besides, maybe if we get them all together in one room they might start getting along."

"If they don't kill themselves first."

"That mightn't be the worst thing, either."

**

The Bishop dropped in and brought a few nuns, selected for their discretion, and quickly dispatched them to the kitchen to make the tea and serve sandwiches to the priests and the politicians.

Nora, as was fitting for someone of her station, had provided well for the day with hams and cold chickens, egg and potato salads, and an assortment of pickles and relish, all paid for in advance and delivered to the house. No detail was left to chance.

She even bought a few dozen Waterford tumblers and a case of beer glasses for those who liked a bottle of stout. "But they're mostly whiskey drinkers and I want everything to be just right," she had explained to Jerry and Jacinta, even as she labored for her last few breaths. She even arranged for Martin to come by and take Danny to the pictures and for burgers, afterwards. He was, she had decreed, still far too young for wakes.

When the gathering had partaken of the tea and sandwiches, the Bishop called for a toast—the cue to open the whiskey.

"To the dear, departed, Nora Boyle, the likes of which we will never see again."

"To Nora Boyle," they all agreed and drank freely from their glasses, except for Fr. Reilly who sipped his.

"She was a great friend to Ireland and to the Church, God rest her soul, and mother to Jeremiah and Jacinta, and grandmother to Danny. May she rest in Heaven tonight."

"Amen," the Boys, the priests, and the politicians agreed again in concert and raised their glasses again.

"And a good and faithful wife to our dear departed friend, Bart. May God rest his soul."

"To Bart," they concurred with their empty glasses and looked around for Fr. Reilly who was charged with serving drinks.

"That curate has a very delicate hand," someone muttered.

"Just be thankful it's him pouring and not the parish priest—he'd charge us money."

But when their glasses were refreshed they were renewed and broke off into small groups and talked among themselves as they waited while Jerry mingled.

"You're the spitting image of your father," the politicians laughed and slapped his back. "Have you ever thought of taking his seat back?" They had lost it in the last election. "With your name, you'd be a shoo-in."

"What would I know about politics?" Jerry laughed as he basked in their attention. He had always felt that they were disappointed in him—that his past failings were still a blemish on his father's name.

"What's to know?" they all laughed. "You just tell the people what they want to hear. Until you get elected, that is, then you tell them nothing. And, when things go wrong, you can always blame the rich—or the poor, depending on who you're talking to."

"That might be how things were done under Fianna Fáil," the local TD interjected. He was from the Labour Party and everyone viewed him with disdain, but Granny had wanted him there, too, because: "it does no harm to know those in the know."

"Come and join us and be a part of the future." He reached out to shake Jerry's hand.

"Do you really think," Bart's old friends bantered, "that the son of Bart Boyle would ever dream of changing coats?"

They all laughed as Fr. Reilly poured some more and Jerry took the chance to slip away.

"He's not a patch on his father," he heard one of them say before he was out of earshot.

"Can I pour you a little more?" Fr. Reilly asked, his eyes soft and his cheeks a little flushed. "I couldn't help but hear what they said. Don't pay them any mind. They're a dying breed and the world will be better off when they're all gone."

Jerry was a little taken aback by the young priest's conviction and also a little embarrassed that he'd heard. "Thanks, Father, and don't give it a second thought. I gave up listening to the likes of them a long time ago. But tell me, have you seen Jacinta anywhere?"

"I think she went upstairs. Her kitchen is overrun by nuns and I think she needed a bit of peace."

Jacinta was sitting on the edge of the bed, smoking and nibbling at her nails. It was all too much for her. Being around the nuns who fussed and treated her like she was incapable brought it all back—the feelings she thought she had left in the hospital.

"Oh Jerry, I'm sorry but I had to come up here to get away from them all. Do you mind?"

Jerry sat on the bed beside her and took one of her hands in his. "Not a bit. Sure I understand. It's like having the circus come to visit but they'll all be gone soon and then it will just be the three of us. We'll have the place to ourselves. It'll be a fresh start, for you and me, and Danny."

"We will be able to manage, won't we, Jerry?"

"Of course we will. We'll have the house and whatever is left—if Ma hasn't given it all to the Church, and the Boys. And I'll get a job, too. Things will be grand from here on. You'll see."

Jacinta squeezed his hand and raised it to her mouth. She kissed it gently and forced herself to smile, chasing all of her wrinkles away. "You'd better get down there before they start pilfering the cutlery and the china. Go on now. I'll be fine."

**

As the Bishop and his entourage prepared to leave, the rest of the gathering waited to bid him goodnight and start their revelry in earnest. The remaining sandwiches were neatly packed away and the nuns had left the kitchen spick-and-span but there was plenty to drink: whiskey and a few dozen bottles of beer.

"Good night, Your Grace," all sides of the political spectrum agreed and loosened their ties and edged toward the table in the corner where the drink was arranged in rows. Fr. Reilly had relinquished his role and fallen in line behind his uncle.

"Good night," the Boys nodded as the Bishop eyed them coldly and departed, down the driveway where his car was waiting, just beyond the unmarked squad car with smoke billowing out the windows.

"Gentlemen," the Bishop addressed the occupants. "Go around the back to the kitchen and you'll find sandwiches in the fridge. You can keep a better eye on things from there."

"That's awful kind of you, Your Grace. We will do so, if you're sure the family won't mind."

"They won't mind a bit. Just tell them that I said it was all right. I'm sure Nora and Bart wouldn't begrudge you a few sandwiches and a cup of tea."

"Good night, Your Grace." They almost kissed his ring as they piled out and went off to investigate the sandwiches.

**

"Will you look at what came in out of the cold," the Boys jeered when the Special Branch emerged from the kitchen, fortified by sandwiches and in search of something stronger than tea.

"C'mon in and have a drink," Jerry encouraged them. "Sure we're all friends here. Isn't that right gentlemen?"

"Come in lads," the politicos agreed. "Come in and relax. We're just getting started. We thought the Bishop was never going to leave."

"Well he's gone now so what about a song? Does anybody know *Skibbereen*? That was always Bart's song, God rest his soul."

"To Bart Boyle," they all agreed and raised their glasses.

They took turns singing the evening away, singing the songs they had in common and careful not to step on the cracks that separated them; chasms of misunderstanding that had torn comrade from comrade.

A young Special Branch man sang *The Croppy Boy* with such a fine voice that he almost brought tears to their eyes. Not to be outdone, the Boys sang *The Foggy Dew* and the men from Fianna Fáil sang *O'Donnell Abu.* The man from the Labour Party sang *James Connolly* and when it fell to Jerry's turn, he sang *The Wild Rover* as they all eyed him blearily.

By the time Martin dropped Danny home, they had shed their jackets and rolled up their sleeves, their faces blotched and red but they were comrades-in-arms once again.

"A Nation once again,

"A Nation once again,

"And Ireland long a province be a Nation once again."

"And who is this young man?" a befuddled Special Branch man asked as he looked up from nosing around the table in the corner but the last bottle was empty. Jacinta had secreted the rest away so that they would all go home before the night—and to have a drink around the house for when she was entertaining.

"That's Bart's grandson," a ruddy-faced man piped up. "I'd know that face anywhere. Come here to me 'til I tell you." He put his arm around Danny shoulders, his armpits damp and reeky and his breath pungent. "Your grandfather and I fought the Black and Tans, so we did. We drove them out of this country."

Danny smiled and tried to wriggle free but the man wasn't finished. "Fought for Ireland, we did."

"Would you leave the poor lad alone?" one of the politicians implored seeing the look in Danny's eyes. "He's just buried his grandmother."

"You're right," the ruddy-faced man agreed as the realization of Danny's plight had a sobering effect on them all. "C'mon then, we should be hitting the road and give these people a bit of peace."

"Stay," Jerry mumbled from the depths of Granny's favorite chair. "Stay and have another drink."

"Ah, now Jerry, it's getting awful late."

"Late me arse. Are you mice or are you men? Stay, for Christ's sake, and have a drink."

They all rose from where they sat and looked at him dubiously. "No, Jerry. It's late and I'm sure your missus has had enough of us and besides, we drank all the whiskey."

"The hell we did. Jacinta? Jacinta get us another bottle, will ya, pet?"

Jacinta stood in the doorway and pulled Danny toward her. "I think these gentlemen want to leave now, Jerry. It is getting late."

"You're right Missus," the gentlemen agreed. "C'mon," they encouraged each other. "Let's go home to our wives and our warm beds."

"Never mind that," Jerry rose unsteadily and tried to embrace them all. "Stay and have another little drink—just a night cap. Jacinta, would you ever go and get us another bottle?" But his enthusiasm flagged and he crumbled back into his chair and began to sing: "We're on the one road . . ."

"Goodnight now Missus and thanks very much." The gentlemen filed past toward their cars, arguing about who should drive. And in the spirit of their recent détente, the Boys agreed with the Special Branch to make it a late morning—so they could all sleep it off.

"Do you see that?" asked the last of the politicians as he steadied himself to pass through the doorway. "Drink can be the unification of this country—or the ruination!

"Will he be all right?" he added nodding his head toward the living room where Jerry was slumped in the chair. "He won't be a bother to you now, will he?"

Jacinta assured him that it would be fine; that she would get him up to bed and that he would sleep it off. She closed the door and smiled at Danny. "Thank Christ that's over."

**

After the funeral party had dispersed, Nora stood in her kitchen, wanting, but unable to touch all that was once her life. The house grew quiet but still reeked of cigarettes. She wanted to rearrange what the nuns had misplaced. Not that she blamed them, God love them, but they could hardly be expected to know how things were done in a normal house where normal people lived.

She had spent years of her life here, cooking and cleaning and sipping cups of tea but she didn't want it to be the place where her family would come to remember her. She wanted somewhere more dignified. Bart had the Garden of Remembrance as the place he could be recalled. She would have to find her own.

"Nora? Shall we be off, then?" Bart had asked from the warm glow that beckoned.

"I'm not ready, Bart. I can't go yet."

"C'mon, *a chroi*, there's nothing more for us here anymore."

"I can't, Bart. They'll need me yet, for a while."

When he smiled at her he looked so young—like when they first started to walk out together.

"They'll have to find their own way from here on in."

"I can't. Don't you see?"

His smile saddened as he faded into the gloom, leaving Nora alone in her darkened kitchen as the whole house slept.

***

I did the right thing, Danny repeated, over and over, as he hurried toward home. But he couldn't really convince himself. He was falling further down the long slippery slope his granny used to go on about. He had been slipping since just after her funeral.

It wasn't really anybody's fault, he decided as he hurried past the cinema in Terenure, lightless as it lingered. *Things just happened.*

There never was any real reason—no divine plan—just the muddle of competing interests and haphazard events as people went about their lives.

They all had their reasons, too; they were just fighting for what they believed in—or just trying to protect what they already had.

He had also figured out that nobody liked to talk about any of that. They were too busy putting bread on the table—or drinks on the counter. "It's all very well for you. You're still young and have me and you mother to look after you," his father used to argue whenever he tried to talk about it, something Fr. Reilly had advised him to do.

"It's all very well for the priests to be talking the way they do. They don't have to go out and work like the rest of us. They never have to worry about being laid off, or having their hours cut back. They are insulated from the reality the rest of us get to live our lives in."

His mother always told him not to pay any attention to his father when he was like that, but she had no answers either. She used to say that that was the way of the world and he better just get used to it.

He did. He also figured out that everything that he had once found warm and comforting was buried with his granny.

He felt better when he looked at things that way and lit another joint. It all made sense when he was stoned. Then he could sit like a yogi, aloof and detached.

He'd been left to find his own way. Nothing he had been taught had any value anymore. It had all been lies; well-meant lies that children were told so that they wouldn't wander off.

As the smoke curled inside of him he relaxed. He had to stop letting it get to him. He just needed to stay cool and let it all blow over, just like he and Anto had agreed.

He had agreed to talk with Fr. Reilly again, too. It would look better for him if he looked like he was trying to change things, and, in time, when the cops had someone else to deal with, he could get out and start his life all over.

He'd do things differently this time. He'd be much smarter.

He took another hit and floated away to a much happier time, though it hadn't started out that way.

CHAPTER 9

A few days after Granny's funeral, as Jerry walked on Talbot Street, the city exploded.

The blast knocked him into a doorway, unhurt but dazed. He watched as shock and horror gave way to frenzy. Bombs had exploded all over the city, killing and maiming Dubliners on their way home from work.

As emergency crews rushed in to sort the casualties, one of them checked Jerry. He told him he was in shock and should wait for someone else to attend to him.

After they did, he went to a pub and drank whiskey to warm the chill in his guts and to blunt the shards of memory that were poking through: images of twisted and blackened bodies lying on a carpet of broken glass, and him sitting in a doorway, crying like a baby as braver men rushed forward to help. There was nothing any of them could do but at least they tried. He just sat there rocking and crying until someone found him and cleaned his face of dirt and tears.

He would never let anybody know about that, and, in time, even he would remember it differently: he had been one of those who rushed forward to save lives in the inferno of it all—with no thought for his own safety.

But for now, his thoughts grew darker as a small flame sputtered inside of him. The man on the news said that the UVF were blamed but everyone knew that they were just the puppets dancing on the end of British strings.

As the flickering flame grew, he could see his mother, rising from her cold damp grave, pointing her long white finger at him. Where his father had stepped forward, Jerry had cowered in a doorway.

He started to shake again until he couldn't take it anymore. He finished his drink and stepped out into the night, still filled with wailing sirens punching holes in the fog of shock that muted the whole city. But he could sense growing anger, too. Soft at first, but liable to erupt into flames beneath a passing breeze.

It was time for him to start doing his part.

**

As the whole country mourned and beat its chest—mea culpas and tribal drumming's—Jacinta kept herself busy packing away all traces of Nora Boyle.

She took some small pleasure from it, that it was she who was packing the old woman's effects and not the other way around.

Yet she was becoming nervous and fidgety, too. The entire city was on edge. It was one thing for the fighting to happen in the North but now it had been brought home to them all. Some wanted to cower away, not wanting to revisit the bad old days when fighting had ravaged the whole country.

Others raged and spoke of bringing the fight to the British homeland; to give them a taste of their own medicine.

Even Jerry was affected. The death of his mother and the bombings seemed to meld inside of him and he never mentioned one without the other.

Jacinta noticed something else, too. He now spoke of his mother in reverent tones that Jacinta couldn't agree with, though she kept her thoughts to herself.

Granny had overshadowed her life since she met Jerry. For years she had walked a narrow path through the greyness with only Granny's clucks and tut-tut-tuts to guide her but now that the old woman was gone, she felt terribly lost. She was going to have to make it on her own. Jerry would be of little help. He would get lost inside of himself again, just like when Danny was born. She would have to be the strong one now—for Danny's sake.

So she had decided that it was best to keep herself busy and organized her packing into stuff that she would go through with Jerry and stuff she would keep for Danny; stuff that could be given away, and stuff that could be stashed to fetch good money from the pawn. Granny didn't need it anymore and it could come in handy on a rainy day.

Granny's solicitor had called and asked that they attend the reading of the will—all of them, including Danny. He also mentioned that Martin would be there and that became a billowing cloud in Jacinta's mind. *What could they want with him there?*

**

"Maybe she left him something, too. She was an awful generous woman and Martin was a great help with Danny." Jerry decided it was grounds for celebration and poured from one of the whiskey bottles they had hidden from the wake. "An awful generous woman," he smiled as he raised his glass and downed it in one.

"Don't be counting your chickens . . ."

But he couldn't be deflated and poured himself another before she could step between him and the bottle. He drank as he watched her put the bottle back in the cupboard. He had another hidden in the sideboard in the dining room and another in the garden shed. It was for when everything became too much for him—when his grief and his fear bubbled up together. A quick belt or two brought everything back into focus and settled him again. But he had to be careful; too many and he would evoke Granny from her grave, rising like a sidhe calling him out to war.

"Now Jacinta, let's not be thinking ill of the dead."

"It's not that. It's just that I get nervous around solicitors."

"And when did you spend time in such illustrious company?" He grinned and drained his glass.

"When I was committed—something we'll have to do with you, too, if you don't stop your tippling."

"Ah, c'mon now, Jass. I'm still in mourning, you know?"

"Is that what you're doing?"

"Do you know what I'm going to do?" he asked as he sidled toward the bottle again. "When we get the money, I'm going to take you over to London—on holidays. We can see Big Ben and Piccadilly. Then we can have afternoon tea with the Queen and have our dinner at the Savoy."

"Don't you think that it would be wrong to go to London after what just happened?"

"I suppose so. I suppose we could go somewhere else like . . . Paris or Rome. We could go and have . . . spaghetti with the Pope!"

"But we don't speak . . ." It didn't really matter. They both knew it would never really happen. Something would always get in the way but it was nice pretending. "You'd have to buy me a new dress then because I can't be going around in this old thing."

She moved a little so he could reach past her to the whiskey.

"I'll buy you more than that." He winked as he poured himself another and left the bottle on the counter.

"I'll need new shoes, too." She casually turned and put the bottle back. "And a purse."

"We'll get you the lot, and a big diamond on your finger."

"Jeeze, Jerry, my sisters will all die of envy."

"Well that settles it then. As soon as we get the money we'll go. We'll fly, too. First class and drink champagne all the way."

**

Afterwards, they stood in the rain on Dawson Street as all their plans melted and dissolved in the pitter-patter, splattering on the ground and rushing off down the gutter. People looked nervously at them as they passed. The city was still edgy.

Jerry threw his cigarette butt into the gush and lit another, the match flickering in his trembling fingers and the spitting rain. "The fuckin' spiteful old bitch of a hag!"

"Jerry! Not in front of the child."

"He may's well hear the truth now. She's been lying to him long enough."

"Maybe," Martin intervened, "I should take Danny and give the two of you some time to yourselves."

"Don't be going to the pictures now, or anywhere else they might be planting bombs. Just walk around for a while—and stay away from crowds."

"Jass, we'll be fine. You know I wouldn't let anything happen to Danny. You know that, don't you?"

Jacinta nodded but Jerry just looked mean. "Why are you even asking us? Didn't you hear what the solicitor said? You're going to be running the show from now on."

"Now Jerry, let's go for a drink and Martin and Danny can catch up with us later."

"Drink? And where are we going to get the money for drink? Are you going to scrimp on the household monies? Well don't let Martin catch you or we'll be up in the 'Joy' for embezzlement."

"Go on, the two of you," Jacinta pleaded with Martin. "Do you have money on you?" She hesitated.

She didn't want to open her bag in front of her husband. The men at the wake had filled an envelope to help defray the costs, unaware of Granny's organization. There was over two hundred pounds and she managed to keep it from Jerry, letting him find the whiskey instead. But now she would have to find a better place to hide it.

"I do," Martin nodded as he steered Danny away by the shoulder.

"Of course you do," Jerry snarled after him. "You were in cahoots with the old bitch all along."

**

"We're not going to be blown to bits, are we, Martin?"

"Don't worry, Danny, everything's going to be fine."

"Yeah, but is everything going to be okay with Ma and Da?"

"I told you, there's nothing to worry about, Danny boy."

"But Ma and Da don't seem to be too happy about it."

"Everything will be fine, you'll see."

"Why do you think that Granny did that?"

"I don't know, Danny. I suppose that she was just doing what she thought was best."

"Do you think she's right?"

Martin sat back as their server placed their burgers before them. Danny was hungry and dove right in as Martin searched for the right things to say. He hadn't risked a trip to the cinema so they went straight for burgers instead, his head on a swivel all the way, but Danny didn't seem to notice.

It wasn't what Martin wanted either but he could see Granny's point; Jerry and Jacinta couldn't even look after themselves. "I'm sure your granny had a good reason and I'm sure that everything is going to work out just fine, you'll see. It's not like I'm going to be telling anybody what to do. I'm just supposed to let the solicitor know if there're any problems."

"That still puts you in charge of them."

"Not really. I'm just supposed to look out for you—that's all."

"Can't my parents do that?"

"Eat your burger and stop bothering me with questions, will you?"

"Do you know who you're beginning to sound like? My granny." Danny smirked and took another bite.

**

By the end of his second drink, a plan was forming in Jerry's mind. Something that would calm his mother's ghost and answer her accusations. He would go to London and blow it up.

They could get away with it. No one would ever suspect the likes of them. He could contact some friends of his father and they would put him in contact. They would probably pay for the trip, too. Jacinta could go with him to make it seem like they were just tourists. They would be like spies in a film. They'd have to get hats—and sunglasses and . . .

"What are ya thinking about, Jerry?"

"Nothing."

"What is it Jerry? You can tell me."

"It's nothing . . . it's just I don't think the English should be able to get away with what they did."

"Don't you think we've all suffered enough? Do you really want other people to suffer the same thing? I heard that they were trying to piece bodies back together for burying and some people got the wrong body parts. Only they didn't know. Just the people working in the morgue knew when they found spare parts left over. My sisters told me and they know someone that's married to a fella that works there."

"I suppose you're right. Life's short enough as it is." Jerry drained his glass in resignation. He'd be haunted by his mother's ghost until he did something. He'd have to make a grand gesture—that's what his mother would want him to do—he'd have to make an example of himself, just like his father.

Perhaps if he did, his mother's will would be changed. Maybe it was like those things you read about where someone has to take the dead father's ashes back to where the treasure is buried—only it's a test of their manhood.

"Get me another, will ya?" He slumped back down in his chair and festered quietly in himself.

**

By the time Martin and Danny got back, Jacinta was smoking and biting her nails. She had taken a few more pounds from the envelope in the privacy of the ladies room but they were gone and she couldn't risk exposing the rest of it. Jerry was drunk. Drunk and mean and spoiling for a fight.

"Ah, here he is," he sneered when he saw Martin and Danny approach. "My own son's guardian that doesn't think me capable of looking after my own flesh and blood."

"Jerry?" Martin pleaded but could see there was no point. Jerry was flushed and slurring and his eyes were burning with a dark fire.

"Don't you fuckin' talk to me—ya fuckin' Judas."

"Would you like me to take Danny home?" Martin ignored him and asked Jacinta but she didn't answer, rocking back and forth where she sat.

Jerry did, almost rising from his chair. "You'll take my son nowhere! Do you hear me?"

"Jass?"

"No," Jacinta looked up from her hands and struggled to focus all of her attention on him. "It'd be better if you go on and Jerry and I'll look after him."

"Unless you don't think we're fuckin' capable?"

"Look, I didn't ask for any of this. This wasn't my idea, you know? This was something your mother worked out with the solicitor. What was I supposed to do?"

"But ya took it quick enough."

"Okay! That's it. I'm leaving. Danny? Do you want to come?"

"No you don't, pet, do you? You want to stay with your mammy and your daddy, don't you?"

Danny didn't answer and just stared at his feet.

"There. See for yourself. Even Danny wants fuck-all to do with you. Go on ya piece of shite! Get out of here now before I . . ."

"Go on Martin. Go on home and we can talk tomorrow after we have had a chance to sleep on the bad news. It's been an awful jolt and we're all still in shock, you know, but we can talk tomorrow."

"Good fuckin' riddance," Jerry called after him as he left. He blew his smoke at the ceiling and turned on Jacinta. "Your own fuckin' brother? What kind of a family did you crawl out of?"

"It wasn't my mother that screwed us."

"How dare you talk like that in front of the boy and his granny still warm in her grave."

Jacinta knew she should have let it go for all their sakes, but her pills and drinking were a bad mix.

"Well maybe it's time that we all faced up to the truth about Granny."

"Ah, Ma! Let's just go home. I don't want us to be arguing and fighting like this. I don't think Granny wanted us to be like this."

Before she could answer, Jerry erupted almost spitting and hissing. "That old bitch! She's probably laughing her arse off at the lot of us."

Danny fought back his tears and looked to his mother for a shred of comfort but her face was hard and creased—the way she used to look when she was in the hospital.

"Look, Danny," his father continued with spiteful earnest. "Your granny did a lot of things to your ma and me. Stuff you know nothing about. And now she goes and does this."

"I don't care. I don't want you talking about Granny like that."

"Like what? Like we should be happy that she screwed us out of what we had coming after all we put up with from her. After your mother and I spent the last few years cleaning her and washing up after her. Christ! If we'd known that she was going to do this we'd have put a fuckin' pillow over her face."

"That's not true. Granny was so good to you and she got Ma out of the hospital."

"Is that what you think? We'll let me tell you something."

"Ah, Jerry, No! Don't bring all of that up."

"It's time the boy knew."

"Jerry. Please. Don't!"

"Your old bitch of a grandmother was the one who put her in there in the first place."

Danny stared at his mother, pleading with her to deny it but she had her head down, sobbing into her hands.

"That's right, Danny boy. She never wanted your ma and me to be happy and right after you were born she got one of her big-shot friends to tell lies about your own mother and had her locked up.

"And she made me leave, too, so she could raise you with all of her fuckin' lies and deceit.

"Your granny," he continued, his venom bubbling out around the corners of his mouth, "was like an ugly old spider in her web, pulling on the strings to make everyone dance to her tune. Even your grandfather couldn't take it anymore and died just so he could get some peace and quiet."

"I don't believe you. You're just drunk."

"You don't have to take my word for it. Ask your mother—she'll tell you. Go on. Ask her."

"Ma? Ma? It isn't true, is it Ma? Ma?"

But his mother didn't answer and cried into her hands as her shoulders trembled. Danny reached out to her as his own tears streamed down his face. "I don't believe it. Granny was always going on about God and being good. She'd never do anything like that."

"Yeah. Your granny was a great one for talking about God, but as you're going find out; those that talk about him are just trying to convince somebody—usually themselves. That's another thing they don't teach you at school."

**

After he had finished his exams, Danny spent the rest of his summer by the river. He left the house early and returned late, after his father and mother had gone to the pub. He didn't want to have to face them and all of the terrible things they had told him. He couldn't sort it out and it churned around inside of him, poisoning everything he had ever believed.

So he sat by the river with a fishing rod, a fine split cane that had belonged to his grandfather. It was made for fly-fishing but Danny didn't care. He never baited his hook—he didn't want to have to deal with actually catching a fish, he just wanted to be left alone. He knew that if he just sat there without it someone would question his state of mind, or suspect his intentions. He had learnt that much along the way: it was all about perception. If he sat there with a rod, he was doing something that was socially acceptable. Without it he was mad—or worse, up to no good.

As he sat there a little hatred grew; a small burning inside of him that almost made his eyes well up with tears. He hated his father for the joy he took in telling him. And his mother for letting him. He wasn't sure about his granny. He still couldn't believe that she would do anything like that but he couldn't be sure.

He couldn't stop thinking about it.

Martin had gone to London again and he had no one to talk to. He thought about Fr. Reilly but he might be a part of it all—the web of lies that he had been told. And he wouldn't want to talk with his granny even if he could. He was alone in the world now and he would never find comfort in the company of others. He just couldn't trust anybody anymore.

Granny had always told him to pray at times like these, so he did. He pleaded for a sign from God. He prayed to him and his mother, to the Holy Ghost, and to all the saints but most of all he prayed for his guardian angel to come out of hiding and lead him, with his sword glowing in the darkness.

"Well look what we have here, boys, all by himself."

Maguire emerged from the bushes, followed by Collins and a few mean-faced scuts Danny had never seen before. They circled him like wolves making sure he had no way out. "There's no teacher to save you this time, Boyle."

"Aren't you catching anything, Boyle?" Maguire kicked at the rod and winked at his companions. "Maybe we can help with that. Let's throw him in the fuckin' river, boys."

They closed on him from all sides giving him no chance to defend himself, kicking him and punching him until he fell to his knees. They were dragging him toward the water and Danny groped around him, his fingers holding tight to any grip he could find. But he was losing. Inch by inch they were dragging him toward the water.

Suddenly they let go, and, as he raised his head, he could see their feet stepping back from him. He waited for a moment. They were probably messing with him and would come at him again when he loosened his grip.

But nothing happened so he raised his head again and glanced around through squinted eyes. His tormentors were gone but someone else was coming through the bushes. Danny knew him by reputation only: Johnny Skelton was a hard man, one of the toughest around. But they said he had changed, that he didn't fight anymore. Some said that he had gone hippie and had gotten into drugs.

"Are you all right?" he asked, picking Danny up.

"Yeah, I'm okay." Danny wiped his face on his sleeve and brushed the dirt and grass from his clothes.

"You're Danny Boyle, aren't you?"

Danny was shocked that he even knew his name and just nodded.

"Your grandmother just died?"

Danny didn't dare answer; his eyes were watering and he knew his voice would quaver.

"So why were those guys messing with you?"

"I know them from school. They're always bothering me."

"Don't you have mates of your own?"

"I have my uncle Martin, but he's in London right now."

"Martin Carroll? Is he your uncle?"

"He is. Do you know him?"

"I do. He's a really cool guy."

Danny's heart puffed up with pride. "Ya, and he's my best mate in the whole world. Only I wish he wasn't away so much. There's nothing to do when he's not around."

"Well I'm just going over to Bushy Park to meet some of my friends. Do you want to come along?"

Danny just nodded and started to follow.

"What about your fishing rod?"

"I don't want it anymore."

"It looks like a good one. Why don't you just hide it in the bushes and get it some other time."

**

"Who's this?" Johnny's friends asked.

"This is Danny—Martin Carroll's nephew. Some guys were trying to throw him in the river so I brought him here instead."

There were five of them sitting in a circle near the edge of the trees; a guy that Danny had often seen with Johnny and three girls, two of them around eighteen and a younger one, around Danny's age. He had seen her around, too, and knew her name was Deirdre.

"I was sorry to hear about your granny," she smiled as he sat down opposite her. He mumbled his thanks as he lowered his head and wished he hadn't come. He knew they all did drugs and all kinds of things.

"But why did you bring him here?" one of the others whispered but Danny could hear. "We were just about to smoke a joint."

"Don't worry. He's cool."

They all looked skeptically at Danny. "Are you sure?"

"I told you, he's Martin Carroll's nephew."

"Oh!"

"C'mon, Danny," Deirdre stood up and walked toward the path that led to the pond, looking back as she went. "Let's go and leave these drug addicts in peace."

"Don't go too far," her sister called after them as the others settled in behind a park bench where they couldn't be seen by anyone passing by.

"Are they really going to smoke drugs?" Danny asked when they sat in the long grasses, side by side, by the rushy pond.

"Yes."

"Doesn't that bother you?"

"No. I smoke too."

"Isn't it bad for you?"

Deirdre laughed and nudged him with her shoulder. "Of course it isn't. They just tell us that so we don't try it."

"Aren't you afraid that it might make you addicted, and all."

"No, Danny. That's just another one of the lies they tell us."

"Are you sure?"

"No, but I think you have to find out for yourself."

"Maybe I should try some then."

"C'mon then," she laughed and took a little joint from somewhere inside her shoulder bag; a red, leathery thing with Indian designs. She probably got it in the Dandelion. "Want some?" she almost winked as she sat behind the trunk of a large tree where no one else could see her.

He looked all around before he sat beside her.

***

He still thought about that day.

When they had finished, he just lay back on the ground and watched the clouds as he had never watched them before. He only had a few hits but it changed everything. The light was brighter and the shadows were darker and all that had seemed so straightforward was now honeycombed. Deirdre leaned over him and began to trace across his face with a brush from the long, bearded grass. Her hair dangled down, too, and tingled along his cheek. Her lips pouted a little and her eyes grew bigger as she looked deep inside of him. And he didn't mind. Being so close to her made everything else fade away. His hatred began to splinter, breaking off and floating away. All the rumblings in his head hushed and held their breath as she lowered her head and kissed him on the lips.

He saw her again the next day, and the day after that. They went everywhere together and weren't afraid to be seen down by the shops where everyone went to notice everyone else.

They toked a lot and talked about everything before rolling off into the long grasses where they could explore a little more. She let him touch her through her clothes, but only above the waist. She let him touch her breasts but he couldn't get her to touch him. At least not for a while.

But he had fucked that up, too.

He almost laughed as he took another hit and decided to cut through the lane that ran behind her house. It was on his way home, but, since the night in the church, he had always gone around the long way.

When she left him, things just got worse and worse. That was when he decided to take Scully up on his offer. That was when he began to slide on the slope.

He was still crazy about her and wanted to stop and look toward her window, just in case she might be looking out. He'd do anything to get her back into his life—after he'd gotten all of his shit together.

But he didn't look up. He'd heard that her father still wanted to beat the crap out of him, and now, with him being called in to speak with cops, and all, he'd want to fuckin' kill him.

He almost wished that he could talk to his mother about it and see if there was any way, but she would only blab it all to her sisters and he had seen the way they were with Martin, always asking him things and making bawdy jokes. He wished he could talk to him. Martin always knew what to say.

CHAPTER 10

Martin lay on his back and stared at the ceiling. David lay across him, his brown skin in contrast with his own. They often joked about Martin's whiteness when they lay in the sun for hours. David teased him, telling him he looked like a piece of white toast. They also joked about being refugees, having had to flee from the rigid righteousness of those who could never accept them for what they were.

"Queers," they were called on the streets of Dublin, or "Nancy Boys" among the rugby crowds. Neither group tolerated human truth in the open, preferring instead to joke about it: "Did you hear about the two Irish queers, Michael Fitzpatrick and Patrick Fitzmichael? Or the Gay-Lick? Or a Pat-on-the-back?"

Martin never reacted. What was the point? They were all repressed one way or another. They sat in the pubs and the churches and pretended that none of it was happening; the wife-beating, the rape of children, and the steady line of young girls that were sent off to the abortion clinics of London.

Those who stood up and looked at it just grew bitter and angry to the point many of them simply left and never looked back. But they all carried wounds that could burst open from time to time. A dull aching accusation that all immigrants felt.

He was lucky. He loved David and the life they shared in Toronto. The city was shedding the vestiges of its staid orange past and was beginning to accept a more diverse future. He felt complete and accepted here, free of shadows and censure. He hadn't wanted anything from there to spill over here, but he couldn't ignore his sister's plea for help. They were family after all, so he lay on his bed, staring at the ceiling, remembering them through the soft veil of separation.

What happened to Jacinta stigmatized the whole family. They all acted like it hadn't, but Martin knew. He had overheard the whispers: "The Carrolls, God love them, are more to be pitied than scorned."

His parents knew what was being said but his sisters pretended they didn't and made things even worse. They didn't have conversations like normal people; they took captives and flailed away with litanies of all the harm the world had ever done to them.

David told him that he was being too hard on them, that he should be grateful that he still had family who talked with him. David had been disowned by his. They only kept in contact through his bank account. An allowance, if he stayed away.

But David didn't know what the Carrolls were really like and probably never would. Martin had no intention of bringing him back there. Their relationship wouldn't survive it. Martin wouldn't survive it.

He had been young when Jacinta was committed, but he still remembered it. Mutterings at first as his parents talked in the little privacy they had. And when he intruded on it, hoping to hear something that might explain it all, they would switch moods in clumsy fumbling. "Poor Jacinta has been taken into the hospital, but don't you worry your head about it, Martin. She's just had a little bit of a breakdown. But you'll see. She'll be right as rain in no time."

It was well meant but it left Martin with a mental picture he could never get rid of: of Jacinta, sitting on the cold steps of Saint Patrick's, in the rain.

"We know what really happened," his sisters told him later. "She and Jerry had a big fight and she attacked him, so his mother had her locked up so there would be no scandal, and all."

He would never forget how she looked when he did get to see her. She was always pale but after a few weeks in the hospital she was pasty. Her hair was a tangled mess despite all the hours she had once spent brushing it.

Even after she had gotten out, she remained "that poor creature." And the rest of them were forever branded "the crazy Carrolls."

It used to get to him when he was younger. And, in his mid-teens, when he started to realize things about himself, things he couldn't talk about with anybody, he started to look outside the little world around him. It was that or spend his whole life pretending. He toked up a lot back then, and it helped. He rarely drank so no one suspected and he was considered to be fine and upstanding and Martin was careful not to do anything to change that.

He took acid one summer and that changed everything. For the first time he saw himself, separate and apart, and knew he would have to go. That was when he used to tell people that he was going to go to New York.

During the last few years he lived in Dublin, he had spent his summers in London, running around with friends, looking for the person he wanted to be in the flashing lights and pounding beats of the clubs in the West End. It was so nice to get away to somewhere where he could really be himself and not be looking over his shoulder to see who was watching.

That's where he met David. They were two frightened boys in a salacious world and clung to each so they would be left alone long enough to find themselves again, slowly. The first summer they fell in love and the second summer they became lovers. He didn't tell anybody at home and that almost felt like shame. But how could he? They wouldn't understand. And besides, he was trying to be there for his nephew.

But he wasn't there when it really mattered. He knew Danny was smoking-up but he thought that was a good thing, a journey of spiritual enlightenment without a dark side. That's why everybody was doing it—everybody that he knew. Just a bunch of heads going against the grain, escaping from the dreary priest-ridden, gossipy, brutal, in-denial existence all around them. They just needed a way out, but it had become seedy—buying and selling on street corners and in back alleys.

Still, it wasn't all his fault—Jerry had barred him after the reading of the will. Not that he let that stop him, and he saw Jacinta whenever she met with their sisters. In the late summer of '74, a few months after the bombing, they had arranged to meet in Davey Byrne's.

He still remembered it. Everyone along the bar turned and looked back, frisking him with their eyes. It had almost become routine—checking on anyone that wasn't familiar. He nodded to the barman in an effort to reassure them all and waved to his sisters who were sitting in the corner like a three-headed Gorgon, dressed in their tacky fineness with hair curled and nails freshly painted in case there were any men about.

He had given up trying to have any kind of influence on them even though they all admitted, and not so secretly resented, that he had a real style about him. He used to help pick out the gloves and the scarves that his mother got for Santa Claus to put under the tree. But he didn't do that anymore. Now he was a bit embarrassed by them and their antics and constant need for reassurance.

They looked over at him and waved back, putting everybody along the bar at ease. But they also looked disappointed as they went back to lingering over their drinks. Jacinta was late and they probably had to make them last. Martin ordered his pint at the bar before joining them.

**

"Thanks very much for offering."

"I barely have enough for my own."

"And what about all the money you were making over in London—if that's what you were doing there?"

Martin ignored the jibe and sipped his lager. "That money has to get me through the next year."

"It's well for you, playing schoolboy at your age while the rest of us have to go out to work—if there was any work."

"You had the same choice as me."

"Will you listen to him—getting awful high and mighty like he's so much better than the rest of us?"

"All I'm just saying is that any one of you could have done the same."

That made them stop and think for a moment, but not for long. "We're just not the learning type," they laughed in chorus as they had done so often before. "And where's all that education going to get you? There's no jobs around here, anyway."

"That's why I'm going to go to Canada." He had started the application process and had been assured that he would meet the requirements after he graduated. People like him were very welcome in Canada.

"Canada? What on Earth would make you want to go there?"

Love, Martin thought to himself but hid his smile as he took another swig on his pint.

"What happened to New York? Wouldn't they let you in there?"

"And we were all looking forward to visiting New York. What's there to do in Canada?"

"I don't know—it could be all right. We could go riding with the Mounties."

They all laughed and sipped their drinks, still careful to make them last. Jacinta was almost half an hour late.

**

She'd had to wait to get Jerry out of the house.

He had promised to get up early and look for work, but, just like every other time, it didn't happen. And when he did get up, he coughed up a storm in the bathroom, cursing and swearing between bouts. She waited patiently in the kitchen knowing he was going nowhere again that day.

She wanted to have a word with Danny, too. He'd been out 'til after midnight and she had no idea where he'd been. She was beginning to worry that he might have been taking drugs.

At least he'd passed his Inter. She was very proud of that and couldn't wait to tell her sisters. None of them had made it that far and they'd all be jealous.

"Any chance of a cup of tea there, Jass?"

She got up from the kitchen table without complaint and filled the kettle. She couldn't help but feel a little sorry for him. He looked terrible. His eyes were sinking into his face and he hadn't shaved in a few days. "I hope you're going to clean yourself up a bit before you go out looking for work?"

"I'm not up for it today, Jass. I'm not feeling too good." He held his head in his hands. "But I'll do it tomorrow," he added when her face clouded over. "I promise."

"What's wrong with you now?"

"I think I'm getting depression."

Jacinta turned to make the tea—and to hide her contempt. *Depression? What does he know about depression?*

"Here," she slid the cup under his downcast face. "Get that into you and you'll feel a whole lot better in no time at all."

"Tea? Do you really think that it's going to fix what's wrong with me? I think I need to go and see the doctor and get some pills. What do you think? Do you think that would help?"

What would help you would be if you got up off your arse and got a job, but she said something else: "Pills? I suppose you could try them."

They worked for her. They dulled all the pain and let her wander through her days without highs and lows—except when she mixed them with alcohol. Sometimes, when she drank, the jagged edge of desperation poked through and her whole life seemed worthless.

But she drank to break from the monotony even if it meant that she said and did things that, later, she wished she hadn't. And it was happening more and more often, but she couldn't dream of going through life without a drink. "I think that's a good Idea, Jerry. I'll phone right now and make an appointment for you."

She knew he'd never do it himself, preferring to sit by the kitchen table complaining and she couldn't put up with another day like that.

**

As she left the kitchen, Jerry reached forward and slipped a few cigarettes out of her pack. They were Silk Cut and they were far too mild for him. He preferred Major's or Carroll's but he couldn't be choosey. He managed to get one lit despite his shaky hands and inhaled deeply, agitating another coughing fit.

He wiped his mouth and sipped his tea. He wished that he had some whiskey left but that stash was long gone. He desperately needed the cure. He heard Jacinta on the phone in the hall and rose as quickly as he could. Her bag was on the counter. He would just borrow enough to buy smokes, and a few pints. She'd never begrudge him that. He had just sat down again when she came back.

The doctor had time today but he'd have to leave right away.

**

After he left, Jacinta sat for a while and smoked. She wouldn't let it get her down anymore. They had taught her that in the hospital. She had to develop the ability to just accept that things would go wrong in life and not allow it to take over. She hadn't been able to do that before.

Since she was a little girl, everything just piled up on top of her and crushed the life out of her.

Everything, like the day the new puppy ran out under a bus.

And the day they all went to the zoo and the elephant took her whole handful of Smarties. She didn't tell anybody and spent the next few days expecting the man on the television to expose her. "An elephant died at the zoo after some little girl gave him Smarties," he'd announce and they'd all know it was her.

The nuns told her that she had to make a good confession and be heartily sorry for that and all of her other sins.

When she was in the hospital, she talked to the doctor about that. He suggested that she might have misinterpreted the message that they were trying to send her but he never explained himself. He wanted her to forget about the past and to focus on the positive side of things—that there would always be people there to help her, and to guide her.

She really wanted to talk about that part of her life that the nuns had molded. She felt it was important to bring it up but he didn't and moved along to asking questions about her father and her mother.

Being a parent was a lot harder than anyone ever said, especially her parents who just accepted everything that happened to them with a stoicism born of faith and hope and fear.

If she had only known what she knew now, she never . . .

But it wouldn't have made a difference. Jerry had assured her that she wouldn't get pregnant just doing it once and she'd had no reason to doubt him. He was in university, after all, and his father was in the *Dáil*, and her father called him "Mister Boyle."

For a while it was like a fairy tale but that didn't last. She'd liked the wedding and everyone fussing over her. But afterwards, when it was just her and Jerry, and her growing belly, it all turned into a nightmare of bickering and him storming out while she cried herself to sleep. Each time made the next one worse until it became a chasm between them.

His mother spoke to both of them and told them to mend their ways but Jerry didn't listen to her. It just made him want to avoid her, and Jacinta could only imagine how he was spending the time he was away from her. When he didn't even come home one night, she broke down and confided in her sisters. They nodded and consoled her but she couldn't help feel that they couldn't wait to be alone and tell each other that they had seen it coming all along.

There was no point in dwelling on all of that so she went up to wake Danny and to retrieve two twenty-pound notes from the envelope she had hidden in the linen closet. There wasn't much left but there was enough for today—and maybe two more after that. She closed the door quickly as Danny emerged from his room looking bedraggled.

"And where were you 'til all-hours of the morning?"

"Out."

"Where? And what were you doing?"

"I was just out with my friends. Leave me alone, will ya?"

"You mean you were out with the drug addicts."

He looked at her like he was totally bored—with her and with anything else she might say—and brushed past her.

"Don't walk away from me like that."

"Like what? I'm just going to get something to eat."

"Isn't it well for you that you have a mother that makes sure there's always food to put in front of you? Maybe you should think about that the next time you're out getting high."

"And you should think about how I let you live in my house. Think about that the next time you're out getting drunk with your sisters."

**

"Well it's about time you showed up," her sisters greeted her with relief.

"I'm sorry. I was having trouble with Danny. Let me get you all a drink." She pulled a crisp twenty and put it on the table in front of them. "And there's another one, too, for when that one is gone."

"Do you see that, Martin? That's how we look after each other in this family."

"That's right. We look after each other and not go running off to Canada."

Martin ignored them and turned to Jacinta. "So how is Danny?"

Jacinta settled herself into the space her sisters had reserved for her and lit a cigarette. She would have to buy another pack; she had only four left. She knew where the others had gone—he had been into her purse, too, but he still didn't know about the envelope. She had a plan for when that was gone, too. Granny's best China, and her silverware, carefully wrapped and stored in boxes in the spare room, under a mound of laundry.

"He's worrying the life out of me, Martin."

"Don't be bothering her with all of that," his sisters interrupted as the drinks arrived. "We're here to get away from all of that for a little while. Cheers, Jacinta. Cheers."

"Cheers," Jacinta agreed, delighted to be the center of their warm attention. Her house had grown so cold to her; Jerry was getting lost inside of himself and Danny's indifference was chilling her heart a little more each day. It was so nice to be with those who loved her unconditionally, even if it only lasted as long as her money held out.

"So?" She turned to Martin. "How was London? Did you meet anyone that tickled your fancy?"

"Him? Are you joking? He'd be afraid of even getting close to a real woman."

"He'd piss his pants."

"Ah, leave him alone, will you?"

They all deferred, retracting their claws as they sat back. Jacinta ruled the roost, for now.

"London was great, thanks for asking."

"And?"

"And what?"

"You have, haven't you? You've met someone?"

"So what if I have? It's just a summer thing." He paused to sip his pint before continuing. "I've decided. I'm going to go to Canada after I graduate."

"I thought it was New York you were going to?"

"I changed my mind."

"She's one of them, isn't she? My little brother has fallen for a Canadian?" She knew that Martin didn't like when they pried in his business but she couldn't help herself. It was how they were together.

"So what's going on with you and Danny? Did he get his results yet?"

Jacinta knew what he was doing but went along with it. "Of course he did—with honors in history, too."

"That's fantastic," Martin raised his glass toward their sullen sisters. "To Danny!"

"To Danny," they responded insipidly, jealous of the bond he shared with Jacinta.

"Yes, my Danny is a good scholar but he'd be a lot better if only Jerry would make him stay at home and do his studying."

"Oh leave him alone, Jass. He passed—after everything—and now I'm sure he'll settle down and get his Leaving Cert, too."

"Do you really think so Martin? You're not just saying that? I've been getting so worried about him. He's getting awful lippy lately and I swear to God that he's taking drugs, too."

"Oh I doubt it, Jass. Why do you think that?"

"He's never at home and looks very shifty when I do catch up with him. He never lets me see his eyes when I'm talking with him."

"That's a sure sign," the sisters agreed and nodded knowingly at each other. "It's no wonder when you look at his father. I'm surprised that he's not an alcoholic, too."

Martin glared at them until they stopped and turned back to Jacinta. "Why do you say that?"

"He's hanging around with those hippie kids—you know the ones I mean, that Skelton brat and the tramps that hang around with him."

"Oh them, they're okay."

"Do you know them?"

"I do, yeah, and you've nothing to worry about. Johnny's a good guy. He's at art school."

"Well in that case would you ever have a word with him and tell him to leave my son alone?"

"Jass, I'm sure there's no reason for you to worry but, if it would put your mind at ease, I could drop by and have a word with Danny, if you like?"

"I don't know, Martin. You know how his father gets. I'd be afraid there'd be a row."

"Well could you get Danny to phone me, then?"

"I would but what if Jerry were to find out?"

Jacinta had no intention of passing the message along. She was happy with the distance that had grown between her brother and her son. She didn't want Danny to have anybody else to turn to until he let her back into his life. And she didn't really want Martin around right now in case he noticed the boxes in the spare room. And if Danny asked, she'd tell him that Martin was busy with his own life. She'd tell him that it was something he would have to learn: that no one loved him like she did. No one, not even that young trollop who was probably dropping her drawers for him after getting him high.

"So how's Jerry?" her sisters asked and sat forward grinning like hyenas.

Jacinta lit up again and leaned toward them. "Wait 'til I tell you the latest. He fell out of bed this morning, at half past eleven, and tells me that he is depressed and that he wants the doctor to give him pills."

"Pills? He'd be better off getting a job."

"Why would he need to do that? Haven't you still got all that money the old bitch left you?"

Jacinta did nothing to dispel their illusions. She wanted them to believe that, no matter how bad things were, she was far better off than any of them could dream of.

"It's not for the money," she reminded them and finished her drink. She wanted them to know that she was now a part of a higher class who never discussed things like that. She waited for her point to register and nodded to the barman. "It's more the principal of the thing," she explained patiently. "Jerry was a victim of politics, you know, because of his father."

Her sisters nodded in sympathy and drained their own glasses. "It must be terrible for you."

They settled into a brooding silence, each with their own thoughts, until the barman brought their fresh drinks.

"Well, we all have our burdens to bear, I suppose."

"Well Jacinta is certainly bearing hers well."

"And she looks great, too. Doesn't she?"

"She looks gorgeous. She puts the rest of us to shame. I'm dead jealous."

They all agreed as Jacinta glowed a little. She knew their affections were easily won, and lost, but she had to take it where she could find it and smiled all around as she raised her fresh glass. "Cheers!"

Martin didn't smile back. His eyes had never left her face, like he was trying to look all the way inside of her. "Getting back to Danny," he tried in a soft voice.

"Never mind Danny," his sisters rebuked him. "He's more than capable of looking after himself. It's Jacinta that you should be worried about. She's the one who is family, after all."

"And what is Danny? He's family, too."

"Okay, okay Martin," Jacinta conceded. "You're like a dog with a bone. Come over on Saturday afternoon. I'll make sure Danny is there and we can pretend that you just dropped in."

"And what about Jerry?"

"He'll be down in the pub. You won't have to worry about him. Are you happy now?"

Martin just nodded, finished his pint, and got up to leave.

"Wait," his sister Gina called out. "It's Ma's birthday next week and we should all pitch in to get her something."

"Sure," Martin agreed and reached for his wallet. "How much are we throwing in?"

"A tenner each."

"A tenner," Martin smiled as he pulled his last two fives from his wallet. "Here. Who should I give it to?" He asked Brenda and Linda but they both just looked to their drinks as they nodded toward Jacinta.

**

Martin had smiled as he walked down the street. It had turned out to be a very expensive day for Jacinta. He knew she had money stashed somewhere and he knew it couldn't last forever. And he hadn't wanted to know where it came from. That way he wouldn't have to lie to Davies.

He never did get around to seeing Danny until after the thing in the church and by then it was too late. He and Danny were never the same again. No matter how hard he tried he couldn't get through to him. It was like Danny didn't trust anybody anymore.

Then, when Danny had to work around the church, so they wouldn't press charges, he pretended to reform and Martin didn't blame him. Everybody was on his case.

That was when everyone started to say that he was more Carroll than Boyle, and they didn't mean it as a compliment. That was when he would have needed Martin the most and he wasn't there. He was too busy moving to Canada.

***

"You're thinking about your nephew again?" David opened his eyes and rolled toward him, wrapping his arms around him and drawing their bodies together. He reached forward and gently kissed Martin's lips. "You can talk to me about it, you know?"

"I know. I just don't know how I feel about it yet."

"What's to feel? The kid's in trouble and needs your help. We can bring him out here where he will be safe."

"I don't know."

"What's to know? Nobody will be able to get to him here. If they try—they'll have me to deal with. Me and a few brothers. I'm from Kingston, man. I know how to look out for my own."

Martin almost laughed. David came from the richest part of town but liked to talk tough, even though he was so soft inside. "I thought your family was rich."

"We are but we have cousins who live down around Tivoli Gardens."

"That sounds like a real tough neighborhood, almost as scary as Rosedale, or Forest Hill."

"Trust me, Toastie, Tivoli Gardens is Hell. People get shot down there for nothing. You look at someone the wrong way and bang, you got yourself another hole in your head." David grew more animated as he spoke. His large broad chest rippled and his face acted out each word.

Martin ran his white fingers gently across David's dark skin. He had a way of making Martin feel that everything would be all right. He used to sing it to him, too, in his best Bob Marley voice: "'Cause every little thing's gonna be all right!"

"But where is he going to stay? He can't stay with us."

"Why not? He's family, man. You look after family."

"Not mine."

"What are you talking about? He's your nephew and he needs a place to start again. He can stay here until he gets set up."

Martin sat up and wrapped the sheets around his torso, turning his back on his lover.

"They don't know about us?" David asked in a softer voice. "Is that what you're worried about?"

"No. They don't"

"What? Are you afraid that they might be shocked because I'm black?"

"No! They'll be so shocked that you're a man that I'm hoping they'll overlook that."

"Toastie, you're one screwed up little Catholic boy. That's why I love you."

"I thought it was because I have such a cute ass."

"That too, but there is nothing sweeter than doing it with a Catholic boy. It just makes it all so much more sinful."

"How many Catholic boys have there been."

"You're my first."

"And the last?"

"Maybe. Is your nephew . . . ?"

"Don't even think about it."

Martin feigned outrage and stormed off to shower but he left the door open for David to follow.

CHAPTER 11

Deirdre was looking out her window the night Danny walked past. She had been smoking a joint and didn't want the smell in her room. She had almost called out but she couldn't do that to him—he had enough problems to deal with—so she edged away from the window and hoped he hadn't noticed. She still wasn't ready to face him after the way she had behaved after their infamous night.

**

After they had been taken from the church, wrapped in blankets to hide their immodesty, her father came to the Garda station. He didn't even speak to her as he dealt with the Guards. Her mother stood between them, interceding for peace, at least until they got home. She even took Deirdre aside and urged her to stay silent until she had a chance to work on him.

By the next morning her mother had done it and convinced him that it was all Danny's fault, that he had led Deirdre astray. She agreed with him that it was shameful and a blot on the good name of the family that he had worked so hard for, but that no permanent harm had been done.

He was somewhat appeased by that but warned that if he ran into Danny, he wouldn't be responsible for his actions. And even as he mentioned Danny's name, he became enraged again until Fr. Reilly dropped by.

The priest had gratefully accepted the tea that Deirdre's mother offered, admitting that he was almost worn out having been called from his bed in the middle of the night.

**

He had declined the car, choosing instead to take his bike. He had wanted to think along the way—to sort out how he was going to deliver the news. Fr. Brennan had told him it would be better coming from the curate, rather than the parish priest, but he couldn't help feel that the old man was shirking his responsibilities.

Patrick hadn't been to the Boyle's house since Nora's wake and was taken aback. Even in the yellowish glow of the streetlights he could see how neglected the garden had become. Nora Boyle's years of attention were being lost to the rush of weeds and litter. He pressed the doorbell and waited. It was late and they would be in bed. After the second ring a sleepy voice called from a window above.

"Who's there?"

"It's Father Reilly. Can I come in?"

"At this hour?"

"Yes, I have news that would be better discussed inside."

"Hold on a minute then, Father. We'll be right down."

They both looked terrible, puffy faced and bedraggled. Jacinta clutched her tatty robe close to her as she led him into the kitchen where Jerry scratched himself absentmindedly and rummaged around until he found a cigarette.

"Well, Father," he asked as he exhaled. "What brings you by at this hour?"

"It's about Danny."

"What's that little brat gone and done now?"

"How do you know," Jacinta snapped over her shoulder, as she fussed with the teapot, "that he has done anything? Did you ever think that something might have happened to him, through no fault of his own?"

"Well," Fr. Reilly interceded and chose his words carefully. "I'm afraid he has gone and done something rather foolish. But he's all right. He's safe and sound but the Guards have him."

"Ah sweet Jesus. Why?"

"Well, they were called to the church after somebody noticed that it had been broken into. They went in and found Danny inside."

"What was he doing there?"

"He was singing *Jesus Christ Superstar.*"

"Ah well, he has become very musical since he got his guitar," Jacinta poured their tea and settled behind her own cup.

"Is there more?" Jerry flicked the ash from his cigarette but missed the ashtray. He leaned forward and blew it away, almost into their cups.

"I'm afraid there is." Fr. Reilly moved his cup to his lap. "When the Guards found him he was standing on the altar in nothing but his underwear."

"Were they his holey ones?"

"Hush you and don't be making a joke out of it. This is terrible news, Father."

"Sure what harm was there?"

"Well, there's more. It seems there was a young lady there, too. She was in her underwear also, and told the Guards that she was Mary Magdalene. The two of them were singing and dancing around like pagans. The Guards think they might have been high on drugs."

"God save us." Jacinta blessed herself and retrieved her cigarette pack and lit one.

"But there was no real harm done, was there, Father?" Jerry pulled the cigarette pack toward him.

"Well, Father Brennan is concerned about the blasphemous nature of the thing. He is very upset and is talking excommunication."

"God save us," Jacinta repeated and blessed herself with her cigarette.

"Will there be any charges?" Jerry asked as his eyes narrowed.

"Well, the Bishop will have to be involved but I will try to have a word with him. He's a very decent man and I'm sure that he'll be able to see his way to having a bit of mercy—for your late mother's sake, if nothing else."

"And well he should after all the money she gave to the Church."

"Don't be talking like that in front of the priest."

"Why not? I'm just saying, you know?"

Fr. Reilly sipped his tea and wished he could take more command of situations like this. It was a very serious matter, though Jerry didn't seem to think so. But he had done what he came to do—to deliver the bad news. "I should be off, I suppose, unless you need me for anything?"

"No, Father. But thank you so much for coming to tell us. I suppose we should go down to the Garda station?"

"Well, if you want my advice—I'd wait until morning. The Guards want to hold him until then. They want to try to scare a bit of sense into him."

"They won't beat him, will they Father?"

"It won't do him a bit of harm if they did."

"Don't you be talking like that. This is your own flesh and blood we're talking about."

"I don't think Danny will come to any harm," Fr. Reilly assured her as he rose to take his leave. "And if you don't mind me saying, it might be better if you both got a bit of sleep and came to it fresh in the morning?"

But Jerry and Jacinta were already squaring up to each other.

"I'll just let myself out then?"

"Fair enough, Father," Jerry rose and walked him to the door.

"Will Mrs. Boyle be all right?"

"She will, Father, after she's had a chance to digest it all."

"Well, don't hesitate to call me if there's anything I can do."

"We will, Father, and thanks very much for coming to tell us."

As Fr. Reilly wheeled his bike down the drive he could hear the two of them tear into each other.

He yawned as the eastern sky lightened and the hedgerows began to chirp. There was no point in going back to bed when he got home. Instead, he'd have another cup of tea before he had to go with Fr. Brennan to face the Bishop.

Later on he'd have to drop in on the girl's family.

**

"It's a bad business," the Bishop had concluded as he sipped his coffee. He had listened impassively as the two priests laid the story before him. The Garda Sergeant had called him, too, and almost seemed to enjoy breaking the news. "And it couldn't have happened at a worse time."

The National Coalition was straining the ties that bound Church and State. The voting on the Contraception Bill had been far too close and needed the *Taoiseach*, and a few others, to vote against their own party. There was even talk of changing the Constitution, too, of giving up the claim on the North. The country was going to the dogs and the last thing he needed was for this to attract the eye of one of those civil liberty lawyer types. It was better that they dealt with it behind closed doors.

Fr. Brennan wanted excommunication, and, if he were given kindling and matches, a public burning at the stake.

"I understand your position on this, Father, but I wonder if it's not an opportunity, too."

"Your Grace?"

"Well, Father. Perhaps it's a chance for us to show God's mercy?"

Fr. Brennan lowered his head so his face couldn't be read. He knew the Bishop well enough, his words were never chosen without consideration. Nor were they open for debate. The Bishop was gently telling them the course they would follow, regardless of how they might feel about it.

"Yes," the Bishop continued after noting his priest's concession. "We can offer this poor, confused lad a chance to redeem himself. I will talk with the Guards, and, instead of laying charges, we will offer to have the boy come and do some work around the church. We can say that we are giving him the chance to atone for his misdeeds. It will allow him to reflect on what he has done and we can give him the chance to offer restitution."

"And what do you have in mind, Your Grace?" Fr. Reilly also knew his uncle well.

"If young Boyle is willing to pay restitution to the church then we can consider the matter closed. He can pay in service. I'm sure, Father Brennan, that you and Father Reilly can find some work for him to do?"

"If that's what Your Grace would wish of us," Fr. Brennan agreed as he made a mental list of tasks for the young and errant Boyle. He was going to have to hire a man to help with odd jobs around the church as old O'Leary was no longer capable and no one else was willing to offer their time. Perhaps this might work out well for all concerned.

"It's not what I would wish, my friend, but what the Holy Shepard would expect from us. We must show some leadership in these changing times and we must show that we can be compassionate, even against those that harm us."

The parish priest and his curate nodded together and the Bishop leaned back and smiled. "Thank you, my friends, for being so accommodating on this matter. I will speak to the Guards and have them make the position clear to young Boyle."

"Would you mind," his nephew asked, "if I could be given the responsibility of looking after him?" Fr. Reilly didn't want Fr. Brennan dealing with him; he didn't think he was well enough.

The Bishop gazed at his nephew while he weighed the options. "I would prefer if both of you dealt with him; it would look more formal. And now gentlemen if you'd excuse me, I have another appointment."

The Bishop closed his office door as the two men left. It was a bad business but it might all work out for the better. His nephew would have a chance to show his mettle, under the supervision of Fr. Brennan. The older man was ready to be put out to pasture and a new parish priest had to be found. He would have preferred not to consider his own nephew given his history with the boy and it was far too papal, but the field of candidates was getting smaller every year.

Perhaps you could give me a sign? he nodded toward the crucifix on his wall.

**

Fr. Reilly, too, had prayed for direction as he approached Deirdre's house. The mother would be fine but the father could be a bit of a handful, especially when he got angry. Most people just stayed away from him when he was like that, but Fr. Reilly couldn't. He had to go in. He rang the doorbell and composed himself. It was all in a day's work.

"Good man yourself, Father." Deirdre's father greeted him and led him into the drawing room where his wife and daughter sat primly on the settee. "The missus and I will just go into the kitchen and make a pot of tea while this one," he nodded toward Deirdre, "gets down on her knees and makes her confession."

"I think," Fr. Reilly hesitated, "that we should just have a little chat, first, and then see where we need to go from there."

"Chat?" her father humphed as he left the room.

"It might be better," Deirdre's mother whispered as she followed, "if you returned her to a state of grace—in case himself kills her altogether."

Fr. Reilly tried not to smile as the door closed, leaving him alone with Deirdre who sat in the armchair opposite him. "Perhaps we should have our chat, then. While we are alone."

Deirdre didn't answer and that unnerved him a little. When she was little she was like a shadow to her older sister and was never seen out on her own. She had changed a lot since then and her mother had once told him that she was learning how to wrap her father around her little finger. Fr. Reilly had no idea how to deal with her so he did what was expected of him. He talked about Mary, the mother of God, and what a great role model she was for women of all ages.

But after what happened with Miriam, he didn't really believe in it anymore. Not that he didn't believe that Mary was the mother of God; what he was beginning to question was the whole way they went about things—asking the people to do the impossible, modelling themselves after saints and the likes. Nobody could ever live up to them. It was no wonder that so many were just giving up.

"There is one thing I do have to confess, Father." Deirdre said when he had finished. Her face was calm but tinged with a touch of contrition. "I was the one who gave Danny the drugs—not the other way around. Only I'm afraid to tell anyone. My father would kill me if he knew. And then he'd kill Danny, too, for spite."

"Now, Deirdre. There'll be no killing or anything like that, but I'm glad you told me."

"Could you tell Danny . . . from me . . . that I'm terribly sorry?"

"I will indeed. When the time is right," he added as her mother knocked on the door. They could have tea in the kitchen—if Fr. Reilly wouldn't mind. Her husband was smoking and she preferred that he did that in the kitchen where the smell wouldn't get all over the new furniture.

"Not at all," Fr. Reilly assured her. "Wasn't I brought up in the kitchen?"

"Don't forget to let Danny know," Deirdre whispered as she passed and followed her mother into the kitchen, where her father sat at the head of the table, with his wife and daughter to his left and Fr. Reilly to his right, where Deirdre normally sat.

"Don't you think it best, Father, that we send her off to board at a good convent school?" he asked as they sipped their tea.

The mother looked like she didn't agree so Fr. Reilly suggested that what Deirdre might need more now was the love and forgiveness of her family. He looked at the wife and the daughter for a moment before he looked back at the father. He could only guess what was going through the poor man's mind.

Fr. Reilly had no idea what it was like to have a daughter. He hadn't even known what it was like to grow up with a sister. In fact, other than his mother, the only woman who ever became a part of his life was Miriam. He wished she was there, sitting beside him. She would know the right things to do and say.

"Well that's all very well and good for Sundays," the father said in a controlled voice. Fr. Reilly could see that it was still surging around inside of him, almost bursting out through his eyes, and the edges of his mouth. He almost sounded like a kettle that was coming to the boil. "But what concerns me the most is my daughter's reputation. I'll not have the whole street snickering behind her back. I only want what's best for her. You understand that, don't you, Father?"

"I do," Fr. Reilly lied a little white lie to ease things along. "But my advice to you is that you show everybody that you still love your daughter, and that you forgive her. You can set a good example for them all."

He regretted it the moment he said it. That kind of talk only worked when they were young—or old. It was funny how that worked out, but it was not going to work on this father. He was starting to come to the boil again so Fr. Reilly decided to stop poking the fire and let everything settle down again.

"But of course, you're the girl's father and I'm sure you know what's best for her. Only I'd ask you to let it alone for a few days, you know? Give yourself time to get over the shock and the anger, and come back to it when you're calmer. I find that when I have something to decide that it is better after I turn it over to the Sacred Heart of Jesus . . ."

"With all due respect," the father interrupted, "to yourself and the Sacred Heart." He paused while he bowed his head briefly. "But I think this situation calls for a more direct approach, Father. It's obvious that she can't get the type of direction she needs from this house."

Fr. Reilly couldn't help it and stole a quick glance at the mother as the father sat back with his arms folded. The poor mother bowed her head with shame. He knew things hadn't been great in the house since Deirdre's sister had left home to go off and live with her boyfriend. The mother had been over to talk with Fr. Brennan, back when he was still sound. Fr. Brennan had told him that the thing the mother was most afraid of was what her husband would do when Deirdre's turn came, as she was sure, even back then, that it would.

"What I might suggest, before any long term plans are made, is that we have Deirdre sit down and have a chat with a friend of mine. She's taking her PhD over in UCD and I'm sure she would be the right person for Deirdre to talk with." He paused as he checked with the daughter who quickly nodded her head.

"And what kind of person is this? She's not one of those psychiatric types?" The father looked worried now—like he was going to have deal with the shame of his daughter being a bit touched, too.

"Well," Fr. Reilly hesitated: this part always raised eyebrows. "She used to be a nun over in Chicago. And she's back in Dublin now, studying, but I'm sure she would be the right person to give Deirdre some good advice."

"I'm not so sure," the father grumbled as he refolded his arms.

"What harm could there be in them meeting?" The mother pleaded.

"Well for one thing, she's . . . defrocked."

"And what's the harm in that?" The mother pleaded again, even more dolefully.

The father didn't react at first. He was looking around and gauging all of their faces. "Okay, let them meet but I'm still going to go ahead and look into getting Deirdre into a boarding school."

Fr. Reilly noticed that Deirdre and her mother both eased a little. He had a good idea what would happen. The father would leave it for his wife to deal with it and she would drag it out until it was too late for this year. It was probably how they dealt with him, pushing everything on down the road before them.

Fr. Reilly knew he had done all that he could for now and rose to leave. "I'll be in touch as soon as I talk with my friend," he assured the mother as he left, as she squeezed his hand by the door. She was almost shivering but smiled again before turning back to the stony silence of the kitchen where Deirdre and her father still sat.

Fr. Reilly happily walked his bicycle to the side of the road where he stopped to put on his clips so his dark slacks would not get covered with oil. Old O'Leary, who looked after Gethsemane, had taken it upon himself to keep the parish bike in the best working order. "You can never have too much lubrication," he always assured. "It's what keeps the world turning."

Fr. Reilly pedaled back up the hill, delighted how things had turned out. Miriam could be just the influence that Deirdre needed and he could get to see her again without it looking bad.

She was Joe's sister, his old friend from the seminary who was now off in Boston working on the guilt of the privileged for the benefit of poor kids—a task he was particularly well-suited to. They kept in touch through weekly letters. "Missals of Disaffection," they called them in which they could privately share their growing disillusionment with their vocations.

But a year back, Joe's letters had changed. His witty and sometimes shocking commentary on all that was wrong with "*the damn fools who were running the world into the ground—present company exempted of course*," started to mention the matter of "*those who gave in. Those that broke under the pressure and quit.*" And among them were men they had known since the seminary: "*The ones we assumed were the least riddled with doubt are often the first to tear off their collars and go out into the world as mere mortal men."*

At first Joe just wrote them as bylines tucked in the post-scriptum, or the post-post-scriptum where he told Patrick how he really was, after pages of enforced joviality.

He had always been the bright cheery one—the one friend that Patrick "*could take his problems to without risking being exposed to an Inquisition!*" It was something they could acknowledge now that they had been out in the world for a while. They lived in fear for themselves, their friends and their Church. It was spreading like leprosy among them, and, as Joe once wrote, "*it is a cause calling for a new Father Damien.*"

Patrick knew Joe was up to something. He had a great knack for knowing how to catch the winds of change in his sails and a happier knack of always landing on his feet a few rungs higher up the ladder. That's how he got to America—that and the fact that he "*had an uncle a bishop in America!*"

Over time he began to write about his growing understanding of, and his inability to cut off forever, those "*who were once good friends and comrades, now fallen in battle because our general staff is comprised entirely of idiots. Well-meaning and pious, and devout to beat the band, but idiots nonetheless. They have forgotten that we are supposed to be a moral authority and not an endorsement of the status quo.*

"*We came into this business to try to do a little good in the world and when we are not allowed—when we are told not to speak out against all the damn injustice in the world—some of us can't take it and we go through the flailing corridors of shame where every ounce of our credibility is stripped from us and we are expelled and defrocked, naked to be abused and ridiculed by the world!*"

Patrick began to think that Joe was about to make his own jump and that was very unsettling. He had always been the one his bishop sent the troubled ones to, when he learnt that they were straying from the path. Joe had the knack of getting people to like and trust him, which was odd as Patrick knew he was the only one that Joe really trusted with his private self.

Then the letter came that cleared it all up. His sister was leaving the convent. She had been in Chicago since the late 1960s and had been considered mother superior material.

But she got herself involved with anti-war protests and into trouble with the American government.

"*She might even have been sent to federal prison were it not for the fact that our race has been blessed with the influence we can bring to bear on our public representatives. We simply mention the possibility of excommunication from the next St. Patrick's Day Parade and our politicians are more than happy to bend a few rules for us.*

"*However, she is, I suppose for the sake of penance, thinking of going back to Ireland. I knew I didn't have to ask, so I gave her your address so she can look you up when she has had enough public humiliation. Be kind to her for my sake as she is too good a soul for this imperfect world.*"

**

He had hardly remembered her when she called, even though he said he did. "Of course I do. It's Miriam, isn't it?" Fr. Reilly lied and tried to sort her from the rest of Joe's family. He had met them all from time to time but now they were a jumble of faces and confused details. "Now which one were you?"

"I was the one with the buck teeth and the pimples."

"I don't remember you like that. You used to have that big shock of red curls."

"That was Claire."

"Sure of course it was. What was I thinking?"

"I would think that you were wondering why I'm calling you." She hadn't been away that long but she had picked up a very American way of talking—very direct and informal.

"Not at all, Miriam. Joe just wrote to me and told me that I might be hearing from you."

"And what did the bishop's right-hand-man tell you about me?"

They both laughed in their shared love for Joe. "Ah now, he just said that you might be coming over."

"Did he tell you that I'm out of the game?" She almost made it sound like she had quit streetwalking and Patrick grew more flustered.

"He did say that you were making a bit of a career change."

"That's a very good way of putting it. I must remember that. Well, what I wanted to know was, now that I'm at the university and living not too far away, and knowing nobody who wants to know me, if you would ever considering risking your reputation and be seen in public with me?

"Nothing complicated," she assured him. "Just a priest and an ex-nun having lunch together in broad daylight so everybody can see there is no hanky-panky."

Patrick hesitated as he tried to sort it out in his mind. He had never been spoken to like this before. He never had a woman invite him out for lunch before, either. What harm could it do as long as it was all above board? He would be doing it as a good priest to one in trouble; as a good friend to a friend's sister, and as a man who was so damned lonely and cut off.

"Well Miriam, it would be wonderful to meet you again. I often go into Bewley's when I'm downtown. Would you like to meet there, sometime?"

"Sure. When's good for you?"

"I often go downtown on Tuesdays. I like to drop into a few books stores around Dawson Street. Perhaps I could give you a call one of these weeks."

"You still buy books?"

"I do," he laughed and his mind was made up. She would know what it was like to be a priest. Joe used to write about all the times she had to listen to his tirades. She would be a perfect friend for him—and she would know what not to do.

"I do have a bit of a book hobby. I collect antiquarian writings about travel and things like that. It lets me try to understand how people were before."

"Does it help?"

"I can spend hours with my nose in my books, as my mother used to say."

"That's nice but I was asking if 'understanding how people were before' helped?"

He hadn't had a talk like this with anyone in years. She was poking fun at him like only a friend would and he was enjoying every minute of it. "Ah sure, Miriam, you know what it's like."

"Patrick? Will my fall from grace be an issue for you?"

He had no idea what to say. If she was a man, one of those that had shed the collar, it would have been a lot easier. He didn't really know how women dealt with their issues. When he was younger he always avoided them and now he had no understanding of them. He could understand the women in the books he read, but, in real life, he had no idea.

"Patrick?"

"No! Of course it won't. Why would it? Sure there's plenty like you, and, if we are to listen to the Boss, we're supposed to show a little compassion and understanding once in a while."

"Like he did with Mary Magdalene?"

"No, no, Miriam. I didn't mean to offer any offence. I'm just not used to talking about things like this."

"Are you sure you're Joe's friend? Do I have the wrong guy? Listen, if this is going to be a problem for you we can just skip it." She paused long enough to force him to dither and decide.

"Not at all, Miriam. What would Joe say if I wouldn't even meet you for a cup of tea? I'll give you a call the next time and we can arrange to meet."

**

But they didn't meet.

He avoided even thinking about her until a letter from Joe arrived. It stressed how worried he was about her and that she was having a rough time settling back into Dublin. He also wanted to know why Patrick hadn't been to see her.

When he got back from Deirdre's house, he did it. He picked up the phone and dialed her number, He had tried to do it so many times that he knew her number by heart. But every other time he stopped on the last number and hung up.

This time it was different. This time he was just asking for her help with a troubled young teenager. No one could doubt his motives now.

He explained the whole situation. Miriam was delighted to be asked and wanted to see Deirdre right away but Fr. Reilly thought it would be better if just the two of them met first so he could give her all the details.

He had hoped to keep the matter private so that there would be no misunderstandings, even though the whole thing was innocent, but he wasn't that lucky.

"Who was that on the telephone?" Fr. Brennan asked as he emerged from hallway.

"A friend, Fr. Brennan. Just a friend of mine."

"Are you always so ill at ease with your friends?" The old man was doddering but had moments of clarity that unsettled Fr. Reilly.

"Can I help you find something, Father?"

"Can I not walk around in my own house without the Spanish Inquisition?"

He walked back into the hall with his open bathrobe billowing around his naked, wrinkled body. Fr. Reilly couldn't put it off anymore. He'd have to make another dreaded call; he'd have to have a word with the Bishop. Mrs. Dunne, the woman who came by to cook and clean for them, hadn't noticed yet, but it was only a matter of time.

CHAPTER 12

The morning after watching Danny walk by, Deirdre lay in her bed. She'd had a night of fitful dreams and blamed it on the joint. She didn't do that very often anymore but sometimes the boredom got to her. The rest of the year had flown by as she immersed herself in her studies but the summer had dragged.

Her father didn't want her to work "like some common shop girl," but she was far too old to spend the holidays as they once did; visiting uncles and aunts and spending a few weeks by the sea at Tramore. It hadn't been fun for any of them since Grainne left.

She was off in Morocco where Johnny was learning how to capture light.

Some of it reflected from the pages of her letters on those days when Dublin was damp and dreary. Their father had cut her off and forbade any contact, but Deirdre ignored him and wrote often. Their mother was involved, too, intercepting the post and hand-delivering Grainne's replies under an unspoken agreement that Deirdre would share the news. "Here's another letter from your friend in Tangiers," she said every time, and, in time, Deirdre stopped correcting her. They were complicit and covert because every time Grainne's name was mentioned her father still sneered: "my own flesh and blood—off fornicating in the desert with a penniless hippie." But her mother was working on him, subtly leaking the better news.

"I read something interesting in the 'Arts' section of a magazine at the hairdressers the other day. It talked about up and coming artists and it mentioned Grainne's Johnny," she casually floated to Deirdre, over dinner while her father sat behind his paper. It stiffened when his wife's tone reached him; it was the tone she used to announce when he had to listen.

"Oh," Deirdre played along, trying not to smile as the seeds she'd sown took root. Grainne had written that his paintings were finally beginning to sell. She also mentioned that she might be pregnant but not to let their parents know—she wasn't sure how she felt about it yet.

They had often talked about it and while Grainne started having sex with Johnny when she was only seventeen, Deirdre was waiting. She wasn't sure if she was ready and Grainne said she respected her for that—just like Deirdre respected her for the choice she had made.

Grainne was the only person she could talk to about stuff like that. She didn't think it fair to discuss it with Miriam, and she tried talking to her mother but all she got was a reminder about the example given by Mary, the mother of God.

She could never really understand the symbolism of the Virgin Mother but she had learned to keep her thoughts to herself. Grainne said that it was typical of the double standards and hypocrisy—that women were supposed to stay virgins until the Church gave them the go ahead to go and breed like rabbits. She and Johnny did want to have children, but only when they felt they were ready.

She did promise to keep Deirdre informed and until she did, Deirdre agonized, too, as she tried to imagine what she would do if it was her. It was all very well for everyone to go around saying that it was a mortal sin of the worst kind but they never seemed to get that upset about all the other killings that went on in the world.

Not that she could ever accept the killing of life at its most vulnerable, but things were far more complicated than that. She understood the morality of it but she also believed that it was a matter for women and not something the clergy should concern themselves with. They would be better off speaking out about injustice and things like that.

She had joined a women's group on Miriam's suggestion and was fast becoming an evangelist. In fact, since she started seeing her, her outlook on many things were . . . not so much changed but more articulated. Things were changing for the women of Ireland and they could now become anything they wished to be.

Her mother was a bit coy on that subject but Deirdre and Miriam discussed it often, something that Deirdre sometimes mentioned over dinner despite her mother's secret signs of disapproval. Deirdre didn't care even though her father grumbled about his daughter spending so much time with "that defrocked nun" but her mother coyly approved. "She's a very bright girl and you should be very proud of her. In my day, young women didn't have all these choices and you should be happy that she has people to help her find the right path. You would if she were your son."

She also reproached Deirdre about going out of her way to upset her father.

Deirdre didn't care. She was just giving them fair warning for when she decided what she was going to do with her life. She didn't want them to be as shocked as they were when Grainne left.

She had no idea what it was that she was going to do but she wanted them to be ready. She had a growing list of all the things she didn't want to become but was less sure about what she did want.

One thing was certain, though. She wanted to do something that would make the world better. She wanted to be a part of the great change that was sweeping the whole world. She wanted to be like Mary Robinson who had shown that women could do it all. She married who she liked, despite the fuss, and had a career and a family. That's what Deirdre wanted for herself—a very full life, full of challenges because that was what it would take to make things better, for everyone.

But seeing Danny again made her stop and think: she had failed that challenge and taken the easy way out.

Still, she had done her penance and now, enough time had passed. She was now ready to right that wrong and, if he was open to it, apologize. She wasn't sure how he might take it—she'd heard how much he had changed. He'd become the local dealer and was hanging out with the wrong crowd. She certainly didn't want to get mixed up in any of that but she had to do what was right.

Of course she couldn't let her parents know, so, after she dressed and went downstairs, she would just tell them that she was going to meet up with Miriam. It was the lesser of the two evils and it wasn't a total lie. She'd planned to meet her later, and besides, she wasn't really sure if he'd even want to talk with her.

"Good morning," her mother greeted her but didn't look up. Instead, she poured more tea and stirred her cup even though she never used sugar, or milk. Deirdre waited. It was how her mother got ready to talk about the things that troubled her.

The news of Danny Boyle's interview with the Garda was percolating through the neighborhood and they both knew how little in life was really private. After the incident in the church, they had walked the gauntlet of unspoken censure and rebuke for months until something fresher came along.

It had taken longer to blow over at home even though Deirdre had agreed to all of her father's conditions and stopped seeing Danny. She had to; her infamous night in the church had shaken them all to their cores and the very mention of it still set her father to huffing and puffing until, at any moment, he might explode and hunt Danny down and horsewhip him.

Her mother was probably torn between broaching the subject and letting sleeping dogs lie.

"Did you hear the news about that Boyle boy?"

"No." Deirdre answered between mouthfuls of toast.

"Well," her mother continued slowly, letting Deirdre know that she knew she wasn't being honest, "it seems that the Garda interviewed him in connection with the Scully murder."

"That's awful."

"You don't think that he might have been involved in any way?"

"I doubt it. Not that I'd know. I haven't seen him since . . ."

"I know dear, but I can't help but think that there must be some mistake. After all, he has always been a most unfortunate boy." Her mother looked up and Deirdre lowered her face. They never really discussed what actually happened in the church.

"I do hope that he has somebody to talk with at a time like this. I don't mean to speak badly about his parents but I'm not sure they can be of much help to him right now."

When Deirdre looked up her mother was sipping her tea, her face was impassive and her eyes were soft and warm. It was how she told her daughter what she expected of her. She always insisted on doing what was right and trying to find a way to do it without ruffling the feathers of propriety. "Of course I'm not suggesting that you take up with him again, but I do think that the boy could use a few kind words right now."

"But what would father say?"

"Yes, it would be better if he didn't know, but what harm can there be in a few kind words—just to let the boy know that people still care about his well-being."

"People?"

"Deirdre, don't be so vague. I just think that showing a bit of kindness can make the world of difference at times like these."

Deirdre finished her tea. She had planned to visit the Dandelion one last time, anyway. And if she did bump into Danny, she would just talk with him—just to let him know that she still cared about what happened to him. Nothing more, but she did owe him that much.

*

The last days of the Dandelion Market were surreal. Everyone wanted to be a part of it again, strolling serenely through memories, or strutting defiantly against the future. It was closing down having lost its space to progress, and Deirdre wasn't too unhappy about that.

It was great when it first began, when she used to tag along with Grainne and Johnny, but now it had changed. Punky looking young men now stood behind the stalls with black spiked hair and safety pins everywhere. And the young women wore pinks with blacks and had neon hair. They wore excessive makeup around their eyes and almost looked snide as she passed in her plain summer dress.

Everybody was a little edgy, but "Peace" and "Love" were still for sale. In amongst the muddle of hats and buttons and torn tee-shirts all sneering at the imminent end of the world, with bits of chains and dog collars everywhere.

She heard him before she saw him, singing *Hurricane* in a wide space where people could stop and listen. Despite all that he had been through, he could still put on a good show and his open guitar case was dotted with shiny coins and a few fluttering pound notes.

She wanted to stand to one side where he mightn't notice, but as she moved he looked up and began to smile. He was wearing his dark glasses and looked pale and thin but when he smiled she only saw his soft, sweet lips. It was one of the things she always liked about him—that he had a shy smile and his lips were huge.

He finished his song and nodded to his crowd as he moved his capo and began a very different rhythm that soon became *Teach your Children*–a song that they used to sing together when they were high.

But the standing crowd soon lost interest and drifted off, dropping a few more coins as they went. Soon it was just Danny singing above the passing crowd, to where Deirdre stood, back against a pillar, off to one side, waiting for the right moment.

She wasn't sure why she was so nervous. Part of it could be guilt. Miriam often talked to her about things like this. She said they were opportunities—knocking very loudly. They were the chances to put right past wrongs.

She had always loved the way he played and sang and that, she reminded herself, proved that he still had a good soul, deep inside him. Miriam would agree. She was always telling her to try to look for the positive in everything. She had also told her that if she still felt badly about what had happened that she would get her chance to make amends, for karma's sake if nothing else.

They often spoke openly but when they spoke about the night in the church, Deirdre was surprised by how much Miriam knew until she realized that she and Fr. Reilly often got together.

That didn't strike her as odd. Instead it made her happy to know that Fr. Reilly had a friend he could talk to. He'd always seemed so lost. Sometimes, she wondered if anything else went on between the two of them but she didn't dwell on that; it wasn't her business.

Besides, everyone needed someone like Miriam in their lives. Deirdre never missed an opportunity to bump into her on campus so that they could go for coffee. Miriam was like having Grainne around again, but she had been away since the beginning of summer, off in Rome, of all places, visiting with an old friend from America. Deirdre was excited about seeing her again. She would have so much to talk about. But first she had to take the chance to set things right with Danny.

When he finished his song, he beckoned her closer and knelt to pick the money from his case. When it was empty he slung his guitar off and gently placed it inside.

"How are ya?" he asked her knees, like he was afraid to look her in the face.

"I'm very well, thank you. And how have you been?" She hoped she didn't look flustered as she tried to recall some of the things she had planned to say, but, when he stood up, he just shrugged.

"Can't complain, ya know?"

She had seen him do this so often, wrap himself in that cloak that men wore against their feelings. She used to be able to get him to open up, but that was before. The cloak was probably so much thicker now—like a wall between them.

"How's university going?" he asked after they had stood in silence for a while.

"It's great. Thanks for asking. I can't wait until classes start again."

She had rehearsed so many better things to talk about but now that he was standing right in front of her she couldn't remember any of them. And when she didn't say anything else, he lowered his eyes.

She had to say something.

"Danny. I wanted to tell you how sorry I am about what happened, you know, in the church."

"Oh that." He rose again and looked her straight in the eye. "Don't be worrying about that. It's all water under the bridge now." He looked like he wanted her to reach out to him to touch him but she couldn't just dive back in.

She had changed and so had he. They'd have to spend some time getting to know each other again before they could do anything else.

She was looking for a way of saying all that but couldn't find it as they both stood awkwardly and tried to understand each other's signals.

"I don't suppose you'd ever consider going out for a drink, or coffee, or something?" He stood back a little, to wait for her answer.

After their night in the church, she became like a nun. And not just for the sake of her parents. She had shocked herself. Sometimes she went too far.

Miriam assured her that it was just part of growing up. "You have to push things and sometimes you will break through—for better or for worse."

She wasn't sure which this was but she did owe him something. But he'd have to become the Danny she once knew before she could consider being anything with him again.

"It's okay. You don't have to if you don't want to." He looked embarrassed, like he regretted imposing on her.

He had misunderstood. It wasn't him; it was the whole seedy reality he was mixed up with. Miriam had talked to her about that, too. About all the suffering and pain drugs were causing in the poorer parts of town. She would probably think that it was judgemental to shun Danny for that.

But was it guilt, or pity?

Miriam would probably say that sympathy and pity had as much to do with love as passion and attraction. "Love," she often said, "is our greatest strength and our greatest weakness."

Deirdre knew exactly what she meant. "No Danny, I would like that. I would like to have a chance to sit down and talk with you again."

He looked like she had thrown him a lifeline but she couldn't be sure; he smirked a lot more now than he used to. It was understandable; life had never really played fair with Danny. But she could do something about that now, with Miriam's help. "I am just on my way to meet a friend in Bewley's. Drop in later, if you like."

*

As she walked away, Danny lowered his head. He didn't want to get all blubbery about it but he felt like he might be finally getting one of those second chances that Fr. Reilly was always going on about.

But everything that he had been through only proved that good stuff never happened to him. He didn't deserve somebody like Deirdre in his life. He wasn't, and it made him smirk to realize, good enough.

Inside, he was full of lies and deceit.

He didn't want to be but it was the only way he could handle things. He couldn't tell Anto to go and fuck himself—and all of his heavies, too. And he couldn't tell the cops anything. Sometimes he thought of telling Fr. Reilly but he didn't really trust him. The Church would condemn his soul—after the cops had beaten the life out of him. Then they'd probably lock him in St. Pat's.

Fr. Reilly said God would forgive him, that He was always happy to welcome a sinner back.

But God knew all of his little secrets. He knew when Danny lied—little fibs at first but getting bigger as he grew.

He knew when Danny stole apples from an orchard and chocolate bars when Mrs. Monaghan's head was turned.

She always said that he looked just like his uncle and that made Danny feel worse. Everybody always talked about how "good" Martin was; what an angel he was and how well behaved he was. They never talked about Danny that way. "Poor little Danny," they'd say when they thought he wasn't listening. "God love him." And, as he grew, it sounded less like pity and more like derision.

Other kids picked up on that and shunned him from the start. They picked on him when his mother was in the hospital and his father was off in England. And they picked on him when his grandmother complained to their parents about them. That was why he had gotten involved in the game. He just wanted to be respected and important but it had all gone so terribly wrong and he was back where he began.

He wanted to believe Fr. Reilly when he told him that if he reached out—if he had a little faith—that things would get better. People who wanted to help would show up when they were most needed. "That," he explained, "is how God's miracles work—through others."

Danny couldn't be sure. Part of him had a bit of a tendency to use people, too.

Being involved with the stuff made you like that. You had to see all the angles. You had to see other people's motives, as well as their intentions. It was how he had learned to survive, only he wanted to change all of that now. He wanted to get back to where people tried to be nice to each other because that's how they believed they should be.

Fr. Reilly had talked about that, the day they walked around Rathfarnham Castle. He told him that, no matter how low a person had fallen, there was always hope. And that God celebrated the return of every sinner, no matter how prodigal they had become. All he had to do was want it—and to not do all the stuff that had led him astray.

But all of that just reminded him of his granny and her angels. It was all very well for the priest to talk about God's forgiveness but the people around him would never forget what he had done.

Deirdre's father would probably not be too happy about him seeing Deirdre again. His views on Danny were well known down in the pub where men gathered to gossip—only they called it something else. They all agreed with him that Danny was a bad seed, only not when Jerry was around. Then they turned their outrage on the drug dealers who were turning their own children against them. Some nights, when enough drink was taken, they still threatened that, one of these days, they would grab their pitchforks and burning torches and drive the devil from them.

Jerry always kept Danny up to date with the current mood in the mistaken hope that it might prod him toward reformation. Danny understood that, but the chasm between him and his parents was too wide.

He strummed a few chords as he searched for a song about getting lost. He had never intended for things to end up like this and in his mind, he joined in with Joe Cocker and began to sing *Lord Don't Let Me Be Misunderstood.*

He sang to the roof, so that no one would notice the little tears that formed in the corners of his eyes and didn't see Maguire slink through the shadows.

He had been there all along and couldn't wait to report back to Anto, who had asked him to keep an eye on Danny.

*

Miriam kissed Deirdre on both cheeks before she sat back and took a little package from her purse.

"I saw this in the Campo D'Fiori and thought of you."

It was a hand-carved dolphin, gleaming white in the sheet of dark blue paper.

"I love it. Thank you so much but please, tell me all about Rome."

"What's to tell? It's full of old relics glorifying past glories—and that's just the Vatican."

They both laughed too loud as the people sitting around them stopped whatever they were doing, sipping their tea or nibbling on their sticky buns. Their laughter the only sound in the little circle of silence spreading around them until it was lost in the swirling cacophony that was Bewley's on a Saturday afternoon, when the older ladies, who shopped on Grafton Street, paused for refreshment.

They were still laughing as the waitress left to fetch their order.

Miriam wanted tea. She had had so much coffee in Rome that she was sure she'd never sleep again. "Now tell me how your summer was. Did anything exciting happen while I was away?"

Deirdre wanted to know more about Rome and the mysterious old friend that Miriam had often referred to as her mentor and guide when she was a nun, but instead they talked about Danny and all that happened.

Miriam absorbed the news without comment, nodding to encourage Deirdre, and seemed very interested in how their meeting went.

She was always asking after Deirdre's love life, which felt strange at first until Deirdre realized; *it must be so hard for her. Almost forty and having to start out again.*

"Do you think that you will see him again?"

"That's entirely up to him. I told him that I would like to meet up with him again—just to talk."

"Do you still have feelings for him?"

"I do. I'm just not sure what those feelings are?"

"Well, I hope you are not expecting me to help you sort them out. That kind of love is not my speciality."

They both laughed and sat back and smiled at each other. This was how they discussed things, laughing at each other while exchanging heartfelt love and kindness—and support.

"Is one of those feelings love–as in man and woman kind of love?"

Miriam had hit the nail on the head. It had been so nice before, when they were younger.

Being in love made everything better. She and Danny could talk about the things they hated and the things they loved. They could share the music that defined them, individually and together, and when they touched, hands, fingers, or even when they brushed their hips together, little sparks ran through them, causing them to shiver. Most of all Deirdre liked closing her eyes and kissing him while they wound their bodies together. Their lips, soft against each other, moist and inviting, fanning flames inside them.

Until he would go too far and try to reach up her skirt, or unzip her jeans. That's when the mood was broken and she would unwrap herself and draw a few breaths while she composed herself.

"Go on. Let me," he'd pester, but she had her boundaries. She wasn't ready to share what lay beyond. He'd plead some more, getting coarser as her shyness grew. He was shy, too, and that was how she knew that they weren't ready. But they were older now.

"Okay. I won't ask." Miriam smiled and poured more tea. She raised the little jug and filled her cup to them brim with creamy white milk. "This is the best thing about being back in Ireland. The milk . . . and the cream . . . and the chocolate. I can't get enough chocolate . . . only now I don't have a habit to hide in anymore."

They were still laughing when Danny approached.

"Oh!" Deirdre was surprised that he came—and a little annoyed that he had come so soon. She still had so many things to talk with Miriam about.

"I'm not interrupting anything?"

"Not at all," Miriam offered into the awkward silence. "And I presume that you are the notorious Danny Boyle I have heard so much about. Sit down and have tea with us, or do you prefer coffee?" Miriam signaled to the waitress to bring another cup, and another pot of tea, and more milk.

Deirdre was flustered and knew she was getting a moment to compose herself. "This," she gestured toward Miriam, "is my friend Miriam and this," she almost blushed, "is Danny."

He looked furtive as Deirdre sat back and tried to see him through Miriam's eyes. He fumbled to put his guitar out of the way and then struggled to fold his legs under the table. He'd probably had a few hits on the way over and more than likely regretted them now. Miriam had very penetrating eyes and was probably trying to look all the way inside of him.

"So," he asked and began to smirk a little. "Do the pair of you come here often?"

Deirdre almost groaned but Miriam just laughed. "Yes, this is where Deirdre and I get together to plan for when women take over the world."

"I'm all for that," Danny enthused, looking grateful for Miriam's show of friendship.

"Good! Because when Deirdre and I are finished it will be a much better place. Won't it, Dee?"

Deirdre just smiled as she tried to figure out her part in what was unfolding. She wanted Miriam to meet him but now that it was happening, she wasn't ready. Danny, however, seemed at ease and reached for his cigarettes.

"Would you mind not smoking?" Miriam asked and smiled to get her way.

"No problem," Danny flustered as he put his pack away.

"I don't mean to be such a bitch but I can't tolerate the smell. You should think about quitting, you know? There are so many studies that say how bad they are for you."

"I am thinking about it."

"Good for you and I'm sure Deirdre is delighted to hear that." She turned to Deirdre and waited for her to say something.

"Yes, you should quit . . ." Her voice trailed off as she thought about it. She wanted him to change, only she wanted him to do it without anybody having to ask him.

Miriam seemed to understand and quickly changed the subject. "So, what do you play?" she nodded across at the guitar while keeping her eyes on Danny.

"I just play a few songs, ya know, stuff that makes me feel better about things."

"I'm sure you are very good. Perhaps Deirdre and I can come and hear you, sometime?"

"I don't do many gigs. I usually just play on the streets, ya know?"

Danny seemed shy—the way he used to be. He wasn't smirking anymore, though he did seem to squirm under Miriam's attention. Deirdre was torn. She wanted Miriam to leave so she could talk with Danny and she wanted him to leave so she could talk with Miriam—about him.

"Well I think that's great," Miriam continued. "I knew some of the street musicians in Chicago. A lot of them had been in trouble, too, but music gave them a way out."

Deirdre was shocked that Miriam had been so blunt but Danny didn't seem to mind. He almost seemed relieved. "I've had a bit of trouble, myself," he quickly glanced at both of them. "Only now I'm going to straighten everything out."

"Good for you. That's great. Isn't it, Deirdre?"

Deirdre just nodded as she realized that Miriam was just trying to put them all at ease and that Danny's troubled past should not be a barrier. Danny seemed to appreciate that and almost smiled the way he used to. Deirdre smiled back as Miriam sat and watched them over the rim of her cup.

Danny had to go. The market was closing and he had things to do, packing the stalls away.

Miriam told him how happy she was to finally meet him and promised to look out for him on Henry Street.

Deirdre was happy. More so when Danny turned to her and asked: "Would you like to go the pictures, sometime?"

She was surprised that he had asked in front of Miriam but she was delighted, too. She was getting a chance to show

Miriam that her lessons on Love and Kindness had been taken to heart.

"Sure. When?" She wanted to sort it out now so he wouldn't have to call around to the house. She wasn't ready for that.

"Tuesday night? We could meet under the clock on D'Olier Street, around seven?"

"Sure. Looking forward to it."

Danny seemed happy as he lifted his guitar and nodded again before melting away into the crowd.

"Are you sure about this?" Miriam asked when he was gone.

"I'm only going to go to the pictures with him."

Deirdre lowered her head so Miriam couldn't see her remembering the nights she and Danny had spent in the Classic, before it had closed down.

"I'm just not sure about that boy. He could go either way, yet."

"You are beginning to sound like my parents."

"Oh God, I must be getting old."

CHAPTER 13

"So, Jerry Boyle?"

Jerry looked up from his pint into the jovial, ruddy face of a man who was feared on both sides of the border. He was the man everyone said could help. Nobody could just contact him directly but Jerry knew how these things worked. He had let the right people know that Bart Boyle's grandson needed help. "That's right. We met at my mother's funeral. That was a good old night."

"It was, indeed," the man answered and sat on the stool beside him, nodding to the barman as he did. "Your father and I used to go way back."

Jerry just nodded, too, afraid that anything he might say would betray his ambivalence toward his father.

The ruddy-faced man settled himself and looked at him through the mirror behind the bar.

"And that's why," he muttered softly from the side of his mouth, so that no one else could hear, though they all sat in silence, smoking and staring off at the television behind the bar, there to drown out the silence. "I have come to tell you directly.

"We found out that your son left his fingerprints on the gun that killed the other little fecker."

He waited while the barman placed his pint before him, and thanked him, before continuing.

"But we also heard that it wasn't him that pulled the trigger. That was done by one of our 'guests' from the North and that's the problem. If we touch him, we'll have Belfast and Derry on our case and the last thing we need right now is another split."

He leaned forward for his pint as his mutterings drifted off and settled into the nooks and crannies.

He glanced around the reflected room as he took his first swig. He knew everyone there and they knew who he was. There were a few locals, unaffiliates, who only listened for a bit of gossip for when they met up with their old friends.

The Special Branch was there, too, huddled near the door, on the other side of a few journalists who could be trusted not to report on such minor matters. The ruddy-faced man nodded to them all in turn to let them know that he knew they were there, and they all nodded back to let him know that they would disregard what he and Jerry were talking about—that they knew it was a private matter.

"However," he continued and lowered his mutterings to a burble. "We can, and will, have a few words with this little Flanagan bollocks. But first we need to know that your son is going to keep his nose clean. We can't be seen to be favoring one of these fuckers just because his family has connections. So can you promise me that you can keep that little bollocks of yours out of trouble for a while?"

Jerry knew what he was asking. They wanted to know if they could trust Jerry, too. He had made a show of himself before—right after Talbot Street—the day he and Jacinta had gone to see the solicitor. He had come in drunk and mouthing off about going over to London to blow the place up.

That had attracted far too much attention and the Special Branch resumed their vigilance of the Boyle family until they were called away to deal with other matters. Banks and post offices were being robbed blind and orders had come down from the top. That was to become their number one priority. The country couldn't afford such carry-on. The mood of the country had changed again and the righteous anger that followed Derry was forgotten, but the ruddy-faced man wasn't the type to forget. That would be a big mistake in his line of work.

"I'll do my best," Jerry enthused and raised his glass. "And thanks very much. My father, God rest him, would be smiling down on us."

They ruddy-faced man raised his glass toward the mirror and took another swig before he rose and put his hand on Jerry's shoulder. "We'll do what we can but you can't expect your father's name to keep getting you out of trouble. One of these days we might get tired of it. Remember that, Boyle."

*

"I'm sure he is doing all he can," Martin reassured Jacinta. She had been complaining about how unconcerned Jerry seemed about Danny.

"Well, it'll be a first if he ever does right by his son."

Martin wished she wouldn't talk like that. It was like that with all of his sisters. They always had to be the wronged-party in all of their dealings with the world, including each other.

Since he'd gone to Canada they all turned to him for his impartial judgement—though they never listened to him unless he was agreeing with them. Normally, he didn't mind too much but this was important—this was about Danny. "Don't worry Jass; he'll be able to come back with me, right after the wedding."

He had followed up with Danny to make sure that he'd filled out all the forms and looked after everything on his end. He had to. He had promised Nora Boyle that he would. He had even taken her money and the solicitor was a witness to that. Martin had gone to see him before he left.

**

"Come in, Martin. Come in." Davies had said as he settled back behind his desk and lit his pipe. "So? This is to be our last meeting. I'll miss them." He added through a billowing cloud. "Mrs. Boyle, God rest her, certainly knew who to pick for the job. I wasn't certain," Davies continued like he was just musing, "when she first spoke to me about the matter. But I can see now that she was shrewd until the end."

Martin lowered his head. He didn't want the solicitor to see his eyes. He wasn't really there anymore. He was leaving for Canada and he was counting the days.

"Now, as to the matter of the money for home repairs, I don't see any problem. The money will, of course, be entirely committed for the said work?"

Martin nodded again but kept his head down. It was all so pointless now. Jerry was working and Jacinta was so much better. They didn't need anybody checking on them, anymore.

"Now there is another matter to attend to. Mrs. Boyle left monies that were to be given to you in the event you were going to leave the country."

Martin looked up immediately.

"It has been invested and currently amounts to a little over seven thousand pounds. I have prepared a cheque which I will exchange for your signature on these papers." He watched carefully as Martin leaned forward and signed each one. "Here," he reached forward with the cheque and a sheet of his office stationary, "is your cheque and this is my son's contact information in Toronto. I have written him about you and he will be delighted to greet you, once you arrive. He has some influence with local politics there and might be able to assist with employment, should the need arise. It never hurts to check in with our own when you are away. We are not such a bad lot when we are abroad."

"Thanks," was all that Martin could think to say. The last thing he intended to do when he got to Canada was to "check in" with anybody remotely associated with anything he had been part of back here.

"It's the least we can do for our young emigrants," Davies continued when he realized that Martin was not going to be more effusive. "Okay then. I won't detain you any longer. I am sure you have much to attend to." He rose and shook the young man's hand and walked him to the door.

Outside, Martin looked at the cheque again. He knew exactly what he was going to do with it. He'd give his father half—things weren't going so well for him. Since Jerry got his old job back, right after the election, he'd been able to send some work his father's way but he hadn't been able to put too much aside, yet.

He'd keep quiet about the rest, and, with a bit of luck, he would have money in his pocket when he got to Toronto. He folded the sheet of office stationary into this pocket, too, just in case.

***

Jacinta decided to let it go at that. She could tell he was trying to get her off the phone. They'd been talking for almost an hour—it must be costing him a fortune, phoning during the day, and all. "Well I'd better let you go then."

"Okay, but promise me that you will call the minute you get any news?"

"I will, and thanks for everything, Martin."

When she hung up, she checked the time and hurried to get ready. She had to pick up something for their tea, but first she'd go in and say a few prayers for Danny' safe deliverance. She'd drop by the church and give thanks on her way to the shops. She'd miss him when he was gone. She'd be broken-hearted, again, but it was the only way to get him beyond harm's reach.

Something was different when she knelt before the side altar.

The sun was out and sparkled through the stained-glass windows near the roof and colored light fell all around her. She closed her eyes and pressed her fingers against them so she wouldn't start crying and have everybody thinking she was going mad again.

She was. The whole thing with Danny had made her world a very dark place again but the refracted light glowed right through her like sparkles of colors and little stars.

Nora's face was rising from the colors and for once, she was smiling.

She didn't say anything. She didn't have to; Jacinta understood. Nora Boyle had finally come back to answer her prayers, mother-to-mother, the way things should be—the way the Virgin Mary would have wanted.

"Thank you," Jacinta whispered through her fingers, sounding like a muffled prayer to the other prayers in the shadows. There were a few of them. Mostly older women interceding for their children, and their children's children. The women of Ireland had a special place in the heart of Mary, and suffered in silence just like she had done when the world crucified her only son.

And as Jacinta prayed, she felt herself filling with a peace she had never known before.

*

Fr. Brennan sat alone in Gethsemane, the verdant little patch behind the rectory. He had wanted to grow vegetables there, but, in deference to the suburbs that surrounded the old church, Fr. Reilly had suggested that they grow flowers and shrubs, instead.

Not that either of them did the growing, nor the planting and weeding; that was the jealously guarded domain of Dinny O'Leary, a crusty old man who had outlived every other purpose in his life.

But his garden was a wondrous creation. It was a small space laid out like a maze, inviting those who ventured in to forget the world for a while, even though it could be heard bustling by on the road outside.

Fr. Brennan spent every fine afternoon there. The doctor, who knew things weren't right but went along with Fr. Reilly's assessment of stress, had told him it was that or they'd have the Bishop pack him off to a home—one of the places where they stored old priests until they died.

Fr. Brennan complained of course, but even the Bishop, who was trying to ignore the rumors he'd heard, said that he thought it was very good of Fr. Reilly to take the lion's share of the work, doing all three masses on Sundays, and all of the confessions. "It's the young buck's world now, my old friend. Take this as a chance to enjoy some of the peace and quiet your years have earned you. I'd do it myself if I had someone like Fr. Reilly to depend on."

It was pure nepotism; Fr. Brennan could see that clearly through the haze that surrounded him. Some days, life became so strange to him and on others, he knew who he was—just an old priest whose mind was beginning to slip, like a worn-out old reel.

His one regret was that he hadn't done enough fishing. Two weeks a year was hardly enough. He had dropped a few hints, back in the spring, but he rarely got to see the Bishop face-to-face anymore. It was like he was avoiding him, and, depending on the day, he was either happy or angry about that. Either day, he'd spend it in the garden, unless it rained.

Everyone knew to leave him alone when he was there.

"You can't come in," he heard O'Leary explain to a couple of old women who had tried to intrude.

"Why not?" they asked, like they were offended by the old gardener's air of authority.

"'Cos it's closed for maintenance."

Fr. Brennan smiled as his eyes began to droop. There weren't many like O'Leary anymore. There weren't many like himself, either. *A dying breed,* he laughed to himself as he drifted off in search of more pleasant times when he was young and full of hope. But a shadow fell across him.

"Are you dead yet, Father?"

"I'm not, Dinny. Are you?"

"I don't think so, Father, but I thought I'd better check. I figured that if either of us knew, it would be yourself."

Fr. Brennan opened his eyes as the old gardener sat on the bench beside him and pulled a cigarette butt from behind his ear. Fr. Brennan had never seen him light a new one but had often seen him take a few puffs and stub one out before putting it back behind his ear.

He lit it with a carefully cradled match, protected from the breeze by years of practice. He could keep one going in the teeth of a gale. It was something he had picked up in the trenches when he went with Redmond's men to "fight for small nations."

"No Dinny, they haven't decided what to do with me, yet."

"Who, Father?"

"God and the Devil. Neither is sure if I would fit in with their crowd."

"Yerra, Father, if the likes of you can't get to Heaven, what hope is there for the rest of us?"

"Dinny, a good gardener is always welcome in Heaven."

"Well, in that case," the old man laughed, a wheezy, choking laugh, "you'd better let me go first so that I can put in a good word for you, Father."

They settled into comfortable silence for a while as the autumnal afternoon cooled. It had been the hottest summer they could remember. It had even set records in Boora, Offaly, of all places. But it was passing and the finer days were becoming fewer, and a bit cooler. Fr. Brennan had to wear his coat. Fr. Reilly insisted on it and would come running out like a clucking hen if he didn't.

Fr. Brennan envied Dinny, who always had something to do, tidying up leaves and taking the last of the flowers, but he always had time to sit and talk and took it upon himself to pick the topic.

"I was just thinking about the Brendan Voyage, Father."

The whole country had been abuzz with the story of "the bunch of crackpots that had set out from Dingle in a replica of the famous boat that found America long before the rest of the world even knew about it." They had reached Newfoundland in June, but O'Leary knew that Dan Brennan never got tired of discussing it. "How did they know how to make the boat?"

"It was all explained in the *Navigatio,* Dinny. It told them how to make it and what to expect along the way."

"And did they know for sure that they would make it all the way?"

"They did, to be sure, though they knew that they'd need a few miracles along the way."

Fr. Brennan waited as the old man's laughter turned to coughing and finally subsided.

On the days when his mind was clearer he could prevail on Dinny for the real news of the parish. He had grown tired of Fr. Reilly's evening reports, delivered over dinner, full of happy or sad news, but never any of the gossip—the glumpy, fatty, delicacies of human interactions.

"Dinny, tell me something. What do you make of the news about that young Boyle blaggard?"

Fr. Brennan had never forgiven Danny for his part in the incident with Deirdre, even though Danny had agreed to their terms and done odd jobs around the church for a year or so, as penance. Fr. Brennan had had nothing to do with him, but O'Leary had. The two had spent a lot of time together, looking after the church and the grounds.

"Well, Father, to tell you the truth, he wasn't the worst of them. He's a bit afraid of work but what can you expect these days?"

"True for you, Dinny, but do you think there might be any truth in what's going around?"

"I doubt it, Father. Since when did the people of this parish ever have a kind word to say for each other? Present company excluded, or course."

"When you're right, you're right," Fr. Brennan laughed and slapped his palm against his thigh. "You are one of the last true wonders of the world—an honest man."

The old gardener was flushed by the praise and when he rose, almost stood to attention. "Well, Father, I'll get back to it and leave you to get on with your meditations."

"You're a good man, Dinny O'Leary."

"And the same to you, Father."

Fr. Brennan settled back into his repose but his hooded eyes were watching Fr. Reilly. He might be able to pull the wool over his uncle's eyes, but Fr. Brennan could see. His curate was always saying how busy he was but always had lots of time for the younger ladies of the parish.

It could have been worse, but Fr. Brennan couldn't help but feel that there was a bit too much "Mary Magdalening" going on. First it was that hussy who used to be a nun, God bless the mark, and now it was that young trollop who had desecrated the altar and had got away scot-free. The whole world was going mad around him.

*

Outside, Fr. Reilly lingered by the door so he could keep an eye on Fr. Brennan who had just suffered another one of his episodes, forgetting himself and wandering around with no clothes on. No one else had noticed it yet but Fr. Reilly knew it was only a matter of time. He would have to let the Bishop know, one of these days. Only he didn't want to end the old man's career. He was due to retire in January. Surely he could keep it hidden until then?

He masked his smile as Deirdre approached. He knew she would be along one of these days—Miriam had given him the heads-up.

"So, did you get to see Miriam since she got back? She mentioned that she was going to meet up with you." He wanted Deirdre to know that he knew so they could talk to each other on the up-and-up and not through veils.

He always got flustered with women when they did that. He had seen it in the films, how women could say one thing but really mean something totally different and, if the poor man misinterpreted, they reserved the right to be shocked and outraged. Speaking to women was the toughest part of his job, especially when they were young and talking about matters of the heart. At least in the confessional he could shield himself with the grill, but, face-to-face, it was hard.

"I did indeed," Deirdre looked demure, like she might be trying to tell him that she knew about him and Miriam.

"And was Miriam well?" He shouldn't have said her name again but he couldn't help it. It felt so nice to be able to talk with somebody about her.

He knew all about their meeting; Miriam had updated him on the phone. She had called him, but it was appropriate on account of the fact that they were trying to help Danny, and besides, Fr. Brennan had taken his medicine and was sound asleep.

**

"I'm not sure," he had ventured, unsure if he had understood. He was always having to remind Miriam that she was back in Ireland now and not off in America where you could say or do anything—where she had got herself into so much trouble. "Not to mention what might happen if her father found out. We are a bit more shy about scandals over here."

"Don't try pulling the priest act with me, Patrick. I've seen it all before. Let's just think about what's best for these two young people. This is just as much about Deirdre, you know?"

"How so?"

"Come on, even a priest must able to tell that they are in love."

Her tone changed and sounded more wistful. He was never really sure what she meant by that but he knew she was trying to tell him something that she couldn't say over the phone. There was nothing for it but that he'd be better off talking with her face-to-face. It was the only way he could be sure. And besides, he hadn't seen her since before she left for Rome.

"You know, Miriam. We shouldn't be talking like this over the phone. If someone was to overhear they might get the wrong impression."

He had heard Fr. Brennan get out of bed and he'd be down any minute—and probably naked, too. "I'll be downtown on Saturday afternoon and we could meet up and have a proper chat."

***

"And tell me," he asked Deirdre, after he had savored every detail of Miriam. "Do you have any news about Danny?"

"That's the reason I've come to see you. I bumped into him the other day and we ended up going for coffee. I can't be sure, Father, but I think he is really trying to change his ways."

Fr. Reilly didn't look directly at her. He stood to one side. He thought about resting his foot on the low part of the wall like Chuck O'Malley would have done, but it might be inappropriate, standing like a bluebeard.

"I'm of the same mind, Deirdre, and I think Danny will need all of our help."

Danny had come to see him the day after he had gone to see the police, after he had some time alone to think about what he should do.

He had started to come back to confession, too, his bless-me-Father evoking older memories.

Until he told him about the night Scully died and how he had been tricked into leaving his fingers on the gun. He knew he had sinned but he was sorry now and wanted to ask for God's forgiveness.

Fr. Reilly couldn't deny him that. Nor could he ever divulge what had been revealed.

"I suppose that all we can do is trust in the power of love."

He wasn't sure but he thought Deirdre blushed before she smiled and thanked him. She told him that she did and excused herself—she had a few errands to do for her mother.

He stood by the gate and watched her walk away. She reminded him of Miriam. She walked so purposefully, too. Though sometimes high-heels made her teeter a little.

Sometimes, with Miriam, he almost hoped she might stumble a bit so he could reach out and steady her.

*

"Are you well, Father?"

Jacinta had just come out of the church and had probably seen him watching Deirdre walk away. He'd have to be far more careful than that and not let his mind wander. They had enough of that with Fr. Brennan.

"Tell me, Father," she asked after he had inquired after her, her husband, and Danny. And she had assured him that they were all as well as could be expected—given the circumstances. "Do you think that there could still be real miracles in the world?"

"I do indeed, Mrs. Boyle." He was delighted that she wanted to talk about something cheery. He never knew how to deal with her when she was depressed—her having been in the hospital for all those years. He was always afraid he might say something that might send her back there.

Sometimes, when trying to deal with the day-to-day, he doubted his vocation but at least he knew how to talk about miracles. "We are surrounded by little miracles every day, only we never notice. We usually have our heads down, praying for big ones."

He waited to see if he had said the right thing, and, after she had wrinkled her brow for a moment, she smiled like he hadn't seen her do before.

"Good, because I think one is after happening to me. I think Nora appeared to me, by the little altar. Not that I'm surprised, mind you, I've felt her there a number of times and today she finally appeared to me."

Fr. Reilly was unsure. If someone else had said it to him he would have been sure that they were speaking symbolically. Not that he doubted Heaven and those saints who could come back to visit a bit of good on those who prayed to them. He just wasn't sure if Nora Boyle was such.

And, if Jacinta was to go around telling people, he would have to let the Bishop know and he could imagine what he might say: *Apparitions of Nora Boyle by the side altar. Should we have RTE over to cover it for the six o'clock news?* The Bishop didn't have time for miracles, he was far too busy trying to carry out God's will.

"And did you find comfort in that?" He smiled as kindly as he could.

"Of course I did, Father. She told me that Danny would be kept safe. She came back from Heaven just to tell me that."

She looked content in that, so Fr. Reilly let it pass. "But I am sure she still wants us all to do whatever we can to help him."

"I realize that, Father. I'm not mad, you know."

"It's not that, Mrs. Boyle, it's that God works His miracles through us and we all have our part to play."

"Sure; isn't that what Nora just told me."

There was no point. Jacinta must have cracked again and he couldn't blame her. The whole thing with Danny must have been too much for her but at least she seemed happy. "Will you tell Danny? It might do him good to know that we are all pulling for him."

"Of course I'll tell him. I tell him how I was able to get his Granny to help, not like his father. He hasn't even raised a finger to help."

He tried to assure her that Jerry was probably doing all that he could, but he wasn't convincing. He rarely saw Jerry anymore; he hadn't been to Mass in years. He felt bad about that. Jerry was lost and there was nothing poor Patrick could do about that, but there was still time for Danny.

"And Mrs. Boyle, would you ever tell Danny that I'll say a Mass for him this Sunday. Only I won't announce it so as not to have people talking."

Jacinta was grateful for that and hurried off because the shops would be closing and her without anything for their tea.

*

As everyone else settled down for the night, feeling that it had been a good day, Danny snuck out his bedroom window. He had to meet Anto at midnight and he was dreading it. Anto had told him that he had a favor to ask and then they'd be even. They were to meet up on Willbrook Road. It was darker up that way and the Watchers wouldn't be about. Anto wasn't afraid of them; he just wanted to have a little chat in peace.

"How are ya tonight, Boyle?" the Driller asked, surprising Danny as he climbed into the back seat. He had never spoken to him before. They were taking the road to the mountains but Danny had nothing to fear. He had kept his mouth shut just like he promised.

Except with the priest, but he wouldn't be able to tell anybody about it.

He still wasn't sure why he had made his confession. A part of him joked about trying to get on God's good side, if He had one, but another part of him was really contrite. That part was the one that wanted to start over and get his life on track again, the way everyone wanted him to be—the way Deirdre would want him. He hadn't really given a shite before, but now it was different.

"I hear that you and your girlfriend are getting back together," Anto smiled over his shoulder.

Danny wasn't surprised. He knew that nothing happened that Anto didn't get to hear about. There were plenty of little snivellers around who reported to him in the hope of currying favor.

"All kissed and made up, Boyle?" the Driller joined in.

"Ah sure, you know yourselves, lads. Am I right?"

They all agreed and relaxed as the Driller changed to a lower gear to climb the hills.

"So what's the crack, tonight?" Danny asked when the silence became ominous and memories of Scully flitted by in the darkness.

"Not a lot. I just had something to do up this way and I thought we could have a little chat."

As the lights of an oncoming car flashed like lightening, Anto turned instinctively and then grinned at Danny: "We are going to need you to go over to London and pick up a few things for us.

"Don't look so shocked. It's no big deal. We'll send you over to watch a football match and the guy who'll sit beside you will leave a few packages. Just stuff them inside your clothes and no one will notice. Nobody pays attention to the football crowd. It's totally safe."

Danny knew the score. He had gone over to see Liverpool a few times and brought packages back. No one ever bothered him. The trick was to wear the team scarf and just hope there weren't any United fans around.

When they got to the mountains the Driller pulled over, not far from where Scully got killed. They all got out and huddled around the boot as the wet winds whirled. Inside, between the spare tire and the repair kit, lay the big black and brown dog. Its eyes were wide open and its red tongue hung from the side of its mouth. It had two holes in the top of its head and dark streaks of red ran from them.

"I had to," Anto explained. "I caught the fucker chewing on a package. We can't have that. We have to have trust—and loyalty. You'd think that a dog would know that."

"C'mon," the Driller beckoned to Danny to take hold of the dog's legs and swing it out. "Danny and I will carry it up behind the trees and dig a hole."

"Thanks," Anto sniffled and Danny was sure that he saw a flash of remorse.

They kept their silences all the way back to Rathfarnham. Anto smoked while the Driller hummed softly to himself.

"By the way," he finally said when they came to a stop outside the Yellow House. He didn't turn around but spoke to Danny through the rearview mirror. "Someone was asking after the gun."

"Not that you need to worry," Anto joined in, still staring at the windshield. "Nobody's going to find it."

Danny wasn't sure, but it felt like they weren't really talking to him—that they were sending messages to each other. It wouldn't matter. He would just do this last thing and then he'd be done with them.

CHAPTER 14

Danny laid out his guitar case and sprinkled it with a few coins—seed money to encourage those who passed to give. He raised his guitar to his chest and ducked his head beneath the strap just like the way priests did with their stoles. He turned into the doorway behind him and tried to tune to the hustle and bustle around him as he took a few quick hits. It was how he got ready for his shows.

Only this time he felt different. This time he wasn't feeling so sarcastic about everything. In fact he was starting to feel better about how things were going to work out. He stood up straight and turned to face the passing crowds.

He took a moment and tried to sense their mood and how they would react. And, as he strummed a few defiant chords to announce that his show was starting, he thought he felt a little flutter inside. He didn't want to go to London, and it wasn't just because he might get caught. For the first time since he was a kid he was starting to think about the right and wrong of things.

It started on the bus, after he had a few hits around the corner from the bus stop where nobody could see him. He couldn't hide from it anymore and just pretend that he was still a teenager doing the stuff because he was bored. It had become a full time job—buying it and selling it—and it had taken over his whole fucking life. Only he had been far too stoned to notice.

What's worse, he was even working with the pushers and the dealers. He had wandered into Hell without even noticing it. Granny had always said that it would be like having his whole body thrown into a fire but she was wrong. It was more like he had fallen in a vat of shit and was slowly sinking.

He couldn't get out on his own. He'd need a fucking miracle, or something.

Fr. Reilly said that they still happened—small miracles that changed lives.

Even Deirdre said that Miriam talked about stuff like that happening all the time.

Deirdre had taken him for coffee after the pictures and Danny didn't get high the whole time. He didn't need to—when he was with her everything was different. It was almost like the way it was in the songs he sang.

And he wouldn't sing wistfully anymore. From now on he would sing about the bit of hope Deirdre had given him. She knew what he was like—better than anybody—and she was still willing to give him another chance. He hadn't had that since . . . his granny got sick.

It wasn't just Deirdre but her friend Miriam, too. She had seen right through him and yet she encouraged Deirdre to help him.

Fr. Reilly was always saying things to him, too. Stuff about doing what was right just because it was the right thing to do—the way Christ would have wanted. He had convinced Danny that what was happening to him was normal for people in his situation. He was, after all, a child of a "not-ideal" family and had to come to terms with that. And, the whole country had to come to terms with everything that happened in the North—and all the stuff that was happening in the South, too. Fr. Reilly suggested that he start looking at everything from another perspective, that instead of thinking about himself as a sinner, he might consider that he was also a victim.

Even just thinking about it as a "situation" made Danny feel better and Fr. Reilly also told him that he had been given absolution for all that had happened before.

Danny wasn't sure how he felt about that part, but he liked when everyone said that they could see that he was really trying to change. They even started saying that he was just an "unfortunate young fella."

His mother said that even his aunts were saying that about him, but, knowing them, they were probably also saying all the other stuff that Fr. Reilly told him he had to learn to ignore.

It was hard because he used to say the same things about himself—all the shite about it being all his fault. A lot of it was, but he had to accept that and put it aside so it wouldn't get in his way further down the road.

He thought about having another hit but he didn't want to risk it in case the Garda-fucking-Síochána wandered by. Besides, he had promised he would give it up—and he would, right after he got back from London.

He thought about starting with *Coming into Los Angeles,* the song he sang when he was trying to have a laugh with himself. Instead, he began to sing *Leaving on a Jet Plane* and all the passing women responded and left a good scattering of coins in his case. Even the sun poked out for a moment. When he was a kid he liked to think of it as God smiling down on him but then when it rained? What was he supposed to think then?

"That's the problem with the way the Church tries to teach: they made you think of normal stuff as bad." Fr. Reilly had told him. He also admitted to Danny that he often wished that people could just talk to God face-to-face so that they could really understand what was being said on His behalf. But he was still on at Danny about going to the Guards and telling them what had really happened.

He couldn't do that. If he did he'd have to spend the rest of his life hiding in shitholes until they finally tracked him down. No matter what the cops and the priest told him, he knew he could never be free of them. Good stuff like that didn't happen in his life.

Except Deirdre, but he'd fucked that up, too.

He was getting a second chance, though, he couldn`t deny that, even though he knew better than to get excited and start hoping. He used to make that mistake when he was a kid. It wasn`t really anybody`s fault; he knew that now. He was just a fuck-up, just like his father. And his mother? He hated thinking badly about her, but really . . . he had been fucked from the start.

He had to go to London and it wasn't going to be so easy this time. Since the thing with Scully he had lost his nerve. Watching him die in his own piss brought it all home—the stakes were so much higher now but he had to do it one last time. He didn't have a choice. They had him by the balls and would probably never let him go, no matter what Anto said.

*

"I think he's really trying to sort his life out."

Fr. Reilly had spent the last few days convincing himself, but he couldn't help but wonder why Danny Boyle had confessed what he did? And what was he supposed to do with what he'd heard? God's plan in this wasn't clear to him. He should tell the police but he couldn't. All he could do was show Danny God's compassion and hope that he would be moved to do the right thing.

"I'm not sure about that."

He looked up, into Miriam's eyes. They were sitting in a small booth near the back, closer than they had been before and he fought the urge to reach across and touch her fingers, just for some human comfort. He envied others that could do that. Hug each other, kiss each other's cheeks, but all of that was off limits to him. A priest had to be aloof so he could pass on God's word free of the slants of emotions.

But sometimes he got distracted and thought about it. That was when he forced himself to remember that they were both just very concerned for their protégé. She was Deirdre's mentor while he was stuck with Danny. Sometimes, he thought he had been given the thin end of the stick, but other times he reminded himself that he should be honored to be chosen as God's vessel in all of this.

It also allowed him to see Miriam above board and to share his feelings, even if they were about other people.

"I just think that Deirdre should go on with her life right now and not wait around."

They were at opposite sides of the table but they were leaning toward each other so they could keep their conversation private in the swirling turmoil that was Bewley's on a Saturday afternoon. It was the only time in the week when he could leave Fr. Brennan on his own. Dinny O'Leary had agreed to keep an eye on him and not let the old man wander away. O'Leary knew what was going on but never let on that he did and Fr. Reilly was grateful for that.

"You might be right but I think Danny would be crushed if she did."

"But you can't expect her to?"

"No. No, you're right there. It's just that I think it might be the only thing that is keeping Danny going these days."

"She'll have to go on with her own life. She will have her degree in two years and I hope she goes on and does her master's—and maybe a PhD."

He knew she didn't dislike Danny. In fact she often said that she wanted to go along with Deirdre and Patrick in believing that his life could be turned around. But she also said that she had seen it far too often. Families and friends torn apart by drugs and all the scourges that came with them.

But she didn't know the whole story and he did not feel it was his place to tell her: Danny had been doomed from the start. He didn't like thinking badly about Jerry and Jacinta, and Nora, but between the lot of them, they had made a right mess of things.

He believed in Danny because his God demanded it. He believed that Danny was in earnest and was doing everything he could to turn his life around and what he needed now was for people to believe in him, and forgive him his past. *I say unto you, that likewise joy shall be in heaven over one sinner that repenteth, more than over ninety and nine just persons, which need no repentance.*

"I don't think that Danny would ever get in her way."

"Perhaps. But he might get in his own way and that would be just as bad."

*

On the bus ride home, Patrick puzzled over all that was said so he would know how to act the next time they met.

But he had to put it aside when he got there, when he had to become the curate of an old man who had lost his mind. He had been so busy with Danny that he hadn't done what he had decided: he hadn't talked with the Bishop yet. He couldn't while they were still dealing with Danny. He knew his uncle had enough to do, and that he felt guilty, like he owed the Boyle family something.

Fr. Reilly felt guilty, too. He hadn't been a good enough priest to them.

They hadn't talked too much about dealing with families like the Boyles during his days at the seminary. And when they did, they were told that they wouldn't have to face it alone, that the Power of God would flow through them—that they'd have Him to guide them all the way.

But Fr. Reilly felt rudderless and useless. He really had no idea what the Boyles must be going through.

Sometimes, he tried to imagine what he would do if he was Jerry but he kept getting distracted when Jacinta turned into Miriam. It was temptation whispering in his ear. It was like when the serpent spoke to Jesus in the middle of the desert, when he was showing them the example of self-sacrifice.

Only evil wouldn't use Miriam; she was more like an angel. An angel that tended to the fluttering flame of his convictions as a priest. An angel who told him, in the cryptic manner of women, that he was being tested. Just like before, when Danny was sent to them after the incident in the church.

He never had much time with him, though; Fr. Brennan saw to that. It was like he didn't want Fr. Reilly and Danny to ever be alone, preferring instead that he spend his time with O'Leary and learn about hard work. Fr. Brennan said it was better for Danny's soul—and the parish ledger.

But when they did have time, Fr. Reilly had asked what on earth made Danny and Deirdre do what they did? He was trying to understand it from a sociological point of view. Why in the church, naked and dancing like pagans? Why there? Was it a symbolic statement?

He always wanted to be the type of priest that young people could feel comfortable talking to. He wouldn't be judgemental like Fr. Brennan and his uncle. He wanted to be more like St. Francis—only with troubled young people whom he'd shelter and nourish until they were healed enough to go out and face the world again.

But Danny wouldn't tell him and just shrugged, acting like he knew the world was full of lies and that he didn't want to be a part of it again after all the lies that he was told as a child, and all—that he was tired of just being set up for disappointment.

Fr. Reilly had tried to tell him about the real truth of Love, but Danny didn't want to know. Why would he? He had never experienced any love from anybody other than Deirdre and she had let him down, too.

If only he could find a way to get her to show a little bit of faith in Danny now—it could make all the difference.

*

"Good night, Father. Himself is sound asleep above."

Dinny O'Leary was standing in the open doorway. He didn't smoke in the house since the night Fr. Brennan thought the house was on fire and set off the fire extinguisher.

"Ah, Dinny. Are you well?"

"Father, after all I have been through, just being alive is well enough for me."

"You have great faith, Dinny."

Dinny looked at his face for a moment and could probably see the grey pall of doubt. "You know, Father, when I was in the trenches, we all believed in God. Even the other side; they believed in the same God as us but we went on killing each other until they told us to stop.

"And every night, when the fighting died down, every last man made some type of a deal with God—that they would never doubt him again if they were spared.

"And then when they all came home they forgot about it all, even their promises. Not all of them, mind you, but enough of them."

"And you kept yours?"

"Of course I did. God kept his promise and I must, too."

*

The Driller sat smoking and avoiding his reflection in the mirror behind the bar. He didn't like the look of himself anymore. He had become fidgety and nervous, always looking around like at any moment somebody might step forward and end him. He was supposed to be lying low but instead he had been doing the opposite.

He knew they'd hear about it and he knew that he'd get hauled in one day, but he also knew they couldn't touch him.

He was sending most of the money back to Derry and they needed him for now. The Dublin crowd might threaten to tell the Derry crowd where the money had come from, but he could rat on them, too. It was all fine and fucking dandy for the old timers to go on about all the support they used to get from friendly houses. These days they were few and far between. And there was never enough money going around. Robbing banks had become much harder—they had called the fucking army out. They hadn't called them out when the Paras were running wild in the Bogside but they called them out to protect their money. Fuck them all. That's why guys like him were freelancing right in front of everybody.

As long as he sent the money back, they didn't care where it came from.

The cops were no better, here nor there. They were just there to make the people feel secure, and, if you were smart and kept a low profile, they left you alone.

But he hadn't and now someone from the Dublin Command had asked to see him. He got the message just before they buried Anto's dog. Only they didn't tell him who it was. They only told him the pub and the time and the day. He'd wait there to be contacted.

He'd been waiting for over an hour but he knew why. They were sending him a message—even before they got there. So he watched the crowd through the mirror. He hadn't been there before and he had no idea who was who. The four guys in corner where probably Special Branch but they didn't seem interested in him. They were busy pretending not to be watching the two guys in the corner. The Driller had heard their accents and knew they were from Belfast and were on their way to London. It didn't really concern any of them—unless they came back.

"So?" A ruddy-faced man asked from just behind him. The Driller hadn't even heard him come in, but he had heard about him and he had heard that he should be afraid of him.

"How's yourself? Can I get you something?"

The older man might have smiled at him, though it could have been a sneer, too.

"I'll stay on my own, if you don't mind?"

"Sure. I was only going to have one more myself."

"How many have you had?"

"Ah sure, you know yourself?"

"I don't and that's why I'm asking. I want to make sure that what I say gets through that thick fucking skull of yours." He was definitely not smiling now. "Understand?"

The Driller straightened his shoulders and lowered his eyes as the ruddy-faced man continued.

"When we agreed to have you down here we were under the impression that you knew how things worked. So it came as a bit of a surprise to hear your name associated with the murder of some local scum."

"I was just doing it as a nickser."

"If you need money you come to us. We can't have scuts like you coming down here and helping yourselves. We decide what goes on down here. Understand?"

"I'm sorry. I didn't mean anything. I was just trying not to be a burden. You know?"

*

The ruddy-faced man didn't answer. He raised his pint and nodded to everyone in the mirror. Sometimes, when he was in on his own, when he was off duty, he'd sit and stare into it. Sometimes, after he had had a few, he could almost see the faces of those who had been the "hard men" when he was younger, as young as the Driller. Recently, he had seen Bart Boyle's face in there a few times.

Bart had been the one who had gotten him out of a few jams when he was young and had done something stupid. "It's all very well," Bart would say, "joining up to fight the British but you have to learn along the way. Mistakes make martyrs and we've had enough of those. What we need now are men who know how to live to fight another day."

"Well, I suppose that no real harm was done but we have the fucking Garda Síochána nosing around, wanting to know about that Scully shooting, and I need to give them somebody.

"Not you," he reached forward to calm the young man's stiffening arm. "We'll give them that other little fucker. We can pin everything on him."

"Well in that case," the Driller gushed as he relaxed. "You should know that he has someone set up to take the fall for him."

"We aren't going to allow that to happen. We want this Flanagan and we'll get him one way or the other." He paused to let the Driller digest what he was saying. "But it would be better if we gave him to the Garda in one piece, better for everybody, you know?"

*

The Driller thought about it. It was no skin off his nose what they did with Anto—he'd never really liked him. Only he'd wait until after Danny brought the stuff back from London.

He could even get someone to intercept him on the way back. He'd sell the stuff and have enough to go to America and get lost in New York or Boston. There'd be people there who'd look out for him—those that still respected the ones that did their part for Ireland.

"I'll be more than happy to do whatever needs to be done," he offered his hand to the ruddy-faced man. They had a deal, for what it was worth but at least it would get the Dublin crowd off his back.

"That's the problem with all you'se young fuckers. You'd kill your own mothers. Now fuck off until you hear from me."

*

The ruddy-faced man waited until he had gone before raising his pint toward the part of the mirror where he had last seen Bart. It was the least he could do for him, but he hoped that his grandson understood that it was just this one time. They had a war to finish and couldn't afford to be getting sidetracked for anyone.

*

Jacinta met Gina at the corner of Henry Street. They were going to spend the rest of the morning in Arnott's. They had seen all the stuff they wanted in Grafton Street but it was much cheaper on the Northside. Gina didn't have a lot of money and Jacinta hadn't told her yet; she'd been able to put away nearly five hundred pounds. It wasn't hard now that Jerry was earning again but she didn't let him know about it. There was no point in upsetting him.

If felt so good to be able to make somebody happy. She couldn't do that with Danny, no matter how hard she tried. He smiled and acted like he was coming around but she could tell; his eyes gave him away. She could see he was terrified and looked out at the world the way he did when he was young and came to the hospital, but Nora told her not to worry about it anymore. She said that as long as Jacinta tried, that's all that really mattered. Nora also suggested that she try to be more loving with everyone.

And her sisters expected it of her, being the one who was doing so well, and all. Linda and Brenda would throw in what they could but it wouldn't be much. They were just getting by as it was.

"This is for the bride," she laughed and handed Gina the envelope that she had kept secret between the pages of Nora's Bible, where no one would look for it. She had confessed to her about it, and about the silverware and the china, but Nora said it was all right. She said that it was better they were put to some use rather than gathering dust in the corner. God knows, she had no use for them anymore.

"There must be a fortune in here." Gina's eyes sparkled like when she was a child. She was the youngest, not counting Martin.

"Well, we have to have you looking your best."

After Jacinta, Gina was the prettiest, but Jacinta didn't mind anymore and was determined to make sure that her sister's day was every bit as special as her own.

She had to hand it to Nora Boyle; she had put on a great show, even if it was just for the sake of appearances. She had spared no expense; like Jacinta was her own daughter. Jacinta could see that now.

She never told Jerry, but sometimes, since that day in the church, Nora used to open up to her and sometimes it almost felt like she was trying to explain herself. "We thought differently in those days," was something she managed to work into almost every conversation, even when Jacinta talked about Danny and what they should do about him. "We did what we thought was best. Only now that everything has changed, our best doesn't seem to have been good enough." She almost sounded like she was looking to Jacinta for some type of reassurance but that was ridiculous. Nora Boyle was reaching down from Heaven to help, them unless . . . Jacinta didn't want to think about that because if Nora didn't get in, what hope was there for the rest of them? Jacinta almost shivered at the thought but recovered before her sister noticed. "So have you picked your bridesmaids yet?"

Jacinta was far too old to be bothered by such things but she still wanted to know.

"I'm just having one. Bernie, from work, you know?"

"Have you told Linda and Brenda?"

"I did, and they're still not speaking to me."

"You know, if you wanted to have more than one, I could get Jerry to fork in a few more quid."

"But you're already paying for my dress. I can't let you do that." Gina shook her head but her eyes lit up. "Do you really think that you could get Jerry to do that?"

"It's not a big deal. He's making good money again and we're more than willing to help. And I could talk to Linda about helping out. There's no point in asking Brenda. She'll agree but she'll never get around to actually coming up with any money."

"Jass! Do you really think I can?"

"You can have anything in the world with that pretty face. Have you picked out your lingerie yet?"

"I was going to look at dresses first."

"You should start with the most important thing. He's not going to remember you in your wedding dress but he'll always remember what you wore the first time."

"Jass!"

"I'm only telling you what I wish I knew when I got married."

"Is that what it was like with you and Jerry? Did you go somewhere nice and romantic?"

"Not quite, but never mind that now; how would I look in this?" She held a frilly set against her and made a few of the moves that she knew men liked.

"Stop it, Jass."

"Or this."

"Stop it, Jass. You're embarrassing me."

Gina was probably thinking that she was too old to be considered a woman anymore so Jacinta put the frillies away and composed herself again as Gina gushed to fill the chasm that had opened between them.

"I'm sorry for saying that. I didn't mean anything by it; it's just that I'm a bit nervous about it all."

"About the wedding night?"

"No, we've already done that. What makes me nervous is thinking if I'm going to be happy with him. I mean I love him, and all, but I hardly know him."

"What's happened?"

"Well, he was all talk about the big fancy wedding that we were going to have, and then, when I asked him if his side might want to help out, do you know what he tells me? He tells me that they want to but his father's business is doing badly, right now, so they can't.

"And then when I asked him how we were going to manage after, you know what he said? He said: 'Don't worry, we always have a few more irons in the fire.' I should have told him to take one of them out and stick it up his arse." Gina broke down and started to cry in the middle of the frillies and the curiosity of the passing shoppers.

"I wouldn't worry about any of that right now," Jacinta offered a tissue and steered her sister toward the change rooms. "Lots of people say stupid things before they get married. Especially men. But you still want to get married, don't you?"

Gina nodded and wiped at her nose.

"See! That just proves that, deep down, you're still in love with him."

"I guess so. But I can't help but worry what he'll be like . . . after. I mean, what if he doesn't want to get married now but doesn't know how to tell me? What if he was just stringing me along?"

"They all do that, Gina. They only start telling you the truth when they know you've heard all their lies. But it's not as bad as it sounds. We're always thinking the worst of them anyway, so it all balances out. Don't you see?"

Gina's face was a mess so Jacinta changed course for the toilets, which just had to be on the other side of the shop and they had to walk past all the staring and nudging of the other women out seeking bargains and a bit of news for when they got together with their friends.

"Don't worry about things like that. It never works out the way you think." She steered her sister through the door and stood her in front of the mirror. "Now let's clean up that pretty face of yours and don't be worrying anymore; everything is going to work out the way it's supposed to and if you stop trying to interfere, you'll stop hurting yourself."

"Ah, Jass! That's so nice of you."

They hugged and held on to each other until they were steady again.

"Jass? When did you get to be so smart about everything?"

"When I was locked up in the hospital. I used to think about everything until it drove me mad. Now I just deal with what's in front of me, and while I'm still mad, I'm much happier about it. No one else can make you happy, Gina. You have to do that for yourself."

"Jacinta?" Gina was almost smiling again. "Do you really think that Jerry could help with four bridesmaids?"

"Why? Who are you thinking of asking now?"

"You, silly."

Jacinta was delighted even though she would never do it. "I'm too old to be a bridesmaid, but thanks for asking."

Gina looked gorgeous in the fifth dress she tried on. It was a little more expensive but Jacinta insisted that they take it. She had a plan for paying for it, too. Nora had said that it was okay.

She had gotten Martin involved again. They had asked the solicitor for money to remodel the kitchen. They would get it done all right; Jerry could get one of the contractors from work to do it, cheap. They might even get it for free if Jerry could dangle a few little government contracts at them. They'd already had a bit of work done on the garden—a few stones laid out like a patio until the contractor had time to come back and finish.

"This is the one, Jass. Isn't it?"

"You look like an angel in it."

"Do you really think so?"

"Well, you would if you smiled more and meant it. You know, one of the other things I learned in the hospital is how little we know about life, no matter what all the experts try to tell us. I think it would be better if we spent our time learning to enjoy it instead of spending all of our time worrying about where we were going after we're dead."

She hadn't really heard that in the hospital—Nora had told her. She hadn't meant to say it aloud. It was something Nora had said when Jacinta asked her if she was in Heaven. She was very terse on the subject and Jacinta could only assume the worst. Not Hell, of course. Nora Boyle was probably in Purgatory—which was just as bad for an old woman who had been so generous in her dealings with the Church. It didn't seem fair.

"Thanks for telling me all that, Jass, but do you know what I really want to do? I want you to help me pick out the right pair of shoes."

"And what makes you think that I'd know?"

"Because I want to look as good as you did. Do you know that Ma used to look at your wedding photo every night? She always said that you were the prettiest bride of all time."

CHAPTER 15

Bart Boyle had never really liked churches and only went there for Mass and funerals and the constant stream of weddings of children of minor dignitaries, all only wanting to be seen and photographed with the elder statesman he had become.

But now that he was there, he had to admit that it was peaceful, except for a few whisperings and the occasional fluttering of sputtering candles, and the sway of little crosses at the end of rosary beads coiled around old, white fingers.

It was where the aged could linger on either side of death. Empty and serene but for the mutterings of hope and despair from the shadowy sinners who toured the stations of the cross, kneeling to dwell on every moment of the suffering that was never really understood. He used to smile at that. "Everyone goes in a sinner and comes out a freshly minted saint," he often confided to his closest friends when they were well-warmed with whiskey. When they put aside all caution and spoke openly and honestly to each other in insinuations and knowing nods and winks that the rest of the world would never understand.

Bart Boyle had never really been a believer, but, try as he might, he could never forget the chill of the water from the baptismal font. Wakening him from wherever he was before. He couldn't remember it, but, when he was alive, he spent a lot of time, subconsciously of course, looking for it.

He had made his Holy Communion and his Confirmation, and for a while, considered the priesthood. There wasn't much else to do back then. He could go to America or he could go to hell. His family's farm had been divided so often that there was hardly enough land left to bury a man, let alone raise cattle or potatoes.

His mother prayed that he'd take the collar but when the fighting broke out, and the Black and Tans came by with their guns and their torches, what else was he supposed to do?

The Church blessed the cause in those days, but afterwards, he found little comfort in that and over time, stopped praying at all. How could he when every time he tried to close his eyes to pray, dead men's faces loomed up out of the dark?

He had never been honest with Nora about that and told her what she wanted to hear—about him going to confession and getting absolution. He never had been able to forgive himself. Not the killing part—he had to do that—but he was never comfortable lying to Nora about it.

He had done his penance, though. Haunting the Garden of Remembrance as all of his old friends moved on while he had to stay. Listening to the voices outside of the wall talking about everything but what Bart and his ilk had done for them. He felt forgotten, except when Nora visited.

Now it was his turn to visit her. He had been released from the Garden and was supposed to move on, but he couldn't just leave her alone again. Not at a time like this.

He had tried talking to her, but Nora was Nora and nothing could turn her once her mind was set. So he did what she wanted—he visited a few old friends and let them know that Danny needed help.

He had his own thoughts, but, as he had learned since he died, nobody was really supposed to judge anybody. Danny was the way he was and they'd all had a hand in that. They had all done things that were regrettable, things that spilled over from the lives of one generation into the lives of the next, filling them in turn, like a fountain. He could have been a better father to Jerry and that would have been better for Danny, too.

That's why he had got involved. He still believed in Nora's faith in their prodigal grandson, who wasn't really all that different from him when he was a young man, though it took a dead man to see it.

"Well?" Nora bustled into the pew after genuflecting as much as her worn-out knees would let her. "It's nice to see that you still remember how to kneel down and say a few prayers once in a while."

"Ah, Nora. Are you well?" He turned around and nodded at her. He wanted to smile but he didn't think it would be fitting, given they were in church, and all. "I was just saying a few prayers for the repose of those poor English souls."

He pushed himself up from the handrail and eased back into the pew by her side. She had her arms folded over her handbag and looked like she did at her kitchen table when he came down to face the morning after a hard night.

"And well you should. Didn't they all have mothers and grandmothers, too?" She pursed her lips to let him knew that she was about to change the subject. "Did you get around to doing what I asked?"

"I did, indeed. I just finished. They all assured me that they're more than happy to do whatever they can."

"It's the least they could do after all that we have done for them."

Bart smiled at her. She was as pretty as the day he first set eyes on her in Herbert's Park one Sunday afternoon. He had heard that she walked there, with her family, and he had been waiting since morning.

"Well it's done now, Nora."

"It's not done yet." She clasped the handles of her purse and held them against her heart. She always meant it as a sign that she was about to become a bit defiant, and stubborn. Nothing ever got in Nora's way when she was like that—not walls or laws and certainly not the unentitled second sons of poor farmers now elevated to bishops and priests. No man was above her and she had little patience for those who thought they were.

But life had fought her every step of the way, too, and left furrows across her brow.

He began to rise and reached out for her hand, to help her up. "It's as good as done and we really should be getting on. We're supposed to have left already."

She pulled away from him and shifted her purse to the other side. "I'm not going anywhere until I see my grandson safe and sound."

As she began to fade away, Bart knew better than to argue. He lowered himself back to his knees and raised his hands before his face and prayed for the deliverance of his grandson, Daniel Bartholomew Boyle, however that might be achieved.

*

"Are you ready for a nice cup of tea?" Jacinta asked and smiled when Danny finally dragged himself from his fitful bed and came down to join his parents in the kitchen. They were making such an effort to be nice and normal about everything. His father lowered his paper long enough to nod to him, muffling a burp as he did.

His mother even took her cigarette out before she tried to kiss him. He almost let her, but backed out and just hugged her so she wouldn't get too close. She didn't look so worried anymore and Danny felt bad about that. If he got caught it'd fuck everything up again.

Still, if he didn't get caught—and he never had before—she'd never know about it and she could go on believing in whatever it was that she was using to get through these days.

"Thanks, Ma." He smiled back. He had to keep it up, too, all the smiling and being polite all the time. He knew the whole neighborhood was just watching and waiting for the latest bit of news about the Boyles.

When his granny was alive, they wouldn't have dared. She would have stared them down with a glance and given them a right earful, too. Almost sweetly at first, until it melted down to its bitter core of acrimony and accusations. Granny knew about them all and was quick to put them back in their place.

He worried about her sometimes. If there really was a Heaven, could she look down at him and see what he was up to? He always told her how sorry he was when she loomed up with the other faces that floated around in the darkness when he lay in bed, afraid to go back to sleep.

Other times it would be Anto and sometimes it was Scully.

Only they'd be looking down on him lying in the back of a car. His eyes would be wide open and his tongue would be hanging from the side of his mouth. He'd even have two holes in the top of his head, with dark streaks of red running from them.

He promised her, and all the saints she knew so well, that if he could just get through this, he never do anything wrong again. He even swore it and sometimes, it almost felt like she heard and she would tell him: "If you promise you are going to start being a lot nicer to your mother and father."

It was just like he was a little boy again and he liked how that made him feel.

He wasn't only doing it for her sake. He was also doing it because of Fr. Reilly and Miriam. He knew they talked with Deirdre and he wanted to make a good impression on them.

Being around Deirdre reminded him of how he used to feel—back when he believed in the Church, and all, and he wanted them all to be able to see some good in him so that Deirdre would see it, too. And besides, it looked so good when the cops came snooping around. Everybody would say what a change they had seen in him, even going to Mass again. He just had to keep it together until after the next run. He had to look and sound like he did when he was a kid—before all the shite started happening.

"I was thinking of going over to London to watch a football match one of these weekends."

"That's nice. Would you like your daddy to go with you?"

"I'm not going to Liverpool," his father snorted from behind his paper, "ever again."

He had been a Liverpool fan for years but the last time they were over, a few years back, he got upset when they wouldn't let them into the club house bar. Danny's hair was too long and they didn't like the look of him, anyway. Even though he was only going to drink red lemonade.

The color didn't matter to them and they pushed them roughly away. His father fumed about it all night as he drank whiskey in the ferry bar. "Well if my son isn't good enough for them they can go fuck themselves. They'll never see me there again."

"Did you ever think that he mightn't be asking you? Well I think it's wonderful, pet." His mother smiled as she passed him a plate of toast all covered with strawberry jam. Just the way Granny used to do it.

"I didn't say anything about taking anybody." But what if he did take his father along with him?

"I might only be able to get tickets for a West Ham game." He'd have to clear it with Anto first—so he'd have time to change the pickup. He wouldn't mind. He'd just be glad of the loyalty.

"Who are they playing?"

"I won't know until I get the tickets."

It would be brilliant. No one would ever suspect him like that. It would just be him and his dad, going to a game together. And his Dad would tell everybody what a great son he had—getting tickets and paying the fare, too.

Just as long as no one asked where he was getting them from. He'd have to get a day job soon—now that the Dandelion was gone.

"Well, as long as it's not Liverpool."

"Can I go, too?"

"Since when do you watch football?"

"Football? I'm just going over to do a bit of shopping. They have far better stuff over there. Gina's wedding's coming up and I want to be able to show up in something stylish—from London, no less. And only we'll know that it was bought in the East End."

"We're not made of money, you know."

*

Jacinta sipped her tea. She'd been down to the pawn with the last of Nora's silver: the prize set that hadn't been used in decades. But it was okay this time; Nora had told her to do it. She also told her that she should spend more time with Danny—to try to give him a normal life.

Jacinta felt guilty about that, but Nora told her not to. She said that the past couldn't be changed, but the future could. Other people had tried to tell her that before but this time it was different. This time it was like Nora was inside of her, speaking directly to her. It would have been disquieting if she wasn't so worried about Danny. Nora told her to smile and go along with him until they could see which direction he was headed.

"If Danny is going to London then I'm going to go along with him whether you like it or not. Besides, I'm owed a trip. Remember?" she nudged her husband. "After Nora died? You said you would take me and you never did."

She was about to pout a little when he shook his head and went back behind his paper.

*

"I might only be able to get one ticket–two at the most."

Danny couldn't ask Anto if his ma could come along, too. That would be pushing it. But he would ask about his father. Even Miriam and Fr. Reilly would think it was so nice, being nice to his family, and all.

He hadn't really lied to them. He just hadn't told them the whole story. Fr. Reilly said that stuff like that was a sin of omission. But he also told him that he wasn't going to get good again over night. "It's like God and the Devil are at war for your soul. And the battle could go either way. God needs us to believe in Good, Danny, not in all the stuff we made up about him. We need to show God that we are worth fighting for so that He can win."

He probably meant it to encourage him, but Danny found it very depressing. If God needed help from the likes of him, He was fucked. And then they'd all be fucked.

Unless those that believed in Him could be stronger. "Faith," Fr. Reilly had tried to explain to him, but Danny didn't want to think about it, although he pretended he was listening. "Faith is the key."

Danny was surprised that he'd remembered that but he couldn't help thinking it was like the type of things people said to get you to believe in what they were saying. People had been doing that to him since he was a child. It got his back up.

Besides, it was better to be unaffiliated until he saw which way the battle was going. Until then he had to do what he had to do.

*

Anto closed the door and lit another candle as the darkness closed in around him, again. His hands shook and his stomach churned but he had kept all of that hidden when Danny dropped in, hidden in the gloom that gathered after the sun began to set. And now that he was gone, Anto sat alone. The newly glowing flame made it all clear: he didn't have too many choices. There was nobody else he could trust with this run. Not that he trusted Danny, but then again, he didn't have to, he had control over him and that was better. But he wanted it to seem like they were both in this together—almost as equals—so he had agreed that it would look better if Danny's father went with him. He was surprised that Danny came up with that on his own. That was the kind of thinking that could run the business—after he was done with it. Maybe he'd give Danny a chance, for a while. He'd take a percentage but he'd be in the background where no one would come looking for him. He'd think about it and decide when Danny got back.

He fumbled with his cigarette pack until he managed to get one out and lit it before he realized that there was one still burning in the ashtray. He had to admit it: it was all starting to get to him.

There was always somebody, somewhere, out to get him and everything he did had to be considered with that in mind. He'd been that way as long as he could remember. There was always someone wanting to fight him; jackasses trying to prove themselves. Or the irate older brothers of those he had previously disproven. Sometimes their parents got involved, too, pointing long bony fingers at him and threatening him with banishment to Borstal, or to Hell.

His father got involved, too, when complaints reached the house, taking his leather belt to his errant son while his mother whisked his sisters away.

The last time, when he was almost eighteen, Anto snapped and grabbed the belt and took it away from him. There was nowhere else to go after that. He moved out and got a place on his own in Ranelagh. He found work where he could, when he could. It was only a matter of time before he drifted into the business and found he had a talent for it and quickly established himself.

Fear. That's how he got where he was. People were afraid of him, and, when the cops were snooping around, no one would speak out against him publicly. He could stay hidden in the dark cloaks he'd spun around himself, but there were those that he feared—those who killed on principal, or for prejudice, or price. He should never have gotten involved with the Driller; he never really trusted him. He got him for his reputation and his willingness to do the dirtiest jobs without complaint or comment. He was just a gun for hire and now others were making him a better offer.

The Driller had given him fair warning with his comments about the gun.

After looking at it from all sides, Anto knew he couldn't outbid them. Guys like him were getting pushed out. It used to be just a bunch of "heads" who'd go over to England to get some stuff. It made sense to bring enough back to make the trip worthwhile. But then more and more people got into it and they had to get organized. That's when the problems began. They had to set up territories and, in time, protect them from heavies who wanted to muscle in. It wasn't long before they started to hire guys who had been involved with the Boys, now cooling their heels, hiding out in plain view.

When these packages were sold off, he would retire. He'd set the Driller up, too, so the fucker would leave him alone.

He was bringing in some heroin this time—not that Danny knew. He probably thought it was the usual run for hash. Anto almost felt bad about that, but when it was over, when he was ready to get out, he'd give the gun to Danny and they could all let bygones be bygones.

But first, he'd rattle Danny's cage a bit, just to keep him honest. Then he'd go to the Gardens and retrieve it. He'd hidden it there, buried beneath the fifth tree on the left. He'd put it there at night when there was no one around. It was freaky. He felt like he was being watched all the time.

That feeling was growing, too, and the only person who knew it was there, besides him, was the Driller.

*

When they got to her bus stop, Miriam asked if she'd be okay getting home on her own.

Deirdre found that so nice, that Miriam was concerned. They had been at a poetry reading near Parnell Square. Deirdre didn't know anybody there but Miriam knew them all and introduced her like she was proud of her—almost like a big sister—boasting about her to everyone.

After the reading, the crowd talked about the deaths of Steven Biko, Andreas Baader, and Hamida Djandoubi like they knew them personally, jostling with each other to seem more informed. Miriam was in among them, augmenting the conversations she approved of and quickly excusing herself from those she didn't. Deirdre admired that about her but could never see herself like that—being able to act so confident and assured.

It was such a contrast to the Miriam she knew in private. That Miriam had so many doubts about herself as a woman and sometimes seemed to be looking to Deirdre for advice or approval. She was really pretty for a woman her age who had been through all that she had been through. When she smiled, everyone around her noticed. She didn't seem to know that about herself even though she was very smart with everything else. But sometimes she fussed a bit.

"I'll be fine from here. Will you be okay?"

"Well," Miriam hesitated and Deirdre thought that she was about to blush. "I was actually going to go back and talk with someone."

"Oh?"

"It's not like that. He's American and I need to go back and get in touch with that part of me. Sometimes I miss it."

"America?"

"Yes, and the person I was there."

"A Nun?"

"No, though it had its advantages. I never had to worry about how I looked back then. What I really miss is being an active part of what was going on in the world."

Deirdre wanted to know more but she could tell that Miriam was anxious to get back. She had heard snippets of stories about the gang she referred to, and, in particular, a Fr. Melchor whom she had gone to visit in Rome.

"Can't you go back?"

"Back? To America? There's no point anymore. Our little gang of conspirators was broken up and scattered to the four winds."

"Go on then. Go back to your American, I'll be fine. The bus will be along in a few minutes."

"Are you sure? I could wait."

"Go on before someone else steals him."

"If only it was like that." Miriam smiled wistfully.

"I am sure you will enamor him."

"Don't be silly." Miriam pursed her lips the way nuns did.

"I've seen you do it before."

"When?" Miriam's pursing was wrinkling at the corners where a smile was struggling through.

"Lots of times. Only I can't remember this exact minute. But there were a few."

"Oh. It's a few, now? So why is it that none of them ever calls or writes, young Miss-Know-It-All? It's God's curse upon me. I'm just like Cain, wandering the wilderness."

"Maybe they're just a little bit intimidated by you."

"Me? How am I intimidating? I'm just an ex-nun that gets lonely."

"Maybe they think you are some type of scarlet woman."

Miriam walked away laughing at that and waved back over her shoulder.

When the bus came, Deirdre sat downstairs near the driver, where the conductor stood when he wasn't collecting fares. The upper deck would fill up with drunks—spilled out from the bars as they closed. Mostly young fellas full of drunken bravado, making lewd comments about her as they passed. It did no good to try to stare them down with disdain; that only encouraged them, so she rummaged in her bag for her book so they could all see that she was reading and they might ignore her. That was why she never saw Anto get on. He went upstairs as she turned her page and she didn't see him until after she had got off and was halfway down the lane that led directly to her house. She knew somebody was walking behind her but she wasn't too concerned. She was almost there. She could see the porch light and the front door.

"Slow down there, Deirdre, so we can have a little chat about that boyfriend of yours."

She turned as he emerged from the shadows. His cigarette glowing in front of him. She wanted to turn again and march quickly up to her door.

"I'm not going to do you any harm. I just want you to tell Danny something from me. Tell him that I was just asking after him. Right?" He grinned and sauntered away.

It always bothered her that he had such poise and arrogance—like he owned the place.

He wasn't ugly the way he should be if the world was the way it was supposed to be.

But he was menacing and looked like the type that enjoyed being that way.

That was another unfairness. Bad people always looked like they were enjoying themselves while the people who were trying to be good always looked a bit miserable—like it was a struggle. That made sense when she considered that the wrong thing was usually easier. People were forgetting to stop and think about that, jumping on to any bandwagon without knowing where it was going to end up. "It's not where things start," Miriam often reminded her. "It's where they finish."

She wanted to believe that there was still more good in the world than bad. She wanted to believe in a God that was more like a parent who let you fall down a few times so that you could learn to walk properly, like her mother.

Her father, though, was more like the God in the Bible.

Perhaps that was why Catholics had clung to Mary, even when they were being persecuted.

They did their share of persecuting, too, and that was something she often wondered about. What was the difference between being misguided and just plain being bad? In Anto's case there was no discussion. He was definitely just pure black-hearted badness.

But he couldn't have started out that way. Nobody did. She knew him when he played football and wondered what had happened along the way that made him the way he was. Probably something like what happened to Danny—only there was no one around to help him.

Then she thought about why he had followed her and why he spoke to her. Was Danny still working for him? Or was Anto just trying to imply that he was? Or was he trying to get him to go back by letting him know he could get to her anytime he wanted?

She watched him walk away and wished that something terrible would happen to him—that he'd be hit by a bus or something. *That is the problem in fighting evil*, she decided as she reached the front gate. *Can you do it without becoming evil, too?*

"Was that little bollocks bothering you?" Her father stepped out of the shadows where he might have been watching them all along. "What did he want with you, anyway?"

*

He didn't believe her but he kept his thoughts to himself for a few days. He knew no good would come from confronting her. Deirdre always seemed angry at him lately. Like he was the cause of all the problems in the world—including the ones that women caused.

He blamed it all on her seeing the ex-nun, although he never did follow through on the boarding school. They missed the enrollment and by Christmas she was behaving like an angel again, doing so well at school and helping out around the house. He had peace for a while and that's what had lured him off his guard.

He had been busy, too, with the Watchers. How could he keep an eye on his own house when he was busy keeping an eye on everyone else's? *That's what happens when you put others first*, he consoled himself as he seethed behind his paper. Deirdre and her mother had both insisted that she was not getting involved with Danny, but they were not telling him the whole story. He said nothing but they had all eaten the rest of their dinners in silence.

He said nothing because he couldn't prove it, and Deirdre and her mother would demand proof. But why else was that little drug-fucker talking to his daughter? It had to have something to do with Danny and drugs and by-fuck was he going to put an end to it, once and for all. He just needed to find out what Anto and Danny were up to.

It didn't take long. A few nights later he was sitting in the local when Jerry Boyle walked in and sat a few stools down from him. He had told Jerry that he held no grudge over what had happened before, but Jerry was still a bit leery around him.

"Come here beside me, Boyle, and I'll get this round."

Jerry joined him eagerly, and, after a few pints, boasted about how Danny was taking him to a football match in London, in a few weeks.

That was all he needed to hear. He could figure the rest of it himself. One of the lads had mentioned something about being amazed how young fellas were able to get tickets and go over—like it was for free. It was Maguire that had said that to him, a decent enough old skin but cursed with the spawn of the Devil for children. They were always getting into trouble. That's why it stuck in his head.

"And are you going, too?"

"I am," Jerry beamed back at him like the fecking eejit that he was.

CHAPTER 16

"Do you really think you should be telling everybody that Danny is taking you over to the game?" Jacinta asked as she placed his dinner on the table in front of him.

"And why wouldn't I?" Jerry looked up from his paper.

Jacinta had heard it down at the shops. Everybody was commenting on it and some of the comments were a little bit snide. Not that that surprised her; they were just chewing on the gossip and spitting out any new juice they could find in it. Still, sometimes she wished he could keep things a bit more private.

"Because not everybody thinks well of our Danny."

"Feck the begrudgers. Let them have a look at their own children—drunks and whores the lot of them. At least Danny is trying to turn over a new leaf. That's probably what has them upset now."

"I know. You're probably right." But she still wasn't happy about it. And neither was Nora. She had made that very clear to Jacinta. In fact she was against the whole thing.

"I had a call from Martin today."

"What time was it where he was calling from?"

"I'm not sure. It's five hours, but I can't remember which way."

"What did he have to say for himself?" Jerry had gotten over the whole thing with the will and was feeling very magnanimous toward the world in general, even toward his brother-in-law.

"Well I'd been saving this so I could tell you when the time was right."

"What have you done now?" He was joking, only he wasn't sure if she could tell. They still, after all the years, and all that happened, hadn't worked that one out.

"Martin is after making all the arrangements for Danny to move to Canada—at least until all this drugs stuff is over."

"And when were you going to get around to fecking telling me, the boy's one and only father? Or do you agree with my mother—that I'm not fit to look after my own son?"

He didn't mean to sound like was getting a bit riled but she seemed like she didn't notice and answered in the same calm voice.

"Nora wouldn't say that about you anymore. She's changed. She also said that she's okay with Danny going to Canada. She wasn't at first but now she has come around to the idea. She thinks it's what's best for him."

He stared at her simple, open face and remembered the way she looked at him the first time they talked. He couldn't help himself and rose and took her into his arms. He was losing her to the darkness again and soon she'd be packed back off to the hospital.

All of this business with Danny was too much for her. She'd always been simple from the beginning—from the day he first went into the tea shop where she worked. He had gone on his own, his university scarf draping down one side and his breath, beery.

**

"What can I get you?" she had asked as he hovered near the counter, letting everyone go before him.

"I'm grand, actually. It's you I've come to see."

"What for?"

"What time do you get off work?"

"Not for a few hours yet. Why?"

He looked around to make sure no one was listening. "'Cos I wanted to ask you something."

She looked like she already knew what he was going to say but was still anxious to hear it.

"Would you ever consider going out with me sometime?"

"I might. Where do you want to go?"

"We could go to the pictures."

They went to see *Rebel without a Cause* and she cried at the end when poor old Plato got himself killed. He even got to put his arm around her and when her sniveling turned to shivering, gave her his scarf. She kept it and still had it somewhere.

He also remembered something else: the night at the dance and the fumbling and the stumbling in the lane out back. He had to coax her with glasses of Babycham and his educated assurance that no one ever gets pregnant the first time.

He also remembered the sinking feeling in his stomach the day she told him she was.

"What are we going to do?"

Jerry had no idea but wanted to sound like he did. He didn't really love her but he did feel responsible.

"We'll be fine; just let me figure out how to deal with it."

"Deal with it? What do you mean by that Jerry? You're not thinking of sending me off to England?"

"No, of course I wasn't," Jerry lied and tried to think. It didn't matter which way he decided; he'd have to tell his parents. He had no money of his own.

His father had blustered and fumed for a while until he was sure there'd be no taint of scandal. Other than that, he wasn't too concerned. His son was a damn fool and Jacinta was no smarter—they'd make a grand match for each other.

After all, it was, as his mother crisply remarked, not unheard of for a young woman to throw herself at a young man when the chance came to climb up a few rungs.

After the shock, they were quite pragmatic and began to make plans for a wedding, even meeting with Jacinta's parents and suppressing any feelings they might have had that it was her fault—for trapping him.

"A wedding?" Jerry had nodded along with them as any faint hope he had of shipping Jacinta off to England, so that he could go on with his life, floated away.

"Of course, a wedding," his mother snorted. "Having bastards might be good enough for kings and popes but it's not good enough for this family."

"You'll find," his father confided in him a few nights later, in the pub, "that one woman is very much like another. And I'm sure from their point of view the same is true about men. There's no reasons why you and your wife cannot go on and be as happy as the next pair."

***

"And when, exactly, was it that you were talking with my mother?" He held her away at arm's length so he could see her eyes.

"I talk to her every day, down in the church, by the side altar."

He could see she was cracked, again, but sending Danny to Canada was as good as anything he had come up with. He hadn't heard back from the ruddy-faced man and it might be for the better if Danny was out of the way for a while. But he also thought about going to see Fr. Reilly to ask if he should be worried about Jacinta and her chats with his mother. There was probably nothing to worry about, but still he did.

*

Miriam had no idea how to get ready for a date but she couldn't bring herself to ask Deirdre.

Secretly, she hoped she might have offered. She'd told her that she was thinking of going out with her American but Deirdre seemed preoccupied. Things with Danny didn't seem to be going so well, but as Deirdre hadn't brought it up, neither did Miriam. Deirdre would tell her when she was ready.

She tried her suit and checked with her reflection but it was still wrong. It was one of the first things she'd bought, but now it didn't say what she thought it had said. In fact it made her look a bit "Thatchery."

She wanted to look like she felt: an ex-nun who was getting out of her shell and meeting someone.

She was friends with most of her colleagues—or at least those who accepted her; mostly the younger women and the more sensitive men. They were the ones who identified with her rebellion. They were in the minority but they made up for it with their unflagging enthusiasm every time she did something un-nun-like. Like when she accepted their invites to parties, and social events, too. She was becoming a bit of a cause-celeb—and a bit of a freak show.

It was good, at first, being able to socialize with people who could see her just for what she was, and not for what she used to be. But it was only a matter of time before the whispers of her fall from the veil spread around the room like an odor, heady to some and distasteful to others.

She just wanted to be Miriam again—even if it was a much older version than she remembered being.

I just want to be with someone who is okay with me and what I have been through, she confided to the picture frame on the table beside her bed.

One of her single friends had told her to do it—to get a picture of her best friend in the world and keep it beside her bed. That way she would always have someone to say goodnight to.

Her brother's face smiled back. It was an older photo of him, taken when he was coaching a bunch of scraggly looking kids that made up an inner-city parish's baseball team. He knew nothing about the game and swung his bat like a hurley. But in the picture he looked so . . . American.

I'm all alone, Joe, in the "Island of a Thousand Welcomes!"

And the family, those that are still in the country—the lumpier, stodgier ones—are always far too busy to be seen with the likes of me.

Joe didn't answer and just stared out of the dugout with his bat over his shoulder and a long slender stalk of grass in his mouth. But she felt reassured.

The worst part of it all, she continued, knowing that he would sit and listen without interruption, *is that I don't like the person I am without the veil.*

You might be shocked to learn that. I certainly was. But you see, back then I was confident. I knew where I stood and I never had to worry about how I looked and what I wore. There are so many mornings, she paused to blink back a tear and sipped wine from the large glass she usually drank her orange juice from—she really had to get organized and buy a few more things for the flat—*that I wish I could just put on the same thing, day in and day out.*

Someone should have warned me, you know? Danger! Entering the convent can compromise your ability to ever become a woman again.

Still Joe didn't answer and just looked past her with his big smile and determined chin.

But then again you'd probably say that it's just like learning to ride a bike—with training wheels. I am a thirty-six-year-old-virgin. I have to start with someone.

She changed again and paused to consider her lipstick. It was far too evocative even though the girl who sold it to her assured her that is was mute.

It was compared to the other ones she had tried to sell her.

**

"Look," Miriam had almost snapped when she lost patience with the girl. "I used to be a nun."

"Well then you might like something dark, like this one."

She held up something that you might wear if you were dating a vampire so Miriam just pointed at the dullest red she could find. "That one will be fine."

"If you were going out with a priest," the girl muttered as she turned to the cash register.

She smiled when she turned back and held out the change and waited. "But it will look great with your complexion, and your dark eyes."

"Thanks, and keep the change," Miriam answered distractedly. She had never really thought about her complexion in ages.

***

I hope I'm not shocking you?

She leaned closer to the mirror to try and get her lipstick right but glanced at the reflection of the picture, to see if he'd answer. But Joe's flipped smile didn't flicker.

You're the one I blame, you know. You and all that idealism you once had. It was like a fire that spread to everyone around you.

She sat back on her bed and picked up the picture. *Joe? Does it still burn inside you?*

He didn't answer and she knew she shouldn't have asked. It wasn't fair of her. He had made his choice just as she had made hers. He was going to stay and try to change things from within.

They agreed to disagree even though he made a point of being seen with her through the worst of what happened. She would always love him for that and she would forgive him anything.

I forgive you Joe. I forgive you for having more strength and faith than I did. And now I'm going to use what little strength I have to try being a woman while I still can. Wish me luck?

She placed the picture back on the nightstand where she could see it from her pillow.

She rose and straightened herself out. She wore a black skirt to her knees and a loose blouse that made her look nice, but not too nice. She wore dark tights, too, and a pair of shoes she had bought that morning. They had heels, but they weren't too high, not compared to what other women wore.

She had makeup on, too. Not too much, just a little around her eyes and her cheeks. Her pimples were long gone but they had left a few pock marks on her face. They were tiny when she was in the convent but since she left, they seemed to be growing like craters.

But it would have to do; she was who she now was. She checked her watch and the mirror one last time, then rose, put on her coat, and twirled around in front of her mirror. If she had a hat she would have thrown it up in the air.

*

Deirdre's father sat behind his paper while his wife watched TV.

She kept the volume down so he could have a bit of peace and quiet to read his paper. Both she and Deirdre had been tiptoeing around him since that night in the lane. That's what convinced him to do it.

He had to. How else was he going to keep Danny out of his daughter's life?

He felt bad for having to get Jerry involved but he had made it clear to the Garda: "the father doesn't know what is happening. He's just going along to watch the game. It's Danny you want and you can catch him red-handed."

The two detectives had sat like stoics until he finished. Then they thanked him for the information and all of his work with the Watchers. They assured him that his contribution was vital and would allow them to crack down on the drug dealers, once and for all.

But something happened as they were leaving and it had stuck in his mind. The taciturn one stopped in the doorway and asked if his daughter was still seeing Danny Boyle.

That got him wondering. Were they questioning his motives?

It also made him wonder if there mightn't be a connection there that led to the grave of Bart Boyle who he always thought of as a big old windbag. He never voted for him. He was more of a Fine Gael man. He had no truck with Fianna Fáil and all of their backroom deals and outright nepotism.

The Boyles had connections with the Bishop, too. Deirdre's father stayed clear of that one. It was one thing to show a bit of disdain to the local TD, but the Bishop—he'd be excommunicated.

And he might yet if Deirdre and his mother found out what he did.

But he had to. It what was expected of him, him being the head of the neighborhood watch, and all.

He was beginning to regret the name "the Watchers." It had even become a playground chant. "The Watchers will get ya. The Watchers will get ya," the children teased each other, but he still believed in what they stood for. They stood for keeping things the way they should be. Safe and sound and not the fiefdom of young bowsies. It was time for a man to stand up—even if part of the reason was his daughter.

He was doing it for everyone else's daughters, too. And their sons. He was going to war on their behalf and things might get tough for a while but he was the right man for the job. He'd show them all and they could quit their gossiping about Grainne running off with a painter.

There was something happening on that front, too, only no one was going to tell him—and him the girl's only father in the world. He was losing his place as the head of the family and had to do something to reassert himself. He thought about telling Deirdre that she couldn't go out on her own for a while but he knew what that would get him.

Besides, he didn't have to. She was staying very close to home at the behest of her mother.

So he sat behind his paper pretending he wasn't there and listened to them whispering on the settee. The two of them were always plotting against him so it was only fair that he did a bit of plotting of his own.

He'd take care of that Anto while he was at it. He had told the detectives about what happened and while he understood that they couldn't react to hearsay, he urged them to keep it under consideration because Anto Flanagan was known to be an intimidator of witnesses.

That almost made the taciturn one smile, but instead he said that he hoped that, after they had interviewed Danny, they could find the link to implicate Flanagan—and that they would be more than happy to implicate him.

Deirdre's father closed his paper and reached for his pipe. His wife let him smoke in the good room now. She said that pipe smoke gave the room a studied air.

Life wasn't as bad as it often seemed. In fact it was better now because he had done the right thing for a man in his position—no matter what anybody might say.

*

"Are you the Driller? I heard about you and the people who were talking about you are not the type of people you even want knowing your name." He was from Belfast so he exaggerated a bit in his wee singsong voice. He was very soft spoken for a big man.

"Locals or our own?"

The Driller had got his name from a friend from Derry. The one he sent the money to. He had told him he needed a bit of muscle for a job.

"We're all the same."

"Not in this particular bit of business, ya know?"

The big man checked over both shoulders and leaned closer. "Go on."

"I need someone to go to a football game in London."

"Do you have clearance for this?"

"It's not what you're thinking. It's a bit of fundraising, ya know?"

"What do I have to do?"

"You have to follow someone and pick up what he's bringing back."

"Why doesn't he bring it straight back to you?"

"Do you want the job or what?"

"I do want the job; I just don't want to step into someone else's shite."

"There's nothing to worry about. You just make contact on the way back and get the goods."

"What are they?"

"Do you really want to know?"

"I suppose not."

"Good. They'll be in duffle bag, a West Ham duffle bag."

"West Ham! Couldn't ya at least make it Leeds, or better still, Glasgow Celtic?"

"Are you sure you're the right man for this?"

"Sorry. I was just trying to lighten things. You're very uptight about this. You're not doing the dirty on someone?"

The Driller pulled on his cigarette and eyed the big man face-to-face. "I suppose you'll be wanting to know what I had for breakfast next. Fuck it. I'll do it myself."

"Now hold on. I never said I wouldn't do it. I was just having a wee fucking joke. What's the matter with you? Has living in Dublin killed off your sense of humor?"

After he left, the Driller looked around but there was no one else there, except for the old guy in the corner.

Derry had given him the clearance and he even had a buyer lined up—someone who was more than happy to fuck Anto Flanagan right up the arse. And they were willing to pay extra for the gun. Someone really had it in for Flanagan.

*

Miriam was waiting in a booth at the back when Fr. Reilly got to Bewley's. There was no one else in that section, except for someone hidden behind his copy of the *Independent.*

She looked a little different. She had more make-up on and her hair was nicely styled. She even had bright nail polish that matched her lipstick.

"Ah, Miriam. How have you been? You're looking well."

She smiled but looked a little flustered, like she wasn't used to compliments. But he meant it, and he meant it as something to boost her confidence. It must be so hard to do what she was doing. He had wondered if he could take off the collar and go out into the world as a man.

"I'm fine, Patrick. And how are you?"

"Can't complain. Anything new with you?"

"Well there is, actually?" She seemed to hesitate before she continued. "I have started to go out with someone."

Patrick struggled for composure and sipped his tea. "That's great news. Is he from around here?"

"God no! He's from America. He's a graduate student. He's working on his thesis."

"Oh is he, now? Well that's grand. He must be great company for you." He really wanted to mean it. She deserved to have someone in her life that she could be in love with. "I'm very happy for you."

But he wasn't. He didn't want to share what he had with her and that was very selfish of him. He had nothing to offer and she had every right to find what she needed somewhere else. Still.

"He knows all about me and he's okay with it." She made it sound like he had saved her from her fate and that made Patrick a little jealous, though he'd never admit it, not even to himself. He wanted to be the one that helped her make her peace with God and the world, as a priest, and as a friend.

"Well that's great news. I suppose you'll be off to America, again, one of these days."

"Oh, Patrick. We just started seeing each other. Don't be trying to marry us off just yet."

"I was just throwing my hat in the ring, you know. I've never done a wedding in America."

In fact he had never been out of Ireland. All of his friends had gone but he was still there and, at times like this, that bothered him. "So how long is he here for?"

"For a year or two."

"You'll be finished with your thesis by then."

"I will."

"And what plans do have for after that?"

"We're thinking of going to Rome. An old friend from the States is there and has suggested that I teach there for a while."

"Rome, you say. Now that will be grand. And is your fella going to teach there, too."

"Karl and I have talked about it but it's far too early to be making plans like that."

"Well, you'll be missed around here."

"That's very Christian of you to say but I think there are many who will be glad to see the back of me. They are right when they say: 'you can't go home again.'"

"You shouldn't pay those people any mind. This is your home. This is where you belong. But, I suppose you have to do what's right for you." He hadn't meant to say that but he couldn't help himself. He'd miss her. "So, Rome, you say? That'll be so nice for you."

"I think so. Father Melchor is getting older now and it will be nice to spend some time with him again. He was the one that led me astray, when I was young and impressionable."

"Really?"

"No! I'm kidding you. Father Melchor was the man who encouraged me to get involved in social issues. They banished him to Rome so they could keep an eye on him."

Patrick tried to look interested but he didn't like the idea of her mixing with her past again. He had hoped that she might find peace and contentment in Ireland. And that he and she could be friends forever.

"Am I shocking you, Patrick?"

"No, Miriam, not at all. That all sounds very exciting and it will be nice for you to see old friends again."

"I must admit that I am a bit nervous about making plans like that. I'm just not used to it. Before, things were usually decided for me and it was just for me to say yes or no. But this is totally different. This is my life and . . ."

"I'm sure you will make the right decision, when the time comes."

"Why, Patrick? I don't have a great track record on that score." She reached across and took his hands in hers. "I'm scared but I'm excited, too."

Patrick didn't withdraw his hands like he should have. He just sat there, staring into her eyes where he could see all that might have been. He was afraid for her, going out into the world that had treated her so harshly. He was afraid for himself, too, left behind without a real friend in the world, growing old under the burden he had chosen until one day it would break him like it did Fr. Brennan.

But what could he expect? He couldn't ask her to share the scraps of his life; the bits and pieces that the job didn't suck out of him. No, he had no right to expect anything from her but he wished he could tell her that the times he spent with her where the happiest he could remember.

"Patrick?" She was still holding his hands and looking into his eyes for an answer.

"Well, Miriam, I'm certainly not an expert on these matters. But from what I know of you, I can only say that you have as good a chance as anybody for finding happiness."

He let go of her hands and raised his teacup between them. How could he talk about happiness? He avoided the subject, preferring instead to dole out assurances to others. But that was the role he had chosen when he put on the collar and there was no point in regrets.

"Thanks, Patrick. I must admit that I was a bit shy about telling you."

"And why was that?"

"Well, you have been such a good friend to me, but I decided—I need something more. I need someone in my life. I never thought that I would, but I'm not used to spending so much time on my own. I just want to have someone that I could go to the movies with and someone I could meet for breakfast on Saturday mornings."

"Sure of course you do. It's the least that you deserve."

"Do you really mean that, Patrick?"

"Of course I do," he lied. Another little white lie to add to his collection but what else could he do? It was for a good cause; something a friend would do.

They sat in silence for a while as the café grew a little busier, mostly shoppers amidst their bags and a few students deep in their notes, and the man in the corner, still behind his newspaper.

"Well," Fr. Reilly announced to settle the matter. "I should be getting back."

"But we haven't even talked about you. How are things with your PP working out?"

Patrick thought about complaining but what was the point? A priest's troubles were his alone and there was no point in burdening anyone else. Besides, she was happy and that was what he wanted for her, more than anything else. "Ah sure, you know, yourself. It's a bit rough at the moment but I'm sure it will all work out for the best."

"Well, Patrick. It was lovely to see you again but I know you have to run. Call me and we will get together again, soon. Perhaps you'd like to meet Karl, one of these days. I have told him so much about you and he is dying to meet you."

"That would be lovely."

He rose when she did and took her hands in his. Without thinking he leaned forward and kissed her cheek, flustering them both.

After he paid the bill and gathered his books, the ruddy-faced man quickly glanced over from behind his newspaper. He had something to bargain with the Bishop—if push ever came to shove.

CHAPTER 17

No matter how often he went back to check, the gun wasn't there. Anto was starting to panic, even though he tried to stay calm and just think.

It had to have been the Driller; he was the only one who knew about it. But what the fuck would he want with it? Except . . .

He sat down with his back to Lir's Children and stared down at the cruciform pool, with the patterns on the bottom. He hadn't liked coming to the Gardens for years. He always felt guilty there—like somebody was looking down at him.

He thought about having another few hits. He was starting to come down again but he didn't dare. The vibe of the place was so against it.

He used to like coming when he was a child. His father used to bring him, to tell him all about his grandfather who had been at Boland's—with Dev. Anto had never met him but when he was younger he was proud of him.

Up until he left home and found out that the Republic they had all fought for was a closed shop and he and his kind were on the outside looking in. It wasn't right and there was no way he was going to do what his father did—work in the dairies, join the union and start a family that's only going to turn against him. He was always going to fight against that. Fighting was the only thing the world understood.

He had always been the type that stood out in the middle of the street and challenged everybody.

He could look back and see that so clearly now, but he couldn't see what was all around him even though it had been haunting his dreams. Blurry images of him running through the woods and then standing alone in a clearing for all other predators to see.

He should never have gotten involved with the Boys, with their minds set like steel and their hearts beating like tribal drums. It was like a jungle all right, and he had been a predator for so long, but now something was coming for him. His instincts were telling him to get under the cover of something. *Even fucking Danny Boyle figured that out.*

That was it. That was how he was going to go into hiding. It was fucking brilliant. Boyle was smarter than he had ever given him credit for.

Maybe he took the gun?

But he didn't know it was there.

Maybe the Driller is holding it over for him?

He was going to have to fight both of them at the same time. He might even have to go to the Garda-Fucking-Síochána but he'd need a go-between for that.

*

Fr. Patrick Reilly settled himself into the booth and put on his stole. He left the light on for a few moments so he could collect himself. He was going to be there all night. Fr. Brennan wasn't able anymore so he had to do it all himself.

He thanked God for Dinny O'Leary. He had agreed to give up his Saturday evening and come over and pretend to be doing a little plastering; repairing the wall that Fr. Brennan had bored holes in when he thought it was the wall between him and heaven. He said that voices of dead people were talking to him from the other side. He said that he could hear Bart and Nora, only he couldn't make out what they were trying to tell him. It took a while to get him to hand over the drill, but, in the end, what harm was there?

Besides, Dinny was more than happy to come over and cover it up for them.

When Patrick turned off the light it would begin. The opening and closing of doors. The squish of the plastic-covered cushion under old creaky knees. The rattle of beads against the grill as the old waited at the window for a bit of comfort and solace, sighing as they waited.

It always began with a "bless-me-father" and a mumble for how long it had been since their last confession. They didn't have to tell him, he knew who they were through the grill. He knew them by their voices and their smells and by the little noises they made that only he could hear.

He tried to let most of it pass him by, but he had to be on the lookout for something in particular to return to when it was his turn to speak. If he didn't, they'd feel cheated and before long someone would try to raise the matter with Fr. Brennan, in person.

But he had that covered, too. Dinny and Mrs. Dunne were always on guard. Dinny patrolled outside and deflected what he could while Mrs. Dunne just followed the time-honored traditions of priests' housekeepers, even though she was just part-time. She acted like she was the keeper of his schedule and told intruders that he was very busy with ecumenical matters. That stopped them in their tracks and they accepted an appointment with Fr. Reilly instead.

Still, he was getting tired carrying the whole load himself. He'd had five calls for "last orders" in the last month. All of them in the early hours of the morning. And he couldn't appear to be put out, not when there was somebody dying.

He did all the funerals, too, and the baptisms, and the weddings and every other reason the Church was called on. He did the three Masses on Sunday, too, and was worn out.

But he couldn't complain; this wasn't the worst of his duties. He just had to nod along and wait for his cue. That was the trick of it all: knowing which transgression to comment on. It was the same thing every Saturday night and, God forgive him, he sometimes wished someone would come in with something big and important once in a while.

He chided himself for letting his mind wander and shifted slightly in his chair. He was just tired. And hearing Miriam's news hadn't helped. Not that he wasn't happy for her. Of course he was but he was a little sad, too. And a bit bitter even though he had no right to be. He slid the grate open and lowered his head.

"Bless me, Father, I was a witness to a murder and I don't know what I'm supposed to do next."

He knew he knew the voice but he couldn't place it right away. He could smell the lingering odor of too many cigarettes and something vague and sweetly pungent.

"Go, on." It was what he was supposed to say and he said it slowly so as not to give anything away.

He remembered the voice, now, and the hard young face that it spoke through.

He listened as Anto retold the story of poor Declan Scully only it was a very different telling than Danny's.

According to Anto, Danny shot Scully for mentioning his name to the Guards. Anto had nothing to do with it except, and he admitted it freely, he was a dealer and he knew that was wrong.

"That's why I can't go to the Guards. It was my fault, in a way. I was the one who brought them together. I was just hoping they could sort it out and be mates again.

"I won't lie to you, Father. Part of the reason was business and that's why I don't think the Guards will want to believe anything I say.

"Besides, Boyle said something about getting the IRA after me. He said his family is connected.

"What do you think I should do, Father?"

*

Fr. Reilly was still thinking about it as he closed the church for the night. He had thought about nothing else. All of the penitents that followed were issued a standard penance and shuffled along. He still had no idea how he was going to deal with it. He had invited Anthony around to the house for a chat but he explained that they would have to discuss it from the beginning as he wasn't supposed to use anything he heard in confession.

It almost felt like Anthony was expecting that and had agreed. That bothered him so he knelt down and prayed for a bit of guidance from his remote and unanswering Boss.

No one answered him, but, as he waited until his mind was quiet, so he might hear God's whisper, he began to think of Nora Boyle. She appeared in his mind with her hands on her hips like she was scolding him. And a look on her face like she was thinking of calling the Bishop directly.

His knees were sore when he finally rose and left the church. He would sleep for as long as he could and when he woke he would know what to. It would be Sunday and he'd have God's ear while he said the three Masses.

*

The football game wasn't bad, 2-2 against Villa. Tailor and Hales scored and had the home fans singing "I'm forever blowing bubbles."

Danny had got great seats and Jerry enjoyed every minute of it, except when they announced the out of town scores: Liverpool was held goal-less by Everton, at home, but at least United got hammered. 4-0, away to West Brom. That was the icing on the cake.

On the way out, Danny bought a pair of duffle bags with West Ham plastered all over them. Jerry would never be seen in public with it, but he couldn't say that to Danny, he was so happy to be doing the treating. He even insisted that they go for a few pints. It was somewhere nearby. One of his friends had told him about it. The Green Man on Plashet Grove. It was run by a fellow from Cork and they had a couple of hours to kill before they had to catch the train to Holyhead.

The pub was all right. It looked like something out of Dickens but the barman was from Dublin. From just over in Templeogue, and he knew Danny from school. He slagged them about their "Hammers" bags but asked to have a closer look at Danny's. He even took it around the corner, out of sight—to show the lads in the other bar.

English pubs were a bit different so Jerry just kept to himself and didn't gawk around like the tourists did in Dublin. The beer was okay, too, but he was anxious to get going and get back to what he was used to.

On the way to the train, they stopped to stock up on cigarettes and a few bottles that were so much cheaper than in Dublin. They filled both duffle bags evenly, only Danny's felt heavier but he agreed to carry both of them. One over each shoulder, for balance in case the sea got rough.

They joked about it on the train, in the bar car, all the way to Holyhead.

Jerry had refused to go by Liverpool even though that boat was so much nicer. And it would have given them more time for drinking. And it came right in along the Quays instead of where they were heading. Dun Laoghaire.

They'd have to take the early morning train into town from there, along with the mailbags and a few Culchies, heading home for a while.

They were bleary when they landed and Danny had gone and lost his bag somewhere on the ship and refused to go back for it—saying that it wasn't worth the hassle.

It was the one that had the bottles of gin for his mother, and all the Silk Cuts. But at least he still had the one with the whiskey and the Player's Navy Cut. Unfiltered. "You're a right fucking-eejit," Jerry chided him as they filed off the ferry.

"It's no big deal. I never liked West Ham anyway."

Jerry would have clattered him across the ear if he wasn't so tired.

And that wasn't the end of their bad luck. The customs man pointed to them as they walked by and they had to go over and show him what was in the bag. He even asked their names as he eyed them with suspicion.

After he had pulled everything out of the bag, including the socks and underwear Jerry had changed on the train, he looked over his shoulder and nodded. They were fucked now. There were uniformed Guards and two men in tweed jackets with leather patches on the sleeves and they all wanted to have a little chat with them.

Not there in front of everybody, though. They led them inside and put them in separate rooms and tried to make them feel like they were fucked now—whatever they were supposed to have done.

Jerry wasn't too concerned, though; it was only a few bottles and a couple of hundred cigarettes. How big a deal was that? He hoped Danny was holding up and began to compose what he was going to say to Jacinta when they finally got home.

*

Danny wasn't the slightest bit concerned, either. He knew what was going down and he had nothing to worry about. He hadn't lost the other bag; he had given it to someone.

It was okay—he had gotten the right password. Anto always wanted them to use passwords and let Danny pick the one for this mission. Danny had chosen "Sarsfield." His grandfather used to use it when he was active.

"Sarsfield?" the big man had said when he approached.

"Sarsfield is the word," Danny agreed as the big man loomed over him.

"And Sarsfield is the man." He answered in a voice that was far too small for him. Small and thin—the way they spoke up in the North.

*

It went down so easy.

All the big man had to do was to tell Danny that Anto had sent him along because the cops were looking out for Danny. Someone had tipped them off.

Danny had nearly freaked out but the big man assured him that he had nothing to worry about. All he had to do was to hand the bag over and go on like nothing had happened. He'd get hauled in but they'd find nothing. He also told him that Anto had said that, if he handled it properly, that they'd be all square. He said that Anto had said that Danny would know what that meant.

Danny was relieved and handed over the bag and strolled off, not once looking back as the big man reached inside and took out the packages and threw them into the sea, just as he had been told to do.

He kept the gin and the Silk Cut. Not for himself; he would sell them and make himself a few quid on the side. Fighting for Ireland just didn't pay the bills anymore.

*

The car windows were getting foggy on the inside and dewy from the sea breeze on the outside, but Anto didn't dare clear them. He didn't want anybody to notice him and his instincts warned him that they were there—that somebody was looking for him.

That's why he sent Maguire instead. He was very anxious to make a name for himself and was far too stupid to fuck it up. Anto didn't dare do it himself; he couldn't risk being around if anything went wrong.

It seemed to be going okay. Maybe he had nothing to worry about. Maybe he was just getting a bit too paranoid. It happened to them all, sooner or later. It was time to get out of the game. He had told the priest the truth about that part.

And if everything went down okay he wouldn't have to worry about anything again—least of all the priest.

But if it did go wrong, if something bad went down, he could get away and get over to the priest's house. No one would look for him there.

And the priest couldn't throw him out if he said he was looking for sanctuary. He had read up on all of that—only it didn't happen so much anymore. But it was worth a try—if things went wrong.

He peered through the fog and the mist and could see Maguire standing near the door, smoking and looking like he was just waiting for someone.

Then he saw the big man come out and get into a waiting car. He didn't know too much about him but he had heard that he used to be a courier. He did the Belfast-Dublin-London run and Anto had heard that he was trusted with all of the heaviest shit. Anto didn't know much else about him—and didn't want to. He knew enough to mind his own business and let other's mind theirs.

He wasn't sure but he thought he had heard something about the big man lying low for a while. He was probably called out for some special assignment. It had fuck-all to do with Anto so he pretended to ignore the car when it pulled away with four men inside. Something heavy was going down. That was for sure. But he had to clear the window when he saw Danny and his father being led out to a waiting car, a dark blue Cortina.

It didn't have any markings on it but he had seen it before—when the two detectives came snooping around. He slid down in his seat as it passed and hoped that Maguire had seen it, too, and was getting the fuck away before anyone noticed him.

When the car had turned at the lights, he sat up and reached for the ignition, just in time to see Maguire being bundled into the back of another car, one that he had never seen before.

He froze and waited.

In time, the train rumbled off toward the city and the seagulls banked against the wind. The rain became a little more persistent but still he waited, smoking one cigarette after another as he tried to figure out what the fuck had just happened. There was no point in going anywhere. The priest said to call after lunch—that he'd be busy all morning, saying Mass or something.

Besides, whatever happened had happened and nobody would think of looking for him here, now. He'd just sit and wait until he had calmed down a bit and then he would take the long way around to Rathfarnham, like he was just out taking a Sunday drive.

He'd go around by Kilternan to Stepaside, past Ticknock and over to Ballycullen. He liked the view along the way and it would kill some time until the priest was ready.

He'd just have another smoke first—to steady his nerves. He thought about having a few tokes but he didn't want to be stoned when he saw the priest. That would fuck up everything.

*

The car that Maguire was bundled into took the same route and stopped, not far from Ticknock, just below the top of Two Rock Mountain.

He was dragged from the car and thrown to the ground that was covered in sheep shit. He didn't care and rolled away like he was trying to roll all the way down to the city.

"Get that little fucker back here."

The ruddy-faced man was in no mood for delay with them parked on the side of the road in broad daylight, though the rain was getting heavier and there was no one else around. Still, he knew, in Ireland, there was always someone seeing what they'd be better off not seeing.

He waited until they caught the rolling Maguire and propped him against a rock, out of view of the road. They held him by the hair and twisted his face around.

The ruddy-faced man knelt when he got there and looked into Maguire's frightened face. "What you need to tell us is: what the fuck you were doing?"

"I was just waiting for my friend who was over at a football match. That's all. I wasn't up to anything. I swear to you'se."

The ruddy-faced man waited while somebody whacked Maguire a few times before continuing. "Do you have any fucking idea who you are dealing with?"

"You're not the Guards?" was all he got from the terrified Maguire.

"No, we're not the fucking Guards. We're the men that the fucking Guards are afraid of. Understand?"

Maguire nodded as his eyes grew wider.

"So just fucking tell me what you were doing and we will happily go on our way and leave you, mostly intact."

He nodded to the man who was holding Maguire's hair and he whacked him a few more times. Only harder.

"No. Wait. I'll tell you anything you want to know."

"There's a good lad. Now who sent you?"

"Anto Flanagan."

"Why?"

"I don't know. He just asked me to do him a favor. I had no idea what it was about."

The ruddy-faced man nodded to the man again and he slapped Maguire a little more, and a little harder.

"Wait." Maguire was on the verge of collapsing altogether and even pissed himself a little. "He asked me to pick up a bag from Danny Boyle. I didn't know what was in it—I swear to you'se."

"Well you tell Anto-fucking-Flanagan something from me. Tell him we want to have a chat with him and it would be better if he came to us. If I have to send one of these boys," he nodded to the men who stood around watching, "they might not bring him in alive. Understand?"

He nodded again and they all got back in the car, except Maguire who sat in his pee-damp trousers and cried on the side of the cold, damp mountain with nothing but sheep to keep him company.

On the way back to the city, the ruddy-faced man had them stop at a pub in Taylorsgrange as he had arranged. The other car was waiting for them and the lads had already gone inside.

The ruddy-faced man had arranged for the Special Branch to meet up with them there, too. Later.

He had given them the morning off and was more than happy for them to follow him around for the rest of the afternoon, once everything had been taken care of. He shook the beads of mist from his coat and stepped inside.

"Did you look after things for me?" he asked the big man while everyone else was busy ordering pints amidst the throng of locals, fresh from Mass with an evangelical thirst on them.

"I did."

"And what's that?" The ruddy-faced man nodded at the duffle bag on the floor beside them.

"It's just some cigarettes and a few bottles of gin."

"What are they doing here?"

"They were in the bag, already."

"Well, they're not yours, then?"

"No. I was going to hock them."

"How much do want for them?"

They stared at each other for a minute.

"I'll take fifty."

"Good man. And here's another hundred for looking after things so well."

The big man pocketed his fee as the ruddy-faced man put the duffle bag under his chair. He would drop it off at the Boyle's house when everything calmed down. They weren't thieves, at least not with the ordinary man.

*

Anto found him when he passed almost an hour later. By then Maguire was soaked and reeked of piss and sheep shit. Anto didn't want to let him into the car but he had to. He had to find out what had happened and Maguire told him everything on the way back.

After he had dropped him off, Anto drove over to the church and parked. The rain had eased off and it was becoming a little clearer. There was no way Danny Boyle had anything to do with it. He was probably spilling his guts right now and it wouldn't be long before they all came looking for him.

Anto had a decision to make. He knew it was all the Driller's doing, now, and he knew he could do fuck-all about it. He'd have to go to the Guards but he'd get the priest to come with him.

*

When Jacinta heard the news she wasn't as upset as she thought she might be. Jerry had called and told her what happened. They were letting him go but they wanted to hold Danny a bit longer. They seemed to think that he might have something to tell them about what was going on.

Jerry asked her to go and tell Fr. Reilly—and to ask him if he wouldn't mind letting the Bishop know. They'd call Davies, too, but maybe the Bishop could get the Guards to release Danny so he wouldn't have to spend the night.

She took it all in stride but wanted to go over to the church to tell Nora. She'd just have to wait until after the late Mass as she didn't want everybody listening while they were talking. People were always sticking their noses in where they weren't wanted.

Other than that, Jerry said they had a good time, only Danny went and lost the presents he was bringing for her but he'd make it up to her when he got home. He sounded so calm and assured – like it was all predetermined.

She took her time getting ready and by the time she got there the church was empty with only one car parked outside. She didn't pay it any mind and went inside to have her chat with Nora.

*

The Driller was waiting, too, for the call from the big man. He should have called already.

They were going to meet and make the swap—the gun with Danny's prints for the packages from London. He knew better than to ask why they wanted the gun, and besides, it had fuck-all to do with him. They wanted Anto and he was more than happy to give him to them.

It wasn't like he hadn't given Anto fair warning. If the dumb fucker had been smarter he would have taken it and disappeared by now, as disappeared as he could get.

But Anto was one of those guys who thought he was bigger than he really was. They were all just pawns and the sooner they realized that, the better.

When the phone finally rang he waited for the third ring before answering. He didn't want to seem too eager.

It wasn't the big man but it was somebody who knew what was going on.

"I have your packages," was all the information he would divulge.

"Does the big fella know about this?"

"Yeah. He was the one that asked me to call you. But if you don't want to meet, you can wait until he gets back."

"Is he away, then?"

"He got called out on another matter—you know how it is."

His accent was Belfast and that was comforting. He didn't want any of the Dublin crowd to know what was going down, even though the gun was probably going back to them. He couldn't afford to cut them in, too. There was enough to send to Derry and a cut for the Boys in Belfast, and enough for him to go to America and vanish like thousands had before him.

"Okay. Where do you want to meet?"

*

He wished it was somewhere else. This was where he'd met the ruddy-faced man. He would have preferred somewhere more neutral but it wasn't up to him. And he didn't want to seem skittish–that would give everything away.

They kept him waiting but he was used to that. And when they arrived there were three of them. They stood around him on all sides and told him to finish his drink, that there was a car waiting outside and that they didn't have all day.

He finished his drink and went along with them because there was no point trying to do anything else. They were the type that would have killed him where he stood and never given it a second thought. He knew the sort—they were just like him. "So where are we off to, then?"

The ruddy-faced man was waiting in the car with a duffle bag on the floor between his knees.

"Is that what you were looking for?"

The Driller thought it over. There was no point in lying to them. They were straight from the Devil and could tell lies from truth. It was second nature to them. He was a bit like that himself.

"It is."

"And what the fuck would you want with a bag full of drugs?"

"I was going to sell them and send the money home, you know, for the lads."

"And you didn't think that you should have cleared it with me first?"

"It all happened so fast. I only just heard that Flanagan was expecting a shipment and I had to arrange everything on the fly. You know how it is?"

The ruddy-faced man seemed to be considering it.

"I do," he finally answered. "Did you get the other thing we talked about?"

"I did."

"Well. Hand it over."

"Hand me the duffle bag first."

The ruddy-faced man laughed and the other's joined in. "You're not in the position to be making demands. Now hand the fucking gun over before I let the boys beat it out of you."

The Driller reached inside of his coat and slowly pulled the gun out, still wrapped in a plastic bag.

"Now get the fuck out of my car and don't ever let me see your face around here again. I'm putting out the word on you: shoot to kill. Understand?"

CHAPTER 18

When Deirdre's mother heard the news it all made sense. She knew her husband had been to see the Guards but she hadn't put all the pieces together, until now.

She was shocked. How could he do such a thing to that poor, unfortunate Boyle who had more than enough on his plate? She never believed that Danny would have gotten involved unless he had to. Flanagan had probably reeled him in slowly and Danny had no one to help him out. The last thing he needed was a neighbor bearing false witness against him.

She knew that her husband would never approve of Deirdre having anything to do with Danny again, but that was no reason to go out and have the boy locked up. She knew he was still upset about the night Flanagan followed Deirdre home and he had a point there, but he had no right to take that out on Danny. Sometimes, her husband could act without thinking. They all could.

She never told him that she had heard him and she hadn't mentioned it to her daughter, yet. Instead, she baked a few scones and announced that she was going to pay a visit to Mrs. Boyle—to show her a little bit of neighborly kindness after all she had been through.

Her husband was dead set against it so she ignored him but agreed that Deirdre should come with her.

They left him fuming in his chair and headed out in closed ranks with their arms entwined.

"So did you ever get to say anything to Danny?"

"Yes, Mother, I did."

"And?"

"And he was very happy about it."

"I'm sure he was, but what about you? How did you feel about doing it?"

"What do you mean?"

"Oh, child. Give me some credit. I know what happened the night in the church."

"But you never said."

"Why would I? We all make mistakes and you've had enough people talking at you about it, led by himself." She sniffed and flicked her head back toward their house as they walked across the road.

*

Jacinta was surprised and embarrassed: she hadn't got to her housekeeping, with all that was going on, and the place was a bit of a mess. Deirdre's mother told her not to worry about it as they had only come over for a cup of tea in the kitchen, just to be with her, and have a nice, pleasant little chat. Deirdre's mother also insisted that Deirdre would make the tea for them, if Mrs. Boyle didn't mind. Which she didn't and they both sat around the fire that Jacinta poked and prodded back into life.

The kitchen warmed quickly as the three women sat down to tea.

Jacinta got a little weepy as she explained that Danny was still being held—for his own protection, of course, and because he might be able to help the Guards with their inquiries. That was how the solicitor had explained it to her, and Deirdre and her mother nodded in total agreement.

"What I don't understand," Jacinta continued through the hanky she had wiped her eyes with, "is how someone could be so mean and spiteful to Danny. Especially now that he is trying so hard to change. And Jerry, too, who never did a bit of harm to anybody."

Deirdre's mother reached out to console her and glanced at her daughter who rose and poured more tea to create a diversion. When they all settled down again she took Jacinta's hands in hers.

"We just want you to know that not everyone thinks badly about Danny. Isn't that right, Deirdre?"

Deirdre didn't look Jacinta in the face. She'd probably heard what Jacinta had said about her being "the one that had first led her poor Danny astray." Nothing that salacious could remain secret in their neighborhood. Instead, she just nodded. "That's right, Mrs. Boyle. Especially now that Danny is . . . trying."

"Well that's very nice of you to say," Jacinta reached over and gave Deirdre's hand a squeeze. Jacinta wasn't sure if she had forgiven her for what happened in the church. She just hoped that she wasn't going to make a big thing of it with Danny. She still hadn't decided how she really felt about her.

"I'll be sure and tell Danny that you said that. It'll do him good—after all the poor lad has been through.

"Well," she cradled her cup in her hand and smiled into the fire. "Because you've both been so nice, why don't you, and your mother and father, come to my sister's wedding? She won't mind, and we are having the reception in the Yellow House. They do a nice spread there and we can have a whole room to ourselves. Will you come? Danny would be delighted if you did."

*

"How are you going to explain this to Father?" Deirdre giggled as they recrossed the street and headed back toward their house, on a bit of a hill, between the trees.

"He will be the one explaining, when I get home." Her mother had her jaw stuck out like a steam engine and huffed and puffed all the way. "When we get home he can sit down before me and explain what was going through his head to pile all that misery on that poor woman? She has enough to deal with, God love her."

They both knew of Jacinta's past but they never discussed it even though everyone else did. Her mother took pride from that. So did Deirdre.

Her father, too, was usually above it all. But lately he had become preoccupied with the "goings on." He was spending a lot of time down in the pub and came home with stories that he could have left there. He said it was important for him, being the leader of the neighborhood watch and all, but her mother wasn't having any of that. She always got outraged when she saw someone suffering. She'd even forget herself, and her propriety.

He was sitting on the couch when they got in and tried to make a joke about checking their purses—since they had been over to the Boyles and all—but her mother froze him with a stare.

"Have you any idea what you have done to that poor unfortunate woman? She's beside herself with tears over there. You should be ashamed of yourself."

Deirdre excused herself and went to her room but she could still hear from there. It was better than having to watch her father having all the air let out of him. She wouldn't add to his humiliation.

She wouldn't take from it either and would go along with whatever her mother decided.

They usually ignored him, like he wasn't there. Or if they did talk to him, they'd be very stinting.

But this time it was going to be different. This time her mother was going to demand her pound of flesh.

"I was only doing what I thought was the right thing . . . for our daughter."

"I see. And did it ever occur to you to discuss it with me before you went around lying about the neighbors."

"I wasn't lying. There was something happening. I'm sure of it."

"There was. A bitter old man was taking out his spite on a poor, unfortunate young lad who, God love him, has had more than enough trouble in his life."

"Oh? Like Danny Boyle is some sweet little angel who would never put a foot wrong? Don't you remember? Don't you remember what he did to our Deirdre?"

Deirdre held her breath. She had no idea what her mother would say to that. They really should tell him the truth—but not tonight.

"He did nothing to Deirdre that he didn't do to himself. Can't you see that? They both made a mistake and while Deirdre got a second chance—what happened to Danny Boyle? Who was looking out for him?"

"He's not my concern. Let his own father worry about him. I've got enough to worry about with my daughters growing up with no morals."

Her mother paused. She was probably trying to maintain some composure but she couldn't.

"May God forgive you for saying such a thing. A decent man would be proud to have my two girls as daughters."

She stomped out of the room and Deirdre could hear her sob as she came up the stairs.

"I'm sorry," her father called up after her mother. "I don't know why I said that."

"You said it because you believe it," her mother turned at the top of the stairs and looked down on her husband. "You always believe the worst of people and that's all you ever get to see. You should be happy that you have a daughter that would cross the road to bring a bit of comfort to someone."

"I am. I am. Only why does it have to be Danny Boyle's mother?"

"Because she is the one who needs it. We don't get to pick who we are supposed to be nice to. There'd be no point in that."

"Okay. But what about the other one?"

"The other one? Do you mean our daughter, Grainne, who is about to have your grandson? Is that the one you want to vent your spleen on?"

"When did this all happen?"

"While you were out minding everybody else's business."

Her father sat down on the stairs and called them both to him. "Tell me they got married at least. Tell me that my grandson is not going to be a bastard."

"How dare you say that about your own flesh and blood. And, for your information, they were married in Morocco."

"What? Did they have one of those Muslim wailers do it?"

Deirdre couldn't bite her tongue in time and rushed to join in. "They are called Imams. And when they get back they are going to have a service here, too. And mother and I are going."

It was her mother's one condition—that they have a church service when they got back. Other than that, she couldn't wait to see them and to hold her grandson in her arms. She had told Deirdre that she would bring her father around. She just had to wait for the right moment to break the news to him.

He would come around, just like her mother said, after he had time to contemplate having to battle against all three of them—five if Johnny and his grandson took sides.

"A grandson?" And even the very mention of it softened him a little. "Can I hold him while they are getting married, properly?"

"You can stay at home with him if you like. Only you'll go over to the church on Saturday and go to confession. Then we can see about going on with things."

Deirdre smiled as she imagined it. "Bless me Father, for I have sinned. I bore false witness against my neighbor." She couldn't wait to tell Miriam all about it.

"And you'll put on your good suit and go to the Boyle wedding, too."

"Why on earth would I want to do that?"

"So your grandson doesn't hear about what a terrible neighbor you were."

*

You've gone and done it again. You're your own worst enemy, Danny chided himself in the small little room they held him in. He was trying to act like he wasn't bothered—except about being innocently locked up—but it was starting to get to him. They had let his father out hours ago and he was still waiting.

After he had been searched, the two detectives had come back for another "little chat" and sat down opposite him like they were Siamese twins, joined at the hip. They just nodded to him and flipped through their notebooks, pausing once in a while to nod to each other. Danny could tell: they had nothing on him. Handing over the bag was a lucky break.

Still, he wished he hadn't done any of it, now. He'd gone and told everyone that he was trying to turn his life around and now no one would ever believe him again.

The detectives didn't look like they did. They made that quite clear. They told him that they knew he was at Scully's execution and that there were some who had even suggested that he might have been the one that pulled the trigger!

They were probably just trying to scare him.

But what if Anto decided to get even and gave them the gun?

It had to have been Anto—the fucker.

The silent one just eyed him coldly while the younger one went on to tell him that they didn't believe it. He said they believed that Danny was there all right, and that he could name the killer. That made him an accessory unless he turned witness.

They told him it would be the wise course of action for him to take. They told him that they wouldn't have to charge him—that they might be able to see their way to getting him out on probation if he did the wise thing.

*

What they didn't tell him was that they had been told by their sergeant, who was told by the chief superintendent, who was asked by a government minister, who had heard from a bishop, that they were to go easy on Danny Boyle. They could squeeze him a bit but, unless they were positive, they couldn't charge him with anything. They could hold him overnight, too, but nothing was to happen to him—nothing!

*

Instead, they suggested that he sleep on it—that they'd be back in the morning and he could give them his statement then. They wished him a good night and left, locking the door behind them.

They turned the light off, too, so Danny sat with the light from the little window above the solid locked door as his only comfort. It was a dull yellow light that left shadows everywhere. And every time he stirred the floor boards creaked and groaned in the empty room. There was just the table and three chairs, a pack of cigarettes, and a box of matches.

That was enough to get him through the night and he had plenty to think about.

But that kind of thing could get to you after a while. He wouldn't let it. No, he was going to use his time to try to figure it all out. The Guards had nothing on him. They were just giving him the old scare-them-straight.

They kept you in an interview room and left you alone for a few hours while you listened to what was going on in the other rooms. Most of the time it was just a drone of conversation. The same old questions. If it was your first time, they didn't push too hard. They just guided you to the path toward reformation. They could get you there, but you were on your own after that.

By the second or third time the questions got much harder. They'd raise their voices, too.

Then it would go quiet. That was when the younger one would sit back and the silent one would take over and start talking in a soft voice. That's when they really got to you. When they took off their civil masks and really bared their teeth.

Everyone knew about it but nobody ever said anything; it was just the way things were done. Even though sometimes it got out of hand—like when the fella jumped off the roof of Pearse Street Station while he was still tied to a chair.

Everyone said it was an unfortunate event but that these things happened. And it only happened to those they didn't know and only read about in the paper, or heard on the news. It didn't happen to them, or theirs. But now it had and the whole neighborhood would be buzzing again about the infamous Danny Boyle, "God love him. Wasn't it his mother that was away in St. Pats for a while?"

"And his father, God bless the mark, had a fondness for drink. And him from such a good family, too. Bart and Nora must be rolling in their graves."

He'd gone and done it again. He was his own worst enemy.

But they had nothing on him. He'd be out in the morning. His mother would contact the old solicitor. The fucking Guards wouldn't be very happy to see him. He was one of the old crowd who could still reach out and have one of them transferred to minding sheep at some crossroad in the middle of a bog in the west.

Danny could sit back and relax and try to figure out what was really going on.

The part that kept eluding him was—how did they know he was bringing stuff in? Anto wouldn't have told them about that, and neither would the Driller. They both had too much to lose.

And why was he intercepted?

He shivered when it dawned on him that all three of them had been shafted, and, as desperation swirled about him he knelt down and prayed to God to save his soul—and his body. And for the first time in years, he wished his granny was near.

"Our Father

"Who art in Heaven . . ."

*

By morning he was a convert. If they would just give him one more chance, he wouldn't mess it up. If he could just get out from under this, he would never put a foot wrong again.

He believed in himself this time. He had found comfort during the night—the same feeling that he used to get when he was a kid and knelt by his bed to say his prayers. It was like someone up there was looking out for him.

He even knelt again and looked up and smiled at the smoke-yellowed ceiling in the tiny room where the only light came from the small window above the solid door. Its frame made a cross on the table before him.

He got up when he heard footsteps approach.

A key rattled in the lock and the bolts were pulled back.

"Boyle," the desk-sergeant barked. "There is someone here to see you. C'mon now."

Danny hesitated, like it might be a trap, despite the assurances of the night.

"C'mon, Boyle. Your solicitor is here."

Danny followed him down the narrow corridor, lined by solid doors, locked and bolted, getting brighter as he went.

After he had been led into another room, a brighter, bigger room, Davies greeted him with stilted concern and asked if he had been mishandled in anyway.

Danny shook his head but didn't raise his eyes.

"I have arranged for your release."

Davies waited like he was expecting Danny to just thank him but Danny forgot himself and hugged the prim old man instead.

"Steady now. Steady."

Danny didn't care. He had been saved, and not just from the cell. He was being given a whole new life and he couldn't wait to get out and start living it.

The two detectives were waiting by the desk as he signed some papers and retrieved his belongings. They had taken his belt and his shoes.

"Remember, Boyle, that you're still a material witness and we would like you to remain available in the case that we need to interview you again," the younger one remarked in a matter-of-fact way.

"Yeah," the taciturn one joined in. "Don't go pulling a disappearing act on us. Otherwise we might start thinking the worst of you."

"Now, Gentlemen," Davies stepped between them, like a wedge. "His Grace, the Bishop, has personally vouched for

Mr. Boyle's character. So unless you have the required evidence to lay charges, I suggest you go on about your day and let my client go about his."

He stepped past them and held the door open for Danny and stood with his arm raised like he was pointing the way. Outside, the sun was shining and the world smelled fresh and clean to Danny.

*

Bart and Nora sat by the small altar and watched with tears in their eyes. They even got to touch each other's fingers. A cold, tingly feeling that stirred old memories.

"Do you need my hanky?" she asked.

"What would I need that for? I just got a bit of dust in my eye. It wouldn't hurt for them to give this place a good cleaning once in a while."

"I think it gives the place a nice feel. I like the way smells linger. You can almost smell last Sunday's crowd."

"Don't remind me. Do you think it might be time to get on with ourselves?"

"Not yet, *a stór.* We agreed that I would wait until Danny was safe and sound and I am not going anywhere until then. Sit where you are and say a few prayers for yourself; I am sure you need them."

Bart sat back. There was no way he could budge her until she was ready. Everything was looked after, but he'd never be able to convince her of that. He lowered his head and let his mind roam free. They'd be a while yet.

*

Anto came to his epiphany sitting alone in his car while he was waiting for the priest. He wasn't sure at first, but it all became clearer as he watched Danny's mother cross the street and go up to the priest's door.

Boyle had been fucking him all along—right up the arse—the little bollocks. That was the thanks he got for not coming down hard when his instincts warned him. That was what he got for even thinking of putting other people first. A mistake that wouldn't happen again. He started the car and headed back into the city.

When the money was pouring in he had bought a place down near Portmarnock—for when he wanted to retire from the business. Where he could look out his front window and watch the sea until he got bored and found something else to do.

No one knew about it and he could hide out there while he figured out what he was going to do with Danny Boyle—the little fucker who had ratted him out.

He'd be let out in a day or two; his family would use all of their connections.

Anto could wait. Then he'd give Boyle a little lesson in loyalty—just like he did the dog.

Only that made him feel bad, but what else could he do? He didn't have Danny's connections. His family had nothing and he'd been left to fend for himself. Fighting back was the only way he could survive.

He'd have to vanish afterwards, though. There was no way he could make it look like someone else had done it. They'd know it was him, but he'd be gone by then. He knew a guy with a boat, not far from his hideout. He could be in England before anybody figured it out.

They'd come after him but he'd have a head start. He knew a few guys from the business. They'd help him out—for a price. They'd help him get to Holland. From there he could vanish and go anywhere he liked. As long as he stayed away from any place there might be Irish—he'd be fine.

He'd started putting the pieces together while he waited. It might take a little while to get a clear shot at Danny. He stopped to call Maguire and told him to keep an eye out for Danny until he heard back.

Maguire was hesitant until Anto offered to pay. Maguire was always a whore but he could trust him. He was too stupid to fuck it up.

*

The Driller was already in hiding in a safe house in Tallaght. No one knew about it so he could lie low there for a while. He'd left a shooter there before—hidden behind the chimney, in the attic. No one would go looking for it there.

There was nothing for it—he had to take Anto out. He couldn't have him leaking to the police. He'd be done for twenty years when they put all the pieces of his past back together. It bothered him, too. That's why he had started toking up. It was the only way he could function anymore.

It was the only way he could go out and not be fiddling with the gun in his pocket every time someone walked toward him. He'd nearly pulled the trigger on a bunch of kids on Halloween. They'd jumped out and scared the shite out of him. Fortunately they thought the gun was fake and just laughed at him as they ran off. They had no idea how close he had come to blasting a few of them.

It let him drive, too, without twitching and turning his head toward every noise.

Though he still turned his head to look down side streets and around corners. He could take in a whole street with just one glance. He'd always been like that, even as a kid. That's what made him so good at what he did.

Except, he didn't want to do it anymore. He wanted to get out and start up again as someone new. Someone with a different past that would shift and change depending on who he was talking to. It would be easy in America. He could get to start over.

He just had one more thing to do and then he'd take the ruddy-faced man's advice and vanish.

Anto was predictable. He did everything in a very dramatic fashion. It had worked for him in keeping everyone in line but now it was going to be his undoing. The Driller just had to keep his ear to the ground. Anto would never go after Boyle himself; he'd hire somebody to do that for him.

He'd be in hiding, too. Probably in that place he had up near Portmarnock. The Driller had never been but he knew about it. He could keep secrets, as long as it suited him.

Maguire! He'd know if there was a hit called. He was like the old women in the post office—the ones that listened in on everyone's calls. You just had to know how to get him talking. And when he was open for business.

Maguire feared him more than Anto. Everyone did. He'd shot his first at sixteen. He still remembered it. He'd been all juiced up on indignity. The Army had broken up the "Free Bogside" and the Brits were harassing everybody. He fired from a distance, the rifle almost breaking his shoulder. He fired more to frighten them rather than hit any of them. They were all so small at the other end of his sights.

The shot echoed around the flats, even after he dropped the gun down the shaft and ran for the stairs. They would be running for cover and he had a few minutes to get down to his flat and hide inside. If you hung about they might start firing back and that would turn the whole place into a war zone. He was just sending them a warning shot—to remind them they were in the Bogside. Free or not, their type wasn't wanted.

By the time he stripped off to his underwear, and dove under his covers, he knew one of them had been hit. It was even on the news. He was a young black guy, from Brixton. He had probably only joined for a chance to get ahead in life but he had no right to come marching through the Bogside like he owned it. He should have known that, growing up in Brixton.

He did feel bad when he heard that Brixton had died. He had been hoping all night, and not just for his own sake. He was hoping that Brixton would make it through, even if he shouldn't have been where he was.

The second one was the execution of someone who was telling tales out of school. He had begged for his life but he died anyway. Orders were orders and the Driller had a growing reputation to live up to. In time, he got his name for kneecapping. That was when they wanted to send a warning without actually killing someone even though most of them would have preferred to be killed. Walking around without kneecaps made you into a leper. No one wanted anything more to do with you after that.

Sometimes, when he toked too much, they all came back to haunt him. When they started to show up, even when he wasn't high, he got worried and moved to Dublin, for the rest. But he got bored and the rest, as they say, was history.

Maguire knew it well, Anto used to retell it every time he was laying down the law—his version of it.

The Driller caught up with Maguire behind the Classic, where no one ever bothered to look. He was reluctant at first but soon saw sense. He agreed to keep an eye on Boyle for a hundred and a bonus if he heard anything of Anto.

The Driller could trust Maguire. He was terrified of him.

*

After the Driller pulled away, Maguire stood in the shadows and smiled. He was making money hand-over-fist.

And he was getting rid of them all; Anto, Boyle, and the Driller. Then he could take over and run things properly. He'd be a lot more careful, though. His trip to the mountains had left a deep impression on him. He still nearly shit whenever he thought about it.

That was Anto's mistake. He got too big, too fast, and started to bump shoulders with the type of people it was better to avoid. Maguire wouldn't make that mistake.

He'd make different ones—like not noticing the car that was parked across the street.

It had been there while the Driller and Maguire were talking and waited until they were gone before starting up and drifting off into the night with four shadowy men inside.

CHAPTER 19

"Are you Grainne Fallon's sister?"

She was standing at the bus stop, looking for all the world like a student as Martin passed. "It's me, Martin Carroll—Danny's uncle. I used to know your sister and Johnny."

He almost didn't recognize her. She had cut her hair to her shoulders and looked like a very serious young woman, bound and determined. He had remembered her as a gangly teen who followed Grainne around like a shadow, aping everything her older sister did. Martin always took time to talk with her but was always careful not to give her any reason to develop any type of feelings toward him.

It had happened with Grainne, before she met Johnny.

That was when Martin realized he was the way he was. And no matter how he tried to explain it, Grainne didn't understand so they avoided each other after that.

Perhaps it was because he was back home, but he felt a need to explain himself to his past.

Or at least those parts of himself that he wanted to show. No one knew about him and David, but at the same time he wanted to address the wrongs of his past. He was getting into karma in a big way and wanted to do a bit of a cleanup.

That was one of the reasons that he had taken Danny for burgers and chips for old times, and it wasn't long before he saw his nephew's childhood face smiling back at him.

**

As far as his sisters were concerned, the jury was still out on Danny. Jacinta was assured of his innocence but the rest of his sisters were holding their verdicts—just waiting to see. "He seems like he is trying to mend his ways but you never know with the young ones of today."

It was all so predictable and he wasn't sure he could tolerate it anymore. But he had to be careful, too, and not speak his mind too openly—they'd say he had turned "American" and he had enough of a problem correcting them. "Canadian," he'd explain and they'd just look at him like he was being a bit persnickety.

"What's it really like?" Danny had been reading all the stuff the embassy sent him.

"What's what like?"

"Toronto."

"It's great. You'll love it."

"Don't you miss Ireland at all?"

Of course he did. Sometimes he'd dress as straight as he could and go to the Irish bars alone. David was upset at first until he realized it was just homesickness. It got to them all—sooner or later.

"Did you get all the paperwork in?"

"I did. I already told you that."

Martin couldn't help it and searched for any flickers, but his nephew was in earnest. He should support him in that. "How did you manage to get the clearance from the cops?"

"Davies. He asked them to provide it and when they got a bit stroppy, he just told them that he didn't want to have to look into laying charges for them falsely arresting me."

"You're not going to be doing anything stupid like that when you get to Canada?"

Danny looked pained as he explained. "I won't. I've learned my lesson. I want to go straight and start over."

"Well you're coming to the right place. We can get you a job no problem. There are a lot of Irish bars in Toronto and they are always looking for musicians. They even pay, too."

"What kind of music, though? I don't want to be playing shite like 'When Irish Eyes are Smiling.'"

"They are going to make you sing it when you get off the plane."

"You're having me on, right?"

"It's that or 'Here I Am from Paddy's Land.'"

"What kind of place are you bringing me to?"

"A place where you can make a new life for yourself. If you're serious about it?"

"Trust me, Martin. I've never been more serious in my life."

"I believe you."

He did. Danny had fucked his life up so badly that even he could see it was time to straighten out. He wasn't a bad kid—he was more the unfortunate kind. Sure he made some dumb-assed decisions, but he didn't really get the direction he needed. None of them did. All they ever got were mixed messages. David used to joke that the Irish were the products of negative reinforcement—all of them.

"Do you, really?"

"I do, Danny, I never gave up on you." Despite the way Danny felt about everybody else, Martin knew his opinion still really mattered to him.

Danny looked like he might cry for a moment so Martin changed the subject. He had to remember, men here still didn't talk openly about their feelings.

Some of the Irish in Toronto were starting to, beerily, usually. A drunken miasma of suppressed feelings about home and all that had happened to them there. Some were just maudlin but others were a bit bitter. Martin didn't mind being the one they spilled themselves on. It was cathartic. He couldn't talk with David and his friends about that. They'd just say it was all part of coming out. It wasn't. It was all about being separated from heart and home.

"So is there anything, or anybody, who you'll miss?"

"Not much, except Deirdre."

***

"Grainne and Johnny are together, in Morocco. Johnny's a painter now and they are getting married." Deirdre looked like she expected him to react differently but Martin just smiled. "That's great news. I'm very happy for them. Tell them I was asking for them."

"I will, of course." She looked uncertain of what to do next and added: "And are you well? How are things in Canada?"

"Great. Thanks for asking."

"I suppose that Danny was very happy to see you?"

He was delighted she had raised the subject. It wouldn't look so bad that way. "Yes. I just had lunch with him the other day."

It sounded very North American but he knew she'd understand. He wanted to keep talking to her until he found a way of bringing it up. He wanted to let her know how important she had become to Danny. Martin didn't think it was right, but Danny seemed to be building a lot of his hopes around her. If she was interested in him—it could mean the world of difference for Danny.

"Is he well?"

"He is. He mentioned you a few times." It was a bit of a risk—throwing it out there like that—but she didn't seem to mind.

"Well, tell him I'll see him at the wedding. I'm looking forward to it."

She smiled sweetly, but still Martin wasn't sure. She'd been brought up to be so polite, just like her sister. Martin had liked that about them. Still, he would have liked to see a bit more of a sign that she cared for him, too.

"I hear your mother and father are coming, too. Tell them I'm looking forward to seeing them again."

He didn't care for the father. Nobody did. Martin always thought he was a bit of a bully, but he liked the mother. He saw Deirdre on to the bus and went about his day, picking up a few things for Gina who was far too busy, and catching up with a few friends.

A part of him enjoyed being home again.

*

After the wedding dinner, Jacinta and her sisters shared a few glasses of cheap champagne as they stood to the side of the dance floor because Gina didn't want them to sit and ruin their dresses.

Linda and Brenda might have complained, but they were shimmering in the long satin gowns and every man in the place was looking over at them. They looked so sophisticated—standing there like royalty and with their hair all made up.

The whole wedding had gone off without a hitch. Everybody who was invited was there, as well as a few who weren't but loved weddings so they came anyway and sat at the back of the church.

*

Fr. Reilly had said the Mass and spoke about the renewal of Hope even though his heart wasn't in it. He kept thinking of Miriam and what it would be like to be standing at the altar with her. He almost let it slip out, too. He almost asked Donal if he took Miriam as his only wedded wife but he caught himself in time. Just as well because Gina looked so nervous as it was.

*

Still, it was grand and they all went to the reception with reinforced beliefs about marriage, either for or against it. And those who had been married the longest assumed places of privilege at their tables, near to the bride's and far away from the young people who were sneaking sips from unattended drinks and cavorting around the edges until the band started.

*

It had cost Jacinta a fortune but she didn't mind. Jerry even gave her extra–to help out. And her father was able to pay his way, a bit. They had all pulled together and done the family proud.

She was hoping the photographer would come by and take another picture of them all standing together. She'd put it up on the mantle along with the one of her and Jerry, on the other side from Bart and Nora who looked even younger than her and Jerry.

Danny's would go there, too, when he got married. Only she'd have to wait and see if she liked her, first. She was beginning to think it might be Deirdre—now that everything was sorted.

"Jacinta?" Linda leaned over. "Would you mind if I asked you a favor? Only there's a couple of men over there who have been giving Brenda and me the eye and it might be better if it was just the two of us standing here?"

*

"C'mon," Jerry met her as she crossed the dance floor, trying to keep her smile. He had been watching her from the bar, where the men had gathered. "Let's show these young ones how we used to dance." And even though the band started to play the Bee Gees, they danced as they did when they first met.

"Would you do it all over again, Jerry?"

"Do what?"

"Would you marry me again?"

"Don't be asking me that; I'm a married man."

She kicked out at his shin as he spun her around.

"But if I wasn't," he laughed as he twirled her back and looked into her eyes. "I would. I'd do it all over again. Only I'd try to do it better."

"We didn't do so bad. Did we Jerry?"

"No, Jass. We did just fine."

"We're going to be okay, aren't we?"

"Do you mean after Danny is gone? Don't worry about it. We'll go over and see him anytime you want."

"I don't mean that, Jerry. Are you and I going to be okay—now that it's just the two of us?"

"Why wouldn't we be? It'll be like the honeymoon we never had."

"That's the nicest thing you ever said to me."

As the song finished, Jacinta reached up and kissed him full on the lips, right there in front of everybody and didn't give a damn what any of them thought. "I love you, Jerry Boyle."

"And I love you, too, Jass Carroll."

"Go on then."

"What?"

"Go and have a drink at the bar. I've seen you looking over. Only come back and dance with me again soon."

Jerry took his wife in his arms and swept her around until she was leaning over backwards and kissed her full on the lips as everyone around them cheered. He blushed a little as he raised her back up. "I will then. Can I get you one, too?"

*

"C'mon," Martin nudged Danny. They had been sitting together at a table across from Deirdre and her parents. Her father had just excused himself and went to the bar and her mother smiled over at them.

"I'm not ready."

"C'mon you only have to dance with her." He pushed Danny forward before him but when they got to their table he leaned across him and asked Deirdre to dance, leaving Danny standing there with his arm outstretched.

"Thank you, Danny. I'd be delighted to dance." Mrs. Fallon rose like a lady and placed her hand in Danny's.

Danny reached out and gently placed his hand on her upper arm. He didn't want her to think he was a groper but he almost stepped on her foot. "Your husband won't mind. Will he?" Danny looked over at the bar but Deirdre's father didn't look back as he bellied up and ordered drinks for all around him.

*

"He's not much of a dancer, is he?" Martin held Deirdre close but not too close. He wanted to be able to talk to her without having to raise his voice.

"My mother wouldn't care. She just loves to dance and my father dances like a bull."

"He's not going to mind. Is he?"

"Him? No. He's far happier at the bar." She smiled up at him and moved a little closer and rested her head against his shoulder. The band had switched to something slower, inviting them to get closer.

But Danny didn't and danced with Mrs. Carroll at arm's length, causing Martin to smile.

"Do you think I should go over and rescue her?"

"And who will I dance with, then?"

"You could dance with Danny."

"Do you think he would want to dance with me?"

"I think he'd want that more than anything."

"Has he said anything?"

"He doesn't have to. You can tell by looking at him."

"Tell what?"

Martin looked into her face and smiled. "He's crazy about you. What do you think has kept him going through all of this?"

Deirdre lowered her head for a moment so Martin asked: "Do you not feel the same way?"

She blushed a little and looked rather shy. "I like him. I always did but . . ."

"I'm not suggesting that you marry him, or anything. I just think it would mean a lot to him if he thought he had a chance with you. It could make all the difference."

He didn't give her a chance to answer and cut in on Danny and danced away with Mrs. Fallon, holding her like the man he was and nearly swept her off her feet.

"I suppose we could dance," Deirdre smiled as Danny stood looking confused. But he brightened up immediately as the band upped the tempo.

"Are you excited about going to Canada?"

"Yeah, I'm looking forward to it, only . . ."

"Only what?"

"Only I'll miss you—now that we're speaking again."

"We could write to each other—at least until you meet some beautiful Canadian girl and forget all about me."

"I'd never forget about you. I never did before."

*

As they danced, Jacinta sat thinking of Nora Boyle. She could almost feel that she was there with her and that Nora was happy with the way things were going.

She also felt that Nora wanted her to invite Fr. Reilly over to her table, to thank him for all that he had done for them. He was sitting alone, just beyond the dance floor, tapping his fingers to the beat.

The poor creature is just trying to act natural, Nora told her, like any priest would do at a wedding reception. *He is lonely, Jacinta. He doesn't want to go home to face the rest of his life.*

God love him, Nora, Jacinta responded. *Isn't there anything that can be done for him?*

Nora knew how lonely he was and why he didn't want to go home and face the rest of his life, but she couldn't divulge it. She had tried talking to Fr. Brennan only he couldn't hear her. He had too many voice in his head already. It was all getting to be too much for him. She had wanted to tell him to stop clinging on when there was nothing to fear, but Heaven and Hell still existed for him. And poor Fr. Reilly was stuck in his own Purgatory.

He came over on the second wave and bowed a little as he sat in the chair opposite her.

"Are you enjoying the wedding, Father?" was all that Jacinta asked when Nora wanted her to say something else. But it wouldn't be fair—putting him on the spot like that. He might start to piddle himself. He still had no idea as to how to talk with women. And that ex-nun was just as clueless, treating him like he wasn't really a man under his robes. Or in his case, priestly casuals: brightly checked shirts and loosely fitting polyester pants. It was his own fault, too. Priests couldn't afford to be going out on dates, even with ex-nuns. He should have known better.

"I'm having a great time, Mrs. Boyle. Thank you for inviting me. It's a credit to you and your family. Fr. Brennan sends his regrets but I'll be sure to tell him all about it when I get home."

"Father," Jacinta interrupted to stop him from prattling on like someone who had just been released from vows of silence. *It must be so hard on him.*

It is, Nora nudged. *You really should tell him how much we all appreciate what he did for our Danny.*

"I wanted to say thanks very much for all you have done for our Danny."

Jacinta didn't know why but she reached out and patted the back of his hand, like a much older woman. "And I wanted you to know that we'll always think of you as a part of our family."

"That's very kind of you, Mrs. Boyle." He leaned a little closer and looked a little sheepish. "I always thought that you didn't like me. Your mother-in-law, God rest her soul, seemed to get the wrong idea about me and I was never able to put it right."

"Do you ever get lonely sometimes, Father?"

He looked right at her as if he was trying to see if she was drunk—or mad. "We all do, Mrs. Boyle, and that's when we should look to Jesus for his . . ."

"I don't mean all that stuff. I mean: do you ever wish you had someone special in your life?"

"We all feel that longing. And some of us get to find that person and marry them, like you and Jerry."

Nora was getting exasperated. Jacinta was very clumsy and the poor priest looked like he thought he was about to be propositioned.

"I know all that but what I'm trying to ask you is that you spend your whole life going around being a part of other people's lives—do you have anything left for yourself?"

He looked like he was afraid that she was having a bit of a breakdown right there in the middle of the wedding.

What Nora was trying to say to him was that he needed to start doing some things for himself. He had to find the time to start reading again. He had always loved his reading time but he couldn't seem to manage it anymore. Nora could tell just by looking at him.

"I chose to be a priest, Mrs. Boyle, and we all have to bear our crosses."

He looked like he regretted bring up crosses—with Jacinta being the way she was.

"I know what you mean, Father. And I even understand what that really means, now."

"Is everything all right, Mrs. Boyle?"

"Everything is as good as we could have hoped for."

"Things with Danny . . . they're still getting better?"

"They are, Father. And we have you to thank for that."

Nora thought about giving him a hug. He looked like he needed one. But before she could suggest it to Jacinta, something started to pull her away. And as the room started to shrink and fade, she realized that Danny was nowhere to be seen.

*

Danny had been standing at the urinal, shaking out the last few drops. He was feeling good about everything and was about to rejoin the party when Anto stepped out of one of the stalls.

"Ah, for fuck's sake."

"You didn't expect me to just walk away from what happened, did you?"

He was right; Danny should have known better. He was never going to be free of this. No matter what the priests said, there wasn't going to be any absolution or forgiveness. Real people just weren't like that.

"And I gotta tell you, Boyle, I was very upset that you didn't invite me to the wedding. I always thought that we were like family, you and me."

"It's still going on. You can come in now if you want."

"It's too late now, Boyle, but thanks for asking."

When he grinned he almost looked skeletal. His cheek bones were poking through his face and eyes were sunken. He must have been hitting the stuff pretty hard—and not just the hash. He looked very edgy, too, so Danny moved as slowly as he could toward the door.

"Where do you think you're going?"

"I wasn't going anywhere."

"You're wrong there, Boyle. We're going for a little drive. Just you and me."

Anto grabbed him from behind and held the gun tight against his chin, like he was ready, at any moment, to blow a hole through his head, and led him out a back door.

It was raining softly as Danny looked to the sky. He would have liked it if the stars were out—that something would witness his end. After all that had happened, it had come down to this; bundled into the back of a car and driven to the mountains where he would kneel down and wait for the end.

Panic grabbed his heart and he would have pissed himself if he hadn't already gone but he was in danger of shitting himself and clenched his arse as they walked, crab-like to the waiting car.

He could still hear them inside, dancing and laughing like life was never going to end.

Anto opened the boot and pushed him inside. Danny lay down and curled up like a dog.

But before Anto could close the boot, the Driller stepped from the shadows and held his gun against the back of Anto's head.

"I'll kill him," Anto threatened without turning around.

"Makes no difference to me. You're still going to die."

"I swear. I'll do it."

"Like I said, go ahead—I don't give a fuck."

"People will hear."

"They'll hear if you shoot him."

Danny wanted to thank the Driller for pointing that out but thought better of it. He'd be better off just lying there and hoping that they might forget about him.

"So what they fuck are we going to do now?"

"You're going to put the gun down, slowly, and then you are going to get in with Boyle."

Danny thought about pointing out that there might not be enough room but decided to stay out of it. He could tell Anto was thinking about it, he could see his hand shake. He was going to go for it.

"Bad idea," the Driller warned. "Now put the gun down or I'll fucking blow you away right here."

Anto must have thought better of it and slowly put his gun on the ground. "You're going to have to kill him, too. You know that?"

"Makes no difference to me," the Driller smiled as he knelt, holding his gun on Anto as he groped for the other gun. When he picked it up, he smiled. "You're after giving me an idea. I'm going to shoot him with this." He waved Anto's gun toward Danny. "And then I'm going to shoot you with mine. It'll be nice. I'll make it look like you killed each other. I might even plant a love letter, too, so the whole world will know that you two were sweethearts to the end. Now close the boot and let's get the fuck out of here. You don't mind driving, do you?"

Anto shook his head and closed the boot and, in the darkness, Hell glowed brightly and a thousand devils rose to take the soul of Danny Boyle to its inevitable end.

*

"Has anyone seen Danny? He's not in the jacks."

"Is he not out dancing? He was there a minute ago."

"He was, but he isn't anymore."

Jerry was going to suggest that he might be out in the back with a girl but he didn't think that Deirdre's father would like that. Besides, Deirdre was still sitting with her mother, like she was waiting for Danny to come back.

I hope he's not out doing drugs again. But he couldn't be. He had done so well and everybody could see that he was really trying, this time. But that was the thing with drugs. At least with the drink you knew where you stood and you could take it or leave it. Even though, Jerry had to admit, that he did more taking than leaving, himself. But what harm was there in that? He wasn't hurting anybody.

"Come here, quick. They're after taking Danny away." Maguire's father stood in the doorway panting.

"What are you on about?"

"I saw them—Flanagan and that Northern fucker. They've just put Danny in the boot of a car."

The entire room went silent. Even the band stopped in the middle of something and the dancers hung onto nothing.

Jacinta rose from her chair, clutching her heart and beseeching Jerry with her eyes. It was like the way his mother looked at him after Bloody Sunday. "Danny?" she screeched and began to wail, inconsolable despite Martin and Deirdre's best effort. "Ah, sweet Jesus. Not my Danny. Not now after everything."

Jerry turned and marched to the door. He had no idea what he was going to do but he had to do something. This was it. This was the moment when he'd get to put it all to rights. All the sins of his life could be washed away by this one heroic and selfless act.

"Hold on, Boyle. I'll not let you walk out there alone." Deirdre's father rose from his stool and held Jerry's elbow.

"Let go of me. I'm going out there no matter what."

"Well then I'm coming with you." Dermot Fallon nudged him with his shoulder. "We're all coming with you."

He rallied the men at the bar and led them outside, collecting their weaponry as they passed the crates of empty bottles.

CHAPTER 20

Fr. Patrick Reilly let himself out and turned toward home, leaving Jacinta and Jerry sitting at their kitchen table, smoking and staring off like neither of them was really there. He had done all he could; assuring them that the Garda were hot on the trail and they would have Danny back in no time.

"And why would they spare him? Don't they always kill?" Jacinta had pleaded like she was coming apart. He mouth had cracked already and her eyes were swollen from crying and wiping them with the hanky Fr. Reilly had given her. It was already wet and snotty.

"To save their own cowardly skins." Jerry had taken her in his arms, rocking her back and forth like a baby. "They know that the Guards are on to them, this time."

Somebody had called them and they came, quickly. They pulled up just as Flanagan drove away. It almost seemed like they had just been waiting around the corner, three car loads of them, two cars of uniformed men and the two detectives in the other. Then, after making sure that nobody had been shot, and after they convinced the men from the wedding to put the bottles away and go back inside, they all took off toward Willbrook Road. They didn't speed away with sirens wailing. It almost seemed like they knew where they were going and what they'd find when they got there.

"They knew," Jerry had added when she looked at him for a bit more hope, "that if they chased them, they might panic them."

Patrick had joined in, too, to bolster the argument. "They are all trained in how to handle hostage situations."

It didn't help. She just kept mouthing the word "hostage," over and over, as she lowered her face into hands and wailed as only a mother can.

"Well," Fr. Reilly had looked at Jerry who looked like he was at a loss, too. "It's getting late and we should all try to get some sleep while we wait for the Guards to call."

***

He couldn't stay any longer. O'Leary might have fallen asleep already and Fr. Brennan might have woken up and could be wandering around the house looking for him.

He wasn't looking forward to it. He was too tired to act out their usual charade: Fr. Brennan berating him about his hours in nothing but his bath robe, and him acting like the scolded curate while he directed the old man safely back to his bed. He'd have to phone the Bishop and tell him, one of these days.

*

The Bishop was waiting for him when he got there. He was sitting by the kitchen table with a bottle and two glasses in front of him. They had been hidden from Fr. Brennan but the Bishop had found them easily enough. "Come in," he beckoned without getting up.

"Your Grace? What a surprise."

"Sit down. There's more."

The Bishop poured them each a generous measure before he sat back again. "I was called by the Guards. They found poor Fr. Brennan out on the street."

"Is he all right?"

"He is. Shivering a bit and completely unaware. But other than that—he's fine."

"I'm so sorry. I should have been here."

The Bishop urged him to sip his drink and waited until he did.

"Even you can't be in two places at one time. He was out on the street because he came down from his bed and found Dinny O'Leary sitting dead in the armchair inside."

Patrick Reilly nearly choked on the small sip he had taken.

"Fortunately we were able to send the two of them off in the same ambulance. There'll be less tongue-wagging this way. Dinny lived alone so we can say that we were called there, too, and found the poor man dead. We'll put on a bit of a show for his funeral, too. He was a good one, was Dinny."

He raised his glass but his nephew still had his head down.

"Tell me. How long did you think that you could keep this secret from your bishop?"

"I'm so sorry, Your Grace. I should have informed you earlier and all of this could have been avoided."

"What's done is done. Dinny would have died anyway. But we'll have to tell everyone that Dan Brennan had a stroke. It'll look better for him when he's in the home—rather than have people thinking he went mad."

Patrick Reilly wanted to apologize again but his uncle wouldn't let him.

"You were only trying to do the right thing by the man and I appreciate that. It's a hard job and some of us break down under it—only we'd never admit to that."

He reached forward and put his hand on his nephew's bowed shoulders and helped him straighten up a bit. "You did the right thing and I know you were busy with the wedding and what happened after that."

He laughed at Patrick's reaction and topped up their drinks a little. "Nothing happens in this diocese without my knowing about it, either after or afore. Go on now and get some sleep. You can have the morning off, tomorrow. I have a few missionaries back from Africa who'll be delighted to come out and say the Masses for you."

He drained his glass and reflected for a moment. "I suppose it's just a sign of the times. The Island of Saints and Scholars is having to call its missionaries back to do God's work at home."

He looked up and smiled at his nephew. "Go on now and take your drink up with you. I'll let myself out. Everything will be as right as rain when you wake up."

Patrick might have argued but he was too tired. And what his uncle said made as much sense as anything he'd heard. And it was as kind as anything he'd ever heard.

*

As he walked out to his waiting car, the Bishop missed the old times when things like this could have been nipped in the bud. He and the ruddy-faced man, or John Joe as the bishop knew him, often talked about that.

They usually met in the graveyard up in Bohernabreena.

They came in separate cars and looked for all the world like they met by accident.

From the road, nobody would be able to make them out, anyway. Just two old men in coats, hats, and scarfs, visiting the graves of lifelong friends. Moving from stone to stone, from either side of the cemetery, until they met somewhere near the middle. Where, sometimes, they chided each other like an old married couple for their past sins against their children, the people of Ireland.

Other times they just came to bare their souls aloud to each other. True confessions before all that was holy to them—the dead around them.

Sometimes they had business, when their mutual interests converged. They were both practical enough to know that they had to work with each other. Otherwise, who would steer the ship now that all the statesmen were gone?

**

"Is it taken care of?" the Bishop had asked without looking up.

"It's as good as done."

"Is it done or not?"

"We're just waiting for them to make their moves and then we'll kill the two birds with the one stone."

"If that Boyle lad comes to any harm . . ."

"Pat? Do you really think that you're the only one that Bart would have looking out for him?"

"Right so." The Bishop turned to walk away but John Joe reached out to him. "Pat. Your nephew."

"And what about him?"

"I think he's getting lonely."

If anyone else had said it the Bishop would have glared them down but John Joe didn't spread idle gossip.

"I'm not saying for sure but it's just I saw him and the ex-nun, in Bewley's one day."

***

Jacinta couldn't face it in case it was bad news, so Jerry answered the door. They knew it was the Guards. It was far too early for anybody else. They'd had sat up all night, smoking and drinking pots and pots of tea.

"Come here quick," Jerry called back to her. "Come and see what the cat's dragged in.

"No offense," he added in deference to the two detectives, standing on either side of a bedraggled looking Danny, shivering and clutching a West Ham duffle bag to his chest.

"Ah, sweet Mother of Jesus. You found him safe and sound?"

The younger detective nodded and nudged Danny forward into his mother's arms while the taciturn one almost smiled.

"You'll come in?" Jacinta asked them as she sobbed and hugged her prodigal son. "For a cup of tea?"

"Or something stronger, if you'd prefer," Jerry enthused as he stood like a curate—the bar kind.

"It has been a long night," the younger detective admitted and waited.

"It has," the taciturn agreed and followed the Boyles into their kitchen. "But we'll just have the one cup. We don't want to be imposing."

"How could you be imposing after bringing our Danny home safe?"

The detectives settled down in their chairs as Jacinta insisted that Danny go on upstairs and she'd follow him on up after she had put the kettle on again. Jerry offered them cigarettes and by the time the kettle was ready they had taken their coats off, too, and looked like a couple of ordinary men.

That's why Jacinta didn't mind rushing off and leaving her husband to entertain them.

"She just wants to make a bit of a fuss over him. You know how mothers can be." Jerry poured their tea and offered to top it up with whiskey.

The younger one declined but the taciturn agreed to a few drops—so he wouldn't catch a chill after spending the night on the mountains.

"And why wouldn't you?" Jerry began to warm to them, a little "But tell me, where did you find him?"

"He was locked in the boot of their car."

"And did they give you any trouble? Did you get to arrest the pair of them?"

"We didn't have to. When we got there they were both lying dead on the ground. They must have had a fight and killed each other."

"And Danny was safe all along."

"He was, but he might be in shock. You'll need to keep an eye out for that."

Jerry gulped his tea and poured some more.

"So they are finally dead—the pair of them?"

"They are," the taciturn answered as Jerry poured another drop to warm his tea. "And what I'm about to tell you must be kept confidential. But as the lad's father you have as much right to know as anybody."

Jerry agreed, totally, and poured a bit extra.

"They were lying on the ground, still holding their guns, and each one had a hole in the back of their heads, as well as the front."

"Isn't that's a bit odd?"

"As far as we can ascertain, they might have both fired again when they hit the ground—as they were falling away from each other . . ." The two detectives raised their teacups to their faces, simultaneously, as Jerry nodded until he realized what they were really telling him.

"There won't be a fuss about it? Danny is just about to leave for Canada. He won't have to be involved in an inquiry, or anything?"

"I doubt it. I don't think anybody is going to make a fuss over either of them. And we've already taken your son's statement. I don't think he'll need to be involved—any further."

Jerry thanked them again and called Jacinta down as they rose to leave. She thanked each one of them with a hug and a kiss and saw them to the door.

"Where's he now?" Jerry asked when they were alone.

"He's having a bath. He had a bit of an accident in his underpants so he's just cleaning up a bit. He's going to go straight to bed after that. The poor lad, he didn't get a wink of sleep."

Jerry held her in his arms and kissed her gently. "Why don't you go up, too, and get a bit of sleep and I'll be up in a minute."

He sat smoking for a while and, in time, wondered what his mother and father would have thought of it all. Before, whenever he thought about them, they would appear in his mind like dark shadows and that used to make him shiver. But that was before. Now, he thought they might have been smiling at him.

He was feeling better about the future, too, and swore he'd spend as much time as he could trying to make things better—for everybody. It was the least they deserved for standing by them through all that happened. Danny's kidnapping was public news anyway—happening right there in the middle of the wedding—and everybody had come up to him and Jacinta before they left.

Some said nice things, but others just looked at him and he could see all the same fears running through them. It could have been any of their children. That was the worst thing about it. It just kept spreading and it was time somebody rose up and did something about it.

He'd talk with Dermot about it. They could set up some kind of thing where they could get all the parents together and Jerry could stand up in front of them and tell them all about his experience.

You never know, he might be able to help some other family from going down the same road.

He'd get right on it—after Danny left.

He tided away the teacups and emptied the ashtrays and was turning off the lights when he noticed the duffle bag, sitting where Danny had left it. He took a peep inside and saw the cigarettes and the gin.

*

Martin had come over to intercept any calls or visitors while they all slept—right into the afternoon. A deep sleep without dreams.

Danny didn't wake until Mrs. Fallon called round. She was wondering—if they wouldn't mind—if they would like to come over to her house for dinner. Jacinta had enough to do and it was no bother, really.

Martin had accepted for them and saw her out before Jerry and Jacinta came down from their beds. Jacinta wasn't sure. She wasn't sure she was up for seeing people just yet but Jerry thought it was a great idea and he'd run out and get a few bottles of wine.

Danny heard his mother tell Martin to go up and ask him first, and then she'd decide.

"Are you up?" He called from outside the bedroom door and waited a few moments before he came in. "You look like crap."

"I don't. I look like shite. Remember? You're back in Ireland now."

"I'm happy to see you, too." Martin ducked behind his fists and threw a fake jab before he reached out and hugged his nephew tightly. "Are you all right?"

"Never better. I guess it was all that fresh mountain air."

Danny knew that Martin knew he was just trying to put on the brave face. He had to; it was far too early to think about it. But he had heard it all. Even Anto and the Driller, pleading for their lives—almost begging.

Nobody answered them—only two sudden shots.

He heard the sound of them being dragged and set into place. Two more shots followed and then someone opened the boot. They had told him that he'd seen nothing and he'd heard nothing. And it was to stay that way, even when he was off in Canada. They could get to him there, too, easier than here. But if he kept his mouth shut he'd have nothing to worry about. They placed the duffle bag beside him and closed the boot, leaving him in a stunned silence.

After they had gone it got worse. All he could hear was the pounding of his own heart and the sobbing he couldn't stop.

That's how the Guards found him. They had put a blanket around him as they asked him a few questions.

*

They didn't discuss it over dinner and Dermot Fallon got over any disdain he might have had and was the perfect host, opening Jerry's wine with flourish and offering Jerry a sample sip—the way they did in fancy restaurants.

Jerry played along and swished it around for a moment before swallowing it and nodded for more.

Mrs. Fallon and Deirdre served in perfect unison, roast lamb with assorted vegetables and potatoes, boiled and roasted. All served on very fine china.

"Everything is wonderful, Mrs. Fallon." Jacinta beamed as the fuss went on around her.

"Thank you, Jacinta and please call me Anne. After all, we're friends now."

"May I say," Martin joined them to keep the conversation flowing. "That I love the china. Is it very old?"

"Actually," Mrs. Fallon almost laughed, like someone who had been caught in a little white lie. "We found them in a pawn shop."

"They are very nice, aren't they, Jacinta?" But Jacinta didn't answer and just sipped from her wine.

*

They chatted about almost everything else until dinner was over and Martin insisted that he and Danny would help Deirdre tidy things away but her father wouldn't hear of it.

His daughter and his wife had done their part and now it was down to the men to clear off while the women went into the front room. It would take them no time at all and he'd be back with a pot of tea and biscuits for the ladies.

He had been on his best behavior and it was a bit of a strain. He needed a smoke. Though he'd probably have to let Jerry have one, and listen to him while they smoked. But it was better than having his daughter spending time alone with Danny—even if his uncle from Canada was there. It was all very well being nice to the Boyles, and having them over for dinner, but he wasn't going to stand for that. He'd be neighborly but he didn't want his daughter going out with one of them.

"Do you see?" Jacinta prodded Jerry. "There's a real gentleman for you. Get up and help him and maybe some of his manners might rub off on you, too," She nodded to Danny before flashing Deirdre a quick smile.

"C'mon then," Dermot Fallon agreed. "You and I can wash and dry while the two lads bring in and put away."

"Isn't it nice for them to be waiting on us for a change?"

Mrs. Fallon laughed and agreed as she led Jacinta and Deirdre into the other room where a coal fire glowed.

*

The morning after Danny left, the Bishop waited for Fr. Reilly.

He had been brooding on it all morning, causing Mrs. Power and Mrs. Mawhinney to remark.

When they heard it was about his nephew they both chided him for always being so hard on the young man. The Bishop let them have their say. The whole world was going mad around him but he was used to that. He waited until they were done and dismissed them with a very formal nod and settled behind his paper.

He wasn't judging Patrick, or any of them. They all went into the seminary modeling themselves after Aidan of Lindisfarne and Ciarán of Clonmacnoise, Kevin of Glendalough and Columba of Iona. Good decent men who spread the word of God through the heathens of Scotland and beyond. They went out with no thought for themselves and served God and no one else, not even the rot that was growing down in Rome.

For him, the greatest of these was Brendan, the Navigator. The man who found America while the Spanish and Portuguese were still praying to Allah. It must have rattled a few mitres down in the Vatican. "It was allegory," they used to remind him with all of their Roman smugness. "Everyone knows that it was our own Christopher Columbus that discovered the New World." That always created a ripple among the Spanish and Portuguese but they could all take a back seat now. It was proven that Brendan's craft was more than capable of making the trip.

Despite all that, he missed the old days in Rome. He had made good friends while he was there. He had studied for a while with Óscar Galdámez who had gone on to do very well for himself. They had kept in touch for a while but they hadn't exchanged letters in years. He should write to him soon, at least to congratulate him. He was an archbishop now, down in El Salvador.

He still got a card from Giovanni Montini, every year, around Saint Patrick's Day. He was one of his earliest friends who had gone on to do very well for himself, all the way to the very top.

They were a mixed lot back then. Idealists and conformists all bound together on the great journey that was service to the Church and all her people. Full of hubris, too, they knew far more than the old men they knelt before, praying that God would take the lot of them off to their Heavenly rewards so the younger men could get on with the job.

The years had taught them all patience and modesty and the sad truth that the world of men was no longer theirs to direct. It was their purpose now to bring attention to what was still good and right in the world. He would have to make sure that it was a feature of every sermon on Sunday. The people needed to be reminded of a time when men gave themselves to the devotion of God instead of bickering and fighting and blowing the hell out of each other. He would call Mrs. Mawhinney and have her dictate a letter.

As if on cue, she peered around the door. "Excuse me, Your Grace. Father Reilly is waiting."

"Send him in, send him in right away." He folded the newspaper but kept it close in case he had to rap his nephew across the nose.

"Patrick, come in and close the door behind you. Are you well?"

"I am, Your Grace, and how are you?"

"I'm an old man whose days are fleeting but there is still a bit of spark in me yet. Can I get you something to drink?"

"No, Your Grace, but you go ahead if you like."

"I will so." He poured a modest dash into the Waterford tumbler he fingered as he sat and studied his nephew's earnest face. Fr. Brennan had been quietly moved off to a retirement home, out of the public eye. "We need to talk."

"Yes, Your Grace, and may I apologize, again, for not telling you in time."

"I was going to talk with you about something else but now that you bring it up: Why didn't you tell me that the poor man hadn't been right in months?"

"Well, at first I was hoping that he'd come out of it. I was going to tell you, of course, but I just wanted to see if it would pass before I brought it to Your Grace's attention."

"I see."

"I felt it was the least I owed Father Brennan, after all he had done for me."

"Well Patrick, that was commendable in one way but, in another, it was very poor judgement."

"I realize that, now, Your Grace."

The Bishop drained his glass and stared at his nephew. It wasn't just the other matter. It was as plain as the nose on his face: his nephew wasn't ready. He was a good curate but he wasn't ready to run a parish. The Bishop would have to find someone else.

"Can I ask you something, Patrick?"

"Anything, Your Grace."

"Are you still happy at the parish?"

"Yes, Your Grace, very happy. Why do you ask?"

"Because I often think that a young man like you should get away and see a bit of the world while he still can. Trust me; they'll have you back here before the end."

"I see, Your Grace. And may I ask where it is you would like me to go?"

The Bishop paused. His nephew had a knack for saying one thing while implying another—it was most unsettling.

"That would be your decision, Patrick. I just thought that you might like a break from parish work. I have friends in Rome, you know? I could ask around and maybe we could find you a position in the Irish College there. You were always a great man for the studying. What would you say to that?"

"I am always happy to serve wherever the Good Lord sees fit to put me."

"There's more to it than just that. You see, a part of my job is to manage the resources of the diocese. That way, when I see a fine young man, such as yourself, who has labored away without thought for himself—well it allows me to reward such devotion. You're overdue a spell in Rome. I firmly believe that we can find the best of ourselves there but I don't want you to feel like I am pressuring you. Just think about it and if you ever feel like giving it a whirl—then we can talk."

"That's very generous, Your Grace," Patrick agreed as he absorbed the Bishop's real message. He was just being given the time to accept it. "Will that be all? I don't mean to be rude but I have a funeral this afternoon."

As he left, he turned in the doorway to ask: "What was the other thing you were going to talk to me about?"

"Ah, it was nothing important."

The Bishop poured himself another little dash of whiskey and leaned back in his chair. He raised his glass to all the old times, to the memory of Bart and Nora and all that they held dear, and to Danny, the prodigal son now deep in the Canadian woods where he might yet make a man out of himself.

*

After all the fuss died down, Jacinta found time to get over to the church. She'd been putting it off but she had to talk with Nora again. They hadn't spoken since the night of the wedding—when Danny went outside.

Perhaps Nora was still mad at her about that, but she still had to talk with her. She had to tell her what it was like to watch her only child get on a plane and emigrate.

Only it was worse. Danny was a kind of a refugee, fleeing from his homeland—from things his mother hadn't been able to protect him from. Part of it was Jerry's fault but she didn't want to be thinking about that when she knelt down to say her few prayers by the side altar.

She wanted to pray for Danny—that he'd come to no harm in Canada. She knew Martin would look out for him but she wanted to get as much help as she could.

She was into her second rosary, the beads slipping through her fingers only to come back around again. Nora was giving her the wait but she didn't mind. It was so nice and quiet with only one other woman, off in the corner, deep in her prayers, kissing the cross on her beads every now and then.

I'm here now but I can't stay, Nora interrupted. *Bart's waiting for me outside. He never was a great man for churches but who could blame him for that?*

She asked after every detail of Danny's leaving, every word that was said and how long they cried. She said she missed that.

"Do you know what Danny said to me, just before he got on the plane," Jacinta whispered through her fingers. "He was talking about when they had him locked up in the boot.

He said that even there, with bullets flying all around, he was thinking of something you used to tell him when he was a little boy. Do you know what that was?

"He said that he remembered you telling him that his guardian angel would always be there for him. He said that after he thought that—he wasn't afraid anymore."

She thought she heard Nora sniffle a little. But that was all.

Then she was gone again, leaving Jacinta alone in the near silent church. Only the slipping beads and whispered prayers of the woman in the corner. And the rustle every time she raised her cross to kiss it. Jacinta looked over and nearly left when she saw who it was—Mrs. Flanagan praying another afternoon away. But Jacinta didn't leave. She thought that Nora would prefer if she stayed—for a while anyway. She had nothing to rush home for.

Mrs. Flanagan never looked over but Jacinta didn't expect her to. She'd give her some time and then one day, when it felt right, she would go over and kneel down beside her and say a few prayers together, for both their sons.

*

Danny called home on Saturday afternoon—just as he said he would. He called around three so Deirdre was able to drop by—just as they had planned, without her father knowing.

"It's got to be about minus twenty," he told her when his mother finally put her on. He was proud of himself—being able to bear it. At home, they'd be clutched around the fire and nobody would go out.

"Ah, ya get used to it." He hadn't yet, but Martin assured him he would, after he learned to dress for it.

He sat by the window, looking down on the length of Balliol Street, a narrow gorge between towers. It was snowing again and he watched the cars struggle to get up the hill. "No. Everything goes on as usual. They're used to it."

One car got stuck and had to be pushed, its rear tires spinning uselessly.

"I haven't got any gigs yet. I'm still finding my way around, but Martin has told me about all the best places. I'm just waiting to make a few connections, ya know?"

The car finally made it up the hill, leaving long, scuttery brown trails. But it was still snowing and they'd soon be covered with fresh white snow.

"I miss you. I don't miss the rest of it," he lied. He was homesick but he couldn't tell her that. It would have sounded ungrateful and he knew stuff like that was important to her. He had told her about his epiphany—the night in the cell—and he didn't want her to think that he was backsliding. He wasn't. It was just that then, he'd been scared. Now that the crisis was over, and the heat was off, he looked at it differently. He had never asked to be what he became. He was just a product of his times.

"I am happy. It's just there's a lot to get used to, ya know?" There was. His slate had been wiped clean and he had been given a fresh new life. Only old habits would be hard to break.

"No. I'm staying away from all that for a while." It wasn't totally true. He had shared a few joints with Martin, but it was different. He was different. Everything over here was different. Here it was more like a normal thing to do.

"There's a few, but none of them are as pretty as you." The snow fluttered down on the balcony outside, soft and fresh. "Or as nice."

"No, I mean it. Knowing that you believed in me made all the difference."

It had. Since the day in the Dandelion, despite all the shite that followed, she had given him another chance. That was all he needed. Everyone else was always going on about God and Love but she was the only one who really showed him any.

"I couldn't have made it without you." He almost started to cry. Loneliness, gratitude, forgiveness, they all fluttered through his heart. Only Deirdre had ever been able to make him feel like that. Only Deirdre could really see who he was behind all the masks he wore. Only Deirdre could love him.

"I love you, Deirdre Fallon," he blurted out when they had wandered into a pregnant pause. "And I want you to think about coming over so we can be together."

Daniel Bartholomew Boyle had come through Hell and high water. But he had left all of that behind. None of it mattered in Canada, where everything was still new, even the old. He was ready now to begin again. He was ready to leave his footprints on the fresh snow and he would become what he never had allowed himself to become before.

"You might? Well that gives me something to look forward to."

Sin a bhfuil

Sin a bhfuil, as the Irish say: that's it. That's the beginning of *Life & Times,* the beginning of the story of Daniel Bartholomew Boyle and I hope you liked it. And before you ask —no! It's not about me, it's about the times I lived through and some of the things that happened around me.

I had the same question from people who read *Lagan Love* and I wasn't in that either. I had a small part in an early draft but I ended up leaving myself on the "cutting-room floor."

I did include myself in one scene in this book —a tiny part —and if you can figure it out, contact me and I'll send you a signed copy.

But back to Danny, the poor little lad who grew from his grandmother's knee to the prodigal returned. What's next for him? How will he fare in Canada? Will Deirdre join him? Will they get to live happily-ever-after?

What of his parents, Jacinta and Jerry, how will they fare?

And Patrick Reilly? Will he go to Rome?

Will Miriam and her American hook up?

I will tell you, but not here. It's all in the next book, *Wandering in Exile.* It'll be out soon and we can have another little chat after you've read it. In the meantime, let me know what you think at:

https://www.facebook.com/AuthorPeterDamienMurphy

Drop by and we can "chat" some more.

– Peter.